HEARTSTRINGS & HORSESHOES

LUCKY SPURS RANCH
BOOK 2

AMANDA JAYNE

Copyright © 2026 by Amanda Jayne

All rights reserved.

This is a work of fiction. Names, characters, places, and events are either the product of the author's imagination or used fictitiously. Any resemblance to actual persons, living or dead, events, or locales is entirely coincidental.

No part of this book may be copied, reproduced, scanned, or distributed in any printed or electronic form without written permission from the author, except in the case of brief quotations used in reviews, articles, or scholarly works.

This book was written by a human, for humans. This book may not be used in whole or in part for the purposes of training artificial intelligence (AI) models, data mining, or machine learning, including but not limited to large language models, without explicit written consent from the author.

Cover Designer: Maldo Designs @smaldodesigns

Copy Editing, Proofreading, and Formatting: @kmortonedits

First Edition: March 2026

To anyone who wishes they'd taken the chance.
Take the chance.

CONTENT WARNINGS

Your mental health comes first. As a person with mental health struggles, I have done my very best to handle all topics with care and respect. This story includes depictions of sensitive topics that have been shaped, softened, or heightened for the sake of the story. Please take caution if any of the following subjects may be triggering for you. This book includes Abandonment (by a parent), Alcoholism (of a parent), Alzheimer's Disease (on page), Cardiac Death (brief reference), Death of a family member (brief reference), Disordered Eating (on page), Drug Use Resulting in Death [including first responder activity] (on page), Drugging a Drink (not consumed), Grief, and Home Invasion (on page). The characters and their choices, opinions, and actions do not reflect my own.

1

"Are you going to tell her?"

"Shhhhh, Connor, oh my god, now is not the time or place. Can we please not do this right now?" Delilah begs.

"If not now, when? Shit's gone too far, and you need to tell your sister," I counter.

It's not like I'm trying to be quiet, so it comes as no surprise when Izzy, the world's nosiest sister, materializes and wraps her arms around Delilah from behind. She's laser-focused on me, eyes narrowed in suspicion and mischief, as she asks, "What's going on, twinie?"

"Nothing!" Delilah answers too quickly.

"Go on Delilah, tell your sister what Ivy did."

I'm fucking pissed. And I know for a goddamn fact how much she hides from her sister, because she confides in me instead.

Delilah blushes red, and regret jolts through me for embarrassing her. I hate pushing her like this, but I'm sick and tired of her dealing with this shit on her own. Delilah's always been the quiet sister. The observant, careful to act, soft spoken sister. Whereas Izzy's always been more gregarious and risk-taking.

The girls are Irish twins, Delilah only eleven months younger than Isabelle, but they couldn't be more different. Izzy left town to get away from her demons. I don't blame her for starting over. I do, however, blame her for leaving Delilah to deal with their piece of shit mother all on her own.

Izzy moved home a year ago and I could breathe again, knowing there was someone in that fucking trailer who cared about Delilah. I wish neither girl had ever been subjected to the abuse from their parents, but at least when Izzy's home, she takes some of the burden off Delilah.

Well, that was short-lived because Izzy fell in love and got engaged to Reid Andersen and moved out of the trailer.

Again.

Izzy's reasons don't matter to me. What matters is regardless of how happy Izzy is, living her little fairy tale life, Delilah was left alone.

Again.

I've put Delilah in a shit position, but she needs to be the one to tell her sister what the fuck happened.

She turns to her sister, and says in a rush, "Mom must've gotten into some gambling trouble again, because last night, some really scary guys came to the trailer and there was yelling, and things were breaking. I was terrified, and I didn't want to leave Mom there, but I snuck out my window and called Connor while I ran to the streetlight off Main."

Shock and hurt crosses Isabelle's face. Delilah stopped relying on her for support years ago and I was more than happy to fill that void. It isn't Isabelle's job to protect Delilah anymore. It's mine. And sometimes, protecting someone means pushing them to move on from a toxic relationship. It's unfair the toxic relationship is with her own mom, her mom's bad decisions, and the bottle.

"She was fucking frozen when I found her, Iz. She's not going back to that fucking trailer. I don't care that she's your mom. Ivy can take care of herself. You've enabled her for too long."

Delilah rears back like I slapped her. Fuck, I meant both sisters have been enabling their mom, but it sure as hell came out like I'm putting all the blame on Delilah.

I open my mouth to correct my mistake when Reid interjects. "Delilah, I've offered before, but now I'm insisting. Come live in the guest house at the ranch. You won't have to pay rent and you'll always be welcome to eat with me and Isabelle, or with my folks at the main house."

"Please, Lilah, I can't stand you living in that trailer. Come stay at the ranch," Izzy pleads.

Ever since Izzy moved to the Andersen's ranch, she's been trying to convince Delilah to come live with them. Anything to get her out of that godforsaken hellhole. Delilah's declined the offer every time, but last night, she might've been pushed too far and might say yes.

Panic floods my system like ice. I'm a selfish bastard. If I only cared about Delilah's safety, I would've moved her out to the ranch myself months ago. Instead, I've tried to keep her out of the trailer, busy with me, her sister, or their best friend, Olivia.

But the sun always sets, and she sleeps in that tin can, avoiding her egg donor. Living in that trailer isn't an option. But I can't bear her being even farther away from me, living out of town on the ranch.

There's no way in hell I'll stand for another man taking care of Delilah.

I take care of Delilah.

My heart hijacks control of my mouth, telling my brain to stay out of it, and I release one of my deepest desires from my vault of secrets.

"No. With all due respect, Andersen, Delilah will be coming home with me."

Today is the one-year anniversary of one of the worst days of my life. But today, Delilah agreed to move in with me, making it one of the best days of my life.

A year ago today, I got a call from my big sister, Quincy. But when I answered the call, it wasn't Quincy on the other end. I was caught off guard by a stoic man's voice.

"Connor? This is Lucas Langford. I'm friends with your sister." His voice was tight with emotion, and my blood turned to ice.

"Is she okay? Is Quincy hurt? Why are you calling me from her phone? Where's Sam?" I couldn't stop the questions tumbling from my mouth. Dread filled my stomach like a lead weight.

Lucas cleared his throat. *"It's Sam."* Silence suspended me in a moment where whatever he was about to say was going to change everything.

The crack in Lucas's voice pierced my heart. *"Sam's gone. He died this morning. I'm with Quincy and the Andersens at the hospital in Laramie."*

I couldn't bring myself to ask what happened. Before he could ask, I threw my jacket on, grabbed my keys and was out the door. "I'm on my way."

I wanted to break every speed limit on my way to the hospital to be there for my sister. I work for the Department of Transportation, practically driving for a living, and my job's taught me you can't help someone if you're dead on the side of the road.

I used the drive to steel myself and lock all my emotions in a box, preparing to hold my sister together. Our parents, Norah and Elliott, were unreachable, so it was up to me to be there for Quincy.

At only twenty-five, I've been the man of my family for a

couple of years already. My dad's rapidly succumbing to Alzheimer's disease, and I've stepped up for my mom and sister in every way possible.

After they got married, Sam took care of Quincy I was able to stop worrying so much about her. For a couple of years, I was able to focus on my mom, my best friend, and every so often, my own needs.

On the drive to Wyoming, I let my duty to care for Quincy seep back into my marrow. I'd do anything my sister needed.

I choked on the pain in the hospital waiting room like a thick, cloying fog. I wove past the Andersens, who were huddled together in various positions surrounding their matriarch. Their suffering was palpable, but my priority was my sister.

Sitting in a cold, hard, waiting room chair sat the shell of my normally vibrant, effervescent big sister. A man, who I assumed to be Lucas, sat beside Quincy, holding her hand in silence.

I knelt before her catatonic form and gently braced my hands on her knees. She didn't acknowledge my presence, meet my eyes, or give me any hint she was somewhere in there.

Trauma does strange things to people, it's unpredictable and uncontrollable. It was like the death of her young husband erased everything that made her *Quincy*. Left in the wreckage was a pale, motionless, shell of a woman.

I connected eyes with Lucas, and he shook his head in disbelief of the situation, and confirming my sister's disappearance. Without having to speak, he and I were on the same wavelength. I stood and bent to brace Quincy by her back. Together, we coerced her out of the chair and onto her feet.

A year's passed, and Quincy still hasn't found her footing. Last May, the two remaining Andersen brothers, Lucas, and I, moved Quincy home to Swiftwater hoping it would help her move on.

Like the cruel bitch it is, time marched on, forcing us into each tomorrow, closing the door on another yesterday. Another day without my sister, lost to her grief. A year's worth of days that refused to pause for her to heal without everyone else moving on around her.

Today was no different in that regard. But it's significant in that she supported her own weight as we walked down to the bank of Whitetail River to honor her late husband's memory with his family.

Our parents were notably absent, as they were last year when Sam's ashes were spread. It kills my mom not to be there for Quincy on hard days like today, but my dad requires constant care which she provides at their home. Quincy understands, but it doesn't make it any less difficult not having their presence and support as we honor Sam.

Delilah shifts in my arms and leans back into my chest for support. The sweet scent of vanilla and jasmine floods my senses as I bury my face into silken strands of sunlight. I place a kiss on the crown of gold nestled against me and am overcome by profound comfort.

On a day not about me, my best friend showed up to support me, knowing how much pressure I put on myself to support my sister. And in the six-degrees-of-separation phenomenon that is small-town-living, my best friend was also there to support someone else.

Sam was the youngest of the Andersen brothers. The middle brother, Reid, and the oldest brother, James, are my brothers-in-law by relation to Quincy. I've gotten to know them in bits and pieces over the years, but despite my sister having been married to the youngest of them, we never crossed paths much. That rapidly changed when Reid fell in love with Isabelle, Delilah's Irish twin sister.

Delilah's been my best friend since I was a pain-in-the-ass little kid. I'm lucky she's still my best friend as a pain-in-the-ass grown man. She served as a bridge of strength today, supporting Isabelle and Reid on one side, and me and Quincy on the other. I don't know what I'd ever do without her.

The memorial gave me and Delilah a reprieve from the argument we'd been having. I know I'm right. She knows I'm right. We both know what needs to happen but wouldn't without a push in the right direction.

"Thank you for being there for me today, doll. I couldn't have been as strong for Quincy if you weren't holding me together." Delilah tilts her head up and smiles softly.

"Forever and ever." Her sweet voice tugs on the heartstring that connects us.

I let her go and we settle onto my couch with her head in my lap. I finger comb her long hair and enjoy the weight of her on my thigh.

"I'm still mad at you," she mumbles.

"I know, doll, but it had to happen. And before you say it didn't have to happen *today*—can you honestly tell me you want to go back to that trailer after what happened last night?" I push.

"No...but I didn't want today becoming about me and my insignificant problems when we were there to honor Sam. Quincy lost her husband, you lost your brother-in-law, the Andersens lost their son and brother. My mom getting herself into trouble is nothing compared to their grief...and you embarrassed me," she says.

"I know, and I'm so fucking sorry. You know I'd never do anything to intentionally hurt you. It was an asshole move to push the issue after the memorial, but I'd do it again in a heartbeat if it meant you'd be living here with me—safe," I say firmly.

"You don't really want me here, Connor. You have your own life and I'm sure you're used to the bachelor lifestyle. I don't want to be a burden."

Little does she know I want nothing more than for her to live with me. She's my world, and I haven't taken advantage of being a bachelor in…shit, over a year. It's difficult to get a hard-on for a woman who isn't the love of my life. My hook-ups have always been hollow and resulted in me scrubbing shame off my skin.

I coax Delilah onto her back, her nape resting on my thigh and cup her cheeks, smooshing them together like a chipmunk, making her giggle.

"You are never, have never, and will never be a burden. I want you to be wherever I am, and it makes me happy providing you a safe and comfortable home. I don't want to hear it again, okay?"

I bend down and suck the tip of her nose into my mouth and release it with a loud pop.

"Connor! Gross! I hate when you do that!" She laughs, wiping my spit from her nose.

I nudge her to get off my lap and pile the throw pillows and lap blankets around her, like a cocoon. She wiggles trying to get out, but I tuck her in tighter. Her laughter shoots me right in the chest.

"You're going to stay here, take a nap because you've got to be exhausted from the shitshow last night, and wait for me, okay? I'm moving you out of that trailer," I say.

"Conn—" she protests but I cut her off.

"It's not up for discussion, doll. You're an intelligent, independent, perfectly capable woman, but you have to let me do this for you." I kiss her forehead and head out the door without looking back.

She's never going back to that trailer if I have anything to do with it.

Delilah belongs with me.

2

Connor age 8, Delilah age 7

I rode my bike way farther than Mom said I could today. But it's the end of summer and I don't wanna go home yet. I rode all the way from my house, through the whole town, past the high school, and now I'm here. My rear tires on the sidewalk, and my front tire is on the dirt road that leads out to the trailer park.

I get off my Huffy and set it down gently, so I don't scare her. Tiny sniffles come from a life-size princess doll. The little girl sitting on the dirt road has her knees pulled to her chin, and her face buried in her arms crying.

I walk over to her. I'm nervous, but it feels like the right thing to do to help her. I plop down beside her in the dirt and pat her shaking back.

"Are you okay?" I ask, looking around for a grown-up.

I can't see her face. It's hidden behind the whitest hair I've ever seen. It's shiny, and straight, and almost touches her bottom. Like the Barbie dolls my big sister plays with.

She slowly lifts her head from her crossed arms but doesn't look at me.

"I'm okay. You don't have to sit with me," she says quietly.

"Do you need a grown-up? I can go get my mom," I offer, hiking a thumb over my shoulder.

"Grown-ups never help. It's okay."

She wipes her runny nose with the back of her hand and wipes it on her pretty yellow dress, already dirty from sitting on the ground. She tucks her doll-like hair behind her ear and shyly looks at me. Her eyes look like diamonds. They're red from crying, but they're sparkly like my mom's wedding ring. My eyes are just brown. I've never seen eyes like hers before.

I pop up from the ground and hold my hands out to help her up. "My name's Connor. What's your name?"

Tinkling like a bell, the little doll says, "I'm Delilah."

I've never heard that name before. It's pretty. She's wiping the dust off her bottom, so I peek at her face a little bit. She's so pretty. Even though her face is all splotchy and red and there's tears and boogers on it.

My mom hugs me when I cry and it always makes me feel better, maybe it works for other kids too. I do know one thing that fixes anything in the whole wide world. My mom's lemonade.

"Do you like lemonade?" I ask.

She's shy but says she likes lemonade and gives me a tiny smile that makes me feel funny in my stomach.

"My mom makes the world's best lemonade. I bet she has cookies too. Come on, you're coming home with me."

3

Delilah

I'm sitting on Connor's living room floor, surrounded by boxes containing my entire life. Everything happened so quickly. I can't wrap my head around my reality.

Not even sixteen hours ago, I was sleeping on the same twin bed I always had—snuggled beneath layers of blankets, because Mom didn't pay the gas bill. Again.

Spring is shining her light brighter every day, but it's still downright freezing overnight in the Rocky Mountains. When I got home last night, as late as I could bear before I fell asleep on my feet, Mom was passed out face-down on the kitchen table. I found a relatively clean blanket to cover her with and quietly pushed the beer cans away from her face.

I fell asleep the moment my head hit the pillow. I've been avoiding home as much as possible since my sister moved in with her fiancé. I can't bear being alone with my mother anymore. It's hard work finding things to do at all hours of the day to stay out of my house, so I'm exhausted every night.

I was a few hours into dreamland when the unmistakable sound of glass breaking ricocheted around the small trailer. I was jolted awake and on high alert.

I thought, *please just let it be Mom stumbling around. Maybe she knocked over some dishes.* How naive of me to think I was safe in my own home.

The front door slammed open against the outside of the trailer, meaning someone broke the glass to reach inside and unlock it. Loud boots stomped across the hollow floor, and shouts of rage filled the air—several different male voices, and of course, my inebriated mother, slurring and crying.

Unfortunately, it wasn't the first time in my twenty-four years of life the sanctity of my home had been destroyed. I knew all too well what type those men were, and what they were after.

I dressed in whatever clothes I could find in the dark, grabbed my phone, and opened the small window in my room. This wasn't the first time I'd had to escape, not my first rodeo, so to speak. I know exactly how to lift and shimmy the window along the rusty track to make the least amount of noise, and gently popped out the screen, letting it fall to the snowpack below.

Things were being thrown and broken, and doors ripped open. I was out of time. I jumped out of the window and was spotted by the man who was standing look-out. He shouted at me to stop, and to alert the thugs inside, but I was already gone.

I ran through the trailer park weaving around homes, cars, junk, and piles of snow. I lost my footing several times in the icy night but had to get as far away from the trailer as possible. Once I was nearing the trailer park entrance, I hid behind a dumpster and called the one number that would guarantee my safety.

Minutes later, tires squealed down Main Street heading towards me. Tires that normally took twice as long to arrive. Connor jumped out of his truck, door swung open, engine running, shouting my name.

I didn't look back as I ran into his arms. He wasted no time getting me into his truck and taking me away.

Like I said, not our first rodeo.

Connor Hayes has been my knight in shining armor since I was seven years old. And here we were again, the brave knight rescuing the damsel in distress from the evil witch.

I didn't buckle my seatbelt. I burrowed under Connor's arm as he drove us to his apartment. No words were needed, we'd said them all countless times before and nothing ever changed.

Violent shivers from the cold and adrenaline wracked my body when we arrived at the drawbridge, so the knight carried the damsel up the castle steps without needing to be asked.

Connor deposited my shaking body on the closed toilet seat and turned on his shower, filling the small bathroom with steam.

He returned with clean clothes for me to sleep in and shut the door behind him. I went through the motions of showering, warming my bones, towel drying and braiding my long hair, and dressing before padding into his bedroom. Connor sat on the edge of the bed in nothing but sleep shorts, head hung low between his shoulders, elbows resting on his knees.

Despite the morose aura in the room, I couldn't help but notice Connor's beauty. Hearing me approach, he reached over to his nightstand and passed me a glass of water and two pain killers.

He flipped back his covers and slid into bed, holding them open for me to join him. I curled into his warm, hard chest and disappeared into a deep sleep.

This morning was far less peaceful. Connor and I have a history of going rounds arguing about my living situation. He wanted me out. I did too but I was never brave enough to make the move. And in the harsh morning light, in the aftermath of yet another close call, everything was game for discussion.

I was inappropriately relieved we needed to head out for Sam's memorial, because Connor wouldn't argue with me there.

I should've known better.

Even when he pisses me off, Connor always has my best interests at heart, and last night pushed him over the edge into raging-alpha-protector-mode. I would've found it sexy had I not been so furious with him.

We tabled the argument during the gathering along Whitetail River where our sole attention needed to be on supporting our loved ones.

But, like the pain in my ass he always is, Connor resumed arguing with me as we left the memorial. That's how my sister found out what our mom got herself into and how I ended up freezing behind a dumpster waiting for Connor to rescue me.

She and her fiancé Reid have been so generous to host me at the ranch for endless hours to keep me away from home. They offer me a permanent place to live on a daily basis. But a little something in me still tethered to my mother always has me declining the invitation.

This morning, however, my world was flipped on its axis when Connor declared I'd be moving in with him. He left zero room for argument.

He took me back to his apartment, forbade me from leaving, and went to my no-longer-home and packed my things. One truck load was all it took to move my world to the other side of town.

Connor stomps into the apartment carrying one last box and locks the door behind him. I open my mouth to protest, but he cuts me off.

"Delilah, don't try me right now. You're staying here and that's final."

I've spent the last seventeen years under Connor's constant supervision and protection. Typically, I'm equal parts embarrassed and grateful. But today, I'm pissed.

"Connor, I'm a grown woman, and can make my own decisions," I snap.

"Clearly not, since you should've gotten out of that hellhole years ago. I decided for you, end of story." His highhanded declaration infuriates me.

"And who are you to make my decisions for me?" But I already know the answer.

"I'm yours. You damn well know that. You've been mine since I found you crying in the dirt in that pretty yellow dress."

His recollection spears me in the heart every single time.

"I don't want to burden you. You work a ridiculous number of hours, take care of your parents, and have been taking care of your sister since Sam died. I can't be another weight on your shoulders." I slide the tarnished sun pendant across the chain I've replaced over the years.

Tears leak from my eyes without my permission. I'm not crying intentionally. My tears have always been Connor's weakness. Since we were tiny kids, he's taken it upon himself to dry my tears and hold them at bay with his love and support.

"Fuck, don't cry, doll. You know I can't take it when you cry. I didn't mean to be an asshole."

He joins me on the floor, sits behind me with his legs bracketing my hips, pulls me into his chest, and cages me with his rainbow-colored arms.

I'm sobbing. "It isn't fair! Why do other people have parents who take care of them when I got left by one, and forgotten by the other? What's so unlovable about me they couldn't take care of me?"

"No, no, no, doll. There's nothing unlovable about you. Izzy loves you. Olivia loves you. I fucking love you. Everyone who meets you adores you. It's not your fault your parents prioritized their vices over their children."

He kisses the top of my head, softly rocking me in his arms.

"It was past time for you to get out of there. Please let me do this for you. Please, doll. I can't stand you hurting, and you being in that trailer makes me sick to my stomach."

Since he has my arms pinned, I smoosh my face into his forearms, rubbing it back and forth on his arm hair to wipe away my tears. I'm so tired of crying over my parents.

I huff a humorless laugh. "Oh, so the move was all for your benefit?"

He pinches my side, making me squirm and yelp.

"If that helps you sleep at night, sure. It'd be doing me a huge favor if you'd live with me so my stress level will drop back below heart attack range. You little shit."

He tickles me along my ribs as I curl away from his fingers. He always knows how to make me smile.

I twist around in his arms to face him.

"Thank you. For everything, Connor. I don't know what I'd ever do without you."

The rich chocolate irises that've always soothed my soul trace across my features. He looks at me like it's the first time he's seeing me, taking in my every detail.

"Good thing you'll never have to find out, because you're stuck with me, doll." He kisses my forehead and hoists us both off the ground.

"Come on. Let's go find somewhere to put all your things."

In his one-bedroom apartment, it goes without saying we'll be sharing his queen-size bed. His parents never allowed boy-girl sleepovers, but I've fallen asleep in Connor's arms more times than I can count. And it's my favorite place to be.

Lithe back muscles ripple beneath his thin cotton shirt as he lifts several of my boxes at once and carries them to his bedroom. He packed them, so he knows better than I do where they need to go.

A pang of longing hits me in the stomach as he walks away. My best friend is the sexiest man I've ever laid eyes on. Just shy of six-feet-tall, he's the perfect height to kiss the crown of my head.

Due to lucky genetics, Connor's golden tan all-year round. He never burns and doesn't resemble a Victorian ghost in the winter like I do.

His hair matches his skin-tone perfectly, a dirty blonde streaked from time in the sun he wears in the most fuck-me hairstyle. It's buzzed to his temples, with thick, straight hair long on top and is either pushed back by running his strong fingers through the strands or hanging playfully over one eye.

I've touched his hair plenty of times to fix it, or to comfort him. But I've never gripped it in the throes of passion the way my fingers ache to.

His body is immaculate, tight and toned—but not bulky, sculpted from hard labor working on the highway.

From his eighteenth birthday forward, he's covered himself with a collage of rainbow-colored art. Tattoos rise from the collar of his shirt and snake around both arms to the backs of his hands. Ink covers his chest, and his back is a breathtaking collage of vibrant images. It wasn't long ago his tattoo artist filled in the blank spaces on his back to weave the pieces into one cohesive back-piece.

I've traced the lines of every single tattoo on hot summer days when he's shirtless, massaging his back after a hard shift, or while we watch movies together. I know his upper body like a map.

How desperately I've wanted to grip his shoulders and kiss

him. To rake my nails down his back while he makes love to me. To kiss and lick the tattoos on his neck and chest with nothing between us.

But it's never been like that between us, and it never will be. He's always seen me as a little sister. Not as a potential partner. Not as a woman.

Based on the girls he's always dated, I'm clearly not his type. He only goes for girls with dark hair and eyes. Unfortunately for me, Connor is my only type.

I'd never jeopardize our friendship by revealing my nearly two-decade-long crush on my best friend. Some things aren't meant to be.

But I'll take any version of a relationship with Connor he'll give me. And that's always been as the best of friends.

We've been inseparable since the day he found me crying in the dirt. Dad went on a bender and Mom was stuck at home with us girls. Taking care of us was her least favorite activity. Izzy was locked in her bedroom, grounded for some asinine reason when Mom spilled beer on my pretty yellow dress. I'd found it in the donation bin near the market and cleaned it the best I could. Mom was furious her beer was wasted, and she screamed at me to get out, over and over again.

I didn't want to leave Izzy, but she was safe behind her locked door. I ran as fast as my little legs could take me. I tripped on a rock and skinned my knees right before I got to the nice sidewalk outside the trailer park that led to town.

I tried not to cry, I really did. But my life was a lot for a seven-year-old to endure, and I collapsed under the weight of my sadness.

That's where Connor found me. Dressed in nice new clothes, with a shiny two-wheel bike, inviting me to his home for cookies and lemonade.

I've loved Connor since before I knew what it meant to love. But he's only ever seen me as a friend, and that's okay.

Or so I've desperately tried to convince myself over the years.

And being the world-class friend he is, I find myself here. About to live with my walking-testosterone sex-god best friend, knowing I'll be sleeping against his bare chest every night. Seeing parts of his life I've never been privy to, private things like the way he brushes his teeth, and when he changes his bedsheets.

Oh god. How often does he change his bedsheets? Does he have women here? What am I supposed to do if he brings a date home? Sit in the living room with noise cancelling headphones and a blindfold on? Or does he go to their place? Does he spend the night with them? Or will he roll into bed with me in the early hours of the morning, covered in their perfume?

I'm going to be sick.

4

I'm unloading a box of Delilah's bathroom products slower than necessary. I need a minute to breathe.

In the past couple of hours, I aired my best friend's dirty laundry out to her sister, demanded she live with me, sorted through rubble from the break-in at the trailer, packed her belongings, and brought them to my 600 square foot, one-bedroom apartment.

My jaw clenches involuntarily and the tips of my ears burn hot mulling over the repercussions of my actions. I finally have Delilah all to myself. She'll be in my bed every night. But most importantly, she's safe after all these years and I don't have to worry myself sick wondering if she's okay.

I get unfettered access to hang out with my best friend whenever I'm home.

In no way will this become my own personal hell—living in intimate quarters with the star of my every fantasy but not being able to touch her or tell her how I feel.

Because how I feel is far more than friendly.

It's completely fine that I've now fingered every single pair of panties she owns and held the cups of her delicate lace bras in my tattooed hands. I've never once imagined Delilah wearing nearly nonexistent scraps of cotton and lace beneath her clothes. It's never crossed my mind, not even once, wondering if she wore thongs, or little cheeky panties.

Why would I wonder about that? It doesn't matter to me. The answer is both. Nope.

Yes, I gathered her e-reader and books beside her bed. But I did *not* find one of the covers intriguing and open it to the page she dog-eared revealing a graphic sex scene of a man pounding into a woman from behind, skirt rucked up over her hips, panties pulled to the side.

I'm entirely unfazed that my innocent little doll has a pile of book-porn, and I do *not* need to know how often she reads it or if her thighs clench together when she does. Nope.

It's totally not a big deal that I found a bright purple silicone rabbit dildo in her nightstand. I'm not at all bothered by how long and thick it is, or that it's given the woman of my dreams pleasure.

I definitely did *not* turn it on and click through the vibration settings or hold it against my nose trying to scent any hint of her pussy. Nope.

I did *not* wrap one of her lace thongs around my throbbing erection and jerk off in her childhood bedroom to the image of her on her knees, those diamond eyes sparkling up at me through tears gagging on my cock.

I did *not* come so hard my knees buckled, and I forgot where I was. Nope.

Shame licks up the back of my neck like flames. She'd be mortified if she knew I hadn't simply gathered her stuff in a big pile and shoved it into a box—but fingered each and every piece, fantasizing about her.

I'm the luckiest fucker on the planet since Delilah Tate chose me to be her best friend. She trusts me implicitly and today will not be the day that trust is destroyed because of my dick.

I find a toiletry bag that has a bunch of shit I don't recognize and hide the vibrator inside. I zip it shut and push it to the back of my under-sink cabinet. Partially to prevent her from finding out I know it exists—but mostly because I can't live knowing she slides it in and out of herself in my bed, beneath my sheets, when I'm not home.

I might die if she's needy, and I'm not the one who gets to satisfy her. Jesus christ, what's wrong with me?

"Hey. Everything going okay in here?" I jump out of my fucking skin, fumbling around to make sure there's no evidence of my depravity out in the open. She laughs. "Wound tight today, are we?"

She has no fucking idea.

"Naw, just trying to get your things put away so you feel at home." Nice save. Her eyes take inventory of what I've unpacked, unfazed.

"Is it okay if I hang my dresses in your closet and put my clothes in your dresser? I promise I won't take all your space," she asks sweetly.

I clear my throat. "Yea, of course, do whatever you need. This is your home now." I rub the back of my neck. "I know it's small, it's only ever been me and I'm gone most of the time. But whatever I have, is yours. And whatever I don't have, I'll get for you."

"You have no idea what this means to me, Connor. I'd never take advantage of you."

Take advantage of me! Please, take everything until I have nothing left.

The shrill alarm on my phone goes off. Shit. I thought I had more time. My lips press against Delilah's forehead for a beat too long, and I give her shoulders a squeeze.

"My shift's in about an hour. I've got to run. I'm sorry to leave you with this mess. I didn't exactly think it through moving you in just to leave you alone."

I'm such an asshole. She's probably scared, and she's never slept here overnight. Shit, I know she's never lived alone before.

Reading my spinning mind, she offers, "It's okay, really. You have an established life, and I'm grateful you're making space for me. Izzy and Liv have been blowing up my phone, so I'll ask them over to help me unpack. If that's okay?."

"Of course. This is your home now. You don't need to ask for permission to have people over." As long as they're female, and don't want to fuck you, I add silently.

I take out my wallet and leave a few $20's. "I don't have shit around here to eat. Buy whatever you need from the market."

She gives me a little smile. God, I love her smiles.

"You don't have to do that, I have money." I give her a pointed look. "But thank you, I'll go grocery shopping and do some cooking. I'll be fine."

I check the time on my phone again. "Fuck, I've got to go." I unwind my house key from my keyring, place it in her palm, and wrap her fingers around it. "I'll make an extra when I get back, but you need to lock up. I want you to always have the door locked when I'm not here."

She nods her agreement. "Be safe!" She always tells me and hugs me tight around the middle. Those sparkling diamonds peer up at me through delicate eyelashes.

"Bye, doll." I kiss her forehead for a beat too long.

She beams at me. "Miss you already."

I walk out the door and the lock clicks behind me. Good girl.

As I walk to my truck, my heart bangs against my ribcage trying to get back to her, like it always does. But this time it's worse.

Because for the first time, I'm leaving when she's all mine.

5

"Holy shit! Connie wasn't joking. He really moved you in." Izzy's eyes are bugging out of her head.

"I didn't think he had it in him. Good for Connie. Finally making his move!" Livy adds.

"He hates when you call him that. Can you drop it?" I'm so tired of this argument.

"Yea, yea, yea. We know. You're just friends. Blah, blah, blah. The only people who believe that nonsense are the two of you," Izzy mocks.

Livy can't help but pile on, "It's okay, we'll float around in denial with you." She claps here hands. "What's first?"

I invited the girls over to help me unpack because I'm overwhelmed by everything that's transpired in the past day. My stomach growls—I haven't eaten since yesterday at dinner, and I only had a small cup of soup—I'm starving. Things were so chaotic this morning, Connor didn't nag me about breakfast, and this moving extravaganza eclipsed lunch.

"Well, he left me some money for groceries. He said it's bare bones in the kitchen. So that's a top priority, but I can do that later, it's not a far walk."

Izzy cuts in first. "No. The car is yours, Lilah. Reid's picking me up later." She drops the car key into my purse on the countertop. "Non-negotiable. Reid and I insist since I've essentially abandoned you, now that you live on your own, you need a car."

I don't like being doted on. I prefer taking care of people, so it's difficult for me to accept acts of good will. Izzy and I saved for years to buy that little car when she turned sixteen. There was no way our parents would provide a vehicle for us. She took the car during her hiatus in Denver, but I didn't mind. She needed it in the city, and I was perfectly content to walk or catch a ride with Connor, or Liv when she was in town.

Olivia Dalton's been best friends with me and Izzy since elementary school. She's just as much a sister as Izzy is.

"Thank you, sissy," I concede and blow her a kiss.

Olivia walks over to her purse next to mine and grabs out her own keys and swipes the grocery money off the counter. "I'll go grocery shopping while you twins unpack." I open my mouth to refuse. "Babe, I'm not going to get into it with you right now, but you're under an incredible amount of stress with so much change. You need calories, love. Dry salads and soup aren't enough." Her compassion shines through her tone.

When I hedge, she adds, "I'll even pick up a gallon of Frank's lemonade." She gets the side eye, because she knows that's my weakness.

I've struggled with food and body image since childhood. I go through phases where I'm better and eat more regularly, and phases where I struggle to choke down even a bite. I know she's right, but it's mortifying, as always, to have other people making decisions for me about my body.

There's no way I can hide my eating habits from Connor now that we live together. He'll realize how poorly I've been managing. The room is tilting, either from the lack of calories, or from the impending anxiety spiral.

I surrender. "Okay, thank you, Livy."

In a red whirl, she's out the door, leaving me alone with my sister. She's looking at me in that way I hate, where she's concerned and frustrated with me. Thankfully, she senses the topic needs to be tabled and moves on.

"Connor packed everything from the trailer he thought was mine. He unpacked all my bathroom stuff already, so do you want to help me fold and hang all my clothes?" I ask.

"You got it. Lead the way." Izzy follows me the few steps to Connor's bedroom. She pauses in the doorway, leans back to look right and left in the hall, and frowns at me. "Is this the only bedroom?"

"Mmhmm."

"No way in hell is he making you sleep on the couch," Izzy bites out.

"No, we'll share his bed. It's not a big deal, Iz." No way, no how will she buy that.

Arms crossed, she purses her lips and narrows her eyes in that disapproving sister way that makes me want to smack her.

"Sure. It's no big deal to share a bed with your male best friend. There's no possible way that could go badly for you. You won't grow even more attached to him and further blur the line you two so precariously toe."

My teeth grind like nails on a chalkboard. I'm too tired for this conversation.

"Can you please save it for a time when I've had more than five hours of sleep and haven't just had my entire life upended?"

She rolls her eyes. Bitch. "Whatever. Show me where you want stuff to go."

We go round and round about my relationship with Connor on a regular basis. I love my sister to death, but I wish she'd let this go.

I've always insisted Connor is just my friend and am careful to act accordingly in public. My feelings for Connor are the one secret I've ever kept from my sister.

Nothing's ever going to happen between us. If something were to happen, I'd first have to admit my feelings to myself, and then to Connor, before I'd dream of telling anyone else. Not even my sister. I wouldn't survive the heartbreak if my secret was exposed, and Connor didn't feel the same.

Our friendship isn't something I'm willing to risk, even if it means never having the only thing I've ever wanted.

We put away clothes, bopping around to music Izzy plays on her phone. We work in comfortable silence, something I've always valued in our relationship. We finish and find there's not much left to put away. I put out my knickknacks, each one widening my smile. Connor won't mind, he bought most of them for me anyway.

"How did you like it?" Izzy asks, holding my newest paperback book.

"I loved it! Thanks for the recommendation!"

"I think this is book two, so I'll order book one and book three comes out soon. So, I'll pass them along once I finish reading them!" Izzy offers.

"Thanks sissy."

Izzy continues stacking my books and I'm jolted by panic. Oh my god. Those books were on my nightstand in the trailer. The nightstand that concealed my vibrator. Shit.

Maybe Connor didn't see it. It wasn't with the toiletries he brought over, and we've emptied the other boxes. There's no way I'm going back for it. I'll have to order a new one and be careful to hide the delivery from Connor.

Olivia returns with arms full of reusable grocery bags. We busy ourselves putting everything away. I don't pay close attention to the items because I'm too overwhelmed to fight my demons right now.

From the last bag, Livy pulls out three pre-packaged salads and sets them out on Connor's coffee table. He doesn't have a dinner table; I suppose there's no reason a transient bachelor would see the need for one. We plop down on the couch and dig into our lunches.

Either to keep it simple, or to manage any possible fights, Olivia bought three identical club salads. I'm hungry enough that each bite of hard-boiled egg, cheese, ham, turkey, and ranch dressing goes down easily.

The familiar itch nags me to calculate the calories in my head. Thankfully, my obsessive thoughts are interrupted.

"Things have been so crazy with the memorial and Deliliah's re-homing, we haven't gotten to talk about the ROCK on Izzy's ring finger!" Olivia exclaims.

Reid proposed to my sister a few days ago. Their love story is unconventional, but I'm so happy my sissy is being loved the way she deserves. After being sexually harassed and mercilessly bullied for years following, my sister swore off men and had never gone on a date before Reid.

I missed her terribly when she was living in Denver, so when I realized how stressed she was about her finances, I did the only thing I could think of. I went to Connor to fix it.

Connor always takes care of things and this was no different. A quick call to his mom and we got Izzy an interview with Swift Property Management here in town. Lucky for us the company is owned by his mom's best friend.

Reid and his older brother James both work for the family business, so I wasn't shocked when Izzy told me she'd be working with Reid. Livy and I poked fun at her for working with her childhood crush. She'd been infatuated with the middle Andersen brother since middle school.

Reid was a royal ass for the first several months Izzy was back home. They were together non-stop for work, traveling across the Rockies and spending nights together at the rental properties.

He better count his lucky stars my sister gave him one last chance after he broke her heart one too many times.

Izzy's extremely forgiving, and ultimately her heart prevailed, and they're madly in love. Now engaged to be married seven months after "meeting," I've never seen my sister so happy. She deserves her happily ever after.

Izzy blushes at Olivia's proclamation but holds out her left hand and wiggles her fingers. She shouts at the top of her lungs, kicking her feet, "I'M ENGAGED!"

We spend the rest of the afternoon plying her for every detail of the proposal and what comes next for the happy couple. From what it sounds like, they have a long road of hard work ahead of them to renovate the Andersen family ranch.

Reid renamed it Lucky Spurs Ranch and has grand plans to make it a vacation destination and to expand his horse operation. Their vision is remarkable, and passion radiates from her like rainbows and sunshine.

The vacation cabin build-out is pretty cut and dry, but Reid's dreams for his horses wander far and wide. On top of offering trail rides and basic experiences for guests, he also wants to rescue and rehabilitate horses.

All the horse-talk around the ranch gave me courage to attend an equine therapy demonstration, and I haven't stopped thinking about it since. It's been in the back of my mind since middle school, but it was never a possibility for me.

Would Reid consider offering at the ranch?

What am I thinking? I haven't even graduated—I have no business indulging in fantasies.

The girls bid me adieu when the afternoon sun bleeds behind the mountain peaks. I love them to death, but I need space to recharge and process the whirlwind of events. Connor's couch envelops me as I close my eyes.

Reality shakes my foundation. I *live* with Connor. I'm trapped in close quarters with the love of my life, doomed to pretend we're just friends. My fragile heart won't survive a million slow deaths. Having Connor in my life as a friend is worlds better than not having him at all.

I'm terrified my heart's going to break and I don't know how I'm going to hide my feelings from him. Our relationship will never be the same; I could lose him if the truth ever comes out, or if I make him uncomfortable living with me.

I can't let my foolish feelings ruin this for me. I should be grateful he's taken me in and rescued me from my circumstances.

I'm safe and comfortable for the first time knowing Connor would never let anything happen to me under his watch.

I refuse to return to the trailer ever again. Mom's in trouble but the state of her affairs isn't my concern. I'll never pay her bills ever again. She made her own choices, and I'm choosing to stop getting involved.

Our relationship may be irreparably damaged, but it's not like there was much left to damage. She and my dad have relentlessly proven we weren't worth sticking around for, staying sober for, or meeting our most basic needs. Part of me is bitter. Why do I feel guilty when she couldn't manage to keep the electricity on or put food in my belly? The other part of me is sad. I've lived a lifetime mourning the parents I should've had.

Sadness and guilt swirl sour in my gut for abandoning my mom. Anger burns that she and my father didn't love us enough to provide for us or give us love or affection.

I'm afraid of getting roped into whatever trouble she's gotten herself into. Thank goodness I have Connor to protect me.

A lightness opens space for relief, now that I'm not burdened by supporting my mom. Connor and I haven't discussed rent, but I know from experience he'll vehemently reject any money I offer him.

Just one more semester and I'll have my bachelor's in psychology. I'm beyond grateful I won't need to pick up a job to cover Mom's expenses.

Izzy and I got jobs as soon as we were old enough and went full-time after high school. I needed every penny to keep our home afloat, so going away for college wasn't an option.

Swiftwater High offered concurrent enrollment with the community college, so I graduated high school with a handful of credits under my belt.

After graduation, I continued chipping away at online classes. I transferred my credits to the University of Northern Colorado's online psychology program and worked towards my degree class by class.

What takes some students four years took me nearly twice as long, but it'll be worth it.

Finals are next month, and my grades will be a critical deciding factor for internship placement during the final semester. My top choice is equine therapy, but the internship options aren't near Swiftwater and I'm nervous to leave my sister and Connor.

Some deep breathing calms my anxiety to a low whir instead of a raging tornado. I grab my bookbag and laptop my scholarship covered and get to work on my coursework.

The stillness of Connor's apartment is unsettling. An unexpected wave of loneliness overcomes me, so I do what I always do.

> Me: Hi!

Studmuffin: Hey dollface, everything okay?

> Me: Yep. The girls got me all unpacked, stocked the kitchen, and fed me.

> Me: How's work?

Studmuffin: That's great doll!

Studmuffin: Work's fine. They've got me up on the pass clearing debris from the tunnel.

Studmuffin: You caught me on break.

> Me: Perfect timing! I'm so glad the weather was nice today. I couldn't handle my first night alone if you were stuck in a storm or on bad roads.

Studmuffin: I feel like shit you're there by yourself.

Studmuffin: I'll try to trade for as many day shifts as I can, so you don't have to sleep alone.

> Me: You don't have to do that. Your busy season is coming up. I'll be fine.

Studmuffin: I don't want you to be fine, I want you to be amazing.

> Me: Okay, I'll be amazing.

Studmuffin: Damn straight you will, because I'm going to take care of you.

Me: You don't need to take care of me. We're roommates now. I AM an adult, just in case you forgot.

Studmuffin: Didn't forget. Just don't care. I love taking care of you.

Studmuffin: And we're not roommates

Me: No, I guess not. I feel like I'm where I belong.

Studmuffin: With me.

Me: With you.

Studmuffin: Okay, doll. My break's over. I've got to get back to work.

Me: Okay! I have to study anyway. I hope you have a good rest of your shift!

Studmuffin: Lock the door.

Me: I did.

Studmuffin: Good girl.

Studmuffin: Sleep tight, doll.

I must look like a lunatic beaming at my phone, so wide my cheeks are hurting from smiling. I love him so much. I read back through our conversation, like I always do, because I'm obsessed with Connor.

I shiver when I re-read his "Good girl" message. He's never said that to me before and I'm all tingly about it. Is that weird?

He was glad I locked the door; it didn't mean anything, right?

The thought of hearing his gravelly voice calling me a good girl makes my sex clench involuntarily.

Now I have *another* reason to crave my best friend, and new fodder for my fantasy bank.

Except, shit. I don't have my vibrator. That reminds me and I order a replacement for express delivery.

Hopefully I'm the one who answers the door when the delivery person comes. They use discreet packaging though, so it should be okay. Connor wouldn't go through my mail.

I make myself a hot chocolate, Livy's an angel for buying me some, and settle in for a long night of studying. Peace washes over me being in Connor's space—I'm safe. I check the time and count the hours until Connor will be home.

It's never soon enough.

6

I fucking hate swing shift. Either give me uninterrupted daylight or let me get a full night's sleep. Swing shift is great for some people, they sleep after they get off until morning, be with their family, and go back in the afternoon.

That's all fine and good, but my assigned locations are often an hour or two away from Swiftwater. So, I have to leave midday and don't get home until the early hours of the morning. It fucks with my internal clock.

Plus, I don't want to scare the shit out of Delilah by knocking on the apartment door at fucking three in the morning because I gave her my only house key. Instead, I drive home and sleep in my truck for a couple of hours. My job wrecks my back and sleeping in my truck after a long shift doesn't help.

I wake to car doors slamming and engines starting as normal people begin their day. Jesus, is it morning already? I'm fucking wiped.

I check the time on my phone; Delilah should be awake by now. The red notification on my messages sends a jolt of energy through me, waking me up.

Only a handful of people text me. My boss, my sister, a

couple friends, and Delilah. And 90 percent of the time, it's Delilah.

I'm like Pavlov's fucking dog. When I get a text notification, I salivate for a treat—attention from my girl.

But I'm disappointed when I open my texts to one from my number two best friend, CJ. I've known the guy since birth, but he got bumped from the top spot the second I met Delilah. He's the best fuckin' guy and I'm lucky as hell he puts up with my bullshit.

He's got that dark hair-skin-eyes combo that makes anyone melt. He's never had an issue making friends, charming teachers and employers, or getting laid.

The best thing about him though, is he's gay as fuck. I say that with the utmost respect, both because he's one of the best humans I know, but also because I didn't have to cut him out of my life for coveting Delilah—like all my other friends did over the years.

Call me a possessive asshole, but the second anyone showed interest in Delilah, they were dead to me. No way in hell was I going to let another guy come between me and my doll.

She's been mine since I was eight years old, and she'll be mine long after we're dead in the ground.

That's one of the reason's I'm so grateful CJ's my right-hand man. He and Delilah get along famously, but he finds her glorious tits repulsive, and that suits me just fine.

He came out to me and his parents in fifth grade. We weren't surprised or affected whatsoever. CJ's always been unapologetically CJ, and the fact he liked boys went over like he was announcing he passed his math test.

When we were in middle school, he didn't just come out of the closet. He decorated it, put on a show, and made it a VIP lounge for anyone who wanted to join. He loved without apologies, wore his heart on his sleeve, and made sure everyone around him was safe to do the same.

He's why Swiftwater High has a thriving LGBTQ+ club and why the whole town comes out for the local Pride festival each June.

You wouldn't necessarily think a middle-of-nowhere ranching town would be so open minded, but I'm proud as fuck to live in the town that accepted CJ and paved the path of safety for everyone else to live their truth.

All I want to do is get my girl in my arms, but he'll come to my fucking apartment if I don't text him back within his acceptable timeframe, and checking the timestamp, I'm cutting it close.

> CJ: Hey Loverboy, how was moving day?

> CJ: I'd already know if you hadn't blown me off for your fucking job. Rude.

> CJ: Don't be a bitch. The buildup is killing me. I need to know EVERYTHING!

> CJ: Okay, I gave you time to come to your senses and spill. If I don't get a text before 8:00 a.m., I'm protesting outside your apartment. I'll make a sign that says CONNOR AND DELILAH SITTING IN A TREE, F-U-C-K-I-N-G.

Goddamn it, this is why he always gets his way. Because he's relentless and has impeccable follow-through.

> Me: Dude, you've gotta chill. Some of us don't work from our phones and can't respond instantaneously.

CJ: Excuses. Now spill or I'm coming over and outing your ass.

Me: I don't know what the fuck you're talking about.

CJ: Mmhmm. Same lie, different day.

CJ: I'm waiting...

Me: What do you want?

CJ: I want to know if your bride was delivered to your homestead.

CJ: Did you carry her over the threshold?

CJ: Oh my gawd, that would be so romantic.

Me: Why do I tell you things?

CJ: Because you love me. Stop avoiding the question.

Me: I got all her shit out of the trailer, and she unpacked while I was on shift.

CJ: How bad did it kill you knowing she changed her clothes in your apartment, and you weren't there to see it?

Me: Fuck you dude.

CJ: Come ON. You can't tell me you didn't picture it. *gag*

> Me: Don't know what you're talking about.

> CJ: Stop being a pussy and make a move. You finally have your shot.

> Me: I'm ignoring you now.

> CJ: Toodle-oo *waggles fingers* say hi to the wifey for me.

I wouldn't be surprised if I damage my phone with how violently I jam it into my cup holder. He's right. I'm a fucking pussy. I can't even admit to CJ I'm in love with Delilah.

I accepted my unrequited feelings years ago and I'm fine rotting away in my pain without anyone else's unhelpful opinions.

But I can't lie, hearing him call her my wife does something to me.

Getting down on one knee. Sliding my ring onto her delicate finger. Pulling her into my arms and claiming her mouth. Delilah walking down the aisle in a white dress.

Fuck. I'm so fucked.

The only reason I've kept my shit in check all these years is because I had physical time away from Delilah.

Any time I got too close to vomiting my feelings or popped a boner, I could escape to my apartment.

Our apartment. She slept in my bed. *Our bed.* A shiver runs along my spine making me jerk in my seat.

Stop.

This can't happen. She's my best friend. She doesn't see me that way.

I lock the poison deep inside and steel myself to face her. One of these days, the poison is going to eat me alive.

I knock on the door and Delilah opens it immediately, like

she was waiting for me. Like she's as desperate for me as I am for her.

"You're back!" she squeals, throwing herself into my arms. I'm fucking filthy, but she never cares, she always hugs me anyway.

"Doll, did you even check the peep hole before you let me in? What if I'd been an intruder? Promise me you'll check next time."

"I promise. But you're here!" She's hopping in my arms. Fucking hell. Her tits are bouncing against my chest, arousal blooms in my veins with every drag of her supple breasts up and down my front.

I escape her grasp and squeeze past her into the apartment. My dick's hard and I need to get into the shower stat, so it doesn't make a surprise appearance.

Surprise, Delilah! My dick's happy to see you too!

I holler over my shoulder, "I'm gonna take a quick shower and then I'm taking you to breakfast."

I don't wait for her response. Instead, I lock myself in the bathroom and turn on the shower. I strip as the water warms and as soon as it's tolerable, I step beneath the spray and fist my cock.

Everyone thinks I'm so chill, that I'm a laid-back, easy-going guy. Truth is, I jack off several times a day, so I don't explode from my pent-up attraction to Delilah.

The days I see her—nearly every day—I blow my load right before we hang out and as soon as I get home afterwards.

If she's particularly affectionate or wearing something irresistible, I have to find a bathroom to abuse myself with my right hand to survive the day. I'm surprised my right arm isn't noticeably bigger than my left from the hours it spends yanking on my dick.

This morning's no exception. In fact, it's imperative I get off because my bathroom's filled with her signature vanilla and jasmine, clouding my brain with lust. I must be a masochist because I use some of the offending body wash and slowly work myself.

I'm usually forced to be quick, but this morning, I take my time. She'll expect me to take a long shower after my shift, so my extended absence won't be suspicious.

My plan for a leisurely orgasm is thwarted by the image of her naked body dripping beneath the shower spray as she runs her soft hands all over her luscious form, and I come in long spurts onto the shower floor.

Holy shit. The wall supports me so I don't collapse from my premature release. I finish my shower efficiently with no reason to linger.

Getting dressed, I can't explain the possessive pride that puffs my chest having all Delilah's belongings blend with mine so seamlessly.

Like she's meant to live here. Like she's meant to be mine.

Calmer, after my shower-fun-time, I snag my girl for breakfast.

"Let's go get you fed, doll."

7

I don't survive one week living with Delilah before my resolve breaks.

She's been skittish all morning, hovering in the living room, compulsively checking her phone, jumping at every sound beyond the front door.

I hope her shower helps her relax because I don't have the willpower today to give her a friendly shoulder massage without cracking.

Someone knocks on the front door. A loud crash in the bathroom follows and I shout, "You okay?" as I walk to answer the door.

Delilah comes barreling out of the bedroom in only a bath towel frantically shouting, "I'll get it!"

"No way in hell you're answering the door in a towel." I reach for the door handle, and she digs a knuckle into my ribs. "Ow! What the fuck?"

She shrieks, "I said I'd get it!"

Yea, that isn't happening. I block her from grabbing the door handle and stiff-arm her while I accept the package from the delivery person who's eyeing me like I'm certifiable.

I've barely pulled my arm back through the cracked door when Delilah yanks the package from my hand.

"What's gotten into you this morning?" My chuckle is equal parts amused and confused.

Her heaving chest tests the limits of her wrapped towel. She has one arm braced against her breasts, pinning the towel closed, and the package-thieving arm pressed against the parted towel at her thighs.

My gulp must be audible.

She's so fucking beautiful—flushed and glistening from her shower and our wrestling match with the door.

Her hair's dripping wet, lips parted from exertion, sending blood rushing to my dick.

Her sun necklace dips into her cleavage, pushed up from holding the towel so tight.

I thought Delilah was the prettiest girl in the world at just eight-years-old. That fact remains, though my attraction now is far from innocent. I've watched her grow from a little doll to a scrawny kid, to a lanky pre-teen.

Then puberty hit. Hormones are relentless motherfuckers.

In a cruel twist of fate, Delilah matured into a fucking bombshell at the same time I became intimately acquainted with my dick.

I've seen Delilah in everything from full snow gear down to a string bikini.

I'd take her in anything, or nothing, every day and twice on Sunday.

My spank-bank is always well stocked from the tight-as-sin jeans she wears, and dresses that skim the tops of her thighs right below her ass cheeks.

It doesn't matter what she wears, honestly.

Her body's straight out of my dreams—because she's my only dream.

If there was a build-a-woman catalog to build the perfect woman, Delilah would be express delivered to my door.

She's the perfect height for me to rest my chin on her shoulder, smell her hair anytime I want, nuzzle into her neck when it's chilly, and to wrap my arms around her right below her tits.

Those. Tits.

I'm proud to say I've never grabbed my best friend's tits. But from countless hours of studiously examining them from a safe distance, and from acute knowledge of her body, I know they're incredible. Just like everything else about her.

Her ass nests against my pelvis when I stand behind her, and from years of hiding boners, I know for a fact her pussy is the perfect height for my cock if I were to take her standing.

Fuck. Me.

Imagining wrapping her luxurious, long, platinum blonde hair around my fist, and collaring her neck as I pound into her tight cunt, has catapulted me into an embarrassing amount of orgasms.

Delilah's the most gorgeous creature I've ever laid eyes on.

Speaking of eyes. Her silver diamond eyes are so full of emotion, sometimes I choke up looking into them for too long. She's seen far too much pain in her years, far too much of the seedy underbelly of society.

Her nose fits her features perfectly. Cheeks that are always rosy are one of my favorite spots to kiss, well, of the spots I'm allowed to kiss.

And those lips. Fuck. Those plump, rose-petal pink lips are the object of my daydreams and nightmares. What I wouldn't give to taste her lips, to pull the bottom one between my teeth, to have them mark every inch of my body.

And now, here she stands—a literal dripping wet dream. She's feet away from me looking like the ultimate present. Wrapped up special, just for me, in a terry-cloth towel.

One tug and I'd unwrap her to feast on her body.

I consume her with a fire that I'm quickly losing control of. Increasing my suffering, my horny-brain sends my eyes to her bare collarbones—right above her cleavage that's threatening to spill from the towel.

My eyes drop to the cause of our morning excitement.

The box she's holding is no bigger than a water bottle and has no identifying markings on it. *What could possibly be in that box to make her act like a lunatic?* Her eyes flick back and forth from mine to the box.

If I'm quiet long enough, she nearly always breaks and tells me whatever she's hiding. But this time, instead of spilling her secret, her thighs press together, and she shifts on her feet.

Holy. Fucking. Shit.

It hits me like a bullet.

Something she'd be embarrassed about.

Something she wouldn't want me to see.

So much so she risked flashing the delivery person.

Her intense demeanor and reaction to my scrutiny.

She bought a sex toy. She couldn't find her purple pal, seeing as I hid it from her, so she fucking replaced it.

My brain's a blur of heat and need. Did she replace it with the same model? What color is it? Is it bigger? Is it textured? How many settings does it have?

Without my permission, my imagination overtakes retinas—Delilah laid out on my bed, legs spread and the box open beside her.

I back up to the wall, frantically grasping for the doorknob.

"I...forgot I have that...thing today. So, I...have to run. 'K bye."

And like the pussy I am, I escape from my own personal hell without my keys, my phone, or my shoes.

I'm so fucked.

8

"And then he ran out the door like his pants were on fire without any shoes on!"

"Oh my god, this is the best thing I've ever heard. Tell it again. But this time, with more pizazz," Livy taunts with jazz hands.

Yes, I called Olivia and begged her to come over immediately to rescue me from this nightmare. No, I didn't call my sister. Sisters tell each other everything, but I omitted telling her about the giant blue dildo I ordered because I'm so horny living with Connor I might combust.

"Livyyyyy, what am I going to do? Do you think he knows? Oh god, he knows, doesn't he? I have to move out. Can I move in with you? I bet my boxes are still in the dumpster!" I move to run out the front door, but Olivia blocks me.

"Slow down, babe. You're talking faster than me and it's freaking me out." She gently coaxes me back to the couch and to sip some water.

"It doesn't matter if he knows or not, honestly." My eyebrows hit my hairline. "I mean, he might've figured out the gist of it, but either way, you have to move forward. Just act like it never happened and let it blow over. He sure as hell isn't going to bring it up, so why torture yourself?"

He knows. I know he knows. Does he know that I know he knows?

I hope there's somewhere nice on the ranch Izzy can bury me because I'm going to die from mortification.

"Livyyyyy!" I repeat, louder and whinier. "I don't have the brain capacity for this! I have finals in a couple of weeks, and I'm supposed to be focusing all my energy on studying. Not obsessing that my best friend knows I need a silicone friend to help me get off!"

"Everyone masturbates. It's not a big deal. You don't think he's choking his chicken on the reg?" Olivia asks plainly, like she's asking what time it is.

When did I miss the day everyone became cool about sex? I'm not a virgin. But I might as well be because it's been years...

Junior year of high school, I wanted to get it over with and lose my virginity on my terms. Izzy's assault two years prior destroyed her, and I needed to control my first time. In retrospect, I wasn't ready. But what's done is done. It's not like I was the only one my age fooling around.

The week before school ended, I went to a ranch party and ended up dancing with a boy I had a crush on. Peter Rickard was sweet enough. He was on the baseball team, didn't get into trouble, and most importantly, looked nothing like Connor.

I've always stayed far away from men who reminded me of the man of my dreams. It'd be like hooking up with the store brand because I can't afford the name brand.

Since I was old enough to know what sex was, I'd dreamed Connor would be my first.

But we'd remained firmly "just friends" and he'd already lost his virginity. He was about to graduate and wouldn't want to waste his time with high school girls like me. So, I settled.

Peter was nice and cute enough, so when he invited me to one of the bedrooms, I went. I wasn't turned on. I didn't know at the time arousal was a key element to enjoyable sex, so I wasn't wet at all. I was nervous but determined to get it over with.

He was as nervous as me, maybe he was a virgin too. We shared a few closed mouth kisses before I took off my panties from beneath my sundress and laid prone on the strange bed. Shoes on and everything.

He stood there staring at me like this couldn't possibly be happening. He met my eyes, and I smiled tightly, giving him whatever permission he was seeking because he undid his jeans and took himself out.

I looked away—which should've been a glaring red flag I wasn't ready—while he fumbled a condom on. He knelt beside me on the bed, and I spread my legs so he could kneel between my thighs.

He asked me if I was okay. I said yes.

He asked if I was sure. I said yes.

He asked if I was ready. I could only nod my head.

I felt foreign pressure, but he couldn't get in because I wasn't wet. He lubricated himself with saliva and started pressing into me again. He met resistance and froze—I told him to just do it. So, he did.

How romantic, right?

He pushed into me, and I cried out in pain. He pulled out in a panic checking if I was okay. We both saw my virgin blood on his penis and that was all she wrote. We straightened our clothes, left the bedroom and I went home.

It was weird though. Monday after the party, Peter didn't show up at school. There were rumors he'd been in an accident and was too hurt to finish the last week of school. I didn't bother checking on him or sending him a "get-well-soon." It would've been a hollow gesture.

Weirder was when I found out later that day Connor had been suspended and wouldn't be walking at graduation. His parents took his phone, so I couldn't check on him until he was off house arrest.

Later, he told me he got in a scuffle with some other senior boys and got blamed for it. It was a bizarre end to the school year.

I tried to have sex again after I graduated the following year. I was dating a cute guy who I worked with at the market, Robby Thompson. Things progressed much more naturally, and we escalated from days spent kissing in the storeroom, to groping over clothing, to touching under clothing in his car, to a mostly pain-free roll in the sheets while his parents were at work.

He disappeared for a week and his parents said he was in some sort of accident. He broke up with me over text and never came back to work at the market.

It was like I was cursed—any guy I touched ended up with some medical emergency and disappeared.

After Robby, I knew anything shy of being with Connor wasn't enough. I've dated casually the last couple years, but I never allow it to get physical.

For years I've tortured myself watching women fawn over my best friend. I have no doubt he's well versed in the bedroom. My stomach churns every time I think about it.

To satisfy my urges, I did copious internet research and tried out a couple of sex toys before I found my favorite one. My trusty purple rabbit was a consistent, complication-free lover.

All he needed was a thorough cleaning and new batteries every few weeks. He was a busy boy. Now he's lost, never to be played with again.

Hours later, Connor returns from his awkward departure.

"Hi. Umm. You're here. Of course you're here. You live here." Connor stumbles around the apartment because he's looking everywhere but at me. His cheeks flush, growing embarrassed.

"Did you have a nice...outing?" I have no clue where he went, and I don't want to know.

"Yep. Forgot I was supposed to visit my family today." He slaps his forehead like *duh*.

His feet are still shoe-less, socks as clean as when he put them on this morning.

"You drove without shoes?" I know he's fibbing.

"Quincy picked me up. Forgot she was giving me a ride."

"Seems like you forgot a lot this morning." I wish he'd forget the image of me in a towel, and that I'm the proud owner of a new sex toy.

He doesn't answer, lips sealed shut. We don't lie to each other, and he's reached his limit for dishonesty. Instead he gives me a tight smile and occupies himself with his Xbox. It's awkward and hurts my tummy, but it's better than the alternative—conversation.

I lock myself in his bedroom, I mean, our bedroom, and unbox my new boyfriend. He's a vibrant electric blue and has bumps and ridges my purple pal didn't have. He's also re-chargeable, so, no more dead batteries.

"Yes, you'll do nicely," I say to my new boyfriend, stroking his silky, silicone exterior. I conceal my new blue bestie in his silk drawstring bag and tuck him away at the back of my underwear drawer. Connor would never go digging around in my unmentionables.

It'll stay my dirty little secret.

9

The weeks following the dildo disaster are blessedly uneventful. After we got over the initial excruciating awkwardness, we locked the incident away in the same box we lock away all the moments we've crossed the "only friends" line.

Thank god my request to permanently move to dayshift got approved. Now I can be home with Delilah regularly.

Every morning, we wake tangled into a pretzel and take turns showering. Whoever showers second makes the coffee, and when we switch, the other makes breakfast.

She studies so much I don't know how her eyes stay open. She's the first person in her family to get a college education and I'm so fucking proud of her.

Until recently she worked part-time at the market. Most of her income went to her deadbeat egg donor, and for several years the rest paid for textbooks while she relied on student loans for tuition.

Last year she got a full scholarship that covered tuition, books, and living expenses. She swears she doesn't remember applying for it, but is grateful, nonetheless. The financial aid allowed her to quit her job and focus solely on her education.

She doesn't remember applying for it because it doesn't fucking exist. It killed me that she was always stressed about money, so I decided she shouldn't have to worry about it anymore.

After she registers each semester, I call the registrar and pay her tuition in full and pre-load her school account to cover anything else she needs.

Covering living expenses proved much trickier. Each semester, I transfer money to her bank account. Lucky for me, I happened upon her account number when I accidentally tore open the envelope she asked me to mail to the power company and found a check inside signed by my doll. Weird how things work out sometimes.

Taking care of Delilah is my greatest guilty pleasure—I get off on it. Now that we're living together and her stress levels are so much better, I walk around in a constant cloud of satisfaction knowing I did that for her.

For my girl.

My girl.

While she's focused on school, I fixate on her, no different from the last seventeen years of my life. The thoughts have rapidly evolved now that I know what she looks like in my bed, and the cute grin she gives me when she wakes up.

And how she looks dripping wet in a towel, clutching a box containing a vibrating dick.

We eat dinner together every night, whether at home—I fucking love that it's our home now—or with friends or family. Each evening, and on my days off, she curls up beside me on the couch reading her dirty books while I play Xbox.

Sometimes she puts her feet in my lap and unintentionally brushes against my cock when she moves. Other times, she lays her head in my lap, and it takes every ounce of concentration I possess not to imagine my dick disappearing between the plump lips that move along with the words on the pages.

I end up taking a bathroom shake-break when she lays on me that way.

My preferred position is when she snuggles into my side so my dick isn't being tortured, and I can peek over her shoulder to see what she's reading.

My girl's a freak.

Never in a million years did I think my little doll read about multiple dudes in love with the same chick and all the ways they fuck her. Or about a couple fucking next to the body of the man he just killed for touching her. Or about the woman being bent backwards over a saddle stand getting eaten out like an ice cream sundae.

All with a docile, placid face, right next to me on the couch, in our apartment.

I've experienced hand cramps, forearm Charlie horses, a stiff right shoulder, and friction burn from jacking off. I need to figure something out or I'm going to wind up in urgent care with a highly embarrassing presenting condition.

I've had a few casual flings over the years. I'm not a monk. But I never hook-up in Swiftwater. It feels disrespectful to Delilah. My friends give me such shit over it.

On principle, I refuse to talk about my sex-life. I'd never want any gossip to hurt Delilah or give our friends and family more ammunition to tease us about being "just friends."

On the rare occasion I'm sent on a long-term assignment, I try to meet a nice-enough woman, or women, in whatever town I'm in and scratch the itch that never fully abates. The itch only Delilah Tate can scratch.

All in all, I love living with Delilah. It's like when we played house as kids, but now she doesn't have to go home early because her mom is screaming, and I don't have to share her with Olivia and fucking Izzy.

It's a dream come true. It's also the sweetest torment having almost everything I've ever wanted but knowing in my soul I'll never have it all.

I'll never get to kiss her rose petal lips or fist my hand into her white silken hair.

I'll never palm her breasts that no doubt fit my hand perfectly or lick the dusty pink nipples that peak beneath her loose pajama tops.

I'll never wrap my hands around her bare hips in a way no friend should and slide my cock into her tight little cunt.

Every night we take turns getting ready for bed and cuddle beneath the sheets on my too-small bed that conveniently presses her against my body. We share pillow talk, and soft, but innocent, touches that burn me with a fire that will never be extinguished.

I watch her drift off to sleep and tell myself it's enough.

It has to be enough—because it's all I'll ever have.

10

Connor age 17, Delilah age 16

I finished my geometry test quickly, so Mr. Sanchez released me early. Connor always meets me after fifth period to walk to the cafeteria together, but I'm going to surprise him today.

I sit outside the boy's locker room, my back against the painted cinderblock, and check my planner for what homework I have this weekend.

It's been a crummy week and TGIF is real. Isabelle's been in an awful mood because the soccer team graffitied her locker with the same slurs she's suffered the past two years. Mom's been on a bender because she lost her job. Again. She spent the little she had left on alcohol.

I try so hard not to hate her but sometimes loving her is impossible. I'm re-writing my list of assignments into a neat checklist when the boys clamor into the locker room after gym class.

The old building's acoustics give me an auditory front row seat to the idiot-teenage-boy show. Laughter and jibes blur together, but one voice stands out amongst the racket.

"Dude, Coach is going to be pissed. You can't miss another practice, or he'll bench you," Connor chastises someone.

"Fuck off, Hayes. It's not my fault Mrs. Lumpy Ass has no sense of humor and gave me detention."

"It's literally your fault. You're such an idiot but you're the best forward on the team and we're gonna get creamed by Ridgemount if you're benched," Connor continues.

Another voice enters the conversation. "Ask your sister to flash him her ass again. Last time the cheerleaders pranced in front of him, his tongue rolled out of his head. He'd forget all about benching you and put you in."

"I'm not asking my sister to flash Coach, you sick fuck." Who was that?

A quieter voice makes my skin crawl. "Don't bother. Just ask Easy Izzy. She's used up but even an old dude like Coach would check her out."

The nickname this school bestowed upon my sister makes me sick. Why isn't Connor standing up for her?

"Don't ask Easy Izzy, ask her sister. She's fresh meat. She'd distract Coach for sure."

"Watch it." There's Connor's baritone.

"Oh right, we're not allowed to talk about Connor's girlfriend."

"She's not my girlfriend," Connor insists. Why does he sound so disgusted at the thought of being with me?

The razzing amplifies and it's difficult to make out who's saying what through the bustling locker room.

"Bet she spreads her legs as easy as her sister."

"She's not even the hot sister." Was that Connor's voice? He doesn't even like Izzy.

"Who would want her anyway?" Wait, was that Connor? I can't tell. Why would he say something like that? Or why wouldn't he stop them from saying these things?

Laughter echoes from the locker room and lockers slam shut. I scramble to stuff my things into my backpack and disappear from the athletics hallway through the nearest exit.

The crisp mountain air tangles my hair and nips at my nose as I sit behind the building, stomach growling angrily.

Izzy and Olivia have a different lunch period than me, so I always eat with Connor. And by eat with Connor, I mean he packs or buys two lunches, so I have something to eat, because we rarely have groceries at home.

But I can't stomach lunch with Connor today. He texted me after fifth period from outside my geometry class, waiting for me like he does every day, but I wasn't there. Because I'm a fool and tried to surprise him and instead overheard things I can never un-hear.

I'm so stupid. No matter how many times I'm slapped in the face with it, I always hold out hope one day Connor will see me as girlfriend material. And today I got bitch slapped.

Not the hot sister? No one will ever want me.

Even if I had money to buy a lunch today, I couldn't eat it because my stomach is burning from humiliation.

My phone chimes for the millionth time. I succumb to temptation and open my messages.

> Connor: Did you leave geometry already?
>
> Connor: Meet me in the cafeteria.
>
> Connor: Where are you?
>
> Connor: Doll?
>
> Connor: You're freaking me out.
>
> Connor: Lunch is almost over. I'll meet you outside your sixth period.

Except, I won't be there. I can't face him with my heart bleeding out of my chest. I shoot a text to Izzy saying I'm sick and walking home. I never ditch class, but there's no way I'm going back inside.

TGIF has taken on a whole new meaning today. Connor has away games this weekend, so I'll have two days to mend my broken heart. Monday I'll come back to school and pretend I'm not madly in love with my best friend.

Because he'll never want me.

11

"Connor's been avoiding me."

After the vibrator incident, I thought we'd move on like nothing happened. Like we always do when things between us cross over the "friends only" line. Like the kiss that never happened.

"There's no way. That boy's obsessed with you. He's followed you around like a puppy since day one," Olivia scoffs.

"He's been picking up a lot of overtime or hanging out with CJ, and when he's home, he says he's too tired to talk, or eat with me, or watch TV together. We've never been this distant."

My stomach cramps from missing him constantly.

The stress from finals and Connor drifting away from me has made eating nearly impossible. I know I'm hurting myself, but I can't stop it. Connor or Izzy pull me back when I drift too far—but neither of them have time for me anymore.

I don't begrudge my sister her happiness. She deserves every success she's finding with Reid and their business ventures. I'm so proud of her. But it's like she grew up without me. I hardly see her anymore, our texts are fewer and farther between, and she rarely calls.

I'm better at hiding my struggles from Olivia because she's so talkative. Not that she's self-absorbed or unobservant, but it's easier to distract her with a new topic of conversation or question about her life.

"I'm don't buy it, but for argument's sake—fuck him. Izzy's still hoping you'll move to the ranch. I've been busier now that I'm full-time at Dad's company, but whenever I'm able, I'm at the ranch with Maisey. Come join our happy little party. It smells like hay and horseshit, but we'll never avoid you." I huff a laugh. Olivia's never been one to mince words.

"I've been living with Connor a little over a month, and things between us are the most uncomfortable they've ever been. Maybe this was a mistake."

"See! It's the perfect solution. Get ready and come to the stables with me for some horse therapy and bestie time. Izzy should be getting home from work soon. Let's all do dinner or something," she offers.

I have nothing better to do than sit here and jump at every noise hoping it's Connor coming through the door.

"Fine. You win. I have a few things to do before I leave so I'll meet you there, okay?

Livy plants a smooch on my cheek and when the door clicks behind her, I flop face down onto the sofa and caterwaul into the cushions. *Why can't my life be easy?*

I can't go back to the trailer. Mom's already been hitting me up for money. I caved and gave her some because I feel so guilty for leaving her—and because I have no backbone.

I'll never hear the end of it if anyone finds out. Connor said I enable my mom. Maybe I do. But I can't shake the nagging obligation to help her, especially when no one else will.

Left alone with my diseased thoughts, endless study material for exams that will determine my internship placement, and lack of sleep, I'm a wreck.

My empty stomach burns, but I can't bring myself to eat.

Food's never felt safe. Because food was scarce, it was safer to be hungry than risk eating something that went bad.

When I was eight or nine, my appendix burst, and the surgery left me with a large, jagged purple scar on my lower abdomen, and I began to fixate on the way my body looked.

Mom was never maternal, but after our dad "went out for milk" and never came back, she became cruel. She threw insults at us like darts at a target full of old holes. Izzy always brushed it off, but I absorbed every word.

Now that Izzy and Olivia are back, I was doing better for a while. Eating like a normal person. Laughing more. But lately... things are unraveling again. And when everything else spins out, my eating habits are the first to crash.

Shame and self-loathing cast a poisoned film over my rational thinking. Everything's sticky and heavy, compounded by stress and loneliness.

Amidst my spiral, I tidy the apartment, run the dishwasher, and pack an overnight bag.

I text Connor letting him know I'm staying the night with Izzy and not to wait up for me. He reads my message, and the three dots bounce on the screen before they disappear.

His lack of a response back hurts worse than it should.

I'm not good enough for him. I never have been. It's not his fault he grew up in a healthy household while I grew up in a booze-soaked tin can. I should be counting my blessings he entertains my presence at all, let alone see me as a potential partner.

No. Connor doesn't want me like that.

He never has, and he never will.

12

"I swear to god, if I work another hour this week, I might die." I moan, lying on CJ's couch holding a bottle of beer, arm dangling off the edge.

"You complain more than my Aunt Sue and she's intolerable. Why are you here again? And by again, I mean, *again*, because you're always here lately. Don't you have a perfectly good apartment with a beautiful woman waiting for you?"

CJ's such a dick. He's right, but still a dick.

"That's *why* I can't go home. She's always there."

"I'm failing to see the issue. Isn't this your dream come true? Living with Delilah? What am I missing?" Patronizing prick.

"She's. Always. There. She's curled around me when I wake in the morning. She's making coffee in her tiny pajamas. She makes me breakfast. Everything's always clean, and my laundry hamper's always empty. She naps on the couch like a cat lounging in a sunbeam. She walks around in a towel after her showers—for like ten steps to the closet—but still!"

CJ scrutinizes at me like he's never seen a dumber person in his life.

"So, you can't go home because your impossibly stunning, sweet, kind, helpful best friend is too good of a roommate?"

"I hate you."

"Mmhmm. Honey, you know as well as I do why you're avoiding her."

My jaw grinds painfully. I'm going to need a dental appointment from the beating my molars are taking. I refuse to engage in this ridiculous conversation. Unfortunately for me, CJ has no such qualms.

"Because you're in love with her, you sad sack little bitch baby."

And there it is. The ugly truth. Of course I'm fucking in love with her. Welcome to the last seventeen years of my miserable life. Wanting someone you can never have is a special level of purgatory. The pain never abates, it just festers.

"Can we *not* right now? I'm fucking exhausted," I groan.

"Yes, because you've been working yourself into the ground and haven't had any Lilah-lovin' to rejuvenate you."

"Don't say *Lilah-lovin'*, please, for the love of god." The last thing I need to be thinking about is any Lilah-lovin', I'm miserable enough.

"You really are a stupid son of a bitch aren't you?"

"Dude!"

"Don't *dude* me. Has it occurred to your teeny tiny hamster brain that your avoidant behavior could be hurting her?"

"What do you mean?" As I ask the asinine question, I see exactly what he means. She's forcibly removed from the only home she's ever known, thinks she's moving in with her best friend but instead, has been living alone during one of the most stressful times of her life.

She misses Izzy terribly and Olivia's busy at her new job. She misses her waste-of-space mom. She's cramming for finals before her last semester of college.

Fuck. I'm a piece of shit.

CJ's face says, *Oh good, the idiot figured out a circle doesn't have corners.*

"Goddamn it. I hate you."

"You love me, don't be ridiculous." CJ rolls his eyes with a flourish.

"Now, if you don't mind, can you please get out of my apartment? I have a date tonight and I don't need tattooed-Adonis answering the door when he gets here."

I nursed one beer at CJ's, so I'm fine driving the mile back to my apartment. Parked at the apartment complex, I bash my face into the steering wheel.

How could I do this to her?

I open our text thread, and my stomach sinks further. Scrolling backwards, the screen is filled with texts from Delilah I managed a one-word response or thumbs up, and many more I couldn't bring myself to answer at all.

After she texted yesterday letting me know she was spending the night with her sister, I picked up overtime and worked through till this afternoon. For as much as it hurts being around her, I couldn't bear spending the night at home without her.

Not seeing her for days has my body physically aching from missing her.

I can't be a coward and sit in my truck all night, so I drag my ass to my front door and hang my head. What am I going to do? What am I going to say? A text distracts me.

CJ: Don't be a pussy.

Fucking CJ. Don't be a pussy. I'm being a pussy.

Darkness greets me when I walk into the apartment. Locking the door behind me, an eerie silence raises the hair on the back of my neck. It's not even 7:00 p.m., where is she? Her car was in the parking lot, unless Iz or Liv drove her to the ranch yesterday and she hasn't come home.

Delaying my suffering, I make something for dinner. My stomach's eating itself after a double shift consisting of gas station garbage, and half a beer at CJ's. I open the fridge and find it nearly bare. Lemonade. Carrot sticks. Hard boiled eggs. A half-eaten dry salad. *What the fuck?*

My pulse kicks up realizing my absence hurt Delilah far more than I anticipated. The pantry isn't much better. Microwaveable rice. Old fashioned oats. A sealed jar of peanut butter.

It takes all my restraint not to break the pantry door slamming it shut, instead, softly clicking it closed, trembling with fury. Not at her—never at my fallen angel—at myself. What kind of man, friend or otherwise, abandons someone like this?

I know Delilah better than she knows herself. I should've seen past my selfish bullshit and realized how badly she's been struggling. I rack my brain for the last time I really looked at her. During the rare times I've been home, I've tried hard to not let my eyes linger because it's physically painful not being able to touch her.

The roots of my hair scream as my hands yank the long strands in agony. My feet are moving before my brain registers where I'm going.

My heart breaks standing in the doorway to our bedroom. The room's dim, lit only by her bedside lamp. She's bent at disjointed angles like a broken doll amidst piles of textbooks, notebooks and laptop.

The blue glow from the screen rips my heart out through my throat. The screensaver's a slideshow of Delilah's favorite pictures. Photo after photo, my face appears on the screen.

Selfies of the two of us at every age, and photos of me I've never seen.

Our life plays across the screen in full color. The occasional photo with Izzy or Olivia provides short-lived relief from my heartache.

She's working herself to death and I haven't been here. Her chest rises and falls with each slumbering breath, but what causes my fingernails to cut into my palms are the dark circles under her eyes, how pronounced her collar bones are against the shadows, and the goosebumps lining her arms from how cold she is.

The apartment isn't cold. She's freezing because she has no calories in her body, and it makes me want to beg for mercy at her delicate feet.

I did this. Another glaring reason I don't deserve her.

I pad silently into the bedroom and gather her school materials and set them on her nightstand. Lifting her laptop, I subject myself to a few more moments of masochism and watch the slideshow of our friendship—each photo a brutal reminder of what I stand to lose.

I crawl into bed beside her, and she instinctually rolls towards my body. She curls around me, every possible point of contact made between our bodies. She sighs like everything is right in her world now that I'm here—and it makes me hate myself even more.

My body heat warms her chilled skin, and her body becomes heavier on mine as she sinks into deeper relaxation. I have so much I need to say, but I don't dare wake her. She needs the rest far more than she needs my excuses.

So, I hold her in my arms and vow to never let her down again.

I haven't waited this long, and worked this hard, to give up on my dream. I plan to give Delilah everything she's ever wanted until my dying breath.

I've been hers since the first time I saw her.

I have to believe someday she'll be mine.

13

My body is languid and warm. I don't want to wake from the dream I'm having. Hovering in the haze between dreaming and waking, I'm weightless and safe. I move to snuggle deeper into the bed when I feel him.

As it does every night, my body's molded to his in my sleep. I need his touch more than food or water. My head's nestled in the crook of his shoulder and the cotton of his shirt bunches between my fingers.

My senses are overcome by everything *Connor*. My nerve endings fire off—there's not a stitch of his warm skin touching my body. *Why is he fully dressed?*

His masculine scent fills my nose, his deep, rhythmic breathing soothes my ears, his heartbeat the metronome setting the rhythm my heart follows.

My leg's slung over his hips, and I don't dare move. I don't want to wake him, and I don't want confirmation the firm ridge below my calf is his erection. But Connor knows my body better than I do.

"Morning, doll," his sleepy voice rasps.

Every muscle in my body seizes up; he knows I'm awake. He

tightens his arm around my shoulders, pulling me closer into his chest. Rough fingers comb hair from my face, and he places a kiss to my forehead.

I barely contain the whimper of pleasure that tries to escape my lips at his attention. I've missed him so much.

I'd give up anything—even move on someday to find a second-rate love—if it meant I could keep this.

I need Connor more than I need oxygen and I refuse to jeopardize our connection. I've swallowed my feelings our entire friendship.

I can keep this in. I have to.

I dare to tilt my head and meet his heavy eyes, but I have no words. What can I possibly say to fix what I've broken?

I'm sorry I'm a burden and you've wasted your life rescuing me.

Thank you for inviting me into your home, but it's best if I leave.

I'm sorry for whatever I did that scared you away. Please don't ever leave me again.

I can't say any of that, so I say nothing at all. His brow furrows when I don't respond.

"What's the matter, doll?"

More confessions threaten to spill from my lips.

I love you but I can never tell you.

I'll do anything to keep you, even if it means ruining myself.

I can't survive without you.

It hurt every second you avoided me.

Connor lifts me from his chest and sits back against the headboard, adjusting me to sit beside him.

"I'm sorry," we both say simultaneously.

"No, I'm sorr—"

"Why are you sorr—"

Our questions collide in the charged air between us.

"Let me go first, doll. I'm sorry I've been avoiding you." His admission stings more than I thought it would. I suspected that's what he'd been doing.

"I was a coward and there's no other way to spin it. Living with you freaked me out—not because of anything you did, but because—I don't know how to explain it. The reasons don't matter. What matters is I let you down and I'll never forgive myself."

"Connor, it's okay..." But he interrupts.

"No, it's not okay. I promised to always take care of you, and I let my own bullshit get in the way when you needed me. I took you from your home, trapped you in mine, and fucking abandoned you."

Self-loathing drips from his pores, a spear through my tender heart.

"Please...please forgive me." His tone and posture scream defeat. And while it hurt he wasn't around, it's my fault he stayed away.

His strong hands wring together, and I place my smaller hand atop his to stop him from hurting himself.

"There's nothing to forgive, Connor. You have every right to a life outside of me and my problems. I'm the one who should be apologizing to you." He tries to interject but I continue.

"You've been so generous taking me in and rearranging your work schedule. You don't owe me a thing. I'm so grateful for everything you've done for me."

Emotion strains the voice escaping my tightening throat. "I'm sorry I made you so uncomfortable you didn't want to be in your own home. If you tell me what I did wrong, I promise I'll fix it."

The anguish in Connor's voice guts me. "Dollface, you didn't do anything wrong. I swear to god. I don't know how to justify my actions. But please believe me when I say it's because of me, not you."

Why does it feel like I'm being dumped by a man begging me to stay? Our relationship is turning into a complete mindfuck. I want to move past this and go back to the way things were.

I un-ball his fists and take him by the hands and do my best attempt at a genuine smile.

"You're sorry. I'm sorry. You love me. I love you. Can we leave it at that and move forward?"

Connor inhales deeply through his nose, brows furrowed, eyes searching, trying to read between the lines. He's not going to find what he's searching for because I'll never tell him the truth about my feelings.

"Okay, doll. We can move forward. Now, can we make a grocery list? It looks like we need a few things."

Of course he noticed. He notices everything. I want to make excuses and promises, but I'm tired of suffering. I can't control my trembling bottom lip any more than I can control the traitorous tears streaming down my cheeks.

Connor gathers me into his lap and cradles me like a child, gently rocking us side to side.

"Shh, shh, shh. It's alright. I'm here now. I know you're stressed. We'll work on it together, okay?"

He pulls a box of tissues from thin air and fruitlessly attempts to dry my tears.

"Here's what we're going to do. You're going to take a nice hot shower and dress in your comfiest clothes. I'm going to make a grocery list of the things I know you can tolerate and call your sister. We're going to meet her and Reid for coffee at Bean & Brew for as much twin-time as you need."

I emit an unattractive laugh-cry-snort at his plan. He always knows exactly what I need.

"Then, I'm going to drop you off at the bookstore to pick out something new to read while I get groceries."

How? How is he so perfect for me, but only as a friend? Why can't he see me as more?

"We're going to take things one day at a time. Our top priority is rebuilding your trust in your body—to listen to your hunger cues and nourish your body, not punish it. Our second priority is annihilating your finals, so you get the equine therapy internship of your dreams."

At that, a laugh bubbles through my tears.

"Sound like a plan, doll?"

"Yes. Thank you, Connor. For everything."

Thank you for finding me.
Thank you for saving me.
Thank you for believing in me.
Thank you for loving me.

14

"Honey! I'm home!" I sing-song as I swing open the door to our apartment. It's a joke, of course, and pretending it's real doesn't hurt anyone but me.

But what awaits in the living room isn't what I was expecting.

"What the fuck! Get off of her!" I storm over to the wall where my doll's cowering.

"Connor, it's okay. It's nothing," Delilah says quietly.

"Like hell it's nothing." I'm not one to get physical with a woman, but I have no qualms grabbing Ivy by the shoulders and yanking her away from Delilah.

"You...stupid son of a...bitch. This is between...me and my kid," Ivy slurs.

Jesus, how drunk is she?

"You don't get to come into my home and come at my girl. I don't give a fuck if you're her mom." I snap my fingers and point at the couch telling Ivy to sit like the bitch she is. Thankfully she obeys because I don't want to manhandle her.

Delilah crumples into my arms just as I reach out for her. Heaving sobs shake her frail body. My arms may be the only thing holding her together right now.

"I'm so sorry, Connor," she sobs. "It's my fault. I didn't check the peep hole like you've been telling me to, and when I opened the door, she shoved her way past me and refused to leave. I know you don't want her here. Please don't be mad."

Oh, my sweet doll. I'm not mad at her. I'm furious at Ivy for putting her in this position. I kiss her forehead, "Never, doll. I'm not mad at you. Wait for me in the bedroom, okay?"

"What? No! Connor, it's okay. I can handle this."

"I know you can, but you aren't going to." I calmy convey this isn't up for negotiation.

Without another word, Delilah peels herself from my body and scurries to our bedroom with her head down. Goddamn it. I hate seeing her shrivel from Ivy's poison.

The witch tilts her head back to see my face, because I'm towering over her seated position on the couch.

"You have thirty seconds to tell me what the hell you're doing here."

"Fuck y—"

"Twenty-five seconds. You're wasting time, Ivy."

"This is your...fault. You...took her away...from me. I need her." She sways in her seat.

"You don't need her, you need her paycheck."

Ivy's eyes dart away, revealing her guilt. She only ever wants one thing. And to scare the shit out of her daughter to get it, is disgusting.

"Get a fucking job, Ivy. You're too old for this shit. Grow up and stop harassing your daughter."

"I just need...a few hundred...and I won't bother...her anymore." Is she fucking kidding?

"She isn't giving you a dime, and we both know you're full of shit. You never learn. Get the fuck out of my apartment." I point at the door and stare her down until she takes the hint. She rises slowly and wobbles before planting her feet.

"You...can't keep her...from me. I'm...her mother."

"I can. And I will. You're not her mother—you're a waste of oxygen. Get. Out."

Ivy stumbles to the front door, flips me the bird, and slams it behind her.

I need to take a minute to cool off before I check on Delilah. I don't want her to see me like this, it's bad enough she probably heard the entire interaction. My hands scrub up and down my tired face, and I roll my head cracking my neck.

It's unbelievable. Just when I think she can't stoop any lower, Ivy proves me wrong.

I find Delilah in fetal position on our bed, clutching her pillow. I climb into bed with her, despite desperately needing a shower after work, and shield her from the pain with my body.

15

Delilah

They say bad things come in threes. Connor and I are falling apart. My mom tore through my new life like a tornado. And now, I've come down with the virus from hell during finals week. Two of my finals are online, thankfully, but the third I have to take on campus.

Depending on who's on babysitting duty, Connor, Izzy, or Livy help me wake up, coax some medicine, food, and hydration into my body, and help me log in to my finals.

I'm not so sick I can't type in a username and password, but I'm disoriented enough I'm terrified to make a mistake and fail a test from a dumb error.

While I'm sure there are options for me if I don't get good grades this semester, the future I want rests on these three exams. I'm already near the top of my class, so if I ace my finals, I'll have one of the first picks for internships. And the internship I want is highly coveted amongst my classmates.

I've worked too hard for too long to fumble at the finish line and lose my advantage.

Despite my mind wading through split pea soup, I manage

to get an A on one online final, and a B on the other leaving me with A's in both classes.

The morning of my in-person final, everything goes to shit.

Connor offered to drive me to Greeley last night and get a hotel so I could get extra sleep before heading to campus. I said no, because he's been doing so much for me already. I hate feeling helpless and weak, and this virus is kicking my ass.

I figured, I've already been sick for days, I have to start feeling better soon. Greeley's a three-hour drive, but my exam is early afternoon, so I planned on waking up early, taking my time getting ready, and studying in the car.

The virus had other plans. Connor got called in for overtime last night but promised to drive me to Greeley as soon as he got home. And because this virus has turned my brain into Swiss cheese, and the nighttime cold medicine I took, I must've forgotten to set my alarm.

"Shit! Delilah, you've got to wake up." I'm jostled awake by a frantic Connor.

"Wh-what time is it?" I ask.

"It's after nine. I've been texting and calling you for hours trying to tell you I'd be home late, and we'd need to hit the road as soon as I got here. At this point we'll barely make it in time for your final."

I shoot up in bed, my head punishing me with brutal throbbing. "Oh my god! We have to go!" I throw off the blankets, but Connor gently holds me down by my shoulders.

"Doll, you've gotta re-schedule your final. You can't take the test like this."

My head tremors back and forth, "No. No, no, no. Not this final. The professor was clear there would be no exceptions." I nervously fiddle with my sun necklace, the familiar warmth from the metal calming me a fraction.

Connor's strong jaw ticks, displeased with my reality, but

relents. "Alright. Get dressed and I'll put together some breakfast and lunch for the road." He helps me from bed and waits until I'm stable on my feet before rushing out of the room.

This can't be happening. I'm so close to getting my internship I can taste it.

The tired, hopeless side of me says there's no point in rushing because I'm going to bomb the test anyway. But the tiny ember in my heart that's never been extinguished—no matter how hard my life has gotten—pushes me to throw on a pair of yoga pants, a sports bra under my favorite of Connor's hoodies I stole years ago and twist my hair into a messy top knot.

I'm slipping my shoes on when Connor tears into our bedroom ripping his clothes off. I freeze, both stunned and ecstatic at the scene before me.

"Let me change and we can go," he rushes out.

Healthy, functioning Delilah would've left the room immediately and pretended not to have seen his bare chest and boxer briefs slung indecently low on his hip bones.

But cold medicine-high, deliriously tired Delilah stands here like a drooling idiot and watches her best friend strip naked before getting re-dressed all too soon. His impressive cock disappears into his underwear just as he turns to face me.

Dear. Sweet. Baby. Jesus. That was Connor's penis. My best friend's dick.

How does he walk with that thing hanging between his legs?

I've always assumed he was well-endowed based on years of gym shorts and swim trunks. But nothing could've prepared me for *that*.

"Fuck! You scared the shit out of me! I thought you went into the living room!" Connor exclaims as he turns back away from me, frantically pulling on jeans and concealing his little—*huge*—secret.

I still haven't moved from my spot in the bedroom, so I have an up-close and personal view of the flush creeping up Connor's neck and onto his handsome face.

His embarrassment triggers my own and I trip over myself rushing from the bedroom. I can never unsee *that*. How will he ever look at me the same? I manage to pack my bag and gather the lunchbox and drinks Connor prepared for us.

He emerges from our room with a baseball cap low over his brows, hunched over on himself, trying to be invisible. He swipes his phone and keys from the kitchen counter and silently ushers me to the door.

We don't say anything for a long while as we head east towards Greeley. I unpack and pass out breakfast and take our trash. Connor's knuckles are devoid of circulation from how hard he's gripping the steering wheel.

My single page study guide sits heavy in my lap as I pretend to review for the test. But the words on the page rearrange into hyper realistic drawings of Connor's cock. They spell out *You saw your best friend's penis, you pervert*. Letters dance around creating black and white images of Connor's naked body taking me from behi—.

"Sorry about earlier." Connor's booming voice startles me in the cab of his truck, and I frantically hide my pornographic study guide before responding.

"Sorry for what? I didn't see anything. I mean, nothing happened. I don't know what you're talking about." Lovely. Now I'm delirious from this virus, the medicine, and horniness.

"Uh...okay." Connor hedges. "Do you want to go over anything for your test or do you want to try to get some sleep? We've still got over two hours left on the road."

He's mercifully offering me an out from our shared mortification. "If you don't mind driving without any company, I might try to take a nap."

"I don't mind. You forget I drive alone for a living. Get some rest, doll. I'll wake you up about a half hour from campus so you can eat some lunch, okay?"

I bob my head like a lunatic and flip up the hood of the stolen hoodie, concealing my lying face. I do my best impression of a sleeping passenger, and for the next two hours, get increasingly hotter and more bothered by graphic fantasies about my best friend.

I doze off at some point, and Connor wakes me up for lunch. We eat in charged silence as we inch closer to my doom. There's no way I'm acing this final, let alone passing it. Not when I've got dick on the brain.

This has never happened to me. Sure, I've dreamed about being intimate with Connor countless times, but the only reference I had was him shirtless plus my active imagination. Now that I know what he's packing, I'm drowning in arousal.

Something is wrong with me, right? Whatever it is had better disappear with the virus because I can't live like this. Who knew horniness could be hell on earth?

"Okay doll, we're here." Connor parks his truck at the testing center. "I know you don't feel good, but you know this shit like the back of your hand. You're gonna crush it."

I risk meeting his eyes for the first time since *the incident* this morning and find unwavering love and support reflecting back at me.

"Thank you. Why don't you try to take a nap, now. I'll text you when I'm done."

Connor rests his elbow on the steering wheel, not a care in the world, and flips his ballcap backwards. Why? Why of all times must this adonis flip his hat BACKWARDS?

We'd normally hug right now, but instead, we stare awkwardly at each other.

Me, because my last neurons went up in smoke at the pornographic scene before me. Connor, because he's watching his best friend lose her mind.

As I get out of the truck, I divert my eyes from the lewd display and offer a clipped "bye" before scurrying away as fast as my virus-infested body will allow.

As I sit for my last and most important final of the semester, my eyes cross at the screen glaring back at me.

My mind's an empty cavern, devoid of everything I've learned and studied. The only thought that ricochets around my empty skull drives me to the brink of insanity.

I want to fuck my best friend.

16

I want to fuck my best friend.

This isn't a new development in my miserable life, but it's all I can think about as I sit in my truck cab in a cloud of her sweet scent.

After I packed the food for our trip today, all I needed to do was change my clothes before we took off. I would've preferred to take a shower, but my fucking job had already made me late picking Delilah up for her exam.

I swore I heard her leave the bedroom as I entered it, and I didn't think twice before stripping down and throwing on new clothes. My dick was flopping around like a dead fish as I pulled on new underwear. And she fucking saw it. My sweet, innocent, forbidden best friend got an eye full of my flaccid cock n' balls.

The pure shock and mortification of the moment were drowned out by the fascination and lust emanating from Delilah's heavy eyes. I waited for her to cover her eyes, squeal, run away, or profusely apologize.

Instead, she drank me in like water on a hot day. If she'd licked her lips, I'd be dead in the ground. We barely spoke on the drive to Greeley. I'd like to chalk it up to both of us being exhausted, but I know it was because of my indecent exposure.

She pretended to sleep but I could hear her mind racing. Things have gotten so complicated since she moved in with me. There's no way in hell I want her to leave, but we can't continue like this. We're walking a tightrope sure to snap at any misstep.

I've tried to think about *anything* else these past few hours, but my brain's an asshole and refused to grant me any reprieve. Instead, my thoughts spun into a web of confusion and arousal.

How much did she see? Did she like what she saw? What I'd do to have her look at me like that all the time. Why didn't I stop her when she ran off? Did I gross her out? That plump bottom lip would feel so good between my teeth. Fuck.

I readjust my hard dick in my jeans. Is there anti-Viagra? Because living with a constant boner can't be good for my health. My brain's permanently deprived of maximum blood flow because my cock can't be reasoned with.

I can't keep fantasizing about Delilah like this. She'd be disgusted if she knew how I'm objectifying her. And my heart breaks a bit more every day I can't have her the way I dream about.

I have to distract myself. I need to get this out of my head before she finishes her test, and we're stuck in this truck for another three hours.

The vibration from an incoming text saves me from spiraling.

> Demon Twin: How is she?

> Me: Fine. She was out cold when I got home but we got here in time.

> Demon Twin: I told her to reschedule.

> Me: I did too. She puts so much pressure on herself. I think she just wants it to be over.

> Demon Twin: Is she doing okay?

> Me: She's still really sick, it's got to get better soon or I'm taking her to urgent care.

> Demon Twin: Good luck with that.

> Demon Twin: Thank you for taking care of her.

> Me: A thank you from Isabelle Tate. Never thought I'd see the day.

> Demon Twin: Fuck you, Connie.

> Me: There she is.

I recline my seat and settle in for a nap, shielded from the sun by my hat covering my face. Delilah said her exam could take up to three hours—might as well recharge before we drive back up the hill.

Knocking on the window scares the shit out of me and I jolt awake, head on a swivel. Delilah stands on the passenger side of my truck, waiting for me to unlock the door. I scramble to open the door for her.

"Sorry doll, I fell asleep." I say, scrubbing my face to wake up.

"It's okay. I figured when you didn't text me back." She hoists herself into the passenger seat, gaunt from exhaustion.

My stomach sinks. Shit. I hate missing her calls or texts. I'm terrified it'll be the one time she's having an emergency and I'm not there for her. Thank god today it was just a quick walk from the testing center to the parking lot.

I can't tell how her test went. She doesn't seem happy or sad, just exhausted. Her silken hair has fallen from her hair tie, framing her face like a halo. I tuck a strand of gold behind her ear, my fingers feathering across her cheek.

"I PASSED!" she exclaims, pure joy overtaking her features.

"Hell yea! I knew you would!" I practically drag her across the center console into my lap before I let her settle back into her seat.

"This virus must've given me superpowers because the test was way too easy. I finished early so I stopped by my advisor's office. Connor. You'll never guess."

Her happiness is like a drug for me, I'll never get enough, which is why everything I do is to make her as happy as possible.

"Tell me, doll." She's vibrating with excitement. Little tease is making me wait, but I'll play along.

"I GOT THE TOP SPOT FOR INTERNSHIP PLACEMENT!" She bounces so hard my truck rocks on its suspension.

This time I succeed in dragging her across the console into my lap, squeezing the life out of her as we laugh and celebrate. She stills and when I lean back to look at her, time stops. Her soft lips part, and she's fixated on my mouth. What I wouldn't give to kiss her.

Like magnets, we drift closer, pulled together by an invisible force. Warmth caresses my lips. Is this going to finally happen? I might die if she pulls awa—

Her ringtone scratches through my desire, like nails on a chalkboard.

"Hello?"

Izzy's voice echoes from the other end of the call. The sisters scream and laugh, reveling in Delilah's fantastic news. Knowing them like I do, they're going to be on the phone for a while.

I start the truck and program my GPS to a chain restaurant Delilah enjoys. I reach across her small frame and buckle her seatbelt. The smile she grants me takes my breath away.

As the truck rolls forward, she checks the screen and sees where we're heading. The smile only grows, and I have to look away or I'll wreck the truck.

I'll do anything to keep that smile on her face. Anything.

17

Connor age 16, Delilah age 15

"Dude, you need to calm down."

"CJ, shut up. How am I supposed to calm down when... I'm missing homecoming?" I hedge.

"Mmhmm. You're about to flip your lid because you're not going to homecoming? Are you sure it's not because you're not going to homecoming with Delilah?" CJ taunts.

"Yea right." Yes. That's exactly why I'm losing my shit.

"You've never cared about a school dance in your life. Why are you in a tizzy over this dance if not because of Delilah?"

"You heard she's going with Roger Mirowski, right? That guy's a douchebag. I don't trust him."

"Roger Mirowski? You mean the brown-haired hunk from the drama club? That Roger Mirowski?" CJ sasses back.

"There's only one Roger Mirowski at school and you know it, you dick. He's a douche, okay? I don't like Delilah going with him." I can't explain it—I could—but I don't want to explain it to CJ.

She's going to look so pretty, I know it. And he's going to pick her up in his stupid car. And hold her hand. And touch her back when he dances too close to her. He's probably going to try to kiss her.

My anxiety morphs into rage and I huck my water bottle across the room.

"Can you text me from the dance if..." I don't even know what I'm asking for.

"Yes, you know I will. I couldn't keep that kind of gossip to myself if you paid me." CJ winks and leaves me to my misery.

"Fuck. You. You cocksucker!" I yell into my headset. Even blowing up zombies on my Xbox isn't taking the edge off. I tap my phone screen again, it's after eight and still no text from CJ. The dance started an hour ago. I can't take it.

Me: Update?

CJ: I don't have an update.

Me: Fuck you. You've gotta give me something.

CJ: Okay. The music is terrible, the decorations are gawdy, and Tina Sutton is sucking face with Tom Milton in the boys bathroom.

Me: CJ! How's Delilah?

CJ: She came with Olivia a little while ago. They've been in and out of the girls bathroom since.

What the fuck? Why did she come with Olivia? Where's her "date"?

> Me: Where's Mirowski?

> CJ: Haven't seen him. Hold on, let me go find out.

I pace back and forth in front of my bed. How long does it take him to get me some answers?

> CJ: Don't freak out, okay?

> Me: CJ…

> CJ: He stood her up.

> Me: He stood her up? What the fuck! Is she okay?

> CJ: I'm not telling you until you promise not to freak out.

Yea right.

> Me: Fine. I promise I won't freak out.

> CJ: She's crying.

Goddamn it. Mirowski's dead. I don't bother texting CJ back even though he's blowing up my phone.

Shoes. Keys. Truck. Headlights. My tires screech around the corner and I throw the gearshift into park. My door hangs open—this won't take long.

I pound on his front door.

"Hello?" *Roger's mom answers the door.*

"Is Roger home?" *No need for pleasantries.*

"Yes. Roger! One of your friends is here to see you!" *Mrs. Mirowski* hollers. Feet stomp down the stairs and Roger's ugly face comes into view. Mrs. Mirowski leaves Roger alone at the front door. Big mistake.

"Uh, hey Connor. What's up man?" Roger asks, genuinely confused by my presence.

I gesture for him to follow me outside. He does, hesitantly, and we stand in his driveway in the shadows beyond his porch light.

"Don't you have somewhere to be right now, Mirowski?" I seethe.

"Uh..."

"Did you forget something? You know, like picking up your date for homecoming?"

"Oh, haha. Yea. I didn't feel like going. You know how those dances are."

"Sure do. That's why I didn't ask some poor girl just to stand her up." Fury blankets my consciousness.

"It's not a big deal. Everyone meets up with their friends anyway. No one will miss me."

"So, it didn't occur to you Delilah might've been excited to go tonight, spent a ton of time getting ready, and waited for you to pick her up? Which you never did?" My voice raises with every way he let her down.

"It didn't cross your dumb-as-fuck mind she would've been devastated when you never showed up?"

Roger flinches as I snap in his face. "Dude, I'm sorry."

"Don't apologize to me. I'd say you need to apologize to her, but I don't want you speaking to her ever again." I back him against the brick of his house, my hands aching as I squeeze them into fists.

By the time I've finished, he's slumped on the ground, and my knuckles are torn to shreds.

Me: How's the dance, doll?

> Dollface: It's okay. I want to go home but my ride isn't ready to leave yet.

> Me: Good thing I'm outside then.

The biting fall wind should be cooling my boiling temper—I wouldn't be surprised if steam's coming off my exposed skin.

My focus hasn't left the gymnasium doors since I got to the dance.

I blink, and she's there. My heart stops.

She's...beautiful.

Her white hair glows in the moonlight, swept into a high ponytail, exposing her delicate neck. Her dress is stunning. The strapless bodice showcases her narrow shoulders.

The dark night casts shadows on her collarbones and the dip between her breasts. Buttery fabric clings to her body like a lover.

I can't stop the dry swallow that bulges my throat.

She's a ray of sunshine in the black of night. The yellow dress compliments her personality perfectly.

My sunshine.

My fallen angel. Just like the day I first met her. I'll never see the color yellow without being flooded by memories of Delilah.

As she approaches, her pace quickens, racing to get to me. Her ethereal face is marred by tear tracks, eyes red and puffy from crying over that asshole. I should've killed him. But I can't protect my doll if I'm behind bars.

"Connor!" Her sweet, broken voice is music to my ears. She collapses into my outstretched arms.

"Shh, shh, shh. It's okay, doll. I'm here. Don't think about him another second. He's nothing to you." I gently grip her ponytail and stroke the rope of gold again and again as she cries into my chest.

Despite my heart breaking from absorbing her pain, it's mended by the way she needs me, trusts me, leans on me. In this moment, I'm overtaken by the delusion I succumb to every now and then. Her being mine.

Would she want me? Does she like me the way I like her? I want her in my arms forever.

"Dance with me."

Delilah's silver eyes snap to mine, pink lips parting on a gasp. I hold her by the nape of her neck and press her face back into my chest and rest a hand to small of her back.

And in the yellow glow from the light poles, we dance.

The vanilla scent of her shampoo makes me high, and I find I'm not cold at all. I'm on fire with need for Delilah. My sweet best friend who's allowing me to hold her in my arms and sway as I hum our song beneath the stars.

We've stopped dancing, frozen in time between friends and something more. Delilah lifts her face to mine and I move without thinking.

I kiss her.

Her lips are warm from being buried in my chest and taste like a cupcake. I've kissed girls before, but nothing has ever compared to this—so right, so all consuming, so inevitable.

We pull apart from the best kiss of my short life and her eyes are filled with...tears.

How did I fuck this up? What was I thinking? She's vulnerable and I kissed her. I kissed my best friend. Fuck!

I look away, I can't bear to see what truth is shining in her eyes.

"Let me take you home," I quietly offer. Delilah simply nods.

The drive is agonizingly quiet. Charged with all the things we should say but won't. I refuse to say the kiss was a mistake. But there's nothing to say that won't break my heart.

A sharp gasp sends my head jerking to find the threat. "Your hands! Connor, oh my god! What happened to your hands?"

My bloody, busted knuckles grip the steering wheel. Shit. I didn't clean up before I got to the dance.

With a pathetic smirk, I joke, "You should see the other guy."

Delilah frowns at me. I've gotten into fights before, but I've always been up front with her. Tonight, I have nothing to say.

After saying goodnight, I wait for Delilah to disappear into her trailer. Once alone, I stumble into the bushes and throw up until bile burns my sinuses.

I've ruined everything.

18

Delilah

"Izzy, this is breathtaking!" I spin in a slow circle taking in the renovated barn at Lucky Spurs Ranch. Izzy and Reid converted it into an event space as they transition the property from defunct cattle ranch to an equine lover's haven.

Fairy lights twinkle from the rafters creating a mesmerizing night sky effect. Tables made from reclaimed wood are scattered across the space, set with a charming array of mismatched antique chairs. Mason jar lanterns flicker with flameless candles amidst small arrangements of wildflowers.

Country music plays softly from a concealed sound system and the barn is perfectly warm on this crisp spring Saturday. My sister's arms wrap me in a hug from behind, and she rests her cheek on my shoulder blade.

"Thank you!" She gives me a tight squeeze and lets me go to face her. "It all came together perfectly! Mr. Andersen jokes I'm the brain and Reid's the brawn, and together we're the perfect reno-team."

"He's right, this is unbelievable. You'll get so much use out of this space—hosting weddings, anniversary parties, birthdays, and graduations. So many memories will be made here because of your hard work."

I'm so proud of my big sister. She was lost and unhappy for such a long time; my heart's full watching her blossom.

"Everything alright, sugar?" Reid's voice booms in the empty barn. Their faces mirror each other's blatant adoration, and jealousy tugs my heart. I'm happy for her, deeply. But standing on the outside of the life she and Reid are building together makes it painfully obvious what I *don't* have.

I don't have a life partner who gazes at me like they need me more than oxygen.

I don't have a partner in crime to make plans for the future with.

I don't have lips I can kiss any time I want.

I share an apartment with my eternal bachelor best friend who's never given me a second glance. Am I hurting myself by holding on so tightly to Connor? I'll never find love if I'm hung up on a man I'll never have.

"Delilah loves it!" Izzy gushes as Reid wraps his fiancée in a bear hug and kisses her.

"We're glad you're our first honored guest, Delilah. The whole family is so damn proud of you. You'll do great in your internship," Reid says as he rubs Izzy's back.

"Y'all didn't have to do this for me. It's not like I've even been placed. Your family is too kind." I'm so thankful for the party, but I'm deeply uncomfortable with the attention.

"Darlin', you became an honorary Andersen the moment I fell in love with your sister. Mom adores you, and you spend more time here than my brother does—and he lives here." He chuckles. "You give any more thought to what we talked about the other day?"

Izzy's brows drop and she looks between us for an explanation. I didn't intentionally keep it from her; I figured Reid would tell her.

"Reid offered to give me basic equestrian lessons this summer, so I'd be comfortable before my internship starts in the fall. To familiarize myself with the horses, proper care, and eventually riding lessons when I'm ready."

"Twinie! I love that idea! Reid's been easing me in with the horses and I'm already a hundred times more comfortable than I was two months ago. Let's do it together!" Izzy suggests.

"Woooooah. I can't handle double trouble. You two will talk my ears off," Reid jokes.

Izzy backhands him in the chest, but he catches her by the wrist and kisses her palm. I turn away, bitter with envy, pretending to look around for someone, but we're the only ones here.

Noticing where my attention strayed, Isabelle offers, "Livy will be here any minute. She can take you to see Maisey while we finish setting up for the party."

I agree and wander off to explore the ranch while they get back to work.

Izzy and I grew up with few friends and even fewer family. Reid isn't wrong, I've been accepted into the Andersen family without question.

I spent Easter at the ranch, and it was the largest, most joyous holiday I've ever been a part of. Mr. and Mrs. Andersen hosted an Easter egg hunt, all ages welcome. The only kids who attended were Olivia's niece, Harper, and some family friends.

Quincy stayed home to help her mom care for her dad. His Alzheimer's is progressing rapidly. Watching his dad disappear day by day is tearing Connor apart.

He wanted to stay home and help Quincy, but she insisted he come to the Easter celebration and get his mind off their reality.

It was an all-out melee for which adult team could collect

the most eggs. They were filled with money, raffle tickets, rental vouchers for Swift Property Management vacations, and of course, candy.

I didn't pay attention to who won what, but it was the most fun I've ever had.

Today's crisp spring wind sends a chill through me, despite the sun shining from the cloudless sky. A shiver races down my arms and goosebumps follow in its wake. Crossing my arms to brace from the breeze, a familiar tingle raises the hairs on the back of my neck.

I feel Connor before I hear or see him. The next thing I know, he's swooped me into the air like a bride and spins me around.

"You scared me!" I laugh. But it stops being funny when he nuzzles warmth into my neck, and I swear he smells my hair.

"Sorry I'm late, dollface. I got held up at my parents helping Quincy."

"It's okay." I try to hide the way my body reacts to his touch. I wiggle so he'll set me down, and we walk side by side back towards the barn.

He's so handsome it should be illegal. Wranglers that hug his ass just right hang casually over his favorite cowboy boots.

Tucked into those sinful jeans is a white pearl snap collared shirt that stretches across his chest and arms, thin enough to tease the outline of the tattoos underneath. Thank god he's not wearing a cowboy hat. I'd combust on the spot and the night would be over before it begins.

The party's in full swing. The music's loud, but happy conversation floats all around. There's a ton of people here I recognize but don't personally know. The Andersens have a vast circle of friends, and it's unreal they're here to celebrate a nobody like me for finishing my second to last college semester.

Connor stepped away to refill our drinks, but I thought he'd be back by now. I circle the crowd, peeking between bodies to find him. Pain freezes me in place when I spot him.

A stunning woman with sleek black hair and an olive complexion is hanging off my best friend. She's got him pressed against the bar and is running her fingers through the long hair that's fallen across his forehead.

My heart fights to launch up my throat or plummet into my stomach. Instinctually, my arms wrap around me, weak protection from the intense pain and threat this woman is posing.

"*It's my party and I'll cry if I want to*" plays in my swirling mind. Even my own brain is mocking my ridiculous unrequited love for Connor. I can't bear to see what happens next, so I disappear back into the fray to find my sister or Livy for a distraction.

I'm rounding the dance floor when a large, warm hand bracelets my wrist. I whirl around, so glad Connor came for me —but the hand doesn't belong to Connor. I tug my arm back firmly.

"Excuse me, do I know you?" I ask the stranger. He's quite taller than me, chestnut brown hair flips at his collar beneath a cream cowboy hat. The perfect amount of stubble covers his face, fair but not pale like me. Vibrant blue eyes gaze down at me, and a wicked grin crooks one side of his mouth. I don't have the courage to look below his neck.

"Jason Beck. Pleasure to meet you." He offers his hand for a shake. I take it briefly but pull away from him. "You're the guest of honor, right? Delilah?"

"Um, yes. This is my sister and her fiancé's ranch." That was a dumb thing to say.

"Yea, I grew up with the Andersens. I graduated between

James and Reid." His words are perfectly polite, but the way his eyes are leering at me is not. I fidget beneath his scrutiny.

I'm not used to having a man's attention on me. At least, not a man who's interested in me. And Jason definitely seems interested.

When I don't respond, he continues. "Heard you're aiming to specialize in equine therapy. Is that something you'll be doing here?"

"I haven't given much thought to where I'll work after graduation. I'm just trying to get through my internship, you know?" He laughs boisterously, though what I said wasn't funny.

"Can I get you a drink?" he asks. I don't want to see Connor with his plaything, so I ask Jason for a lemonade.

I find a high-top table and wait for him to return with our drinks. He's decent looking. Objectively speaking, he's attractive. But my standard of male beauty is Connor—and Jason doesn't hold a candle to him.

Jason swaggers back, a devilish gleam in his eyes and my stomach drops uncomfortably.

One of his hands offers my drink while the other casually slips too low on my back. I resist squirming beneath his touch when his fingers dig into my hip.

"Here you go, sweetheart." The tart lemonade zaps the tip of my tongue but is snatched from my hand.

"Get your fucking hands off her," Connor growls.

"Back off man," Jason quips calmly, cocky as can be. But Connor doesn't take no for an answer, especially when it comes to me.

This time, Connor's demand is accompanied by a shove. "I said get your disgusting hands off her."

Jason postures like he's going to retaliate when Reid plants a hand on each man's chest, pushing them apart.

Reid hisses furiously, "Keep your voices down. What the fuck's going on?"

Connor shrugs away from Reid's barrier. Not bothering to follow Reid's order, Connor speaks at a normal volume, unafraid. "I'll tell you what's going on. Your buddy over here slipped something into Delilah's drink and now I'm going to kill him."

I gasp. *What?* Why would someone spike my drink at my party, at my sister's ranch.

"Get. Off. My. Property. You sick fuck," Reid growls.

"You believe this kid over me? Seriously, Reid. You know I'd never do anything like that," Jason says, unbothered.

I have no desire to stick around and see how this plays out. Izzy will understand why I have to go, especially after Reid tells her what happened. I sneak away from the testosterone cloud and jog to Izzy's cabin. Thankfully, I chose to wear cute tennis shoes with my sundress instead of heels.

The door's locked, so I sit in the wooden rocking chair on the covered porch and wrap my cardigan tighter around my body to ward off the evening chill. My phone's going off like crazy. I set it on my lap and watch as the notifications pour in.

> Missed Call: Studmuffin
>
> Studmuffin: Where are you?
>
> Reid: Are you okay?
>
> Missed Call: Studmuffin
>
> Studmuffin: Delilah. Where are you?
>
> Missed Call: Sissy

Sissy: Where did you go? Are you okay?

Missed Call: Studmuffin

Livy: I'll fucking kill that sleaze ball. Do you need a ride?

Why would Jason spike my drink? How did Connor even see Jason when he was preoccupied with his little girlfriend?

I'll get the answer to that question sooner than later because Connor's storming through the shadows to my hiding place.

He drops to his knees in front of the rocking chair and covers my bare knees with his warm hands.

"Don't touch me." My words shock me and bite Connor. I've never told him not to touch me. He yanks his hands back like I've burned him. I can't have his hands on me right now.

It *hurts* being so close to him but not having him. It *hurts* when he touches me because it's never in the ways I'm desperate to be touched.

I don't even want to look at him right now.

Connor's normally strong voice cracks under my rejection. "Doll? What's going on?"

I turn my head away from him and stare into the black night.

From the corner of my eye, Connor wars with himself on whether to touch me again.

"Doll. Please look at me. *Please*. I'm not going to touch you if you don't want me to—but you've got to look at me." The agony in his voice widens the crack in my heart that's been forming since childhood.

"I can't do this anymore." The admission slips from my tongue without permission.

Connor sits back on his heels, knuckles white, fisted restraining from touching me.

"I don't understand," he rasps. I don't understand either, but the truth-door is open, and I can't stop now.

"I can't keep doing this with you. You have me, but I can't have you. I'm yours, but you're not mine."

"What are you talking about?" Frantic eyes scan my face trying to read between the lines.

"Thank you for protecting me, but why were you watching me when you had that woman…" I can't bring myself to say it.

"What woman?" he asks. Is he serious?

"The woman who couldn't keep her hands off you at the bar. Or was there more than one and you're not sure which one I'm talking about?" I snip.

My pain and embarrassment are turning into anger. Connor says nothing.

I stand, forcing him to shift away from my feet.

"Forget it. I'm tired. I'm going to wait for Izzy to let me into her cabin. I'm going to stay here for a while." My impromptu plan surprises me nearly as much as it does Connor.

"Delilah, what? No, you aren't staying here. You're coming home with me."

"No. I need some time."

"Some time? For what?"

"Some time away from you." Connor jerks back like I've stabbed him.

My heart aches, hating hurting him. But I *can't* anymore. I can't keep living in a delusional bubble hoping he'll want me some day.

It's past time I accept our relationship for what it is.

And what it will never be.

19

"Some time? For what?" I ask, heart in my throat.

"Some time away from you," Delilah chokes out.

My heart stops. I die from her sharp rejection but somehow, my punishment is to live in eternal purgatory without her.

How did tonight go sideways so fast? I went to refill our drinks when Carolyn from the liquor store cornered me. She's always been blatantly clear she wants to fuck me. Thing is, I have no desire to fuck anyone other than Delilah, let alone a cougar like Carolyn.

I couldn't have been away from Delilah more than five minutes. Fuck. Was it longer? What does she think she saw? Because I told Carolyn in no uncertain terms I wasn't interested and to keep her hands to herself.

That predator slipped something into the drink he picked up from the bartender and I followed the fucker to stop him from hurting whatever poor girl he was hunting.

When he gave the drugged glass to Delilah, I saw red. Rage. Protectiveness. Jealousy. Possession. Why's another man buying my girl a drink? And why's she accepting it? And who the fuck does he think he is to hurt what's mine?

"Delilah, I don't—what happened? Whatever it is, I'll fix it. Please. Just come home with me," I beg like a fool.

"You can't fix it." Pain lances through me as her dagger pierces through my chest.

I get to my feet and move to hug her but jerk my arms back. She doesn't want me to touch her. She doesn't want me.

We stand in deafening silence. What am I going to do? I can't lose her. Not even for one night. I won't survive it.

"Oh, thank god. Reid! She's over here!" Isabelle yells, running towards her house. Mounting the porch, Izzy's eyes eviscerate me, furious Delilah's hurt, and certainly blaming me.

The sob that bubbles up Delilah's throat twists the knife in my chest. "Can I...stay here for a while?" she asks her sister, delivering the killing blow to my heart.

Reid reaches the porch, looking as furious with me as Izzy does. He locks eyes with his fiancée, some telepathic couple-conversation passing between them.

Izzy wraps her arm around Delilah's shaking shoulders and leads her into the cabin. She gives Reid a pointed look before shutting me off from the love of my life.

"Thank you," Reid says, shocking the shit out of me.

"What?"

"Thank you for being there for her. I didn't know Jason was a predator. If I did, I would've killed him a long time ago. I'm sorry Delilah had to go through that. You're a good man, Connor."

"She doesn't seem to think so." I'm disgusted such a petty thing came out of my mouth.

Reid leans against the porch railing, crossing his arms in a "dad" stance. "Don't be fucking stupid." *What? Is he serious?*

"You're in love with her."

My ears ring and my eyes blur hearing my deepest secret spoken so clearly for the universe to hear.

"Don't bother arguing. I've known since your birthday party

last year. No man looks at a woman the way you look at Delilah unless he's in love," Reid says like I'm dumb as shit.

I can't bring myself to admit it. It won't do any good. The less people who know the truth, the better. If Reid's known all these months, surely, he's told Isabelle.

Has she told Delilah? She couldn't have. If she had, Delilah wouldn't think she's anything other than mine.

"She loves you too, you know." That gets my fucking attention.

"You don't know what you're talking about. She loves me as a friend."

"Yea, that's what Isabelle said when I asked her. But I don't buy it. So, what are you going to do about it?" I scowl at Reid, daring him to continue.

"You're going to lose her if you don't tell her how you feel. Take it from a guy who almost lost the love of his life." His eyebrows raise, the scarred one not quite as high.

"How did you fix it?" I ask quietly, but my words reverberate loudly in my muddled brain. I have to fix this. I need her.

"It was a different situation, but same principles should apply, I'd bet. First, I admitted to myself all the painful, ugly, terrifying truths I'd been burying. Then, I told her everything and hoped like hell she'd give me another chance. I've spent every minute since trying to be the man she deserves."

Reid stands from the railing and pats me hard on the back. "You've got to admit it to yourself before you can tell her. And pray it's not too late." And with that, he slips inside to guard my girl, my heart, for the night.

Sleep eludes me. The bed smells like her. The sheets are cold and still without her beside me. The walls of this damned apartment are haunted with her voice, her laughter, and her love.

No matter what I do next, my life will never be the same. But if I had to choose a life with Delilah or without her, I'd choose her.

Every. Single. Time.

20

Studmuffin: I miss you.

I stare at the text Connor sent this morning like if I look at it long enough, I'll miraculously know what to do.

I've been staying at Lucky Spurs Ranch for the past five days. After the barn party, I cried myself to sleep in Izzy's bed, and Reid was kind enough to sleep on the couch.

I was mortified inconveniencing Reid in his own home, so Izzy arranged a room for me at the main house.

Always gracious hosts, food is abundant. Eating to not offend the Andersens and ignoring the feelings I refuse to face has had an unexpected side effect.

I've gained weight. Typically, when I'm stressed, I control my intake even stricter. But there's something healing being at the ranch, spending my days in the sun with my sister, having no contact with my mom, and hiding from my problems.

It's been nice pretending to be a normal, well-adjusted human being. At least during the daytime. Nights are when my mask falls. Nights spent in a bed without Connor. Nights without the pillow talk I've greedily cherished.

I miss him so much it hurts. I felt his heart breaking when I told him I needed time apart. It broke me to say it, but it was true. It isn't his fault I want more, but I can't keep pretending what we have is enough for me.

He goes to the ends of the earth to care for me, provide for me, and protect me. He even brought Reid a bag full of my necessities while I stay at the ranch.

He finds ways to keep me away from other men but dates other women and lets them touch him. The mixed signals have knotted me up for years, and my rope frayed so far I cut loose to save myself from drowning.

Connor texted me steadily our first night apart. The next couple of days were filled with missed calls and texts I didn't respond to. Now, I get one or two texts a day like the one I'm staring at.

I miss you too...but it doesn't change anything.

"Twinie?" Isabelle's sweet voice floats into my temporary bedroom. "I brought you coffee."

"Thanks, sissy." We sit side by side on the bed and sip our morning caffeine. She's been uncharacteristically quiet during my stay here. I feared she'd be in my business, but she's given me as much space as I ask for but welcomes me when I'm ready for company.

"Want to come down to the stables this morning?" she asks.

We've spent time with Reid every day familiarizing ourselves with the horses and it's incredibly soothing. These few days have reaffirmed my desire to work in equine therapy.

"I'd love to. But it's time to face the music. I need to go home and talk to Connor. We can't stay in limbo forever. We've been friends for too long to let a wound like this fester."

Izzy narrows her icy blue eyes, searching for answers I don't have.

"Okay, I'll drive you."

I stand outside our front door, unable to enter the apartment. Connor's truck was in the parking lot, so I know he's home.

Whatever happens next will irreversibly change the course of our relationship.

The decision is made for me when Connor opens the door and nearly bowls me over.

"Shit, Delilah, are you okay? I'm so sorry, I didn't see you." His hands hover awkwardly, careful not to touch me.

Purple and blue color the bags under his hollow eyes. His hair is a mess, and he must've slept in the clothes he's wearing. He looks as bad as I feel.

He clocks the bag at my feet and his sorrow-filled eyes meet mine for an explanation.

"We need to talk." The dreaded four words that leave my lips taste like poison.

Connor's face breaks further, but he takes my bag and follows me into the apartment. It looks exactly like I left it. Either he's kept it meticulously clean, or he hasn't moved a thing in my time away. Both options plague me with guilt for leaving him.

He sits on the edge of the couch, elbows on his knees, hands clasped, and head dropped between his shoulders. I'd normally sit beside him so close our thighs would touch. But it feels wrong today, so I sit with a cushion between us—which also feels wrong.

I'm not meant to be away from Connor.

His back tightens, hating the cavern of space separating us as much as I do. I'm the one who came home unannounced and declared we need to talk—but I have no words.

"Are you okay?" Connor asks. My sweet man. His first concern is always me.

"I'm not sure."

"What can I do to fix this? I'll do anything," he pleads, head still hanging low, jaw clenching rhythmically.

Not anything.

The only fix for this is if he wants me like I want him—and he doesn't.

"Can you at least tell me what happened at the party that upset you? I couldn't stop that prick from spiking your drink, but I stopped you from drinking it. I swear to god, I was already on his heels to confront him. I lost it, Del. I didn't mean to scare you." His head lifts enough to see me through his mop of hair.

"You didn't scare me, Connor. You saved me. That isn't why I left," I explain.

"Why did you leave?" he rasps.

"Where were you when Jason spiked my drink?"

Connor blinks rapidly, caught off guard by my question.

"I was at the bar."

"Why were you still at the bar? You went to refill our drinks, and you didn't come back. If you'd come right back, Jason wouldn't have ever approached me."

"I went to get us new drinks and I got caught up chatting."

I smile placidly at him. "I know. I saw."

"What do you think you saw?" Connor asks dumbly, but with a hint of irritation.

"I saw a gorgeous woman with her tits in your face, fingering your hair."

"Shit. Del. That was Carolyn. She works at the liquor store. I'm not involved with her. Hell, I don't even like her. I told her to get her hands off me."

"That's not what it looked like to me."

"Doll, it meant nothing. Why are you pissed at me about Carolyn when you let Jason get you a drink?" Connor snaps.

How. Dare. He?

"Oh, I don't know Connor. Maybe because it felt nice to have a man show interest in me. Maybe because I haven't been on a date in years. Maybe because I'm so tired of waiting."

Connor's shock is palpable. "Waiting for what?"

I can't tell him the truth. He doesn't want me. He's never wanted me like *that*.

My voice is barely audible. "Please don't make me say it."

Somehow Connor's crept closer and is right beside me. His clammy hands frame my face, forcing me to look at him.

"Don't make you say what?"

"Connor...please." It comes out as a pained whisper.

"Delilah...I—"

My phone rings cutting the tension. I scramble to answer it, desperate to wake up from my worst nightmare.

"Hello?" I answer too chipper.

"Hello, is this Miss Tate?"

"Yes, this is she." I stand from the couch and pace the living room.

"This is Angela from Blue Mountain Rescue and Rehabilitation, is now a good time to talk?"

My eyes bug out of my head, and despite the awkward state of our relationship, I turn to Connor to ground me. He's watching my every move.

"Yes. Now's a great time to talk."

"Congratulations on earning top of your class this semester. Your advisor tells us you are a shining star in the psychology program."

I blush at the compliment. "Thank you so much..."

"As I'm sure you know, you were awarded the top internship selection among your classmates, and based on the interest form you

submitted, we'd like to offer you a fall internship shadowing our licensed clinical therapists and equine specialists."

Tears spring from my eyes and the biggest smile overtakes my face.

"Yes! Oh my goodness! I mean, yes, I accept, I'd be honored!" Connor stands before me, rubbing his rough hands up and down my arms. His touch immediately soothes me.

"*Wonderful, just what we like to hear. I'll iron out the details with your advisor and either she or I will reach out closer to September. It was a pleasure speaking with you and we're looking forward to having you at Blue Mountain Rescue and Rehabillitation! Bye now.*"

The call disconnects and I stand dumbstruck.

"I...I got the internship. I GOT THE INTERNSHIP! OH MY GOD, CONNOR!"

I leap into his arms, wrapping my legs around him like a baby koala. He holds me tight and spins us in circles in the middle of our living room.

Connor's voice is muffled, his breath hot against my neck. "I knew you could do it. I'm so fucking proud of you."

We stay locked in our embrace for longer than appropriate for our precarious relationship. I shimmy to get down and he lets me drop gently to my feet. The weight of what we've left unsaid hangs heavily between us. But neither of us are brave enough to tell the truth.

"I'd better go unpack..." I hedge.

"Yea. Of course. I was heading out when you got home, so, I'll see you later?" he asks.

I'm unreasonably wounded he's leaving already, but it's for the best we ease back into living together.

"Bye, doll." He waits for my customary response but leaves when I say nothing.

The door snicks shut, and my lungs allow me to whisper, "Miss you already."

21

I'm so fucking tired. When I got my job with the department of transportation, I assumed the busiest months would be during winter.

As it turns out, at least in my position, summer is my busiest season. Which fucking sucks because asphalt is hot as balls after baking in triple-digit heat.

My busy season couldn't come at a worse time. My relationship with Delilah is upside-down, underwater, in a car with the window cracked.

I'm slowly drowning in agony having her so close, but we've never been further apart. Everything's gotten so fucked up.

I thought living with Delilah would be a dream. Instead it's been a nightmare, unraveling me day by day and I'm about to snap.

I can't touch her the way I want. I can't look at her the way I want. I can't tell her the words bursting from my heart. *I LOVE YOU! I've loved you as long as I can remember, and I've been IN love with you for nearly that long.*

Regardless of how messy things are between us, nothing will

stop me from working toward her dream. Someday, the long shifts and overtime will pay off. It has to.

The soft click of the front door is barely enough to rouse me from my sleep-deprived wallowing. Tentative footsteps approach our bedroom and stop outside the doorway.

This is what I mean. She's *right here* but she might as well be a million miles away.

Hell, I've fucked things up so badly she's afraid to come into her own bedroom for fear of facing me. I hate myself.

"I can see your shadow, doll. You can come in, I promise I won't bite."

The light from the living room casts an ethereal glow around her, and I forget to breathe. I unconsciously drag my knuckles along my sternum to ease the chronic deep ache.

"I don't know how to do this," she says.

"Come here." I pat her side of the bed, and she eases onto the comforter beside me. "What don't you know how to do?"

She hesitates, fear marring her features. "This. Us. From the day I met you, our relationship has been effortless. This scares me."

"What are you afraid of, doll?"

"Everything. What happens next. What happens to our friendship."

I'm not stupid, I know what she's getting at, but I refuse to accept it. I wrap my arm around her shoulders and pull her down to rest on me.

"Let me tell you what's going to happen. I'm going to be away a lot this summer, so you'll have space. But don't think for a second I'm going anywhere, or that you're going anywhere. What happens next is you preparing for your internship and leaning on the Andersens and Olivia to indoctrinate you into horse-land." I finger comb the strands of white-gold silk draped across my chest.

"And nothing happens to our friendship. We made it through the Great TV Show Cheating scandal during high school." She jolts up to argue with me, but I hold her tightly against my body.

"I maintain we had no such agreement about not watching episodes seven and eight over the weekend. But as I've apologized for the last decade, I'm *sorry* I found out about Jennifer's baby before you did."

Delilah's slight body trembles beneath my arm, containing her laughter. Her delicate fingers clutch at my shirt.

"We've made it through hundreds of tiny disagreements and insignificant fights. I don't see how this is any different," I explain.

Her warm breath penetrates the thin cotton of my shirt. "This isn't a tiny disagreement...or an insignificant fight," she whispers.

She's right. Of course she is. But I'm sure as hell not ready to put words to what's broken between us.

"No, you're right. But I'll never let anything, or anyone, come between us—not even ourselves. I don't regret moving you in here for a second, but I won't lie, it's been a big adjustment for both of us. We're treading in uncharted waters, but there's no one I'd rather have by my side." I hug her tighter against me and she melts into my hold.

"What's happening to us, Connor?" Her question breaks my heart.

"Nothing we can't handle, doll. Nothing we can't get through together." I kiss her temple and drag in her vanilla jasmine scent for longer than I should.

We sit in relatively comfortable silence, soaking in each other's company. Being with Delilah has always recharged my soul, and despite our current predicament, I feel infinitely better than I did ten minutes ago.

"I'm sad you have to work so much this summer," she says quietly.

"I know doll, but summers are always a bitch."

"I know. But...this is the first summer in years I haven't had classes. I get a real summer, and I wish you could be a part of it."

Fucking *ouch*. Heart, meet waffle iron.

"I'll try to get back on night shift so we can have days together," I offer desperately.

"No, no. You'd be exhausted. I'm sorry, I shouldn't have said anything. I don't know why I'm being such a baby about this. Things have been so weird between us...I thought some summer fun would help. It sounds stupid when I say it out loud."

I do mental math to calculate the minimum number of shifts and overtime hours I need to hit my savings goal by the end of summer.

"Let me see what I can do, okay? There's a lot of seasonal guys looking for extra work and I bet I can get out of one or two of the longer trips." I expect her to tell me not to bother, because Delilah always puts everyone else's happiness above her own. But she surprises me.

She lifts from my chest, propping herself on one arm and traces the collar of my shirt with one finger. Electricity courses from her body to mine.

"I'd really like that. If it's not too much trouble. I want to be with you as much as possible before my internship takes over my life."

Does she have any idea the effect her words have on me? I want nothing more than to be with her.

But she doesn't mean it the way I wish she did. I can't formulate an appropriate response, so I go with the simplest truth.

"I want to be with you too."

22

Connor age 14, Delilah age 13

"Oooo," the class taunts.

"Quiet, class. Delilah, take the hall pass and go straight to the guidance counselor. No messing around or it's straight to detention," Mrs. Harbach says. Yet another teacher who hates me for no reason other than for having the wrong last name.

I work hard to go unnoticed, so I'm worried why the guidance counselor wants me to come see him immediately.

I knock on the open door and wait to be invited in.

"Ah, Miss Tate. Please take a seat," Mr. Richards says. I do as I'm told and try my best not to fidget.

"Do you know why you're here?" he asks.

"No, sir."

"Now's your chance to tell me anything you want to say. It will stay in this room, I promise," he says. Behind me, the door is still wide open and the gossipy teacher's assistants are sitting in the main office.

I stay silent and he shakes his head in disappointment.

"This is your last year of middle school, Miss Tate. The administration takes the success of its students seriously and need to ensure you're ready to enter high school in the fall."

What's he talking about? I get good grades, and I stay out of trouble. Why wouldn't I be ready to go to high school? Cold sweat beads on the back of my neck and I squirm uncomfortably in the hard, plastic chair.

"Your teachers have reported an upsetting trend. You've been falling asleep in class and aren't keeping up with the material as easily as usual," Mr. Richards says.

I flush with embarrassment.

Dad left, and Mom stopped taking care of us. There's never enough safe food to eat.

So, yea, when my stomach's burning from being so empty, and Mom's up all night drinking and wailing about my dad being gone, sometimes I fall asleep in class...

And being so hungry and tired makes it hard to pay attention... and I've gotten a few bad grades on assignments and tests recently.

"I'll try harder, I swear. Please don't be mad. Please don't hold me back in eighth grade!" I plead.

Mr. Richards regards me with such scrutiny, like bugs crawling all over my skin.

"See that you do. You'll be stopping in for weekly visits with me until your teachers are satisfied. If things don't improve, administration will need to get involved." He raises one bushy eyebrow over his tortoiseshell glasses.

"Yes, Mr. Richards." Keeping my head down, I rush from the office, giggles and whispers from the teacher's assistants already following me out the door.

Hoping I have enough grace period to use the bathroom, I lock myself in a stall and allow myself a minute to cry.

This is the worst year of my life.

Izzy and Connor are both in high school now, so their schedule is different than mine. Izzy goes to school earlier than me, so, I walk to school by myself. And I don't see them after school as much because Connor has sports, and Izzy has a lot more homework.

Livy's still in middle school like me, but her lunch period is different than mine and her specials are on a different rotation than me, so when I have gym, she has art. Or when I have art, she has music.

I've never been this lonely in my whole life.

My dad left. My mom doesn't love me. I can't do anything right—not even eating...

"Why the long face, dollface?" Connor says, nudging my side with his elbow.

I plaster on a fake smile and keep walking, hoping he'll drop it.

I had another counseling session with Mr. Richards today. They're bad enough, but today the school nurse was there. It felt like she saw inside me and learned all my secrets.

"I don't have practice today, and it's warm out. Do you want to go do homework at the park?" Connor asks.

I readily accept because though I'm so hungry I might faint, especially in this warmer weather, I'll do anything to stay out of our trailer as long as possible.

We sit at an old table with green rubber coating peeling off the diamond pattern of the seats. Izzy has detention and Livy has riding lessons, so it's just us today.

Time alone with Connor is my favorite. He always makes me forget about the bad things in my life for a little while.

I watch him closely as he pulls his books from his backpack. He got a lot taller this year, and his arms are bigger. He has fuzzy hair growing on his face and sometimes his voice cracks and sounds deeper.

High school looks good on him. I flush at the thought and cover my face with my hair, digging into my backpack.

I've been having these feelings more often lately. I've always loved Connor; he's my best friend in the whole world. But now when I look at him, he's not just my best friend. He's my extremely cute best friend who's becoming a young man...just like I'm becoming a young woman.

One time I thought Connor was staring at my boobs, but then he tripped and fell, so maybe he was just distracted.

"What are these?" Connor asks, grabbing the colorful pamphlets that've fallen out of my backpack.

I scramble to gather them up, but he holds them over his head so high I can't reach.

"Nothing," I grumble. But Connor never takes that as an answer.

He knows me better than I know myself and I can't hide anything from him.

He flips through the pamphlets, and I sink deeper into mortification, burying my head in my arms on the sticky table.

Connor gets on his knees next to my seat and pries my head up from my arms. His eyes are shining with tears and seeing him hurt breaks me.

I burst into tears and collapse into his arms, joining him on the pavement.

"Shh, shh. It's ok, Delilah-doll. It's gonna be okay. We'll get you through this, I promise," he soothes, rocking me in his arms, not caring if anyone's watching.

"Why didn't you tell me?" he asks, pain lacing his cracking voice.

I can't bear to look at him, so I burrow into his chest and talk into his tear-soaked shirt.

"You already worry about me too much. You bring me snacks and your parents invite me over for dinner all the time. I didn't want to bother you..." I admit.

Connor pushes me back by the shoulders and tips my chin up. "Hey. Stop it. You never bother me. I like helping you. It's always hurt my stomach when you don't have enough to eat, and my mom and dad hate it too. It's not your fault your parents...your mom, sucks."

I huff a laugh through my tears. "Sucks" is the understatement of the year, but he's right.

"Talk to me. Please, doll," Connor pleads.

Taking a deep breath, we get off the ground to sit back at the table. He holds my hands atop the worn green diamond tabletop.

"I don't know how to explain it..."

"Try. You can tell me anything. I wish you hadn't kept this from me. I could've tried to help sooner..." he says sadly.

"It's not your job to fix me."

"I know. But I can't not help...I can't stand you in pain." He smiles, perhaps revisiting the day we met, me sitting in the dirt, crying, and him riding up on his bike like a knight in shining armor.

"Mom doesn't really buy groceries anymore. She used to... sometimes."

Connor looks so angry, his knee's bouncing under the table like a basketball.

"I was so hungry all the time, I ate what we had, but lots of times it was spoiled, and I'd end up throwing it up later."

"Oh, Delilah..." I've hurt him by hurting myself and it breaks my heart.

"I hated throwing up, so instead I got more choosey with the foods I ate. I already avoided the rotten and spoiled food at home. But then I started avoiding treats, like I wouldn't take a cupcake at the class party, or the chips from your lunchbox. Well, when we were at the same school." I wince, chagrined because it's not his fault he's a year older than me.

"Soon I was only eating oatmeal, frozen vegetables if the freezer was running—if we had electricity—or canned. Dried beans are cheap, and they keep me fuller, so I always try to buy those when Mom gives me grocery money." I'm embarrassed admitting all this out loud.

I've never told Connor the full truth and I didn't tell Mr. Richards or the school nurse, but they figured it out anyway.

I pull a pamphlet from the front-zipped pocket of my backpack. The one I thought might help me.

Equine Therapy.

"We don't have insurance or even a doctor."

Connor's wracked with sorrow. I hate myself for burdening him with my stupid problems.

"I only eat foods I think are healthy and safe. Fresh food spoils too fast. Foods like noodles, rice, lunch meat, cereal—those will make me fat. When I eat my safe foods, I don't gain any weight, and Mom doesn't have to buy me more clothes. I'm in control of what I eat.

"But...I guess I'm not eating enough of even my safe foods since I've been falling asleep in class and getting bad marks on my homework."

Connor's at a loss for words, everything I say makes him sadder and sadder. This is why I didn't tell him...I knew I'd hurt him.

He picks up the equine therapy pamphlet and flips through it.

"Would this help?" he asks, motioning with the colorful paper.

"There's no way we could afford something like that, and I have no way of getting there." I snatch it back and crush it into a ball doomed to die at the bottom of my backpack.

"Let me talk to my mom, I'm sure she—"

I cut him off. "No. Thank you, Connor, but no. I can't take anything else from your parents. I promise I'll try to eat more foods, okay? The school nurse said hard boiled eggs are healthy and can last a week in the fridge...if we have electricity. She promised me peanut butter was safe. And Mr. Richards said if I ask the grocery store people, they should have foods in the back that are less money since they're trying to get rid of it."

He regards me carefully, not knowing what to say or how to help.

"Promise?" he asks.

"Promise."

23

"Are you listening to me?" Olivia asks across our table at The Flying Pig.

I drag my mind out of this lust-filled haze to meet her emerald eyes. "Sorry, what were you saying?"

"I was asking if you want to carpool to the ranch after dinner to visit Maisey. I know it's not one of your lesson days with Reid and Izzy, but if you don't have anything else going on, I'd be happy to share my Maisey-time with you." She winks.

"That sounds good. The temperature will be a lot more pleasant after the sun goes down." I try to sound enthused, but my mind is miles away.

Olivia's feline eyes cut through me like an X-ray. "What's going on with you lately?

"Hmm? Nothing. My mind wanders to my internship every minute of the day. I'm supposed to be enjoying my first summer off in forever, but I wish I was already entrenched in work, you know?"

"I do. You know I'm a prima-workaholic. Once you're comfortable with the horses, and have some hands-on experience under your belt, you'll be golden."

Olivia has a way of brightening your day, and I'm grateful for her especially on days like today when my hormones are trying to catapult me into Connor's pants. Spending time at the ranch will be a good distraction anyway because Connor is away on a three-day trip, and I miss him like crazy.

"Do you want to make a whole night of it and sleep over in the guest house? Steal Izzy away from her fiancé for a night and have a slumber party like the old days?" The plan forms in my head, exciting me more with each word that comes out of my mouth.

I finish my lemonade, and Lou Ann drops a refill off like magic. I've been obsessed with anything lemon since Connor's mom's lemonade first tickled my tongue. She doesn't make it much anymore; they live a life of quiet survival with Connor's dad's Alzheimer's disease.

Since moving in with Connor, I dread the nights I sleep alone in our bed. He doesn't need to know I big-spoon his pillow, or sleep in his shirts. Those secrets will stay between me and the walls of our apartment.

Livy looks...guilty? She fidgets in her seat across from me at the pub and doesn't meet my eyes when she responds. "That sounds amazing, but I have plans with..." She stops abruptly. Panic filled eyes shoot to mine.

I'm not one to push. I have no room to pry into other people's lives when I've been hiding a hopeless crush on Connor for years.

"I'm proud of you. I hope you know how much I admire you." She changes the subject abruptly. "I know you were struggling this spring, but you seem to be doing much better."

She's right. I take inventory of my plate and find I've eaten nearly everything without consciously lifting each bite to my mouth, forcing myself to chew and swallow.

Between the twenty-four seven showing of *Connor Dicks Down Delilah* my imagination's concocted, and distracting myself from said film, I ate my entire lunch without a thought. My pork green chili is dregs in the bottom of the bowl.

"Thanks Liv."

"Let's blow this pop stand and go to the glitter factory. Lucky Spurs Ranch has a special blend of horsehair and hay bits with our names on it."

I allow myself to check my phone once we're on the road. Olivia is performing a one-woman Broadway show in the driver's seat, so I'm safe to indulge my masochism.

> Studmuffin: You should've seen this huge ass elk today. It was as big as my truck!

> Studmuffin: Thanks for picking up those drinks I like from the market.

> Studmuffin: Our song was on the radio today.

I close my eyes and let the notes and lyrics of our song crash over me like a wave.

As long as old men sit and talk about the weather. As long as old women sit and talk about old men.

Maybe it's strange two little kids latched on to a country ballad about endless devotion. But it spoke to us. It tugged on my heartstrings in an inexplicable way and wove itself into the fabric of my being. I'll eternally think of my life with Connor every time I hear our song.

> Me: Must've been a big elk. Pics or it didn't happen.

> Me: And you're welcome. They were in the cooler by the register so I grabbed as many as I could carry.

> Me: Forever and ever, right Connor?

> Studmuffin: Right, doll. Forever and ever, amen.

> Me: I miss you.

Three dots bounce on my screen and my heart stops beating, waiting for his reply. Maybe I shouldn't have said that. But I do miss him, terribly.

The dots stop dancing. The pavement gives way to dirt road and the bumps beneath the tires reminding me what I should be focusing on. My education. My career.

I may not ever have the love of my life—so this dream will have to be enough.

"You useless piece of shit!" The good for nothing gigantic blue dildo thuds against the wall before sadly wiggling around on the floor. I didn't turn it off before my orgasm-denied temper tantrum. My purple pal never let me down like this.

Unsatisfied and pissed off, I turn the damn thing off and throw it into my underwear drawer.

I cover my sweat dampened skin with a light dress and throw my pillow ruffled hair into a top knot. A few muttered curses and my sandals accompany me out the door and into the blazing summer sun.

Do you know why summer is the most miserable, godforsaken season of the year? While children are frolicking around in swimsuits, and adults are enjoying the bright Rocky Mountain sunshine, I'm taking cold showers and leaving half-moon scars in the palms of my hands from how tight I clench my fists.

Everyone has *their thing*, and *my thing* has always undoubtably been Connor. Connor's eyes. Connor's lips. Connor's laugh. Connor's touch.

But summer is a real bitch because she brings the most tempting version of *my thing* out to play.

You know those douchey shirts the gym bros wear? The tank tops that've been cut to reveal every rib, or the T-shirts with the sleeves cut off, split nearly the bottom hem. Like, why bother wearing a shirt at all when the entire world can see your useless man-nipples.

The PROBLEM is that on Connor, those shirts aren't douchey at all. They're like the most expensive La Perla lingerie money can buy, made specifically for my tatted-up, muscles chiseled from hard labor, golden as a god, best fucking friend.

His arms are always out to play. I have a front row seat to the gun show every time I open my eyes. Droplets of sweat drip down his ribs into his low-slung jeans. I want to trace their salty path with my tongue.

My god, what's wrong with me? Women complain about being objectified, but my lizard brain can't do anything but objectify my best friend.

My. Best. Friend. I'm a creep. A pervert.

But he's so pretty I could cry!

I suppose the only saving grace is he works so much during the summer, I'm saved from being a Peeping Tina, at least during the light of day.

If I'm lucky, the mountain air cools enough once the sun goes down and Connor puts on a full shirt or a hoodie. My fingers still itch to touch him, but the visual temptation is concealed.

Connor's intolerably attractive at his *worst*. My brain short circuits when he's dressed and groomed for a normal day. The ball cap goes on and dear god...

I've gotten in the habit of dabbing the corners of my mouth like a nervous tic for fear I'm drooling over him.

And because lady universe is a raging bitch, she likes to compel Connor to flip that goddamn hat backwards. I've been known to suddenly have somewhere I need to be, or a phone call I have to take when his hat is backwards. He's so attractive it's categorically unfair.

My self-control only stretches so far. And apparently, that distance is the one-eighty degree turn of the brim of his cap from front to back.

I swear to god, if he ever put on a cowboy hat, I'd spontaneously ovulate. My eggs would jump the cliff down my tubes screaming PICK ME! PICK ME!

Unsatisfied, I check my phone and am crestfallen to find no text from Connor. Even with the widening distance between us, he texts me every day, and I don't like this one bit.

A hot-cold flash of anxiety coats my skin in a sweat. Three days. I haven't heard from Connor in three days. He was supposed to be home from this job three days ago. I would've understood if he was too tired to drive home after his shift ended and he found somewhere to sleep. But it's the night of day three and he should've been home by now.

His absence and the cavern of distance between us is why my blue bestie is getting re-charged daily. When I'm not masturbating for distraction, I'm stress cleaning at eleven at night. Our downstairs neighbors must hate me for the noise I'm making pacing around the apartment.

My cheeks are tight from dried tear tracks, eyes are bleary from exhaustion.

I've texted. I've called. I called CJ incessantly until he answered. Quincy hasn't heard from him either.

It's taking everything in me not to take off on a one-woman search and rescue mission. But I have no idea where this job even took him. My head pounds with unanswered questions.

What if he's hurt? What if he's dead? Why didn't I tell him I love him? What if I never see him again?

I blindly fumble around for the wall for support as I collapse onto the floor. Panic and regret consume me. My lungs refuse the gasps of air I'm struggling to pull in. Dark spots obscure my vision, and I know I'm about to pass out or have a panic attack.

The deadbolt on the front door clacks open and I jump to my feet, leaning against the wall for support.

I've never been so relieved as when Connor's tattooed hand opens the door.

Our bodies have always had a sixth sense about where the other is, and his eyes find me immediately, like they always do.

"What's wrong?" In a split second, his bag is on the floor, and he's rushed to me.

My face falls and uncontrollable sobs wrack my tired body. I'm in his arms before I know what's happening and he coos comfort and reassurance into my neck.

I draw back to get a good look at him to see if he's injured in any way.

Chocolate eyes skate across my face, concern written all over his. Furrowed brows silently question what's wrong. My brain tells my mouth to say I'm fine. That I was worried but am happy he's home safe, but no words come out.

My heart has no words. It has a strong, steady beat, screaming his name.

The pounding of my heart's desire is too loud to ignore, and my mouth crashes against his and I kiss him with every ounce of desire and regret I've suffered these past days, weeks, months, and years.

I pull away when my brain registers...he's not kissing me back. I slap a hand over my mouth, back out of his hold, and flee. The bathroom door slams behind me, and I sink to the cold tile floor.

What have I done?

24

Delilah's pretending to be asleep when I come to bed. I can't blame her.

What the hell happened tonight? She kissed me. *Delilah* kissed *me* unprovoked.

I dread a sleepless night laying inches from her warm body, too afraid to cuddle up to her like I want to. But my body overrules my mind and the exhaustion from the past few days drags me under into a fitful sleep.

I wake to comforting sounds coming from the kitchen and a cold, empty bed. I squeeze my eyes closed, not trying to fall back asleep, but to shut out the inevitable pain coming my way.

All I know is the love of my life, my best friend, kissed me, and I'm afraid of what it means for us.

Nearly ten years have passed since her lips first met mine. But last time, it was my impulsive actions that led to our kiss. I was furious at the kid who stood her up for homecoming and devastated by how hurt and embarrassed she must've been.

In that moment, dancing beneath the stars, my knuckles still bleeding from bashing his face in, I was overcome with a surge of possession. Delilah was mine.

Delilah's always been mine. She'll always be mine.

I can't reconcile the possibility she might have feelings for me beyond platonic friendship—but last night has got me all fucked up.

When we got stranded behind a rockslide, the first and only place my mind went was to Delilah. Would she worry I wasn't texting her? Was she waiting up for my call? Was she afraid when I hadn't come home on time, or the next day?

But she's been spending as much time as possible away from the apartment—away from me. Maybe she wasn't even sleeping at our place and couldn't care less about where I was.

I was safe but unanchored without any way to contact her. When I trudged my tired body up the stairs last night, I expected to find a quiet, empty apartment.

What I found instead was a broken angel. I can't lie and say it didn't feel good to see evidence she still cared, but I never want her to worry or suffer, especially on my account.

I intended to profusely apologize for my extended absence. Instead, she melted into me, right where she's meant to be. Just holding her would've been enough. I'll always take whatever I can get when it comes to Delilah.

But she tipped her tear-filled eyes to mine, love emanating from her and kissed me.

One moment's all it took to flip my life on its head. I would've kissed her forever, but she pulled away too soon.

Why did she pull away? Does she regret it? I fall back into the moment, reliving every micro sensation. Her lips pressing to mine, insistent, hot, and greedy.

And I...fuck. I stood there like an idiot and didn't kiss her back.

Did I really not kiss her back? God fucking damnit!

I fly out of bed and pace our bedroom, nearly ripping the

hair from my scalp. She didn't run away because she regretted kissing me. She ran away because she thought I didn't want her.

Little does she know, she's the only thing I've ever wanted. I've been wrapped around her delicate finger since I met her. There isn't anything I wouldn't do for her.

Except, apparently, fucking KISS HER BACK!

How the hell do I have this conversation with her? How do you find the right time to have a life changing discussion? Is there ever a right time?

So instead of being the man she deserves, I tuck tail and move forward as if nothing happened. Just like I did the first time we kissed.

The birds haven't woken to catch their worms, yet the sun still rises over the eastern horizon. Reid and Izzy asked us over today for breakfast and for some help on the ranch. Izzy will be showing Delilah the ropes—or at least the few ropes she's learned from Reid—while I help him with some projects on the property.

Today will be the perfect distraction from the storm of emotions swirling in my mind. Time with Isabelle should offer Delilah a reprieve as well.

"It's unreal out here, man," I say to Reid as we work along the eastern fence line of the ranch. They're planning to build a few small guest houses to rent out to guests and Reid needed a second set of hands to clear organic debris from the staked area.

"Nothing will ever compare, that's for sure. All I wanted was to share it with other people. All Isabelle ever wanted was a place like this to escape to, or to call her own. We're lucky to have the chance to make it a reality."

"Not sure it's luck. More like determination, and a hell of a lot of hard work," I offer.

"Meeting Isabelle sure feels lucky to me. Couldn't do any of this without her," Reid says with such affection in his voice, I envy everything he has.

Meeting Delilah felt the same way, lucky, life altering. I sure as hell couldn't get through this life without her.

A weird fucking bobblehead bounces around on the dash of his truck as he drives us back to the main house.

"What's with the anteater?" I ask, unable to hold in my curiosity.

Reid chuckles. It catches me off guard because he rarely laughs.

"It's an armadillo," he says, a fondness softening his harsh features. "Did your sister ever tell you about Sam's weird obsession with armadillos?"

I shake my head no. Quincy and I have a good relationship, but we've never shared much about our personal lives. Chalk it up to the age difference or her moving away, but I don't know much about her time in Wyoming, aside from the basics of meeting and marrying Sam.

"A school project on the stupid creatures turned into a lifelong, hilarious obsession." He sobers, because what a short life it was. "Now it's all we have left of him, other than memories."

We bump along in choked silence, contemplating the harsh loss of his little brother—my sister's young husband—hell, my brother-in-law. I didn't just lose Sam that day. I lost my big sister too. She's a shell of who she used to be.

It hits me how alone I've been feeling. My dad isn't all there anymore. Alzheimer's is a real cunt. Mom lives for him and barely takes care of herself. Quincy's buried in grief. Delilah and I are falling apart—and I fear our pieces will never fit together the same again.

"The land we just cleared was his, you know. Our parents gave us each a plot of land to build a home on and Sam never got the chance. Isabelle and I are building these cabins not only for our dreams, but for him. Someday soon, loved-up couples and happy families will make their own memories on Sam's land. My hope is his memory will live on forever in the memories made by our guests." Reid's love for his brother shines through his emotion-clogged throat.

I don't know how to respond. I wasn't prepared for a deep heart-to-heart with Reid Andersen this morning.

As lush greenery passes outside the window, I wade through the dreams Delilah's shared with me over the years. It makes me wish I could give her a home like this.

Breakfast turns into brunch, and we eat way too much. Mrs. Andersen is a fucking Michelin star chef, I swear. I'm thrilled to see Delilah poking in bite after bite without the anxiety that often plagues her during meals.

"Do you want the last croissant Mrs. Andersen sent home?" I ask back in our kitchen.

"No thank you, go ahead. If it was one of the mini quiches, you might have to fight me for it." Her smile guts me.

I'd do anything, give anything, be anything for her to always smile at me like that.

"I'm sorr—" we say at the same time, the apology hanging between us.

"You go first," I say.

"No, you go first," Delilah insists, and it's well known I can't deny her a damn thing.

I drag in her sweet scent faintly hanging in the air, holding it in my lungs while I gather my courage.

"I'm sorry things between us are so fucked up. I didn't mean to scare you these past few days. There was a rockslide that blocked us from coming home. My phone died, with no way to charge it." I study her face for any hint of what she's thinking.

"I was safe, but we were stranded until the emergency crew could dig us out. I drove straight home as soon as we could pass. All I wanted was to get back to...home." I nearly said to get back to *her*, but I don't know how she's feeling about me.

We stand on opposite sides of the kitchen island, but there might as well be an ocean between us. I fear her diamond eyes see right through me.

"It's okay. There's no reason to apologize. Of course I was worried sick, but as long as you're safe, none of that matters. I'm the one who should be apologizing," Delilah says as a bashful blush colors the apples of her cheeks.

"Doll, you have nothing to apologize for," I insist, but she continues.

"I'm sorry I...kissed you." My heart cracks, the brittle string connecting us ready to snap. She's sorry she kissed me. Does she regret it?

"I was so scared something happened to you, and I was so relieved you were home safe. I just...reacted. Can we pretend it never happened?" That heartstring is held together by my last shred of hope she doesn't regret kissing me.

She looks down, a silken curtain of hair obscuring her beautiful face from me. I reach across the narrow island and tuck her hair behind her ear, allowing my fingertips to graze her pulse point and down her neck.

What's there to say in this moment? We're both concealing truths and veiling lies about our feelings.

"Sure doll, consider it forgotten." My mouth turns sour at the lie.

Because I'll remember that kiss until my dying breath.

25

"Show us your tits!" Livy hollers as we sip iced tea from camping chairs shaded from the harsh afternoon sun.

"Yea baby! Take it off, cowboy! But leave the hat on!" Isabelle piles on, cat-calling her fiancé.

Reid, James, Greyson, and Connor are framing the first new guest house at Lucky Spurs Ranch. Contractors will build the remaining cabins, but it was important to everyone they have a hand in building Sam's cabin.

Thank god for that because let me tell you, we have front row seats to the gun show. Greyson's rightfully perturbed. His baby sister has the most vulgar mouth of us all and is currently using it to harass his best friends.

It's hot as sin out today, so I can't blame the guys when shirts come off one by one. Tanned, muscular mountain men in only jeans, cowboy boots and hats, sweating, doing hard labor, is better than any Magic Mike show.

James rips his sweat-drenched shirt off, swings it around his head and flings it right into Olivia's face.

I'm laughing so hard I nearly fall out of my chair and the

three of us devolve into a heap of hysterical, hormone-raging, horny females.

"Oh my god, James! Are you kidding me? This shirt reeks! I'm going to smell like your sweat for days!" Olivia complains.

"Just how I like it, kitten," James retorts.

The flirtatious familiarity between them is nothing new, but it never fails to send Greyson into a murderous rage. He's already got a hand clamped around the back of James's neck, leading him away from the peanut gallery.

Reid twists his soaked shirt and snaps James and Greyson in the ass in rapid succession, both men yelping like little girls and chasing after him. Boys, I swear.

A water fight ensues, and we try to take cover from the onslaught, but it's too late. Izzy gets a bottle of water splooshed into her face and she tackles Reid to the ground. They're covered in dirt and sawdust, but my sister's never been happier.

Greyson continues chasing James because James is an idiot and keeps poking the bear, making lewd comments about Olivia, which she joyously joins in on.

Amidst the chaos, Connor's doubled over, laughing his ass off as these men ten years older than him act like children.

I don't dare voice what I'm thinking, because I'd earn a first-class ticket to horny jail.

Connor's downright edible today. Those goddamn cut-out tank tops—they're Connor's stripper uniform during the summer. He looks like a tall drink of water on a hot sunny day, and I'm dying of thirst.

His skin turns the perfect golden tan during the summer, decorated like a mural from his tattoos, and the sun streaks his hair with lighter blonde.

But I only get to see his hair when he takes of his FUCKING BACKWARDS HAT to wipe his brow with his forearm and fit it over his head again.

I swear to god, I drool over him so much I've become dehydrated.

Connor's eyes catch mine and flit away as the water fight continues. Greyson's fuming mad, having returned to hammer the shit out of some nails, but Connor's leaning against the cabin framework, arms crossed, serenely watching the scene.

My hands ache to touch him, to trace the swirls of his tattoos, follow the path of each drop of sweat down the grooves of his abdomen, smooth back his sweat-soaked hair before putting that slutty little hat back on his head.

It's not fair! Why does my best friend have to be irresistible? And why does the most caring, sweet, attentive man I've ever met, have to be off limits?

I can't take the sexual tension clouding the worksite, so I gather the discarded water bottles and empty pitcher of tea and head for the kitchen.

The walk isn't far, but it's not exactly close either. I don't mind, I need the time and space to get my head on straight. I've spent the summer here, learning everything I can from Reid, shadowing Olivia and Izzy, and helping with chores around the stables. I'm much more comfortable around the horses. I've become a half decent rider, if I say so myself.

My mornings are spent at the ranch. Afternoons are filled with consuming everything I can get my hands on about equine therapy. And evenings are spent drowning in loneliness, even when I'm surrounded by people.

Some nights there's a barbeque or bonfire at the ranch, and we always have Sunday dinner at the main house. Other nights, Connor and I cook dinner, eat together with forced conversation, and pretend I didn't leap into his arms and kiss him.

I asked him to forget it happened, and it seems like he did. But I think about it every day. His hard body pressed against mine, soft lips molded to mine...and how badly it hurt when he didn't kiss me back.

With each awkward day that passes, I'm convinced moving in with Connor was the worst decision I've ever made. To be so close to but not have him is torture.

When he's at work, fear claws at the back of my mind that he's going to get trapped again or hurt, taking my heart with him.

Any time he's off work, but not at home or with me, I obsess whether he's with other women, dating, and enjoying his summer like a man of his age should.

Noxious green poison of jealousy floods my veins, and to survive his absence, I go to the ranch, rage clean, or read an extremely smutty book.

Connor's never been secretive, but he's also an adult and doesn't have to tell me where he is at all times. Sometimes he says he's going to hang out with CJ, his sister, or his parents.

But sometimes he doesn't mention where he's going, and my gut sours with envy he's sowing his oats.

Why do other women get his time and attention when I'm the one desperate for him?

"Delilah! Wait up!" Connor shouts from behind me. Damnit. Why did he have to follow me? I can't be alone with him while he's covered in glittering sweat and masculinity. Why does he have to smell better when he's all sweaty and dirty?

Fucking pheromone bitches.

I quickly calculate where I'm at in my cycle, and I'd better be ovulating for how feral I am for this man. His hand grazes my lower back, and I nearly leap out of my skin at the contact.

"Woah, sorry, didn't mean to scare you. I thought you heard me," he says.

"Sorry. Lost in thought," I lie. It's not like I can be honest and say, *I heard you, but I'm running away from you, so I don't beg you to carry me over the threshold and put a baby in me.*

We walk in stilted silence the rest of the way to the main house.

"Sam's cabin's really taking shape. You guys are doing great work." I break the tension.

"Yea, it's coming along. I hope Reid keeps letting me help. I want to be part of the build from start to finish."

"Yea? I never knew you were interested in construction." My interest piques.

"I didn't either. But working for the highway's getting old and I'm ready for a change. Watching you chasing your dreams inspired me. I'm proud of you, doll," he says bashfully.

"Liv's working with her dad, Iz found her place in the Andersen's businesses, Quincy's trying to find herself after losing Sam. Everyone's moving on but me."

His words send me into a panic. Moving on? Connor wants to move on...without me?

No.

I can't let that happen. Not when things are so weird between us. How can I keep him here—with me? He's happiest helping out on the ranch, and he gets along well with Reid.

I'll be spending the rest of my life at the ranch in some way or another to stay close to my sister. The cabin construction will only take so long, so it wouldn't make sense for Connor to make that his career, especially if it takes him away from me like the highway work does.

It hits me square in the face. What was Livy saying when she was teaching me about Maisey's hooves? The need for a qualified farrier and how hard they are to find.

I'd been at the stables with Livy trying to take my mind off Connor. Unfortunately, it didn't take my mind off it for a second.

Instead, a radio station blared in my head telling me how

stupid I am and how he'll never want me, all while learning how to check Maisey's hooves.

But there's a neon arrow pointing to one thing Livy said. Good farriers are expensive and hard to come by, and with Lucky Spurs Ranch expanding as rapidly as it is, Reid's mentioned hiring one full-time.

Without a second thought, I blurt, "Reid's looking to hire an on-staff farrier to tend to the horses."

Connor takes the crushed water bottles from my hands and opens the door for me. I busy my hands rinsing out the pitcher and refilling it with ice water for the group.

"A farrier? Like, the horseshoe guy?" Connor asks.

"They maintain their hooves and fit them with horseshoes. Olivia said horses can go lame if their hooves aren't properly cared for," I say.

"Lame like…injured?"

"Painful joints, cracked hooves, even abscesses. It messes with the way they walk, affecting their whole body," I explain the little I know.

Connor takes out his phone and gets lost searching for information on farriers while I put lunch together for everyone. Some simple sandwiches, potato chips, watermelon slices, and Oreos. I search the cupboards until I find a large picnic basket and pack everything in.

"This is really fucking cool. It's not just trimming the hooves. You have to know how to adjust for their gait, pressure points, shit like that. If their feet are fucked up, it hurts all their joints and their spine." His face lights with interest.

He follows me out of the main house, still buried in his phone. As we walk back to the construction site, he tosses out his findings, growing more excited by the minute.

"Damnit." He huffs.

"What?"

"You have to take a bunch of classes with hands-on training to get certified, and then apprentice under an experienced farrier. The process takes over a year, and it's a full-time commitment." Dejected, he pockets his phone and jerks his hat off to run his hands through his hair in frustration.

"If you're not happy working on the highway anymore, maybe it's time for a change. A year is nothing in the grand scheme of things. You're twenty-five, not fifty. Changing careers is super common when you're this young. You'd already have two careers under your belt by the time I freaking graduate." I sigh.

"Hey, don't say shit like that. You've worked your ass off. It's not a competition." He takes the heavy picnic basket, and we walk the rest of the way in silence.

"It ain't a bad idea," Reid says, scratching at his beard. "I've been thinkin' about hiring a full-time farrier. The ranch is at a crossroads. To grow, we have to make some big moves like acquiring a lot more horses, which means we'll need to hire a stable manager and ranch hands and bring in specialists. I take tireless care of my horses, and with a stable full, I'm going to need help to sustain the expansion."

"What kind of expansion? I thought it was just the guest houses?" Connor asks.

"Some people will come to relax, but having more activities will draw in a wider customer base," Reid says.

Isabelle joins in, "We want to offer trail rides, riding lessons, school field trips, and teambuilding activities. And we'll need horses and guides if we ever want to offer daytrips or camping."

"Not to mention Delilah will be graduating soon and will be

the best equine therapist this side of the divide," Izzy gushes. Heat rises to my face, and not from the summer sun.

She turns to me. "You know, Reid and I have talked about it a lot, and we'd love to offer equine therapy at the ranch—but only if you'll take the reins."

My eyes bounce back and forth between the two of them. "Are you...serious? You'd let me start a program here?"

"If it's something you want. We have the resources. This is something we'd like to do for you," Reid offers, his generosity surprising me.

"It'd be easy enough to set up the logistics. I can check on zoning and you'd need to beef up your liability insurance. Waivers, forms, shit like that doesn't take any time at all," James helpfully offers. The Andersens and their businesses are lucky to have a lawyer for a son.

"I don't know fuck about shit, but I grew up here with these dickheads. Me and Liv would be happy to pitch in any way we can," Greyson offers. Olivia echoes her support.

This found family of mine blurs together from the tears filling my eyes.

"Y'all would do...all of that for me? What if I'm terrible at it? What if no one comes and I waste your money?"

"Never going to happen," Connor says, sternly. "Everyone here has complete faith in you." He squeezes my bouncing knee, grounding me.

"What do you say, twinie?" Izzy asks, hope blooming on her face.

"Yes. I say yes! Oh my god! This is a dream come true. I couldn't ask for anything better!" I exclaim.

Izzy meets my eyes, and I use our twin telepathy to tell her this could be a perfect solution all around. My eyes flit to Connor, and that's all it takes. She moves to sit in Reid's lap and wraps her arms around his neck.

"Thank you, baby." She kisses him.

"Anything for you, sugar," he replies.

Izzy toys with the hair at the back of his neck, luring him under her spell. "We're already in desperate need of a stable manager. It might be nice to have someone we trust, keep it in the family…"

"Everyone's got full-time jobs, sugar. I don't think keeping it in the family's an option," Reid says.

I nudge Connor's knee with my own and scream at him with my eyes *this is your chance!*

He clears his throat and speaks confidently. "If you're lookin', I'd be up for the challenge. Haven't consistently ridden since I was a kid, but I'd love to get back in the saddle."

"Don't you work for the department of transportation?" Olivia asks.

"I do. But I'm ready for a change. Don't want to spend my life alone on the road. I want to be here, with my family." His eyes twinkle at me, turning my insides to jelly.

"I mean, he's already family. His sister married our brother," James offers.

Reid scratches his beard in contemplation, Izzy softly finger combing his hair, whispering in his ear. Olivia, Greyson, and James chatter excitedly about the possibilities.

"If you're serious, you're hired," Reid decides.

"Fuck yea!" Connor shouts. "I mean, yes, I'm serious. Thank you for the opportunity. Delilah and I were talking about me becoming a farrier and working on the ranch that way. But this'll be the perfect way to learn my way around the ranch and the horses. If it's alright, I'd still like to look into a farrier program. I could do both," he offers, hope filling his voice.

"Didn't think you'd be the solution to all my problems, Hayes." Reid shifts Izzy off his lap and comes to stand in front of us. Connor gets to his feet and the men shake hands, sealing the deal.

"Welcome to Lucky Spurs Ranch."

"I'll put in my notice Monday morning. There's always a surplus of folks wanting seasonal work, so I doubt they'll make me work my notice. Can I get with you once I have a solid end date?" Connor asks.

I disappear into my head, tuning out the logistics, the excitement, and the planning. Everything's fitting together like a jigsaw puzzle. Everyone's finding their place at Lucky Spurs Ranch, and it feels right.

It's too easy. Too convenient. But maybe life doesn't always have to be hard. Maybe sometimes things fall into place the way they're meant to.

Connor transforms before my eyes. He wasn't unhappy before, but he wasn't fulfilled or challenged, either. This may be the perfect solution to make his life complete.

If only I got to be in that life as more than just a friend.

26

I never considered myself a city boy. I worked in the mountains with fucking asphalt for god sake—but I was sorely underprepared for what waited for me at Lucky Spurs Ranch.

Working on a ranch is a whole new level of exhaustion. My days begin even earlier than before—too early to be called morning in my opinion—and end later.

I'd complain about the long hours if it weren't for loving everything I'm learning from Reid and from the farrier program I signed up for. Never would've guessed I'd find my place with horses, but here I am, covered in their shit and smiling about it.

Reid started me out taking over the day-to-day care of the horses and facilities. Took me a few days but soon I was a pro at feeding, watering, and turning the beasts out for the day.

Now he's got me managing supplies and coordinating with the veterinarian and other folks that work with the ranch.

He's still managing the boarding schedule, but I've been shadowing him on all boarding activities since day one, so it's a matter of time before he sets me loose with that responsibility.

I didn't realize how burnt out I was working on the highway, but the slower pace at the ranch soothes my soul. Each morning, crossing over the property line onto the ranch drops my shoulders from my ears, and I can *breathe*.

Don't have anything to rush home for each night since Delilah carpools with me nearly every day to do her own learning on the ranch. I'm more at peace than I've ever been that she's safe and happy both at home and out in the world.

I'm comforted that on top of my already obsessive claim on Delilah, Reid takes over-protective to a whole new level. Nothing goes on at the ranch without him knowing about it, and he'll kill anyone who comes to harm his family, which includes Delilah, and strangely, me.

On the odd day I'm not at the ranch or am separated from Delilah, I'm relieved her sister, Reid, James, Mr. and Mrs. Andersen, and often times Greyson or Olivia, are nearby.

Our busy schedules have helped Delilah and I ease back into spending time together, and the awkwardness has faded. We aren't back to where we were, but it's better, and that's all I can ask for at this point.

It's quitting time on Friday and the whole family's coming out to celebrate Reid's birthday with a bonfire. Mr. and Mrs. Andersen are tucked in for the night, babysitting Greyson's daughter Harper, so he can let loose tonight.

"Thirty-four, huh? Last year of your early thirties," James taunts his younger brother.

"Still younger than you, dickhead," Reid retorts.

"Dickhead? Seriously? That's all you've got? Isabelle's made you soft." James teases.

"I'll show you soft." Izzy grabs a s'mores skewer and chases a laughing James threatening to stick it up his ass.

I thought liquor would be flowing at an end of summer birthday bonfire, but that's not the case at all. I rarely drink because it makes Delilah uncomfortable. Reid quit drinking when he got with Izzy because he'd been using it as a crutch to drown his sorrows. The others are enjoying a few beers.

Living in a house where you don't know where your next meal is coming from, if there'll be hot water for a shower, or light when you flip the switch, fucks a person up.

I watched Delilah crumble year after year because her parents drank and gambled everything away, and she tried desperately to hold her family and home together.

I vowed a long time ago she'd never live like that again. Having her in my apartment is only the first step.

She's not bothered that Liv, James, and Greyson are kicking back beers like it's water. It speaks to how safe she feels here, and that makes me happy.

The birthday bonfire is the perfect way to wind down after a long week, surrounded by the best people I know. But the relaxed atmosphere doesn't last long.

In elementary school, we learned about Rube Goldberg machines, where one action set off a complex series of reactions. But I've never seen it happen in real life quite like this.

James goes to get another beer, and on his way back tickles Liv's exposed armpit, causing her to spray a mouthful of beer into Greyson's face.

Greyson launches out of his chair, tipping it backwards, knocking over the camping table stacked with food.

Upturned dishes slide off the table onto the picnic blanket Izzy and Reid are cuddling on.

Isabelle springs to her feet and shakes her hands to get the sludge of mixed foods off her hands. The splatter hits Delilah in the chest.

It. Is. War.

"You did *not* just ruin my dress!" Delilah shrieks as I try to dab the food off her chest. *Don't touch her tits. Do NOT touch her tits.*

"It's not my fault!" Izzy yells.

"Greyson, what the fuck, man?" Reid growls, trying to clean the food off himself and his betrothed. Reid gets up and takes Izzy by the hand, now laughing.

We aren't far from their cabin, and based on the amount of fondling happening, they'll be cleaning each other off in the shower.

"Are you fucking kidding me? Don't blame me. I was minding my goddamn business when Liv spit in my face!" Greyson roars, looking around for his sister.

Liv and James are in a heap on the grass laughing hysterically, trying to pour beer on each other.

"That's it!" Greyson shouts. "Goddamn it James, how many times do I have to tell you to keep your hands off my sister?"

"I don't remember. Can you tell me again?" James chuckles.

Greyson takes off, chasing James into the woods, Liv hot on their trail egging them on, leaving us alone by the fire.

Now that the chaos is over, I turn to check on Delilah. She's got a weird expression on her face.

I take off my hoodie and offer it to her. "Here, put this on over your dress, at least you won't get cold."

She doesn't take it from me. Crackling of the fire' the only sound in the eerily quiet night.

"Then what will protect you from this?" she asks as she smashes a destroyed lemon-bar pie into my face.

I'm momentarily stunned. My sweet little doll doesn't know what's coming for her.

Before she can scramble away, I tackle her to the blanket. She screeches and flops around beneath me trying to get away.

"Get off me! You weigh like a thousand pounds!" Delilah laughs.

"I don't think so!" I hold her hands over her head and smear my gooey face all over hers.

Her laughter fills me with light. My sunshine in the dark of night.

Giggling and squirming, we make a sticky mess. We're covered in lemon-goop from our hair to our chests and have pastry in places it should never be.

Delilah bucks her hips into mine to lift me off and lets out a sharp gasp.

My fucking traitor of a dick's hard and pressing into the thin fabric of her dress, most of which has risen over her hips.

I freeze. What do I do? Roll her off me and pretend it didn't happen? Deny that my hard cock wants to press deeper into the juncture of her thighs?

Instead of doing anything sensible, my body takes the wheel, and I roll my hips in to her, dragging my erection along her seam. Her pupils blow out and my dick twitches. Did she like that? She doesn't want me like *that*—does she?

I'm still holding her hands captive above her head, so I take the opportunity to take in her heaving chest. The lace of her bra is peeking out from the neckline of her dress, askew from our wrestling match.

Her hot cunt rolls against my dick, and I see stars. She's dry humping me back.

I meet her eyes and find pure desire. I must've lost my goddamn mind because instead of ending this before it goes too far, I dip my head and lick a path from her tits to her neck, sending a full-body tremor through her.

Something inside me snaps—something that's been drawn too tight for too long. And I take and take.

I release her hands and plant mine on the ground for better

leverage as I pump my hips into her relentlessly. Her hips roll beneath me, hands frantically clutching at my shirt.

For a moment, I think I've died, and this is my reward in heaven for living a good life. But even heaven wouldn't be as divine as Delilah's hot pussy dry fucking me.

"Co...nnor. Oh my god. Don't...stop." She moans between pulses of pleasure.

Fuuuuuck, I've never heard anything sexier. My girl, the one I've always wanted, but thought I'd never have, is begging me to make her come.

I hope this isn't a one time "let's forget it happened" thing like the two times in our lives we've kissed. But if it is, I'm going to make the most of it.

I'm afraid I'll ruin everything if I open my mouth, so I tease kisses and licks across her neck and chest. I can't cross any more invisible lines tonight, so I stop myself from pulling down her bra cup and sucking her tits into my mouth.

Over the clothes, no kissing on the mouth is working for her, so that's what I do.

Nothing's ever felt better than this. I've never been so turned on and I know it's because of the woman moaning beneath me. It's always been her.

"Please, please Connor. I'm so close."

Her sweet begging is my undoing, and I rut into her like an animal, triggering a body shaking orgasm from her, unintelligible moans falling from her lips.

"Fuuuuuck! Baby, you feel too fucking good." I can't keep it in.

It's all too much, feels too incredible, and before I can back off, pure, blinding pleasure overwhelms my entire body, and I come in my jeans.

Hot spurts of cum are trapped by my boxer briefs, and my

continued humping smears it everywhere. I don't give a damn because that was hands down the best orgasm of my life.

Our movements slow and I rest the weight of my lower half between her spread legs, taking a moment to catch my breath.

Feet stomping through the woods get me up off Delilah in an instant, and I do my best to help straighten her dress and hair. Thankfully, the intense blush on her face is obscured by the dark and lemon pie filling.

The group filters back in, all laughter and shit talking. Izzy tosses Delilah a pack of wet wipes and a sweatshirt.

"Figured you might want to clean up," Izzy says.

Delilah and I don't look at each other for the rest of the night.

Back at the apartment, we take turns showering and silently get ready for bed. I can't have her pull away from me after what we did. So when she crawls into bed, I extend my arm, offering her my shoulder as a pillow.

I might die if she rejects me. There isn't a world where I make her come and we go back to being just friends. But tonight isn't the time to make life changing decisions.

I've never been more relieved than when she snuggles into my side and relaxes into me.

Can she feel how hard my heart's beating beneath her palm? Does she have any idea how earth-shattering tonight was for me?

Neither of us are brave enough to say goodnight, so I flick off the bedside lamp, plunging us into darkness. We'd normally have pillow talk until she falls asleep.

Typically, once she's asleep, I kiss the crown of her head and smell her vanilla-infused hair—greedy for any piece of her I can get.

But tonight, my girl surprises the hell out of me. Just when I think she's ready to fall asleep, she turns her face into me and places a tender kiss on my pec.

That kiss tells me she's open to what happened tonight, and she's not closing the door on this new level of intimacy.

Her small offering sealed her fate.

Delilah is mine.

27

What am I doing? Something must be wrong with me. I've never been this horny.

My blue bestie gets a workout nearly every day. That's a lie. It's every day, sometimes more than once.

What do you expect when I'm living and working with the sexiest man alive and now have been dry humped by him to completion. My blue bestie does a bang-up job, but nothing compares to the way Connor made me come beneath the stars that night.

It didn't matter we were covered in sticky pie filling or were in the wide open and anyone could've seen us—it was profoundly intimate. We weren't naked, he wasn't inside me, but it was the best sex I've ever had.

I'm painfully disappointed that like the two kisses that "never happened," *this* never happened either. Is there an award for denial and avoidance? Because if there is, we both deserve the gold.

But it *did* happen, and it's all I think about. My body aches for him every minute of the day. I longed for Connor before, but now knowing how he feels between my legs, my suffering is unbearable.

Naturally, I'm currently straddling Connor's pillow with my blue bestie situated just right, and I'm questioning every decision I've ever made.

I need to come. I can usually orgasm with my vibrator but it's like a tickle when I need a deep itch scratched. No matter how hard I try, I can't replicate Connor's hard dick grinding against me like he'd die without having me.

The thought that he might want me in that way was intoxicating. I gave in to my desire and took as much as he was willing to give.

I've been at it for a half hour already and I'm nowhere close to satisfied. Connor's at the ranch today helping Reid with the guest cabins but I stayed home so I wouldn't be subjected to him prancing around in front of me in his slutty little tank top and backwards hat.

And his ass—dear god, his ass is magnificent. His jeans sit just low enough on his hips to reveal that tempting "V," making my mouth water involuntarily. Drool isn't attractive on anyone, let me tell you.

I used my day of solitude to take an everything shower, exfoliate and moisturize every inch of my body, and indulge in some good old-fashioned masturbation.

I give up, tossing my blue bestie off to the side and remove myself from Connor's pillow. I can't forget to wash his pillowcase...

My phone goes off on the bedside table and I flop over to check it.

> Studmuffin: Hey doll, how are you feeling?

Funny story, I've been so horny for him, I couldn't survive a day of watching him do hard labor, so I told him I wasn't feeling well. The guilt from lying is worth not being subjected to his abs today.

> Me: I feel fine, sorry I'm not there to help!

> Studmuffin: You feeling better is all that matters. We've got it handled over here.

> Me: Is it going okay?

> Studmuffin: [selfie of a shirtless, sweat-glistening Connor covered in sawdust standing in front of the nearly framed guest house]

Why? Why must he torture me? Does he realize what it does to me when he sends me pictures like this? I have a locked folder in my phone full of photos he's sent me over the years and I'm not ashamed to say they make an appearance when my vibrator comes out.

Lust muddles my brain. Am I perpetually ovulating or something? This is ridiculous. I blame my hormones for what I do next.

> Me: [selfie naked from the shoulders up, lying in bed with evident post-pillow humping hair]

The bouncing dots appear, and disappear, over and over. Is he going to reply? Did I take it too far? It's okay for him to send flirty selfies but not me?

> Studmuffin: Please tell me that was meant for me.

> Me: Who else would it be for?

> Studmuffin: I don't know, but I don't want to think about it.

> Me: Good to know. Yes, it was for you. If you can send me topless selfies, why can't I?

Again, the bouncing dots spike my anxiety.

> Studmuffin: What are you doing at home that left you looking like you've just been fucked?

Oh. My. God. Did he really say that? I read the text repeatedly to confirm that yes, my best friend just referenced me and being fucked in the same sentence.

Confidence sparks and I'm running with it. I'm tired of living in limbo with Connor, so I'm pushing the issue.

> Me: Maybe I was.

> Studmuffin: Don't fuck with me Delilah. Are you alone?

> Me: Nope.

> Studmuffin: Who's in our fucking apartment?

> Me: Just me and my blue bestie.

> Studmuffin: Your what?

> Me: [photo of blue bestie laying discarded on the rumpled bed next to his used pillow]

> Studmuffin: Delilah…

> Me: Yes?

> Studmuffin: Did you fuck yourself with that vibrator?

> Me: Mmhmm, but it wasn't enough.

> Studmuffin: No? Don't like this one? You must miss the purple one I found in your nightstand at the trailer.

He did *not*...I thought it got left behind. Connor found it and has known about it all this time? I might die from mortification if we hadn't blown past that into uncharted territory.

> Me: It's an upgrade from my purple pal. This one is longer. Thicker. Textured. And vibrates so hard I come every time.

> Studmuffin: Fuck. You're killing me, doll.

> Studmuffin: What are you doing to me?

> Me: I'm trying to tell you it isn't enough.

> Studmuffin: What would be enough?

Now it's my turn to type a response just to delete it, over and over. What am I supposed to say?

This was fun but nothing's changed between us? I'm in love with you but you see me as just a friend? We had a heated moment by the bonfire, but refuse to talk about it? I don't know how much longer I can live like this?

Instead, I don't say anything at all.

28

"Thanks for taking her today, I appreciate it," Greyson says.

"It's no trouble at all. We get along like biscuits and gravy, don't we Harper?" Mr. Andersen says. "Let's go find the checkers set and play a few games before we set the table."

Harper bounds off with her pseudo grandfather. Greyson's dad died a long time ago, and he's got a tenuous relationship with his and Olivia's mom, so Harper's only consistent family is the one here at the ranch.

"How many nannies have you been through this summer, Grey?" James asks.

The family gathered for Sunday dinner. Collectively, we managed to convince Quincy and my folks to come too. Mom's got Dad settled in the den with one of his shows. I sat with him for a bit, but I never know what to say. Mom talks to him like he's lucid. Quincy reads to him or tells him stories. I stay until I can't bear the silence any longer. What a shit son I am.

Reid took Quincy to see the progress on Sam's cabin.

Delilah and Izzy are in the kitchen with Mrs. Andersen whipping up what will no doubt be an impressive spread for dinner. That leaves me on the deck for this awkward exchange.

"I don't even know," Greyson grumbles.

"Six," Olivia pipes in.

"Ain't no way it's been six," Greyson snaps.

"Yep, six. First was your regular nanny, Cara, when she skipped town with her boyfriend. Second was Beatrice who'd just retired from the doctor's office. She lasted what, a week?" Olivia muses.

"Alright, you can stop," Greyson interjects.

"Third was Sabrina from the boutique. You made her cry on her first day and she never came back. Fourth was Rochelle, Harper's old teacher."

"Dude, how did you lose Harper's old teacher as a summer nanny?" James asks. Greyson locks his jaw, refusing to answer.

"She dared to bring arts and crafts to do with Harper," Olivia says smugly.

"The house was covered in fucking glitter. That shit is the devil of craft supplies—it never goes away," Greyson says. James is barely concealing his laughter.

"Fifth was from an agency. Greyson didn't even let her in the house," Olivia says.

"She was carrying a case of essential oils. No fucking way I'm letting that nonsense around Harper," he argues.

"Oh, so is now a bad time to tell you she's had an essential oil diffuser in her room for months? I gave it to her for her birthday, you moron," Olivia pokes. Before he gets another word in, Olivia finishes her list.

"And six. Whoever you fired today. When I called the agency for you, I told them to send their best nanny, that cost was no object. What could she possibly have done to upset you?" Olivia asks.

Greyson presses his lips together tightly, not wanting to answer. James elbows him in the gut, eager to know what ridiculous reason Greyson found to fire his sixth nanny.

"She reorganized my kitchen," he says.

Everyone, including me, bursts out laughing. Insults and jibes are being thrown left and right at the absurdity of it all.

"I can't find fucking anything now!" Greyson snips.

He turns to his sister with disturbing puppy dog eyes I never want to see again.

"Livy, could you take some time off from work and help me out until the school year starts? It's only a few weeks. I'm begging you."

"Stop making that face. You're creeping me out, you weirdo. I'll make it work, and if there's a day I can't, I'll plan with the Andersens," Olivia promises.

"Thank you so mu—" Greyson's cut off when James of all people interjects.

"I can help." We all gawk at him like he's nuts. "I mean, if Liv needs a second set of hands or some back-up...I can move my schedule around any time," James says sheepishly.

Why is Olivia bright red? What the fuck is that all about?

Before Greyson blows his lid—because even I've noticed how James can't follow Greyson's one rule to *stay away from Olivia*—my angel pops her head out the front door to tell us dinner's ready.

"Dinner was incredible, thank you Mrs. Andersen," I say as Delilah and I head out for the night. We're the last to leave—Quincy took our parents home in the middle of dinner when my dad got confused and overwhelmed. The sorrow on my mom's face broke my heart.

"Don't thank me, this young lady did most of the cooking," Mrs. Andersen says, causing Delilah to lightly blush.

"Well either way, Sunday dinner's always a highlight of my

week," I say truthfully. I love my family, but it's been years since I've relaxed and enjoyed time with them.

I sweep Delilah's hair off her bare shoulder—my finger snagging on the thin strap of her tank top and grip her by the back of her neck.

She stiffens under my palm. I've always touched her like this, so it's nothing scandalous, but she's clearly on edge.

Mrs. Andersen doesn't miss a thing, her eagle vision taking in our every movement. Her eyes twinkle and she purses her lips, holding back a smile and winks at me. "G'night you two."

As soon as we get home, Delilah curls into my side, exactly where she belongs, and we turn on an episode of one of her trash reality shows.

I've never minded giving up control of the remote because it's always meant time with my girl in my arms, relaxed and content.

"Can I have my phone?" she asks.

I've always carried her shit. She hardly ever carries a purse and always wears clothes without decent pockets. I take our phones from my pocket and hand hers over.

We indulge in mindless scrolling while her show rolls into another episode.

"No! No, no, no, no, no. This can't be happening!" Delilah cries, sitting up rapidly, a death grip on her phone.

"What's going on?"

"I haven't checked my e-mail all day. My advisor says my internship sponsor had to pull out at the last minute." Heartbreak floods her eyes.

"They can't do that, can they? You signed an agreement."

"They can. Either side can terminate the internship at any time. They're giving their time voluntarily without compensation. This hardly ever happens...why me?" Her hands cover her face, blocking me from seeing her tears.

"Shh, shh, shh, doll. Deep breath. We'll figure something out. Everything happens for a reason. Something better is on the horizon," I soothe.

I get her into bed, and she falls into a fitful sleep, nestled against me. I've been stroking her hair for so long my hand's numb, but I don't care. I'd do anything for her.

Checking the time, I know my message won't be seen until morning, so I shoot it off before I second guess myself.

> Me: Need to talk to you about something tomorrow morning away from the twins.

> Reid: ☾ Reid has notifications silenced. Notify anyway?

I plug my phone in and settle against my sleeping doll. *I'll fix this for you, baby.*

"How's she doing?" Delilah asks.

"Not good. I didn't want to leave, but she kicked me out. Said she wanted to be alone."

Today would've been Quincy and Sam's fourth wedding anniversary. I can't fathom the grief she's suffering on the day meant to celebrate her marriage. I tried to keep her company, but she was stone-faced and insisted she didn't need to be babysat.

"Poor thing. She's got to be hurting. I wanted to send her flowers, but I didn't know how to appropriately recognize a widow's grief," Delilah says.

"I don't think any of us do." I flop back onto the couch with a heavy sigh. We sit together in the quiet, taking comfort in each other's company.

"Oh my god!" Delilah shouts, launching off the couch.

"Jesus! Scared the shit out of me. What?" I ask, my heart knocking against my ribs.

"I have *so* much to tell you. You'll *never* guess what I saw today," she says, bursting with excitement. I love when she's happy like this.

She's sunshine personified and I'm one lucky bastard to bask in her light.

"Tell me," I say, happy to indulge her love of gossip.

"I ran to town with Izzy this morning to get her dirty chai, and while she waited, I walked down the block since the weather was so nice. I got to Clark's Hardware and popped inside to say hi to Greyson." She's vibrating with excitement.

"I asked how things were going, and he said the arrangement with Liv and James is working well and what a relief it's been not worrying about Harper during the workday. He said he was waiting for them to come get Harper for a day at the stables."

She's dancing around like she's going to piss her pants. Now I'm buzzing wanting to know what she saw.

"When I left to walk back to Bean & Brew, James was walking around the back of the hardware store to Grey's apartment. I figured he was heading upstairs to get Harper." She's like the cat who got the cream, smug satisfaction on her face.

She's about to burst but I wait her out. I'm not coaxing it out of her. She *wants* to be the one to tell the secret and it's fucking adorable.

"Olivia came from behind the building, and they started MAKING OUT!"

"Are you serious?"

"Yes! He had her pressed against the brick wall and they were going to town on each other. I ran away before they caught me spying. I barely kept my shit together when I got back to Izzy. I told her I didn't feel good and asked her to bring me back here because there's no way I could keep it a secret all day." She's talking so fast she's out of breath.

Them fooling around isn't really our business, so I'm good watching this play out.

"Is that it? Was there something else you were excited to tell me?" I ask, damn well knowing what happened to her first thing at the ranch this morning.

"The whole Best Friend's Little Sister scandal has drained my brain power today. I forgot to tell you what happened this morning!" she says.

"Before the scandal, or after?" I ask.

"Before! After you dropped me off at the ranch this morning, Izzy said Reid wanted to talk to me and brought me over to the stables. He was grooming Hope, a new horse they just rescued. She's a black paint, her color contrast is brilliant—as if night was splattered across her pristine white coat. Connor, she's beautiful, I'm in love with her."

And now I'm jealous of a fucking horse—I'm pathetic.

"Did you know Hope is Izzy's middle name? How crazy is that? It's like fate brought her to Lucky Spurs Ranch," she continues, her joy like a drug to me.

"Anyway, Reid said my advisor contacted him since he's making a name for Lucky Spurs Ranch and their new equine program, and he agreed to be my internship sponsor this fall! Can you believe it?" she squeaks.

Yes, I *can* believe it, because I orchestrated it.

When Delilah's internship fell through, I got with Reid and told him the situation. He wasn't sure how he could help.

I had to tell the truth and let him in on my secret sponsorship of Delilah's education. He was stunned to say the least, but impressed I'd gone to such lengths to take care of my girl.

Yea, he knows she's my girl. Perceptive bastard. Thankfully, he's kept it to himself.

I worked it out with her advisor for Lucky Spurs Ranch to facilitate her internship, and they'd bring in licensed therapists to work with Delilah. It took some convincing, but after also confessing my secrets to the advisor, they agreed. Everyone loves a good love story.

I'll pay Reid directly for any out-of-pocket costs—since Delilah thinks she's on a full-ride scholarship—as well as the equine therapists brought in to mentor her.

"I'm so happy for you, doll. See, I told you everything happens for a reason."

The reason just happens to be that I'm in love with you.

29

Connor age 11, Delilah age 10

Livy's mom's driving me and Izzy home. We went home with Livy after school, but it's time for us to go back to the trailer while they have a nice dinner as a family, and we hide in our bedrooms and pray our parents don't notice us. There'll be no dinner for us tonight.

The school week passes with grumbling tummies and private tears. Sometimes Connor's mom packs extra snacks and he shares with me. I try to save half for Izzy.

Thankfully we had hot water this week, so at least I'm clean. But the electricity went out last night, Mom must've skipped paying the bill again. I just want a regular home with a nice family and not fear for my basic survival.

"You okay, doll?" Connor's concerned voice stops my mental spiral.

"Oh…yes, I'm okay. Sorry."

"You don't look okay. You look sad," he says.

"I am," I tell him honestly. We're at the park by the school. His mom dropped him off while she does the weekly shopping. He walked to my house, and we came here together.

He swings beside me, keeping perfect pace.

"Why are you sad?" he asks.

"It's stupid," I say, embarrassed to voice my feelings.

I tell Izzy everything, but this is different. This is Connor. I love him...but he won't understand. He has a normal, happy family. It's uncomfortable sometimes when I tell him things.

Connor stops swinging and grabs the chain on my swing, lurching me to a stop too.

"Tell me or I'll tickle you," he says, holding his hands up like claws.

"No! I hate it!" I whine, curling in on myself to protect my ribs from his fingers.

"Then you better tell me," he threatens playfully.

I hop off my swing and take him by the hand, leading us over to the big oak tree shading the field. We sit in the soft grass, plucking blades and tying knots in them.

"You know that house by the library? The white one with the blue door?" He nods.

"Someday, that'll be my house. I'll plant flowers by the front porch, and I'll have a rocking chair. The cute picket fence is old and broken, but I'll fix it and paint it bright white. I'll walk to the library every day to check out a new book." I pause, growing emotional.

Connor laces his fingers with mine, holding my hand tightly.

"I'll have a job that makes enough money that I always have fresh food and hot water, and my lights will always be on." I smile sadly. I'm only a little kid and I know how pathetic it is to have such basic dreams.

"I know you will. It's okay, Delilah. My family can help more, and I bet if you told the school what's going on—"

"No. We can't. Izzy will be fourteen in three years, and she'll get an afterschool job. You only have to be fourteen to get a job, did you know that?" I ask.

Connor shakes his head no. "I wish I could help more," he says sadly.

"I know. Someday you can live with me in the white house with the blue door," I say with false hope.

Connor gets on his knees and brings me into a warm hug. He whispers into my ear words I'll never forget.

"Someday you'll have the white house with the blue door. I promise."

30

"Casanova! Where's my update? I'm dying of thirst without any tea," CJ whines. Despite telling him no several times, he showed up at the ranch today.

"CJ, I don't have time for this right now. I'm trying to prove to Reid he made the right choice hiring me."

"Psh. You won't even notice I'm here. Talk to me like we're on the phone with your earbuds in," he says with a dismissive flip of his hand.

"No, because when we're on the phone I can hang up on you," I quip, flinging muck into the wheelbarrow with a little more force than necessary.

"Stop being a whiny bitch and talk to me. Come on, you can't tease me with hints that things are heating up with she who shan't be named and then shut me out! Connorrrrr."

Sometimes I forget how fucking annoying CJ is when he wants something.

I stab the pitchfork into a mound of shavings and manure, the crunch masking CJ's incessant voice for all of three seconds. Sweat rolls down my neck despite the early hour. My lower back's aching and I'm not even halfway through the stalls yet.

"You know, this whole brooding cowboy thing would be hotter if you didn't smell like horse shit." CJ plugs his nose dramatically.

"Then get the fuck out! Jesus. I'm serious, things are going well for me here and I can't afford to get distracted," I snap.

"Distracted from what? Shoveling shit?"

"Don't be a dick," I grumble, moving to the next stall. Scoop, toss, repeat.

I haven't worked this hard, for this many years, to buy the damn white house with the blue door to lose sight of it now. It's not an option anymore, but I refuse to give up on Delilah's dream. I just haven't figured out how to pull it off yet.

I must be a fucking fool to have spent my life saving money to buy a house for a woman who wasn't even my girlfriend. I made good money with the highway, and I gave it all up to start a whole new career at Lucky Spurs Ranch. I can't fuck up my chance.

"Daddy Reid working you this hard, or are you trying to impress someone?" CJ waggles his eyebrows.

Instead of answering him, I push the full wheelbarrow outside to dump it and return to lay down clean shavings. CJ follows me around like a petulant child offering lots of opinions, but zero help whatsoever.

"Where is Princess Delilah anyhow? Isn't she here somewhere becoming the world's best equine therapist?" he asks.

I warm at the mention of her name. And he's right, she's here working her tight little ass off. She's blossoming as her confidence grows and her skills improve. I can never thank Reid enough for what he's done.

Guilt mounts for going behind her back. But I've been making her life easier behind the scenes our entire relationship, so it's easy enough to swallow the unpleasant sensation.

"Reid's got her out on a trail ride. Part of her internship is learning to be comfortable around the horses, and Reid's like the horse whisperer."

CJ grows bored with his line of questioning and begins prattling on about the new guy he's dating. I half listen while I check the automatic waterers and sweep the stable aisle clean.

By the time I'm finished refilling grain bins, I know far more than I ever wanted to about his new boytoy's proclivities.

Checking the clock in the office, I don't have much time to inspect the section of fence Reid mentioned before lunch.

God, I'm so fucking tired and it's hot as shit today. It's been unseasonably warm, and I'm reminded every day how much more difficult ranch work is than I expected. But the aches, pains, and smashed fingers are worth it because I love working here.

My farrier training is surprisingly interesting, and I love every minute I spend with the horses. It's no wonder Delilah chose equine therapy as her career path. I get the same calming energy around the horses I do when I'm with her, because they're both pure of heart.

I grab my bucket of tools and toss it into the UTV.

"Hey! Are you seriously leaving me here?" CJ shrieks from behind me.

I toss a wave over my head and start the vehicle.

I holler, "Hey! I thought you weren't supposed to wear white after Labor Day," to CJ as I drive past, kicking up dust onto his pressed chinos.

I laugh my ass off at his bitching and moaning before getting back to work.

"Who's ready for boy's night?" James claps his hands and rubs them together eagerly. Olivia kidnapped Delilah, Iz, and Harper for a sleepover at her parent's mini mansion.

Being the ultimate hostess she is, Mrs. Andersen made homemade pizza and hot wings for the Broncos game tonight and brought them over to Reid's cabin, before she and Mr. Andersen retired for the evening to the main house.

"Will someone put some food in his mouth and shut him the fuck up?" Greyson grumbles.

"Dude. What crawled further up your ass than usual?" James chuckles.

Reid claps Greyson on the back, moving past to load up his plate. "Aww, Greycie, are you still salty you caught James checking out Liv's ass the other day?"

Greyson wheels around, sucker punching Reid in the gut, who nearly drops his plate.

At the same time, they bark—

Greyson with "Shut the fuck up."

And Reid with "Party foul! You don't mess with hot wings."

James is cackling, dropping behind the kitchen island to avoid the wing Greyson hurls at his head.

I'm happy to sit back and observe these clowns and enjoy my beer. I don't have one often, but it's the perfect way to end the day I've had.

First thing this morning, I walked in on Delilah changing, her ass jiggling as she shimmied on her Wranglers. Mucking stalls with a hard on isn't exactly comfortable.

Then, fucking CJ was poking around, running his mouth. I love the guy but he's worse than a helicopter parent sometimes.

To top off my discomfort, I pinched the shit out of my hand in the fence I was repairing. Hurts almost as much as when I smashed it with a hammer the day Delilah sexted me for the first time.

Both accidents are evidence I don't work well distracted—and I'm too close to my goals to get distracted.

When Delilah left with the girls this evening, she lingered longer than usual hugging me goodbye and I swear to god she pressed her hips into me, like my aching dick was a magnet for her cunt.

A beer can clunks down on the coffee table in front of me.

"Looked like you could use another," Reid says, sitting beside me on the couch. The football game's playing on the flat screen, but we're all so used to watching sports we don't need the volume very loud.

"Thanks man," I say, downing the rest of my beer and cracking open the new one. "This'll be my last one, still have to drive home tonight. Ain't close enough with y'all to have a slumber party yet."

"Good choice. Those two are fucking ridiculous, bickering over Olivia," Reid says, shoving a chicken wing into his mouth whole and sucking the bone clean.

I'm tempted to fish for gossip to share with Delilah, but that's not my style, and it's important to me to earn these men's respect.

We eat in comfortable silence, periodically shouting at the ref or after a good play.

Reid tosses his paper plate onto the coffee table and settles back into the couch cushions.

"You've been doin' good work. Probably don't say it enough, but things have been running smoothly since you came on and my stress levels are lower. Isabelle sure thanks you for me not being such a cranky asshole at the end of the day anymore."

Recognition from Reid is unreal, his approval fulfilling a need I didn't know I had. Dad's been disappearing for so long, Mom's been so preoccupied with his care, and Quincy's been grieving—so I haven't gotten much attention, let alone praise, these past few years.

Delilah's always proud of me, and her opinion means more to me than anything, but approval from Reid is a close second. I've come to admire him and wouldn't mind if I was more like him.

I catch an elbow to the back of the head, jerking me from my conversation with Reid. James tumbles to the floor behind the couch. He bumped me trying to dodge Greyson's wrath.

"Will you both knock it the hell off? Christ. Hayes is a decade younger than both of you and he's more mature than you on his worst day," Reid chastises.

"Don't lump me in with that asshole," Greyson grumbles, righting himself and acting like he *wasn't* trying to bitch slap his best friend five seconds ago.

Having zero survival instincts whatsoever, James pokes the bear. "Olivia doesn't seem to mind my maturity level."

He yelps and dives over the back of the couch, landing on Reid's and my lap, fleeing from Greyson's swinging fist.

We shove him off us onto the ground and turn up the volume on the game.

Despite dodging two thirty-five-year-old men fighting like children, I'm happier than I've been in a long time.

Here with this family I've found.

31

Delilah

Rounded eyes the exact shade of root beer peer back at me. The gelding patiently waits while the therapist explains the goals for our session today. I need to build a strong foundation reading and interpreting equine body language before building up to helping others.

"Wonderful!" Tanya, the therapist, says softly, combing her fingers through the gelding's black mane. "Biscuit's mirroring your energy. Do you see how he's standing relaxed—his head's hanging low, ears are pointing outwards, eyes are sleepy and he's resting one hind leg."

"Yes," I say gently, cautious not to get overly excited about crushing my first lesson.

That's a gross exaggeration, but as a girl who grew up with zero positive feedback, the smallest grain of praise lights up my brain like a carnival.

I've been relaxed around the horse, and he's comfortable enough to mirror my energy.

Tanya motions for me to follow around Biscuit's side. My boots crunch in the dirt and Biscuit's ears flick towards me. I pause, but she urges me forward.

"You'll learn more from him today than you will from me."

Tanya guides me to walk slowly in a wide arc around Biscuit. He moves calmly and quietly, following me like a shadow.

The sun glints off his silken coat, a mesmerizing pattern of sorrel and white. He'd be the most beautiful paint horse I've ever seen, had I not met Hope first.

I've been sneaking over to see her every chance I get. Lucky Spurs Ranch is working its healing powers on her already.

"Good. Now step closer to him," she says.

I tense slightly, and step forward softly. Biscuit halts his movement, shifting away.

"He's giving you space. Do you feel how your body told him what you needed? He feels your hesitation and senses the shift in your mood."

Deliberately, I relax my shoulders and neck and breathe easily. This time when I step towards him, he stays in place and his ears relax.

I've loved meeting all Reid's horses and learning how to care for them. But it isn't until now that I understand what Olivia, Reid, and Isabelle have described. Horses have a way of *speaking* to you without any sound—and I feel what it means to be *heard*.

I've regaled my first session with Tanya to my sister and Olivia. The three of us are at The Flying Pig for Queen Olivia's twenty-third-birthday dinner and I've never been happier.

I have to tell myself this because if I acknowledge the giant missing piece of my perfect life, I crumble. Connor and I are good—great even. But we're still dancing in the grey area between friends and something more.

I internally smack myself because tonight is about Olivia, not my life-long, undying, unrequited love for my best friend.

Livy's acting odd, though. She's her typical boisterous, bubbly self—but she's distracted. She's been checking her phone every few minutes, all night. It's not like she needs a ride home. Since neither Izzy nor I drink, she always has a built-in designated driver.

She asked for the check as soon as the food arrived, which Izzy insisted on paying, so we've just been sitting chatting, enjoying our precious time together as a trio. Life's had us running in different directions and I miss my girls.

Right on schedule, Livy picks up her phone and opens a text. "Shoot. I'm so sorry but I have to go! One of my dad's biggest clients moved their meeting to first thing tomorrow morning. I need to head home to sleep off the pitcher of margaritas I just consumed."

"Do you need a ride?" We gather our things.

"No!" Livy practically shouts. "No. My, uh, mom's waiting out front."

With no further explanation, she disappears into the bar leaving Izzy and I staring stupidly at each other.

"That was fucking weird," Izzy says, finishing her Cherry Pepsi. "Do you want to stay? Or should I take you back to Connor's?"

I can read my sister like a book, and she wants to get home to Reid.

"I'm ready to leave. Let me pop into the restroom first. I drank way too much lemonade."

I take off into the crowded bar making a beeline for the ladies room. The door handle jolts against my grip—locked. I lean against the opposite wall for a minute before something, or someone, slams into the ladies room door.

I rush forward to ask if everything's okay when I hear a laugh I'd know anywhere followed by a chastising *"James!"*.

Oh. My. God. Livy's hooking up with James in the bathroom. That sneaky little bitch. Client meeting my ass.

I return to our table and Izzy slides out and links her arm in mine. I'm dying to tell her what I heard but for some reason, I don't.

I know what it feels like to want someone I can't have. And Olivia clearly wants someone forbidden. I'll keep her secret—from everyone except Connor.

Lying in bed at the end of a long day is the pinnacle of relaxation. Clean skin against cool sheets, snuggled beneath a soft blanket is glorious. What makes it heavenly is curling up against my Greek god best friend and having pillow talk until one of us—me—falls asleep.

"You've got to be kidding? In the bathroom at the pub? They need to be more careful if they don't want Greyson finding out. They aren't exactly great at sneaking around if we've caught them multiple times. It's gonna get back to Greyson," Connor lectures.

"The heart wants what the heart wants." I'm all too familiar with the sentiment.

"Yea," he says sullenly.

I prop up on my elbow, my hair fanning out on his tanned shoulder. "What's going on? You seem off tonight."

Connor sighs heavily and rubs his hands up and down his face and through his long hair, bleached from hours under the sun.

"I popped by Quincy's earlier to check on her. I haven't seen her in a couple weeks, and she hasn't been great about returning my calls or texts. She wasn't home, and since she's ignoring me, I tried to reach her another way."

He gets a boyish glint in his eye that flips my stomach.

"I rang her video doorbell nonstop until she answered through the camera." He chuckles.

"You did not!" I say, slapping his hard, bare chest.

"I did. Turns out she's in Laramie visiting Lucas."

"Lucas?" I question, struggling to place the name.

"Her and Sam's best friend from college," he says.

"Oh, right. That's nice she has him to lean on. I can't imagine how difficult the past year and a half has been for her."

"Yea. I guess. I'm glad she has Lucas's support, but isn't it weird she's spending so much time alone with her dead husband's best friend? Shit, that was callous. You know what I mean. It's not...appropriate," Connor says, visibly uncomfortable.

"That's one way to look at it. Or you could choose to look at it as Quincy getting the love and support she needs in her time of grief.

"Grief isn't linear or logical. Like I said earlier, the heart wants what the heart wants—and maybe right now Quincy's heart wants comfort and familiarity. Maybe she feels closer to Sam when she's with Lucas. I'm sure they have countless stories to reminisce about."

"Maybe. I have a gut feeling it's something more," he says.

We chat until my eyelids are too heavy to stay open. The last thing I remember is Connor pressing a kiss to the crown of my head and telling me he loves me.

If only he loved me the way I love him.

Biscuit's back and I'm bubbling over with excitement for the session today. Tanya's introducing a group of teenagers to

Biscuit, and I'm standing beside a lanky boy with his hood pulled over his head.

"Isn't he beautiful?" He glances at me like *Why is this weird lady talking to me*.

"Hi I'm Delilah. I appreciate you coming out, you'll help me learn a lot today."

The boy scoffs. "Good for you. I didn't ask to be here."

I let his saltiness roll off my back. Tanya explained this program is for kids who are at-risk of heading down the wrong path. Their parents, or a judge, enrolled them. She's graciously invited me to participate.

Tanya asks for a volunteer and when no one offers, I raise my hand and guide the surly boy towards Biscuit.

The gelding's tossing his head and clapping his hooves against the packed dirt. I've learned enough to be confident interacting with Biscuit, but this kid hasn't, and he looks nervous.

"He's agitated...I'm so sorry, I didn't catch your name," I say to the boy, embarrassed needing to ask.

"Jake."

"Okay Jake, thank you for volunteering." I wink at him, and get an eye roll in return, his crossed arms tightening around himself.

"What do I have to do?" he mumbles, uncomfortable standing before his peers.

"Breathe. Inhale slowly, exhale softly. Drop your arms and relax your shoulders. Don't think too hard about it, just relax your body," I instruct.

Jake is just as agitated as Biscuit, but with all eyes on him, he reluctantly follows my direction. I do the exercise with him and Tanya quietly guides the other kids to do the same.

The crunching of Biscuit's hooves slow and his heavy breaths stop, leaving the pen quiet.

"Did I do that?" Jake asks out the side of his mouth.

"You did. You told him you weren't agitated anymore."

"But I didn't say anything."

"Exactly. He heard you without you saying a word." I smile at Jake and sneak a peek at Tanya who gives me two enthusiastic thumbs up.

The session passes in the blink of an eye, and I'm filled with joy witnessing the beauty of these kids communicating with Biscuit with their spirits.

Watching Tanya load Biscuit into his trailer and pulling away from Lucky Spurs Ranch, it sinks into my bones what it'd be like to create a space people could be safe, seen, and heard.

And maybe even become whole again.

My post-success glow doesn't last long. When I show up to the stables the next morning, I walk in to my worst nightmare come to life.

Mom's drunk off her ass, or strung out, pacing like a caged animal along one end of the stables. I entered from the opposite side, behind the cavalry that already arrived.

Reid's holding Izzy back from our mom, trying to deescalate the situation.

James is talking to my mom trying to figure out why she's here.

Greyson's standing between James and Reid, who now has Izzy's arms pinned to her sides, despite her furious thrashing.

"What's going on?" I try not to stammer.

All heads whip around to me slowly walking into the chaos. Everyone talks at once and the onslaught has me backing towards the door.

"ENOUGH!" Greyson barks—bringing the stables to an abrupt silence.

Izzy calms enough for Reid to let her go and she comes to stand beside me, hand in hand.

"She showed up some time overnight. Reid found her sleeping in one of the empty stalls when he came out for morning chores," she sneers.

"We've been trying to get her to tell us why she's here and what she wants but she's been incoherent and combative," Reid adds.

"Think her ride left her here. I got the impression they were here to steal shit to sell."

Panic grips me deep in my chest, so I do what I always do when I need help.

> Me: Emergency! Mom's at the ranch

Studmuffin: What the fuck?

Studmuffin: I'm in town for Reid.

Studmuffin: Fuck. I'm on my way.

Studmuffin: Stay away from her, Delilah. I mean it.

> Me: The guys have it under control, I think. But she and Izzy might try to kill each other if they get the chance.

Studmuffin: Take Iz to the main house and wait for me there.

I tuck my phone away and against my better judgment,

disobey Connor and approach my mom. I've always been the one to talk her down from her benders or redirect her rage.

I walk past a protesting Izzy, again held back by her fiancé, past a fuming mad Greyson, to stand beside James. I assure him I've got this, and he backs away a few steps.

In the absence of these three men's intimidation, my mom settles a touch.

"What are you doing here, Mom?"

"You little bitch. That's all you have to say to me after you abandoned me?" she slurs.

"I'm just asking you a question, I'm not judging you or attacking you. Okay?" I try to soothe. She mumbles nonsense and resumes pacing the aisle.

"We can't help if we don't know the problem," I say. Izzy scoffs loudly because the last thing she cares about is helping our mom.

"Here y'all are, fat as pigs, eating like kings at this godforsaken ranch, while I starve to death in that freezing cold trailer." Her words hit their mark. She always complained how much Izzy and I ate, which in reality, was barely anything at all.

I'm sucked back in time to living in that trailer, suffering through her beratement.

There's no winning with her. Some people will never be happy, and they want nothing more than to make everyone around them as miserable as they are.

Losing my patience quicker than I used to, I ask, "What do you want?"

She's not used to me talking back or standing up to her.

"You stuck-up cunt. You and your whore of a sister will open your legs for anyone for a free meal, but don't bother sharing any of your good fortune with the woman who raised you."

"Raised us?" Izzy shrieks. "We raised ourselves, Ivy. Why should we help you when all you ever did was neglect us?"

She and Mom get into a screaming match and all three men jump in to deescalate the situation.

No good will come of this. All I can do is walk back to my car and wait for Connor.

I don't have to wait long. A knock on my window scares the shit out of me. My door's wrenched open and warm hands envelop my tear-stained face.

"What's going on? Are you okay? Fucking Ivy..." Connor trails off, furious as ever.

"Come on, let's get you inside. I bet Mrs. Andersen left some of her baking around."

I follow him inside like a zombie and plop down at the kitchen island. Connor bustles around the kitchen, comfortable in the space from spending so much time here. A plate slides in front of me, but I don't look at it.

"I'm going to take care of this. I refuse to let her hurt you anymore," he says resolutely.

A kiss on my temple and he's gone to save the day like he always has.

I roll his words around in my muddy head. His love clashes with my mom's hatred and I want to stick an ice pick through my head to stop the voices—Connor's, my mom's, Izzy's, and my own, battle to be heard above the others.

The kitchen window frames rolling pastures yellowing from the below-freezing temperatures overnight. My pulse jumps as my eyes focus on the beautiful black and white paint horse in the distance. As Hope grazes, I center myself and for the first time, my voice wins out over the rest.

I refuse to let Mom take from me anymore. She took my childhood, my confidence, and my health. The plate sitting on the island in front of me holds a thick slice of homemade banana-walnut bread, the crust dyed from the berries Connor spooned next to it.

Stealing one last glance at the horse I wish was mine, I get up to find what I need. I slather butter on the banana bread and without hesitation, take a bite. Pleasure dances on my tongue and I savor the flavors and textures.

Watching the beautiful mare, I eat every morsel of food on my plate.

For the first time in a long time, I have hope.

32

"It's done."

"Thanks Grey, I owe you one." I sigh with deep relief.

"Don't mention it," he says, and I smirk thinking he means it was no issue.

"Seriously, Hayes. Don't. Mention. It." And now I'm afraid.

"We've all learned when Greyson says he'll handle something, it's best to leave him to his 'Bruce Wayne by day—Batman by night' persona, not ask questions, and pretend it never happened," James jokes.

"Shut the fuck up, James. You're already on my list," Greyson snarls.

"Your list of best friends? Yea, I know. I've been in the top spot for decades." James ducks in time to miss Greyson's bitch slap.

Not for the first time since I joined Lucky Spurs Ranch, I laugh at men ten years my senior acting ten years my junior.

"What'd my asshole older brother do now?" Reid asks, coming in from the grill.

The smoky scent of hickory wafts in behind him and my

mouth waters. The racks of ribs he slathered with barbeque sauce earlier smell irresistible.

"Ran his fucking mouth," Greyson says.

"So, nothing new," Reid jokes, pulling macaroni salad from the fridge. On his way to the dining table, he claps Greyson on the back.

"Thanks again, man. I might get some sleep now that Isabelle's safe."

Greyson waves a hand dismissively before disappearing out the front door. Sometimes I forget he runs his own business in town, since he's here most mornings and some evenings.

"What happens now?" I ask the room.

James steps into lawyer-mode and gets serious.

"After the deputies hauled her off the ranch, they held her at the station until I got in front of the judge. She offered Ivy two choices. Voluntary rehab, or a luxurious overnight stay in jail, a trespassing charge, and a temporary restraining order."

"Of course, Ivy didn't choose the option that would benefit her or her daughters. So, for the next fourteen days she can't come within five hundred feet of the ranch, or her daughters, no exceptions.

"Assuming she doesn't show up to contest the order, the judge will likely grant my request for a six-month protective order," James explains.

I can't express the relief of knowing Delilah's safe, at least for the next two weeks.

The front door swings open and Izzy walks straight into Reid's arms and buries her face in his chest. Jealousy burns—not because of their embrace, I hug Delilah all the time—but because that's all I'll ever have, and watching Reid get all of Isabelle grates on me.

My focus shifts behind Izzy to my fallen angel, brighter and livelier than I would've expected after everything that went down this morning. Izzy kept Delilah busy while we handled the Ivy situation.

She gives me a soft smile and my stomach flutters. If you did an MRI, no doubt you'd see a swarm of butterflies, tired and tattered from a lifetime taking flight every time Delilah's looked my way.

"Hey, doll, you doing okay?" I ask, folding her into my arms.

I'm enveloped by her familiar vanilla-jasmine sweetness and savor this stolen moment.

"I'm doing better than I thought I'd be. She's needed help for a long time and if she refuses to accept it, I can't hold myself responsible for her anymore," Delilah says.

"I'm so fucking proud of you." I kiss the crown of her head and release her from our hug, instantly hollow without her.

"Serve up," Reid hollers

We sit around his small farmhouse table and as a blended family—Andersen, Tate, and now Hayes—to enjoy sticky sweet ribs, extra dill pickle macaroni salad, and smoky baked beans.

This is the first in a long time I've seen her eat so much, and so casually. She cleans two ribs to the bone, spears every last baked bean with the tines of her fork, has seconds of macaroni salad, and cleans her fingers with her tongue.

I stare at her tongue swirling around her delicate fingers for so long Reid catches me and clears his throat.

You'd think James would be the fifth wheel, with Reid and Izzy paired off, and Delilah and I being whatever we are. But instead, I'm the fifth wheel aside the two brothers and Irish twin sisters.

I know how much pain the Andersens have endured losing Sam, and how badly the Tate twins were treated by their parents. It's not a competition, and irrational to compare, but I can't help grieving the relationship I used to have with Quincy and my parents.

As soon as we started losing my dad to Alzheimer's, we lost our mom along with him, because she devoted herself to his care and we got left behind.

I still had Quincy, even though she was married and living hours away with Sam. After Sam's death, it's like my sister died too.

Despite the bone deep sorrow over what I've lost, I'm grateful for my found family. All I've ever wanted is to build a family with Delilah—to give her everything she dreams of—the house, the kids, the nights rocking on the porch. But I remind myself this is enough.

It has to be.

Her small hand squeezes my thigh, and whispers, "You okay?"

"Yea, doll. I'm right where I want to be."

"James, oh my god!" Livy scolds playfully.

The idiot's been tossing tiny balls of smashed bread at her for the past five minutes. He's acting like a middle school boy with his first crush.

"Pull her pigtails, they really like that," Izzy says.

"That's what she said," Delilah pipes in.

I love her so happy and carefree.

We've gathered for this not-a-triple-date at The Flying Pig. It's such a joke. Anyone with eyes can see something's going on between James and Olivia—they're shit at hiding it. And Delilah and I are what we've always been—not just friends, but nothing more.

It's late, so instead of ordering six entrees, we opted to load the table with dishes to share. I'm picking at the last bits of hatch green chili nachos. Delilah and Izzy thumb wrestle over who gets the last soft pretzel bite, and Reid nearly stabs the back of James's hand with his fork when he reaches for the last jalapeño popper.

I raise my hand and snag Frank's eye to get a refill of my cola and Delilah's lemonade.

"Everything sounds perfect, Izzy. The wedding's going to be out of a storybook." Livy claps her hands together, bouncing in her seat.

"I hope so, but even if it isn't, it'll be perfect to me and Reid. As long as we're married at the end of the day, that's all that matters," Izzy says, mooning at Reid.

I'm a prick for being jealous, but all I've ever wanted is for Delilah to see me that way—to want to marry me.

She shines her light on each person at the table, none of them realizing how lucky they are to bask in her glow.

The fact she's been eating better than ever has added color and fullness to her cheeks. I've loved her at every stage of life, every awkward phase, at her best and at her worst—but I love to see her thriving.

This fall has been transformative for her in more ways than one. Her internship has given her purpose and direction. Delilah's drive is inspiring, and she's going to help countless people with her equine therapy education.

Being out from under Ivy's influence has made her self-confidence soar and damnit if that isn't attractive as hell.

The screech of Delilah's chair being shoved back startles me; before I can ask what's wrong, she's up from the table and rushing off to the restroom.

I was lost in my head and wasn't paying attention to what was being discussed.

Four sets of yes ping pong between each other's and mine. I raise my eyebrows and jut out my chin like, *what the fuck happened?*

Izzy breaks the awkward silence. "She was gushing over how beautiful the wedding's going to be, and I said hers will be beautiful someday too."

She bites the corner of her mouth and Reid massages the base of her neck glaring daggers at me.

Is Delilah embarrassed or sad she isn't getting married? Despite my desperation to be her husband. Izzy's broken-up over inadvertently hurting her sister, and Reid's furious because my dumb ass is at the center of the problem.

He knows how I feel about Delilah. I'm getting some real 'shit or get off the pot' vibes, but there's no right move for me to make.

I can't make her want me.

I can't make her fall in love with me.

I've long accepted these facts. Why's she sad about it not being *her* wedding? It can't possibly because of me…right?

When Delilah returns from the bathroom, she's folded in on herself. We need to get out of here. "Hey doll, would it be okay if we take off early?"

Brows furrowed, she says, "Of course, are you okay?"

"That second plate of nachos was a mistake." I rub my stomach and feign a grimace.

I toss some cash onto the table, and we say our goodbyes. I help Delilah into the truck and have a silent meltdown cursing the stars as I walk to the driver's side. The only sound in the cab of the truck is my head repeatedly knocking against the headrest.

"Do you want me to drive?" Delilah asks, voice laced with concern, gently rubbing my thigh.

"No, I'm not sick." Her brow pinches with confusion.

"Something upset you and I wanted to get you out of there."

Delilah looks down, and a ghost of shame mixed with anger passes over her delicate features.

She says nothing, and we drive home in charged silence.

I suffer walking behind her up the stairs, her pert ass swaying back and forth in denim cut-off shorts that've always driven me wild. Her crop top hangs loosely off one shoulder, her trim waist twisting with each step. She stops at our front door forcing me to reach around her body to unlock the door.

Our boots go onto the rack by the door, and she plops down on our couch, dejected. Kneeling, I remove her socks and gently rub the balls of her feet—her dressier cowboy boots don't fit as well as her everyday boots.

I sweep the curtain of white gold from her face and tuck the priceless strands behind her ear.

"I don't know what's going on in that pretty little head of yours, but if I did something to upset you, I'll fix it, I promise. I'm going to take a shower and give you some alone time."

I grab her socks from the floor and remove my own. I stand and walk towards the bedroom, stripping off my shirt as I go.

"Connor."

I whip around and find tears in her crystalline eyes.

I'm on my knees again in front of her in a heartbeat.

33

Tonight was perfect—food, friends, and not a care in the world. I love seeing my sister so happy, and I have a big, gruff cowboy to thank. Izzy had a crush on Reid for years. It took him way longer to realize she's everything he needed.

She, Livy, and I have been scrapbooking and giggling like little girls planning their wedding. She'd be happy in flip flops at the courthouse, but Reid wants to give her the wedding of her dreams and I'm determined to ensure she gets it.

I know Izzy didn't mean to hurt me tonight, but her comment about my future wedding cut me to the quick.

I won't have a wedding. Because the only man I'll ever want to marry isn't in love with me and never will be.

Connor kneels before me, vowing to do anything to make me happy. As he rubs my legs, more tears fall from my traitorous eyes. Doesn't he realize the kinder he is to me, the more it breaks my heart? Every day he shows me the life we could have, but it's an illusion.

"It kills me when you cry. Talk to me, doll. What's going on?" Connor brushes the tears from my cheeks with his thumbs.

I can see my future in the depths of his eyes, so dark I get lost in them—but it's a future I'll never have.

Someday he'll meet someone and fall in love with her and there won't be room in his life for me. What woman would tolerate a man having such an intimate friendship with another female? I wouldn't.

"It's not fair," I lament, choked by my tears.

"What's not fair?" he says, pain lacing his voice. "I can't fix it if I don't know the problem."

I nudge him back by the shoulders so I can stand, and round the back of the sofa to pace. My fingers tangle in my hair, gripping so hard my roots scream.

I'll explode if I keep it in any longer. But if I risk everything and tell him the truth, I could lose him.

I always thought having a part of him was better than nothing—but my soul has been dying from not having all of him.

The gilded heartstring that's connected us since the day he found me crying in the dirt has frayed to a gold fiber about to snap. Hope and denial can't hold us together anymore.

"Is this enough for you?" I blurt, my heart overriding my head.

He stands to his full height but doesn't dare cross the barrier of the couch to reach me.

"Is what enough?" he asks, confused and in pain from the distance I've created. He's so beautiful it hurts. Hair mussed from taking off his shirt, jeans slung low on his hips revealing the band of his black boxer briefs, a golden canvas inked with masterpieces immortalized beneath his skin.

"This. Us," I say, unable to meet his eyes.

"You're scaring me. What's going on?" He rounds the couch and blocks the path I'm wearing in the floor.

"I thought after the bonfire things would change between us, but they didn't. Everything went back to the way it's always been, and I can't take it anymore. It's too painful. I can't do this anymore," I ramble, frantic, bordering on a meltdown.

Connor gently grabs me by the upper arms, not allowing me to flee.

"Can't do what? I can't lose you, Delilah. I'll do anything, give anything, be anything to make you happy. All you have to do is ask," he says with such confidence he can't possibly know what I want to ask for.

"Please," I beg, my voice laced with desperation. He's standing so close my nipples graze his bare chest with each inhale.

I can't meet his eyes, so I fix my gaze on the intricate sun tattooed over his heart. It's my favorite of his gallery of ink.

Aching need thrums through me as he tilts my chin up, cupped in his calloused hand.

"Please, what? Baby, anything you want is yours."

My heart's too big for my rib cage and my lungs aren't filling with enough air. My chest burns with the words I can't say.

I barely get the words out. "Not *anything*."

His eyes frantically search my face for an answer, brows creased in frustration and concern. The pieces fall into place for him, and his frown deepens in disbelief.

"What are you saying?" An emotion I can't name laces his voice.

Is he really going to make me say it? My mind's made up.

It's always been Connor.

I can't wait another day, another minute, without knowing if he wants me back.

His massive hands wrap around my waist, tremoring fingers biting into my flesh. I want to be confident and strong, but my words come out as a whisper.

"Please kiss me."

I'll die if he rejects me—the pain would be too great to survive. He has to feel the chemistry between us. I refuse to accept this pulsing need is one sided.

Doubt, my ever-present companion, creeps in reminding me if Connor had feelings for me, he's had years to make his move.

Oh god. Is this all in my head?

I've ruined everything. Connor doesn't want me. Why would he want *me*?

My panic is snuffed out. One second my heart is breaking, the next it stops all together.

Connor crashes his lips to mine.

It's more than anything I've conjured in my wildest dreams. His mouth is plush and hot, firm and sure. Our lips move together in a dance they've always known but were never allowed to perform.

His hands slide up my arms and shoulders, one gripping the back of my neck, his fingers tangling in my hair, tilting my head exactly where he wants me—the other pressing my sun pendant gently into my chest.

I'm floating—his grip the only thing tethering me to reality.

His tongue doesn't request access to my mouth, his ironclad self-restraint doesn't demand entry, but the kiss is perfection, forever imprinting on my DNA.

His lips stop and pull away from mine by a breath. Another soft kiss is pressed to my lips and the love of my life lifts his head to look into my eyes.

"Is this real?" Connor asks.

My brow furrows in confusion, silently asking him what he means.

"It's impossible. Everything I've ever wanted is..." His words cut off and he clenches his jaw to stop them from tumbling out.

"Baby, I need you to hear me because I meant what I said."

He pauses and the world stops spinning on its axis, my heart hangs by a thread, about to be cut by whatever he says next.

Leaving no room for interpretation, Connor vows, "Anything. You want. Is yours."

I'm paralyzed by fear of losing him—I'll lose everything if I'm misreading him. So, I say nothing.

A kind smile takes over his face. The same smile that's always comforted me. The same smile he gave me that first day sitting beside me in the dirt.

"I've been yours since the day my bike led me to a fallen angel, and every moment since." Calloused fingers brush my hair from my face.

"I was yours when I punched Danny Parker in the stomach for pushing you off the swings." A gentle kiss to my forehead.

"I was yours every day I packed your favorite foods for lunch to share with you." Lips trailing to my temple.

"I was yours when I went to the nurse's office when you got your first period." My face flames at the memory.

"I was yours when Roger fucking Mirowski stood you up for homecoming and I picked you up with split knuckles from bashing his face in." His lips trail down to my hot cheek.

His hands were wrecked that night. When I asked what happened he said, "you should see the other guy," and gave me a lopsided grin. I had no idea he was being literal.

"I was yours when I danced with you in the moonlight and kissed you for the first time under the stars." He chuckles with mirth.

"I was so nervous I'd ruined everything. After I took you home, I puked in the bushes."

There it is. The moment we've ignored for nearly a decade. Our first kiss.

I always assumed it meant nothing to him, and I was too embarrassed to bring it up.

But he remembers.

He pauses and I think he's finished confessing, but he takes me by the hands and interlaces our fingers, his aura darkening.

"I was yours when I nearly beat Peter Rickard to death when I found out he'd taken your virginity." Rage and sorrow seep from his pores.

But why? Because I didn't give myself to Connor? He'd already had sex by then and I was convinced he didn't see me that way after the kiss that "never was."

"I was yours when I broke all ten of Robby Thompson's fingers after he dared to touch your naked body. He's lucky I didn't break his tiny dick too." Connor's seething.

My mind's spinning with his confessions, putting together missing pieces from the puzzle of my life.

It's impossible he's felt the way I have all these years.

How much time have we wasted lying to ourselves that we were just friends? It makes me ill with grief for the life we could've had together.

Connor composes himself and kisses the tip of my nose.

"I was yours yesterday, and every day before. I'll be yours every day my heart is still beating. I'll be yours if there's an afterlife, and in every future life and universe for eternity."

He presses a soft kiss to my parted lips and wipes the tears trickling down my cheeks.

His eyes soften and his voice wraps around my heart with the unadulterated adoration with which he says, "I'm hopelessly in love with you. I have been since before I understood what it meant. I'll die from a broken heart if I wake up and this was all a dream."

I shake my head furiously, gazing up through tears at the man I've always loved.

Sweet kisses punctuate each word as he says, "I"—*kiss*—"am"—*kiss*—"yours."

Heartstrings & Horseshoes

We stand in silence, holding on to each other for dear life. The final boundary between us obliterated. His eyes search mine quiet and pleading, begging me to feel the same.

He's laid himself bare and I haven't managed to say a single word. I wipe my eyes and pull myself together enough for the truth to rise from my battered heart.

"All this time. We could've been together all this time. For every moment you've been mine, I've been yours. Every breath I've breathed has been for you. My heart has always beat in time with yours.

"I wanted all those memories to be with you. Every year I wished you'd ask me to the school dances. I wanted you to be my first time...but you'd already given yours away, so I settled. I only dated other guys because I couldn't have you. You always had another girl on your arm, stealing the attention I was desperate for."

Tears stream down my face unbidden.

"Why?" I barely croak. "Why didn't you ever choose me?"

I'm just as guilty. I never made a move either.

Torment radiates from him. Regret, frustration, confusion, and grief mingling.

"I thought my feelings for you were plain as day, and I wasn't what you wanted. Having you as my best friend had to be enough, since I couldn't have all of you," Connor admits.

He links his pinky with mine and leads me to sit on our couch. He turns to face me, one arm slung over the back of the sofa, fingers gently playing with the ends of my hair.

"I was scared. The way I wanted you was ugly and all-consuming. You were so good, and pure. I thought there was no way you'd want me. If I acted on my desires and you didn't want me, or I fucked things up and hurt you...it was too big of a risk.

"I fell into the same safety net I think you did. Having you as my friend was better than not having you at all, and I promised myself I'd never do anything to jeopardize our friendship."

Connor patiently waits for me to say something—anything, but I can't.

He continues. "I was stupid. I tried distracting myself with other girls, that's true, and I'm so fucking sorry I hurt you. I never would've touched another girl if I knew you wanted me. I honestly don't know how you sat by and watched me be such an idiot. I nearly went to jail each time I found out another man touched you. I couldn't handle it."

My best friend pours his heart into my hands. He's completely transparent, releasing a flood of pent-up sadness, disappointment, and anger from years of denying his feelings.

"If I knew you wanted me to be your first time, I would've waited forever." He tugs on his hair, visibly distraught.

"I'm so fucking sorry. Did that piece of shit hurt you? Did he force you?" His temper's rising, he's about to lose it. Connor's protectiveness has always been one of my favorite things about him.

I squeeze his knee in reassurance. "No, he didn't force me, and he didn't hurt me—well, beyond the pain that's unavoidable your first time…"

His jaw's clenched so tightly he could crack a molar.

"You'd already lost your virginity, and after what happened to Izzy, I wanted to control the situation. I know that's a terrible reason to have sex for the first time, but it felt like the only way…" I've never been ashamed of my sexual choices until now.

"He was nice, it was safe enough, we didn't kiss—"

"Stop. Please. I can't hear about another man touching you," he growls, tortured.

"I want you to know I was okay…even if it wasn't really what I wanted. I can't take it back any more than you can take back any of the women you've been with."

His molten chocolate eyes shine with shame and sorrow.

"I'm so fucking sorry. I wish I could take it all back, but I can't." He looks away from me, trying to compose himself.

His coarse beard tickles my fingers as I pull his face to me. When he resists, I climb onto his lap, straddling his legs. I hold both sides of his face, forcing him to look at me.

"I take it back," I say softly. Connor jerks back in panic.

"No! I mean, I take back saying we wasted so much time being apart. We've had the most beautiful friendship, and every choice we made led us here."

I pause, because I can't take back what I'm about to say.

He loves me. He wants me. He's mine.

And I leap.

"I'm in love with you Connor, I always have been. I'm yours, forever and ever."

And with my deepest secret hanging between us, he closes the distance once and for all, wrapping his arms around me and irrevocably binding our souls together with an earth-shattering kiss.

34

She's everywhere. Her hands are on my face, in my hair, gripping my shoulders, nails scratching down my bare chest. If it weren't for the bite of pain, I'd think I was dreaming.

Delilah's lips move in tandem with mine, punishing kisses that border on desperation.

Her hips move against mine, my aching dick thickening between us. My hands are as anxious as hers, taking in as much of her body as I can—roaming from her ass, up the slope of her hips and back making her shiver, and into her hair, controlling our kiss.

"Baby, I love you so much. I can't believe this is happening," I say into her mouth, unwilling to stop kissing her. I fist her hair and tip her head back, leaving her delicate neck vulnerable.

I lick and kiss and suck down the lithe column, across her collar bones and up to that tender spot behind her ear. She gasps and rolls her hips into me when I take her earlobe between my teeth and bite gently, licking the sting away.

She whimpers with pleasure from my attention. "Is this real? I've wanted you for so long, this doesn't seem real."

I hold her to me tightly as I stand and flip her to her back on the couch, my hips cradled between her legs.

"Dollface, nothing's more real than you and me. We were always meant to end up here, it just took us longer than we wanted." Her arms wrap around my neck and brings my mouth down to hers.

I haven't been with so many women to be an expert by any means, but I can tell she's inexperienced from the way she kisses me. It turns me on to be the one to teach her, play with her, and learn with her.

I pull back, not wanting to go too far too fast. She huffs adorably in annoyance and tries to drag me back down.

I sit on my knees between her spread thighs, massaging up her thighs to the crease of her hips, my thumbs teasing beneath the frayed hem of her jean shorts. Her hips tilt upwards seeking more, but I deny her.

"We don't have to do anything, doll. There's no rush. Today's been a lot." Goddamn it, I hate being the good guy.

All I want is to plow my dick into her until my balls slap her ass, but instead, I'm pumping the brakes.

Her face falls and she withers beneath me. "You don't...want to...with me?" Delilah's doubt breaks my heart.

"Baby, all I want is to"—I waggle my eyebrows suggestively—"with you." Her laugh shoots sparks through my veins.

"I don't want to push you into anything you're not ready for."

Mischief glimmers in her eyes and I know I'm in trouble. She shrugs and feigns indifference.

"You're right. I'll just go to bed and make myself come all over my fingers. Alone. I've gotten by for *years* without your cock. What's one more night?"

The little she-devil. The word cock coming from my angel—the way her mouth rounds into the perfect "o"—makes mine jump in my pants. She wants to play? I'll play.

"Is that what you did when I worked nights?"

"Mmhmm. Every night before I went to sleep."

Fuuuuuck.

"Since you stopped working nights, I touch myself as soon as you leave for work in the morning. The bedroom's humid from your shower, and all I smell is you," she taunts.

"That so?" I gulp, struggling to keep control of the conversation. My thumbs no doubt pressing too hard into the crease of her hips.

"Mmhmm. Your side of the bed's still warm, so I take off my pajamas and lay in your spot, rubbing my bare skin all over the sheets that smell like you."

I'm so hard I can barely pay attention.

"I make myself come with your pillow between my legs."

Did I die? I think I've died and gone to heaven.

"Remember the day I sent you that selfie from bed?"

Yes of course, I fucking remember, I smashed my hand with a hammer because it's all I could think about.

"Is that what you were doing? Fucking yourself, texting your best friend?" I ask, afraid to know the answer.

"I tried and tried to come, but I couldn't. I needed more. You send me shirtless pictures sometimes, so, I returned the favor," she says confidently, her blush betraying her.

"You needed me between these thighs, baby?" I squeeze them harder, my hands having been mindlessly stroking them. She's so fucking soft.

"I've been going insane since I had you on top of me at the bonfire. I've never come so hard, and we were fully dressed. You felt so good, Connor. I wanted you so bad, I was afraid to say anything or move the wrong way for fear you'd stop."

"I blew in my pants, baby. You think I felt good? You felt fucking incredible. Even as a horny virgin, I never busted in my pants. I didn't care I was sticky with my own cum, because I finally had you beneath me."

I pull her by the hips, so her ass is propped up in my lap, spreading her legs even wider, exposing her barely covered cunt to me.

I gently run the back of my knuckles along the seam of her shorts, right along her center and she bucks into my touch, gasping.

"You need me here? That toy of yours not enough since I fucked you into the ground?" The sexiest whimper escapes as I press my knuckles a bit harder into her covered pussy.

"You want this? You want me inside you, baby?" I ask, in disbelief I've been granted the opportunity to even ask.

She nods softly, her eyes never leaving mine.

"I've waited my whole life to hear you say it, doll. I need you to be a good girl and tell me what you want," I command gently. Her eyes flash—I think my girl might have a praise kink.

"You like that? You want to be my good girl?" Her pupils overtake the blue of her eyes, and I have my answer.

"What do you want, Delilah?"

"I want you to make love to me," she says, as easy as breathing.

Goosebumps cover my skin hearing her say those words. I was sure she'd say she wanted me to touch her, make her come, or fuck her.

She wants all those things, but she wants me to love her more.

Suddenly our little game isn't amusing. I'll give her whatever she wants.

It just so happens making love to her is all I've ever wanted.

35

Without another word, but with some exaggerated grunting and giggling, I gather her into my arms and stand from the sofa. I carry her to our bedroom, her legs wrapped tightly around my waist. The denim of her shorts overstimulating my bare torso.

Night casts our room in darkness. I need to see her face, every expression when I take her for the first time—I fumble to flick on the bedside lamp. Climbing onto the bed on my knees, I carefully lower her to the pillows, her white hair fanned out like a halo—my fallen angel.

"Tell me what you like. I want to make you feel good," I pant, struggling to hold back.

"I...don't know. It's never been good for me. I don't know what I like," she admits.

A dark, primal part of me revels in the fact no man has ever brought her pleasure—that I'm the only one who ever will.

The two dipshits who were lucky enough to be inside her have no clue what they lost. Not that I would've let them live if they tried to keep her.

"What do you like when you touch yourself?"

She blushes deeply and pinches her lips closed.

"You can tell me anything. I'll do anything, be anything you want. There's nothing to be embarrassed about," I say.

She gulps and her doe eyes cut right through me.

"I have a folder on my phone with pictures of you." She stops, waiting for my reaction.

I nod, encouraging her to continue, when my internal reaction is jumping up and down, high fiving myself like a douche.

"I was telling the truth. I get naked and lay on your side of the bed. I look at your pictures, especially the ones without a shirt"—her eyes devour my bare chest—"and I tuck your pillow between my legs, or straddle it, and use my vibrator to get off."

Sticky pre-cum escapes my slit, envisioning what she's telling me.

"What does your vibrator do that you like?" I ask.

"It goes inside me, and that part vibrates. And the piece on the outside vibrates against my clit. I need both to get off."

"The piece inside vibrates against your G-spot?" I ask, holding on by a fucking thread.

"Maybe? I don't know where that is."

Oh, this is going to be so much fun, learning her body as she learns how to take her pleasure from me.

I shift from between her legs to stand beside the bed. I unbutton my jeans, giving my throbbing cock a reprieve.

"I want you to undress me," Delilah says quietly. And fuck me if that isn't the hottest thing I've ever heard—my girl owning what she wants.

"Good girl. I'll do whatever you want, you only have to ask," I praise, the flush returning to the apples of her cheeks.

I unbutton her shorts and tug them over her ass and down her long legs. Fuck me, she's wearing a simple ice blue thong, the center darkened by arousal seeping through the fabric.

It's irresistible, I can't stop myself from licking her through her panties.

The action's purely selfish, something I've fantasized about. I also need a second to get my shit together. I'm dizzy having everything I've ever wanted served to me on a silver platter.

"Connor!" she gasps, covering her face with her hands but I pull them away.

"Don't hide from me. I want to see everything. I'm not missing a second of this."

"Lift up." I slip her crop top off, revealing her bare breasts. "Jesus, Delilah. You didn't wear a bra today?"

"It was hot today," she says shyly.

"Don't be embarrassed, that's so fucking hot. You walked around all day in front of the men at the ranch with your tits out?" Her smirk tells me what I need to know.

"Fuck. My good girl was naughty today," I tease, possessiveness and arousal roaring inside me.

I knead her tits, the perfect handful, and revel in how heavy they are.

"If you only knew how bad I've wanted to see these tits"—*kiss*—"suck these nipples"—*suck*—"and watch them bounce while I make you scream." Her breathy moans nearly undo me.

I shuck off my jeans, my dick barely contained by my boxer briefs.

"Shit, I don't have a condom." The biggest moment of my life and I'm unprepared.

"I haven't been with anyone in years—but I'm not on birth control," she says.

My cock throbs as an image of Delilah, round with my child, flashes before my eyes. Fuck. Why do I like that so much? I've never given much thought to having kids, but I'd have them with her, no question.

"I haven't been with anyone in a long time, and I'm clean, I swear. I'd never put you in danger," I promise.

"I know you wouldn't." Her trust in me means everything.

"I want to feel you inside me with nothing between us. But... can you pull out before you come?" she asks.

My girl wants me to take her bare. What did I do in a past life to deserve this woman?

"Of course, baby. Whatever makes you comfortable. Besides, I've been dreaming of painting you with my cum," I say, palming my dick through my underwear for some relief.

"Then do it."

That's it. She wants my cum? She's going to get it.

I slide her damp thong down her legs, delectable arousal stretching from her glistening cunt to the fabric. I shed my boxer briefs and climb onto the bed between her legs, my cock bobbing between us.

"You're so goddamn beautiful." I'm weak in the knees for this girl, and she's offering herself to me.

She smiles sweetly at my compliment but won't meet my eyes. She's struggled with body image her whole life, and I don't know how to make her believe me when I tell her she's perfect. So, I show her with my body—something I only dreamed I'd be able to do.

I drink her in, and she squirms under my focused attention. Her skin impossibly soft beneath my calloused fingertips. I take my time exploring every part of her I can reach, worshiping her body with silent praise.

When I get to her scar, her hand is there in an instant, covering her biggest insecurity. She tenses—face pinched, head turned away from me.

"Look at me," I demand softly. She immediately complies.

"Good girl. Now listen. You are perfect. Every inch of you.

Now watch," I command. I carefully run my tongue along her scar, kissing it, stroking it gently.

"Please, stop," she whines.

I stop immediately and sit up.

"I'm sorry, it's just a lot and—" she rushes out.

"Never apologize for telling me what you need. At any time, if you say stop, we stop. No questions asked, no apologies necessary, okay doll?" I say firmly.

She relaxes back into the pillows. I press her butterflied legs into the mattress and massage the crease in her hips—never touching her where she needs me, driving her wild.

Impatience gives her a burst of bravery and she circles her tiny hand around my cock, stroking me slowly.

A whimper escapes me. "Baby, you have no idea how long I've fantasized about you touching me." *Fuuuuuck. Nothing's ever felt so good.*

"It's not going to fit," Delilah whispers, my ego explodes at the compliment.

"We'll make it fit," I say, as I shuffle backwards and bury my face in her pussy.

I learn her body as I lick arousal from her skin and slide my tongue between her folds. She tastes like mine.

She moans the loudest when I circle the stiff tip of my tongue around her clit. And she pulls on my hair like it's reins when I suck the bud into my mouth. Her pussy flutters and her legs box my ears when I spear my tongue inside her hole.

"I love how responsive you are for me," I say into her cunt.

"Only for you. Only ever you," she pants, and I double down on my efforts.

I focus my attention on her clit until she's shaking and incoherently chanting my name. She said she can't come unless she's full and has clitoral stimulation.

I'm going to learn her body so well she'll come from me sucking her tits, but until then, I'm happy to oblige.

I swipe two fingers through her dripping folds, gathering her slickness, and gently thrust into her cunt.

"Oh my god! Connor!" she shouts.

Delilah screaming my name is *everything*.

My fingers pump in and out, working her higher. I curl my fingers behind her pubic bone and press deeply into her G-spot as I suck her clit between my lips and abuse it with my tongue.

She comes silently, her body tensing, nearly levitating off the bed.

As I release her from my mouth, she sucks in a ragged gasp of air and untangles her fingers from my hair, my scalp stinging from how hard she was pulling.

I'll go bald with a smile on my face if it means I can live between her legs.

"Such a good girl coming for me," I praise.

I get to my knees and position myself between her boneless body, moving her around like a ragdoll. Relief hisses from me as I pump my cock. Rutting into the mattress while tongue fucking her was divine torture.

"You want this dick, baby? You want me deep inside this pretty little pussy? Once I'm inside you, there's no going back. You were already mine, but once I claim you, you're never getting away from me," I say, surprised by the feral possession searing my veins.

"I want it. I want you. Please, Connor. I can't wait anymore. Make love to me."

The head of my cock breaches her tight hole, my whimper filling the space between us.

I push into her in one smooth thrust. She cries out, hands flying up to tangle in her hair.

"Fuuuuuck. Delilah, you feel so fucking good."

She's panting and writhing beneath me, full of my cock. I'm drunk from the overwhelming pleasure. It's never been like this for me before.

"Oh my god, you're huge. I've never been this full," she moans.

"That's fucking right, you were made for me, made to take this dick." I pull out to the tip and push back in deep.

"I told you we'd made it fit. All it took was making your pussy cry for me, and your cunt was pulsing, begging me to fuck you."

Though, as I say that, I know what we're doing is so much more than fucking—it's life-changing, soul-altering lovemaking.

I slide in and out of her tight wet heat, delirious from the pleasure she's giving me.

"Take me harder. You won't break me," she moans.

"I don't want to hurt you, you're too precious to me. I want to do this right," I say, struggling to hold back from pounding her into the mattress.

Her delicate hands frame my face as she drags me down for a gentle kiss.

"You'd never hurt me. I've wanted you for so long. Make love to me like you've always wanted. Take everything—it's always been yours."

And with her permission, I fuck her brains out.

My mouth's on her tits, marking her chest, biting her neck, my thumb frantically working circles over her swollen clit, while my cock thrusts in and out of her perfect body.

"Fuck. Your cunt's heaven, baby. I'm not going to last," I pant.

"I can't tell…if I'm still coming from your mouth…or coming again. You feel so good. You're such a stud, filling me up, taking everything from me." I nearly shoot my load from the filthy words leaving her angelic mouth.

"FUCK!" I pull out and in one—two—three pumps, I'm spurting hot cum onto her tits and her soft belly until I'm spent.

I carefully roll off her tiny body onto my back atop the tangled sheets.

"That was better than I ever dreamed it would be," Delilah says to the shadows dancing across our bedroom ceiling.

"You're everything I've ever wanted. I never thought I'd have you. I wasn't kidding, now that you've let me inside your body, I'm never letting you go." I reach out and take her hand, lacing our fingers together like we always do—somehow familiar but also brand new.

I shouldn't be surprised our sexual compatibility is on fire. Our pieces have always fit together like a puzzle. Once you know everything about your person, any walls and barriers to intimacy are already gone. We can revel in pure, unabashed, carnal desire.

"So, don't," she says, squeezing my hand.

Little does she know I'd die before letting her go. I sit up to get her a washcloth to clean my mess from her skin, but she pulls me back down.

"Stay. I'm happy evidence of your love is covering my skin. Stay."

Fuck. I've never been able to say no to her and there's no way I can deny her when she says things like that.

I lay beside her and arrange her in to lay on my shoulder like we sleep every night. She curls into my side, stroking my sweat-cooled chest. Her fingers absentmindedly trace my tattoos, like she's done a million times.

"I love all your tattoos, but this one's always been my favorite," she muses, her touch a soothing balm along every line and curve of the sun inked above my heart.

"Yea? It's my favorite too," I say wistfully.

"Why's that?" she asks.

"Because it's you." Our eyes meet—this moment frozen in time. "You're my sunshine. You always have been."

"Thanks, brother. I hope you know what this means to me, and what it'll mean to her. Living near Izzy, and her therapy horses... thank you." I shake Reid's hand, sealing our deal.

"James will draw up the paperwork. I'll reach out to the architect we've been using and set up a time for y'all to meet. Congratulations, and welcome to the family, again," Reid says, clapping me on the back and heading back to work.

In a weird twist of fate, I'm lucky to be Reid's brother-in-law from Sam's marriage to my sister, and now from each of us planning to marry one of the Tate twins.

As I walk back to my truck, fallen leaves crunch beneath my boots, my fingers running along the curved metal in my pocket. Parked in front of what will someday be my home with my girl, I sit on the tail gate and allow myself a moment of calm.

Every penny has brought me closer to making Delilah's dreams come true. It's still heartbreaking I can never give her the house by the library.

Every year since I turned eighteen, I've asked the couple who owns it to sell it to me. And every year, they've told me no.

The husband died a few years back and I helped the wife with maintenance and upkeep until she passed earlier this year. I thought I finally had my chance. I was wrong. The couple had no children, so they gifted the home to the city to become a museum for Swiftwater history.

That was that. Delilah's dream would never come true. Everything I did wasn't enough.

All these years working my body into the ground was for nothing. I saved every spare penny to buy that house for her.

The only thing I ever wanted was for her to be happy, and that house would make her happy. I was devastated I'd failed her so profoundly.

Reid's giving me a second chance at making her dream come true. It may not be the house by the library, but it'll be white and have a blue door. I'll plant flowers by the porch and get a rocking chair that fits us both. I'll install a white picket fence out front if she wants, even though Reid's selling me two acres.

We'll build our lives on the ranch we've both come to love, and put our blood, sweat, and tears into.

I'm going to make her my wife.

Delilah Hayes is the name that's haunted my dreams for years and I'm going to make it a reality.

I remove the warm metal from my pocket, an old ring from Delilah's jewelry box, one I know fits perfectly on her ring finger.

Reid recommended the jeweler that made Isabelle's ring, and if I can leave unnoticed tomorrow morning, I'll get to the jeweler and back in plenty of time.

I never thought her happiness would include me.

Now that I have her, I'm never letting her go.

36

"You got a tattoo for me?" I sit up, admiring Connors handsome face. The tattoo I've admired since his eighteenth birthday, was for me.

"I've gotten several tattoos for you. But the sun was first." Connor brushes my sex-tousled hair from my face.

If there was any lingering doubt about Connor's feelings for me, it just evaporated. The first thing he did when he turned eighteen was permanently mark his body with a symbol of me.

"So, does this mean I'm your girlfriend?"

The devotion in his chocolate eyes melts me. "Yea doll, you're my girlfriend. You're the sun in my sky and light of my life. I've been in love with you for so long, you're woven into my soul. You're so much more than my girlfriend—you're my world. Always have been, always will be," he vows.

"Delilah, you are mine just as much as I am yours. I need to hear you say it."

I love him so much it hurts, but some of the pain releases when I say, "I am yours, and you are mine."

"Mine," he says, kissing my forehead.

"Is this really happening? I'm afraid to go to sleep because if

I wake up and this was a dream, I'll never recover." My throat's tight with emotion.

Connor pops the comforter open for us to slip beneath. I lay beside him, covered only from the waist down, uncharacteristically comfortable with my body on display. His eyes rove my naked skin, but only for a moment.

"Tomorrow when you wake up, I'll be right here, holding you and kissing you good morning. I'll remind you every day for the rest of our lives how real my love for you is. I'll tell you with my words and prove my words with my actions."

He motions for me to settle into the crook of his shoulder—my spot—and curls his strong arm around me.

"Go to sleep, doll. And trust me to still be in love with you when you wake up."

Instead of the normal kiss to the top of my head, I tilt my face, and Connor places the sweetest kiss on my lips.

Connor Hayes is in love with me. He's finally mine.

The frayed heartstring connecting us weaves back together like braided steel cable.

I fall asleep with his taste on my lips, dried evidence of his love on my skin, and peace in my heart.

After waking me up overnight to fill my body and lavish me with pleasure, Connor insisted I take the day off from the ranch. I wake long after the sun had risen, a stark contrast to the pre-dawn start our days have had since adopting ranch hours.

I pause as I reach for my phone. A crisp note is neatly folded and propped against my favorite water bottle.

Hydrate. I've got big plans for you tonight.

Pamper yourself and spend the day oversharing with the girls.

But be ready for me to pick you up at seven.

I'm finally taking you out on our first date.

Love, your boyfriend.

My ears ring like my eardrums have burst. Izzy and Livy are screaming like preteens. My god, the high pitch may cause long-term hearing loss.

"I KNEW IT!" Izzy screeches.

"Oh my god, will you shut up! I don't want Reid or anyone else hearing about my sex life," I chastise.

We're in the privacy of her and Reid's cabin, but the ranch is one giant revolving door. Someone could come in and hear us at any minute.

They resume screaming and while I want to bury my head and hide, I'm a hundred times more excited than them. So, I join them.

My voice grows hoarse from screaming but I'm floating on a cloud.

We settle into the chairs on Izzy's back porch with glasses of iced tea and a sleeve of double stuffed Oreos and can of Pringles each.

"Spill. Tell us everything. Don't leave out a single detail." Livy bounces in her seat.

"Not *everything*...I don't want to know what Connor's junk looks like." Izzy gags.

"Speak for yourself," Livy says, waggling her eyebrows. "I bet he's packing."

The flaming blush that saturates my cheeks answers for me, eliciting a squeal of joy from Livy and disgusted groans from my sister.

"Start from the beginning," Olivia demands. "You left dinner last night in such a rush, we were worried."

"I'm sorry if the wedding talk went too far. I didn't mean to upset you," Izzy says, taking my hand.

"Don't be ridiculous. I'm over the moon happy for you sissy. Sure, for a minute there I was upset by how far away marriage was for me, but it was the push I needed to finally tell Connor I'm in love with him," I assure my sweet sister.

"All the things we've held back over the years bubbled to the surface and once everything was out in the open, I asked him to kiss me."

Livy flails her arm out in excitement and sends her glass of iced tea careening to the ground. We flinch, expecting the glass to burst but Izzy says, "Shatterproof. Reid says you can't grow up on a ranch with three boys without having shatterproof dishes." Izzy dries the floor and picks up the glass without a second thought.

"Anywayyyyy," Livy pushes.

"Kissing led to grinding, which led to the bedroom. To be honest, the sex was the least important thing that happened last night. We admitted we're in love with each other. And aside from rings and a marriage license, we're committed to each other for life," I say wistfully.

"Who cares!" Livy says. "YOU FUCKED CONNOR!"

A deep voice from the sliding glass door scares the pee out of us. "I told you so," Reid says to Izzy, reaching over to drain her glass of tea.

"I told you at their birthday party last year and you didn't believe me," he says smugly, but with no malice behind the words, my sister making moon eyes at him.

Reid pats his front and back pockets—"Where's my phone? James owes me a hundred bucks"—and disappears back into their cabin.

We dissolve into giggles, and I don't care if it's at my expense. I have everything I've ever wanted.

I check the time on my phone for the millionth time this hour and nearly cry. Connor will be home to pick me up for our first date in twenty minutes and I'm nowhere near ready.

I've tried on every piece of clothing I own, styled and restyled my hair, and am now so sweaty I need to take another shower. Why am I so nervous? Connor's taken me out for dinner before.

But this is different—we aren't going out as friends. He's taking me out as his girlfriend and I'm freaking out.

I want to impress him and make tonight perfect since he's been dreaming of our first date as long as I have. I don't know where we're going and I'm afraid to be underdressed or overdressed.

I'm spiraling into a panic attack when my phone chimes.

> Studmuffin: I'm on my way. I can't wait to see you. You're probably freaking out, so I want to remind you I'm madly in love with you and you are perfect exactly the way you are. Don't overthink it, dollface.

And just like that, the tornado in my chest settles to a dust bunny. As I thumb through my discarded outfits, I reflect on our relationship, and if he's loved me the way he says he has, that means he loved me when I've been ugly, sick, sweaty, dirty, angry, and puffy from crying.

Connor loves me. I can do this.

You can never go wrong with a little black dress, so I choose my favorite one. It's flattering and not too tight, so I can eat comfortably. The stretchy fabric slinks down my body, caressing me seductively.

I'm careful to pull the bodice up to cover the bra I'm wearing. It's a sinful set I bought for myself as a reward for landing my internship but haven't had a reason to wear. I hope Connor likes it.

I slick my hair back into a high ponytail and put on my favorite earrings and an extra spritz of perfume.

I'm sitting on the edge of the bed, putting on my dressy cowboy boots when someone knocks at the front door.

Who'd be knocking our door? Connor has a key, and everyone else texts before they come over. I pause on my walk to the door. What if it's my mom? She's not supposed to be anywhere near me. Quietly, I take the last few steps to the door and peer out the peephole—to find Connor on the other side, holding an enormous bouquet of flowers.

His eyes drink me in as soon as I swing the door open, admiring every detail I fretted over. It was silly getting so worked up. This is Connor. He'd never make me feel anything less than wanted.

"You're...beautiful. So pretty, Delilah." He gulps, a blush tinting his cheeks.

"These are for you," he says, offering me the flowers.

The heady, floral scent invades my senses, and I swoon like a fool. I've never gotten flowers before, and these are my favorite. Carnations are often overlooked, but I've always loved them, and Connor remembered. Shades of yellow are accented by the occasional light pink carnation. I want to take a picture to keep them forever.

"Are you ready to go?" Connor asks, clearing his throat nervously.

"I need to get these in some water," I say, turning back towards the kitchen, but Connor gently cups my elbow.

"It can wait—but I can't." A sinful smile curves one side of his mouth and my stomach erupts into butterflies.

I set the flowers on the counter as Connor tucks my phone and other things into his pockets. I've never needed a purse around him, and I love he's my same Connor tonight.

He escorts me to his truck, opens my door with a flourish and helps me inside. He reaches across my body to buckle my seatbelt, and on his retreat, kisses the sun pendant hanging between my collar bones.

The breath I suck in is masked by the door shutting, and as we drive away from our apartment, Connor's hand never leaves my thigh.

Water nearly comes out my nose from how hard I'm laughing.

"You did not!" I exclaim.

"I did. Your freshman year, I scared off every guy at school who dared to look at you. The school nurse had never been busier because boys at school had come down with a severe case of clumsiness. Jammed fingers, bloody noses, skinned knees," he says with the brightest smile on his face, as if he didn't assault half the student body.

"So, I have you to thank for never being asked out on a date?" I ask, dabbing my eyes from laughing.

"Hell yea. I thought I couldn't have you but there was no way I was going to let any other asshole get near you. You forget I was a teenage boy too, and I knew the depraved shit going on in my own head. Anyone else fantasizing about you the way I did made me murderous," he admits.

"Why do I find that so attractive? I had my own bodyguard and didn't even know. I should be alarmed by how many people you've hurt on my behalf, but instead I wish the waiter would bring our check so I can thank you properly, at home," I say, twirling my tongue around my straw with a wink.

"WAITER!" Connor hollers, standing so fast his chair crashes backwards.

I can't stop laughing. He's the perfect man, and he's mine.

The next few minutes pass in a whirlwind. Our bill is paid, he practically tosses me into his truck, and we make it home in record time.

Rounding the front of the truck, Connor opens my door and unbuckles my seat belt. He scoops me up like a bride, kicking my door shut behind us. We laugh and make out through the parking lot and up the stairs.

He sets me down long enough to dig his keys out of his pocket and unlock the door, but then I'm back in his arms, and he's booting the door open, carrying me over the threshold.

I. Am. Swooning.

Connor locks the door and as we pass the kitchen, plucks a yellow carnation from the bouquet. I kiss, suck, and bite his neck, driving him crazy. He carries me to our bedroom and gently sets me on the bed.

"You're so fucking beautiful, doll. I've wanted to take you out on a date since middle school but as soon as you opened the door tonight, I wanted to say screw the date and take you to bed instead." He gets on his knees and deftly removes my cowboy boots and socks, pressing his strong thumbs into the balls of my feet.

I fall back with a groan of relief. He sets my feet down and I prop myself up on my elbows to watch my favorite show—Connor undressing.

My eyelids fall heavy and mouth parts as he takes off his cowboy boots and unbuckles his belt. His attention is fixed on me, the power heady. He unbuttons his shirt and takes it off, reaches one arm behind his neck and pulls his undershirt over his head in a pornographic display.

"Like what you see, baby?" he taunts.

"You're so sexy, Connor, and I get to touch you whenever I want." His eyes flash with satisfaction.

"I hope you do. I want your hands on me constantly." He hooks his thumbs into the waistband of his boxer briefs, pulling his underwear and pants down at the same time.

He stands gloriously naked like a tattooed, golden, chiseled statue.

Needing his body on me, I sit up to strip out of my dress.

"No," Connor barks.

"I want to feel your skin on me," I breathe.

"I undress you." Holy shit that's so hot.

"Stand up." I pop to my feet eagerly, not trying to hide my submissive nature.

"Good girl," he purrs and my sex weeps in response.

The carnation he plucked from my bouquet twirls by the stem between his deft fingers. Connor circles me like prey, dusting the flower up one arm and down the other. Silken petals drag up my exposed neck, down my throat, across my collar bones and tease my cleavage. I squirm under his attention and the tickling sensation.

"Open your mouth." I do so immediately, and Connor places the stem horizontally between my parted teeth.

"Close," he growls.

With his hands free, Connor peels the straps of my dress down my shoulders painfully slowly, stretching the fabric to its limits. My bra grips the neckline of the dress, and he tugs it down roughly with one finger between my breasts.

The motion makes his heavy cock bob between us flooding my mouth with saliva.

The slip dress pools at my feet, leaving me in barely-there lingerie. Connor steps back to admire his handiwork. He scratches his bearded jaw, licking his lips like he's starving.

Taking the carnation from my mouth, Connor dusts it across the swell of my breasts and down my stomach, making my muscles dance away from the sensation.

"This wasn't in the drawers I packed from the trailer." Fire lights in his eyes.

"And why would you know that? Didn't you just sweep all my clothes into boxes?"

Connor sucks his teeth, restraining himself and it's intoxicating.

"No, dollface. I didn't just sweep your clothes into boxes. I fingered every bra and thong in your drawer." My eyes go wide, and my pulse quickens.

"I wrapped one of those slutty little lace thongs around my cock and fucked my hand in your childhood bedroom." My gasp encourages his honesty.

"Did you ever wonder where your purple vibrator went?" I nod, transfixed.

"I found it in the nightstand where you kept your smutty books. All I could picture was you fucking that toy while some fictional man turned you on and I lost it. I wanted to be the only cock to give you pleasure."

"You are. No other man's ever made me feel like you do. My toys were okay…but I always fantasized it was you sliding in and out of me."

A small groan slips between his lips, weakening his cocksure attitude. He fists his dick and strokes himself as I speak. It's so erotic I might come without ever being touched.

"Who'd you buy the lingerie for, Delilah?" He crushes the carnation in his hand, dropping the dead flower at my feet.

"Who were you planning on fucking when you bought this cocktease bra and panties?"

"Honestly, no one. I wanted to feel desirable, even if no one wanted me." He tries to argue but I hold up one finger stopping him.

"I didn't know you wanted me, Connor. I bought these for myself. But you'll be the only one to ever see them or take them off me."

I step to the man I now call mine and scrape my nails down his solid chest, holding his molten gaze as I drop to my knees at his feet.

My nails dig into his muscular quads and his erection fills my vision. I've never understood when women say a dick is attractive, but Connor's is immaculate.

Thicker than any vibrator, so long it's intimately acquainted with my cervix, with throbbing veins trailing from the base to the flared head. The pronounced ridge between the shaft and head makes me want to lick around it like a ring pop.

"I want to make you feel good." I circle my hand around his girth and stroke him root to tip gently. A full body shiver courses through him, and he jerks his head cracking his neck.

"You always do. You don't have to do this." He gulps, his Adam's apple bobbing.

I squeeze his cock tighter, and he groans. "I want you in my mouth. Please, may I have your cock?" I ask, deviously innocent.

"Fuck yes. Suck my dick, baby. I've been dreaming about having your lips wrapped around me for fucking ever." His hands hover in the air, unsure whether to hold my hair or tangle in his own.

I make the decision for him and lead his hand to my ponytail—he immediately wraps the long rope around his fist.

"I've never done this before," I admit, licking my lips, still stroking him.

"We'll go slow, only do what you're comfortable with. I'll love every second of having your mouth on me."

I hold his base steady with my hand, my man vibrating with restraint. With unbroken eye contact, I flatten my tongue and lick the broad head of his cock like an ice cream cone.

The sexiest whimper escapes him and my pussy floods with satisfaction I made him lose control.

Unsure what to do, I lick every inch of his shaft making his legs tremble. Emboldened, I suck a deep breath in through my nose and take the head into my mouth and lower my mouth until I gag.

"FUCK!" Connor barks. The strangling sensation of my throat closing around his tip makes him feral. My scalp burns from how hard he's pulling my ponytail, and I love it.

His pleasure encourages me, so I repeat the process. In. Gag. Out. In. Gag. Out. Tears run down my face, my makeup destroyed.

"I'm going to come, baby, tell me where you want me to come right fucking now before I blow," he says, on the brink of ecstasy.

I won't be able to swallow, so I release his cock with a pop and jerk him off until he explodes across my breasts.

With the little energy he has left, Connor drags me into the shower to clean us off, gently massaging soap across my body, careful not to get my hair wet.

He makes love to me until the early hours of morning and we spend the day together in bed, learning each other's bodies better than we know our own.

37

Connor age 10, Delilah age 9

"Now kiss the princess!" *Izzy says.*

"STOP. That's not what you say," *Livy complains.*

"Livy..." *Connor whines.*

"You say, 'Now do the kiss!'" *Livy exclaims.*

We've played wedding every recess this week. Livy was the flower girl in her cousin's wedding and now all she wants to do is play wedding.

Connor's my bestest friend. I love him so much. Almost as much as I love Izzy. Connor doesn't want to play-marry Livy, and Izzy doesn't want to play-marry Connor.

I want to play-marry Connor a lot. I want to real-marry Connor when we grow up like a mommy and a daddy. Not like my mommy and daddy since they're mean and make a lot of noise at night.

But like Connor's mommy and daddy. His mommy is the prettiest lady and she's so nice to me. Sometimes she brings me a treat after school and on the best days, me and Izzy get to go home with them, and we get real dinner.

Mommy says mean things about Connor's mommy when we get home from his house. I don't know why...she's so nice.

Livy's mommy and daddy are nice too. Her house is always clean and warm, and there's so much food to eat they throw lots away.

Maybe having a wedding is a happy thing if the people getting married are happy and make each other happy. Mommy and Daddy are never happy and yell at each other.

The bell rings and recess is over.

After school, Izzy and I wait with Livy and Connor for their mommies to pick them up. Sometimes they drive us, but Daddy threw a beer can at the car last time we got dropped off, so me and Izzy are gonna walk.

Livy and Izzy are playing with a bright pink bouncy ball, and Connor's sitting with me on the grass.

"I don't want to play wedding anymore," I say, plucking pieces of grass and ripping them apart.

"I like playing wedding. You smile at me a whole bunch. Maybe someday you'll marry me, and we'll have a for-real wedding. My mom and dad have a whole book of pictures from their wedding, so I know all the stuff. You'll wear the prettiest dress, and I'll wear the outfit that looks like a penguin. We'll have a big, tall cake, and soda pop, and dance till bedtime."

He paints a beautiful picture, one I'll remember forever, but Mommy says good things don't happen to people like us. I have a pile of shredded grass on my lap, and I hope I can scrub the green off because this is my nicest dress I got from the donation bin.

Izzy plops down in the grass next to me, Livy's mommy took her home. A car horn beep-beeps and it's Connor's mommy.

"Bye Izzy, bye Delilah-doll! See you Monday!" Connor hollers as he skips to his mommy's shiny blue car.

"Miss you already!" I holler.

Izzy helps me up and I brush the grass pieces off my dress. We hold hands on the way home, but we don't talk much. Weekends are a bad time at our house. The trailer's so small and so many people come to our house on the weekends to play cards with Daddy, and it smells like smoke and sour beer. It's loud and I don't sleep good. Izzy and I share her bed since her door locks.

My tummy grumbles loudly, and Izzy makes a sad face. We won't eat much till school Monday. The teachers give us free breakfast, and Connor packs extra snacks and always gives me some.

At bedtime, I stare at the ceiling in Izzy's room and imagine what it'd be like to for-real marry Connor when I grow up.

38

Delilah

"It's no wonder they call it the Dreamhouse." Connor gapes out the windshield.

The Andersens named the property aptly because it's the quintessential dream house. The cabin sprawls the bank of an ice-covered private lake, surrounded by snow dusted pine trees as far as the eye can see.

Thousands of fairy lights decorate the roofline and are strung between the cabin and the nearby trees, creating an idyllic fairytale.

Izzy and Reid came on a work assignment last year, and it was here their connection bloomed. He brought her back for Valentine's Day for a romantic vacation ending with them officially being a couple.

Their love story's come full circle, and they get to say their vows where they began.

The four-hour drive passed in the blink of an eye. Now that Connor and I are official, we spend most our time—that isn't spent naked—reminiscing over our lives and sharing long buried secrets about our unspoken love.

The Rockies are already entrenched in winter and will be a

snow-covered paradise well through March. Thanks to the dedicated men and women Connor used to work with, the highways were safe to travel. It wasn't until we were navigating the back mountain roads that it became more adventurous.

Connor took it slow and repeatedly asked if I was comfortable because he wanted me to feel safe. I've never felt safer than when I'm with him, regardless of the setting or circumstance.

He rounds the truck cab with a skip in his step that warms my heart. My golden retriever with a surprisingly wicked protective streak. Frigid November air whooshes in and I shiver.

"Let's get you inside and I'll bring in the bags," Connor insists.

The interior of the Dreamhouse is out of a magazine, and I'm filled with pride Izzy's applied her vision to properties like this across the Rockies. A crackling fireplace greets us, instantly warming my chilled skin. Connor drops a kiss on the crown of my head and goes back out to get our things.

No one's in the main room to greet us, so I take my time wandering through the space admiring the woodwork and unique artwork gracing the walls. A door shuts behind me and I whirl around.

"Twinie!" she shrieks running into my arms, as if we don't see each other every day.

At the same time, we say—

"You're getting married!"

"I'm getting married!"

We laugh and hug and twirl around the living room like children.

"I never dreamed my life would turn out this way," Izzy says, with a spark of sadness.

"I never dreamed it either, but you deserve it, sissy. We went through too much, suffered too greatly, and worked too hard to claw our way out of that trailer. You deserve every happiness and luxury life affords you." I comfort her, gently rubbing her back, the white ends of her hair tickling my hand.

Her hair's grown so much this past year. She kept it short for ages as a result of her trauma, but once she felt safe with Reid, she let it grow and regained her bodily autonomy.

"Christ, it's cold out there! It's not even December, what's going on up here?" Connor groans, toeing out of his boots and hanging his canvas work coat by the door.

Even fully clothed, his body makes me weak. He's next level gorgeous and all mine.

"Let me take you to your room and I'll give you the grand tour!" Izzy says with a delighted clap of her hands.

Somehow, the Dreamhouse is larger on the inside than it appeared from outside. Five suites are sprinkled throughout the property, along with the opulent master suite. Everyone was happy to double up, but there's the perfect amount of space for the small wedding party.

Mr. and Mrs. Andersen will sleep the farthest from the center of the house, the quietest room for when they're done of an evening.

Olivia and her niece Harper will be sharing an adorable suite facing the front of the property. Harper will be delighted to see the fairy lights from her window.

Connor and I have a corner suite overlooking the lake. I wish we could come back in warmer weather to take advantage of what must be the perfect lakefront.

James and Greyson get their own rooms—Greyson closer to Harper and James closer to the master where the bride and groom are staying.

Izzy jokes that James might want to shack up with Greyson

because they have no intention on being quiet on their wedding night. She gives an exaggerated nudge-nudge-wink-wink and Connor feigns throwing up. She punches him in the arm, on par for their relationship.

"Reid's parents just got here. There's nothing planned until dinner, so go relax in your room. Take advantage of the jacuzzi tub—trust me." Izzy bops off to greet her future in-laws and Connor snicks the door shut to our suite.

"Thank god we're staying in a different room than they've used," Connor says with a shiver of disgust. "I did *not* need to hear about Iz and Reid fucking in that tub."

I snort, because I didn't need to hear about it either, but it was hilarious how Connor grew more uncomfortable the more Izzy overshared.

He gathers me in his arms, pressing me into his hard chest and spins us like a madman until we flop onto the giant king-sized bed in a heap of giggles.

"Hi," he says sweetly, peering down at me.

"Hi," I say back, utterly charmed by this man. Seventeen years later and he still gives me butterflies. The difference is, I can act on them now.

We spend the afternoon making love and fall into a blissful nap.

Raucous laughter wakes us, and I'm surprised the sky is fading into pinks and oranges as we near sunset. I didn't mean to sleep so long.

The rehearsal dinner is informal, and Izzy said to dress comfortably, so Connor and I change into fresh clothes that weren't rumpled during a four-hour car ride and make our way to the dining room.

I can't hold back my laughter. Every surface of the kitchen is covered with open pizza boxes, liters of Cherry Pepsi, and an adorable tower of Hostess cupcakes. Plates are passed around and loaded with greasy, cheesy goodness.

When it's my turn through the line, I hesitate for only a moment. In the past, pizza was a strictly no-food for me. Just the thought of eating it used to give me hives, but the anxiety is a ghost of what it once was.

Food's been easier lately, probably because of how happy I've been. When Connor told me he loved me, something clicked into place, and I felt whole. Every day that he showers me with love, I heal bit by bit.

I take a slice of cheese, Izzy's favorite, and meat lovers, Connor's favorite. It's been years since I ate pizza, and I didn't want to overwhelm myself with new options.

Connor kisses my temple and whispers, "I'm proud of you" as he fills his plate.

He pours me a bubbling glass of Cherry Pepsi and gets a dessert plate with two waxy cupcakes for us to enjoy after dinner.

"James, if you don't shut the fuck up right now, I'll kill you and send you to a watery grave in the frozen lake, I swear to god," Reid seethes.

James is cackling like a hyena, nearly tipping backwards out of his chair.

"What? You don't want your blushing bride to hear about the time you got Little Reid stuck in your zipper trying to cover up getting caught in the hay loft with Marcie Gossler?"

Reid lurches from his chair to strangle his older brother but Izzy holds him back, laughing. Even the normally stoic Greyson is laughing.

"No, you dumb fuck, why would I want my *wife* to hear about any of my past sexual experiences?" Reid snaps.

"It's okay baby, I know you weren't a monk before me. Plus, now I want to hear the story," she says with glee.

He tickles her sides but relents, waving a dismissive hand for James to continue.

"That's the whole story. He was in the hay loft with Marcie doing god knows what, heard me and Sam come into the barn, panicked, and got his dick pinched in his zipper. He screamed like a little bitch and Marcie flew down the ladder like her ass was on fire," James regales.

"Never thought I'd take my son to the emergency room with a penile injury, but such is life," Mr. Andersen says chuckling. Mrs. Andersen bats his chest with the back of her hand.

Connor laughs with the family we've been adopted into. I'm so lucky to have his love.

"How're we supposed to fit into these dresses after that brunch? My god!" Livy complains, cradling her food baby.

"Hush, you're gorgeous. Maybe James will ask you to dance," Izzy taunts.

Livy turns beet red, stuttering, "I don't know what you're talking about. Gross. I mean, like...shut up!"

Flustered, she takes her dress to the bathroom and the lock clicks behind her.

Izzy and I share a knowing look but drop the subject. Today's about Izzy and Reid, and in the end, Livy's love life is none of our business.

"It's so nice of Mrs. Andersen and Harper to finish the decorating," I say.

"I know, luckily this place is stunning as it is. Some flowers and candles and we're set!"

Izzy's an angel in her wedding dress. Blush pink chiffon drapes like a waterfall from her waist to the floor. A high slit allows her leg to peek through with each step, showing off hot pink cowboy boots. The bodice is made of intricate lace, with a sweetheart neckline held by delicate straps that meet at her waist, leaving her back exposed.

I stand behind her, finishing her hair, overflowing with happiness for my sister. A somber expression crosses her face.

"Hey, what was that? Today's a happy day," I say.

"It is. I'm over the moon, I can't wait to marry Reid and become Isabelle Andersen. His parents being here for him—so happy and involved—makes me sad for what you and I don't have," she says to me in the mirror.

Moments of grief like this come out of nowhere. Having a difficult relationship with a parent is a minefield to navigate. Though they're alive, you mourn the death of the relationship you wish you'd had. Our parents cared more about gambling and alcohol than to be there for us. The way we were raised was worse than negligent, it was abusive.

"I know, sissy. I think about it sometimes too. But look at the family you've built for yourself. Your life is full of support and love, and we'll always have each other," I say.

Izzy turns around and wraps me in a soft hug.

"I love seeing you so happy," I say to my sister, choking back tears.

"None of that, I don't want to redo my makeup." She laughs. "You look amazing. Connor's going to lose his mind when he sees you." Izzy fluffs my breasts, and I slap her hands away.

A knock sounds on the door and Livy shouts from the bathroom, "Five minutes!"

I open the door to find Mrs. Andersen's smiling face—the kind of mother I wish we'd had. Izzy exits ahead of me and her future mother-in-law brushes a tendril of hair from her face.

"Oh honey, you look lovely. My son's a lucky man." They leave to set up before the ceremony and I follow behind, Livy still shouting from behind the bathroom door.

I bump into a wall of muscle, and Connor's arms shoot out to catch me.

He immediately yanks his arms back, nearly dropping me, to dramatically cover his eyes.

"It's bad luck to see the maid of honor before the wedding," he says.

I have no such qualms. Connor's edible in dress cowboy boots beneath tailored dark grey slacks and my favorite white pearl snap. His hair's slicked back, and I have an uncontrollable urge to dig my fingers in to mess it up and grip it while he kisses me.

"Ok, studmuffin," I say, patting his firm chest on my way past.

"See you in a few," he says, still dramatically covering his eyes.

"I'll be the one next to the bride." I slap his tight ass and saunter off to find the rest of the wedding party.

39

The ceremony's set to take place before the magnificent fireplace I'm told has special meaning for Izzy and Reid.

Simple flowers and candles adorn the mantle. A funny little bobble head armadillo sits proudly front and center.

The dining room chairs are set in a neat arc around the fireplace, each with a pink satin bow tied on the back. A photographer dressed in all black moves through the space like a phantom.

Mr. Andersen walks his wife to her seat, kisses her reverently, and takes his place in front of the fireplace, hands clasped in front of him. I sit on the end opposite of Mrs. Andersen, leaving room for the family between us.

Harper's a little princess in her puffy pink dress and glimmering tiara, sprinkling rose petals on her short walk to the fireplace and comes to sit beside her pseudo-grandma.

I don't know a ton about Reid's history, but from what Delilah's told me, he used to be extremely private as a result of an accident that disfigured his face.

There's no trace of that insecurity as he walks in. His longer hair is slicked back away from his face, beard is neatly trimmed, and his dress shirt's unbuttoned at the top to not irritate the scarring on his neck.

The groom comes to stand beside his father, who claps him on the back proudly. My heart jolts, grief flooding me from missing my dad. Who he used to be, who he'll never be again, and most of all, that he won't remember when I get married.

James leads Delilah to her place beside the makeshift altar. He flanks Reid with a squeeze to his shoulder.

I can't take my eyes off my girl. Her dress is slinky pink satin, draped like water across her fair skin. A cowl neck teases her breasts, making my mouth water. Her hair's pinned to one side, revealing the delicate column of her neck.

She's breathtaking.

Greyson leads Liv to the altar, and they take their places beside their rightful best friends.

A sharp intake of breath has people turning to watch Izzy walk to the altar, but I look at Reid. It's earth-moving when a man so openly loves a woman. He beams with joy as she makes her way to stand before him.

He pulls her into a hug, unable to resist touching his bride and kisses her tenderly. They whisper sweet nothings to each other; they deserve as many private moments as they want on their wedding day.

Warmth spreads in my chest seeing Izzy so confident in her own skin. She suffered for so many years at the hands of cruel, ignorant people and disappeared behind a façade. She looks like the Izzy I grew up with, but older and herself again.

She tenderly caresses the scarred side of Reid's face, and he leans into her touch, a balm to his old pain.

I envy him, standing before the love of his life, about to make her his forever.

My attention's consumed by this woman I loved in secret,

who I now love loudly and openly, standing proudly with her sister on the most important day of her life.

Mr. Andersen invites the wedding party to take their seats. Harper moves a spot down by her dad, and James sits beside his mom, lovingly holding her hand.

Greyson and Liv bookend Harper, showering her with praise for her excellent performance as flower girl. And Delilah takes her place beside me. Where she belongs.

Mr. Andersen welcomes us all to this joyous day and says a few words before giving the floor to Reid.

"Go ahead, son," Mr. Andersen says, choked with emotion.

Reid takes a folded piece of crisp paper from the inside pocket of his suit jacket. When he unfolds it, a tattered piece of paper is revealed and Izzy's hands fly up to cover her mouth, holding back a sob.

Delilah tenses, her sister's emotions rippling through her. I wrap my arm around her shoulders, pulling her in tight.

"Come here, darlin'," Reid consoles, pulling his bride into his arms, whispering into her ear and kissing her temple.

When she's composed herself, he gives her an adoring smile, the corners of his eyes crinkling deeply from the peace she brings him.

He clears his throat and reads.

"Isabelle, words can't express how lucky I am to marry you. I'm not going to question it, because I'm afraid if you dig too deep, you'll run for the hills." Light chuckles fill the room.

"I thought I had a good life, but I wasted it caring only about myself. At one of the darkest times of my life, you brought me back from the brink." Reid wipes away a stray tear.

James takes his mother's hand, and Mr. Andersen moves to stand behind his wife—a family strongest together.

"I wish Sam could be here today, and in a way, he is because he lives on in our hearts." He reaches around his dad to boop the armadillo, whose head bobbles merrily.

"Sugar, you rescued me from my grief, and you didn't even know it. I can never thank you enough for bringing me back to life."

There's not a dry eye in the house, and Izzy wipes the tears from Reid's cheeks, smiling softly at her groom.

"It's fitting, getting married at the place I realized my feelings for you. I was slower to come around, but I promise I'll spend my lifetime loving you the way you deserve. It was here I opened up about my dreams for the first time, and you not only listened, but you made it a reality when you drew this." He holds the worn piece of paper reverently.

"I like to think Grandpa's lucky spurs brought you to me, the same way they brought him Grandma. But instead of a girl wearing a red dress in the stands at the rodeo, their luck brought me a firecracker in pink and combat boots." They both chuckle.

"You made my dreams come true, Isabelle. You gave me a second chance at living, the courage to make my plans a reality, and most importantly, your love. I'm honored to be your husband." Reid cups Izzy's cheek and places a soft kiss to her lips.

Delilah looks to me, her adoration clear as day. She gives me a sweet kiss that sends warmth to my toes.

Mr. Andersen resumes as the officiant.

"Isabelle, sweetheart..." he leads, indicating it's her turn.

She has no paper to read from, or memento to share—she speaks directly into Reid's soul, her eyes brimming with love. He takes her by both hands, his thumbs brushing across the backs of her hands gently.

"When I was a little girl, we used to play wedding." She shoots a playful grin at Olivia, Delilah, and me.

"It was a fun game, but I never thought it'd happen for me.

The only love I was given was conditional and toxic. For many years it was just my sister and me against the world."

Delilah rests her head on my shoulder, wiping away tears.

"No boy ever caught my eye because it was a young man destined to steal my heart. The moment I saw you in the middle school hallway, I was smitten. Many years and heartaches later, the universe brought us together in the most unexpected way. You mended my broken heart, and I fell for you more each day." Her smile's so wide, I can't help but smile with her.

"You fought my demons, believed in me, and accepted me for who I am. You saved me as much as I saved you. You're my best friend, my lover, my person, and now, my husband. You've given me a life I never could've dreamed of, and every day you love me unconditionally. I said yes beneath the sign representing our new life, and I'll say yes every day for the rest of my life. I promise to love you with everything I am, forever," Izzy finishes.

My attention shifts to Delilah as Mr. Andersen has Reid and Izzy repeat the traditional vows, to have and to hold, so long as they both shall live.

Her eyes meet mine, pure love shining back at me. As the happy couple exchanges rings and seals their commitment with a kiss, one truth overtakes me.

I'm going to marry Delilah.

The wedding party floats away in a cloud of laughter to take wedding photos, leaving me alone with my thoughts.

This decision was inevitable. I've known Delilah was it for me since I was eight years old. It's long past time I make her mine permanently.

I lock myself in our suite, ensuring privacy while I do what I need to do. Checking the time, my best friend's still at work, but I know he'll respond.

> Me: Hey.

> CJ: Aren't you supposed to be basking in merriment?

> Me: You're gonna want in on this.

> CJ: Color me intrigued.

> CJ: Proceed.

> Me: Remember that summer you made me watch every episode of "Four Weddings"?

> CJ: Yesssss. I'm listening.

> Me: Remember how you insisted you'd plan a better wedding than any of the contestants?

> CJ: Please tell me this is going where I hope it's going...

> Me: Could you help me plan to marry Delilah in approximately 36 hours?

I wait impatiently for his response.

> CJ: Sorry that took me so long, I was so excited I threw my phone, and it cracked against the ceiling. It shut itself off from the impact and I've been screaming at it to turn back on to text you back!

> CJ: YES OH MY GOD I WOULD LOVE TO PLAN YOUR SUPER SECRET SURPRISE WEDDING!

> Me: Do you think you can plan it all from home?

> CJ: *scoffs* Do I think I can plan it all from home?

> CJ: Does Taylor Swift make grown men cry?

> Me: Like babies.

> CJ: Exactly.

> CJ: Send me your ideas and leave the rest to me.

> CJ: Oh, and add me as an authorized user to your credit card.

> Me: Done. I want it to be perfect, but please don't bankrupt me...

> CJ: Did you forget you're talking to the Bargain Queen of the Rockies? Now leave me alone to make magic.

> CJ: But still send me stuff. Leave me alone after you send me stuff.

I pocket my phone, roll my shoulders, and shake out my hands to get some of the buzzing energy out of my body.

I'm going to marry Delilah Tate.

In two days, she'll be Delilah Hayes.

40

In a delightfully unorthodox turn of events, Izzy demanded everyone change into pajamas before dinner. In her words, "No one wants to eat tacos in a dress that requires double-sided tape." Despite the odd request, everyone was grateful to shed their formalwear, especially in such a cozy mountain cabin.

She and Reid surprised everyone with hilarious matching pajamas—flannel bottoms and fuzzy socks in each person's favorite color, and an inappropriate T-shirt.

Reid's wearing a shirt that says, POUR SOME SUGAR ON ME, and Izzy's replies, I'M SUGAR.

Connor and my shirts bear the classic SAVE A HORSE and RIDE A COWBOY.

Mr. Andersen's shirt reads, THIS WEDDING IS BROUGHT TO YOU BY MY SPERM, and Mrs. Andersen's says, I GREW THE GROOM.

Harper's shirt is half a lyric, IT'S A LOVE STORY, with Olivia's replying BABY JUST SAY YES. Greyson was less than thrilled Harper was dragged into the nonsense, but she was ecstatic to be included.

My favorite pairing is James and Greyson—who adamantly

refused to put the shirt on until Reid threatened to unearth an ancient embarrassing story.

Greyson's says, I BETTER SHAPE UP 'CAUSE YOU NEED A MAN, as Danny Zuko, and James's responds, I NEED A MAN, WHO CAN KEEP ME SATISFIED, as Sandra Dee.

We all laughed so hard the clothes changing was delayed a solid five minutes—I nearly peed myself laughing. Connor loved their shirts so much he snapped some pictures to show CJ, and then Greyson tried to break his phone.

The photographer takes a series of adorable couple's shots. The T-shirt pairings will live in infamy forever. Izzy insists she take a break and join us for dinner, which she gratefully accepts. That woman's been on her feet all day capturing every moment for the happy couple.

An elaborate taco bar's exploded in the gourmet kitchen. Mrs. Andersen whips up a batch of virgin margaritas, and I catch James, Greyson, and Olivia slipping tequila into theirs.

I love that no one shames me or my sister for choosing not to drink. Reid stopped drinking for Izzy, and Connor avoids it for me. Even the scent is triggering sometimes, but we trust this group with our lives and don't mind them imbibing.

Extremely relaxed and happy, I load my plate with warm corn tortillas, grilled shrimp, lime cabbage slaw, garlic-jalapeño crema, and cotija cheese. I don't finish my plate because I'm too busy picking off Connor's plate because his are to-die-for. He chose carne asada tacos, overflowing with guacamole and chili corn salsa.

I can't eat another bite, but Mrs. Andersen brings out chocolate covered strawberries in every variety—milk, dark, and white chocolate, salted-caramel chocolate, and more.

I nearly clear them out of the peanut butter and jelly strawberries. It's like they melted chocolate peanut butter cups and dipped the strawberries in the decadent concoction. I jokingly try to bite Connor's fingers off when he tries to take one from me.

I love that Izzy and Reid had no one to impress or anything to prove, and chose the food and desserts they love instead of a giant cake they wouldn't enjoy.

As dessert is wrapping up, Reid crawls beneath the dining table, cracking his head. What in the world? Reid isn't the horse-around type of guy. Izzy giggles, shoving her hands under the table, squirming from whatever he's doing down there.

He bumps his head again on the way up, shoots to his feet and victoriously holds a pink garter above his head. The room fills with hoots and hollers until Reid stretches the garter like a slingshot and points it back and forth between James, Greyson, and Connor. James dives under the table to avoid being shot and Greyson hides behind his daughter, who's laughing like a hyena.

As he shoots the garter, I swear he winks at Connor who jumps out of his seat to catch it like a wide receiver before tumbling back into his seat, nearly taking me down with him.

"I'm saving this for later," he whispers into my ear, goosebumps pepper my arms.

My sister shoots to her feet and shouts, "Let's dance, bitches!" Music plays from hidden speakers, and we make our way from the dining room.

Reid swinging her around the makeshift dancefloor surprises me—he doesn't strike me as a dancing kind of guy. But he'd do anything to make his wife happy, and for that, I'll be eternally grateful to my new brother-in-law.

Greyson has Harper dancing on the tops of his feet, and I nearly melt from how adorable they are. Mr. and Mrs. Andersen slow dance to every song, no matter how fast the beat is, until they turn in for the night.

"You motherfucker. How many times do I have to tell you to keep your hands off my sister?" Greyson barks, chasing James around the small space threatening him within an inch of his life.

Ever the instigator, Olivia started the whole thing and now she's conveniently shuffling Harper down the hall to get her ready for bed, all the while giggling.

"They're going to get caught," Connor whispers. He drags stray hair back from my face and a spark runs down my spine.

I lean back into his chest, and he runs his warm hands from my hips up my ribs until his fingertips tease the sides of my breasts. I gasp from his touch and grind into where his cock is contained by the thin pajama pants. Massive hands tighten around my hips and grip me tightly, halting my movement.

"If I get hard right now, you're taking care of it, doll. Your actions have consequences," he growls into my ear, nipping my earlobe as he pulls away.

Holy shit, he's so sexy.

Very interested in these consequences, I hook my arm around the back of his neck and grind my ass into his hardening cock to the rhythm of the music.

"Does my good girl want to play?" he whispers. "You want to leave your sister's wedding reception early and have everyone know exactly what we're going to do?"

I shiver at his words but grind back into him harder. His hands travel aimlessly along my sides, around my stomach, and up my torso across my breasts to lightly collar my throat.

"Do you want me to fill you up down the hall from everyone we know?" His free hand lowers to my stomach, fingertips trailing the waist of my pajama bottoms. My muscles jump beneath his touch, and he presses tighter into my flesh.

He's impossibly hard. He may be teasing me, but the only way he's leaving this room with his pride intact is if everyone simultaneously looks the other way, or if he uses my body as a human boner-shield.

Deciding two can play at his dirty game, I rest my head on his shoulder and grab his hand to collar my throat. His fingers twitch against my pulse point, and I know I've got him.

"I do want you to fill me up...but not in the hole you've been using," I taunt.

"That's it," he snaps, his head darts around taking inventory of the remaining partygoers.

Izzy and Reid are in their own world dancing, kissing and reveling in wedded bliss. Greyson must've stormed off because he's nowhere to be seen. As a matter of fact, where did James go?

With the bride and groom occupied, Connor spins us around and grips the back of my neck, marching me towards our suite.

I'm so hot for him I might light on fire, and I'd happily burn if it meant he'll touch me.

Connor softly closes the bedroom door behind us and locks it. Now alone, face to face, he prowls towards me. I back away as if he's a fearsome predator and I'm his very willing prey. He backs me up until my legs hit the edge of our bed.

"You want me to fill all your holes, baby? I've already claimed your cunt"—He cups me roughly through the thin flannel pants—"which hole are you offering to me tonight? Your virgin ass? Or your mouth?"

I never pictured myself having anal sex, but now I'm panting for it. Anything for him.

"My mouth. I want you in my mouth. I want to make you feel as good as you do when you lick me," I moan.

"Fuuuuuck, baby. I've been dying to get back inside this hot mouth." He grips my jaw so tightly it drops, opening for him.

He licks into my mouth possessively, with no finesse, only animal need. A whimper rises from my throat when he sucks my tongue into his mouth.

I gently push him backwards and try to drop to my knees as

seductively as I can. His hands grip my biceps and pull me back to standing.

"As much as I love you on your knees for me, there's no way in hell you're sucking my dick without my tongue deep inside your pussy." He reaches over his head, tears off his naughty T-shirt and unties my pajama pants.

"Wh-what? How can I...while you..." I stammer, my face burning with embarrassment from my inexperience.

"Do you trust me?" he asks sincerely.

"With everything I am," I answer honestly.

"Let me show you how good oral can be." I shudder at his intensity.

I scramble out of my shirt and unhook my bra, tossing it across the room. I hook my thumbs into my untied pants and thong and slide them down my legs, snagging my socks as I step out of them.

I crawl onto the bed on my knees and sit on my heels waiting for Connor to strip.

His eyes devour me, taking in every naked detail as he takes off the rest of his clothes. My nipples harden to tight peaks beneath his gaze.

His hard cock bobs between us and I can't wait to take him in my mouth—but he told me to trust him, and I want to do this right.

Connor positions his pillows further down the bed and lays back, his body bared to me like a buffet. I take him in my fist and lick the head of his cock. He bucks into my hold and lets me play with him for only a few strokes.

"Come here," he demands.

I crawl closer to his shoulders before he says, "Turn around."

My brows furrow, and in my moment of hesitation, he slaps my ass. I turn around so I'm facing his feet when he grips me by the waist and drags me to straddle his chest.

"Back up, baby. I want you to sit on my face."

I whip my head around. "You want me to what?"

I know what sixty-nine is...but I've never done it, and my inexperience is showing.

Dragging me backwards by the hips, he situates me exactly where he wants me, with my knees spread indecently wide on either side of his head, and my fluttering pussy above his face.

He pulls me down and spears my center with his tongue. I cry out in surprise and fall to my hands for support. Suddenly, my inexperience is the last thing on my mind.

Connor licks me like his favorite dessert and when I open my eyes, his dick is right in front of my face. I may not have read the book, but I understand the assignment.

Supporting myself with one arm, I fist his cock stroke him firmly. He groans into my pussy, his tongue rimming my entrance.

I've never sucked him off from this direction, but it shouldn't be too different, right? I brace my weight and take him in my mouth, surprised this side of his cock feels different against my tongue.

I take my time exploring and experimenting. I love learning Connor's body. I want to play him like an instrument and make him mindless with pleasure.

It's difficult to concentrate when every flick of his tongue brings me closer to heaven. I hadn't registered my hips were grinding shamelessly into his face, his beard scraping addictively against my clit. I pop off him to catch my breath, saliva trailing from my swollen lips to the head of his cock.

"Baby, oh my god. What are you doing to me? Your beard feels so good." I roll my hips, greedily taking my pleasure from him.

He lifts my pussy off his mouth enough to speak. "I'd live between your legs if I could."

He licks a warm path from my clit to my ass. I jerk away from the sensation, but Connor doesn't let me. He does it again and again until I relax.

I shamelessly ride his mouth, losing myself in pleasure. My blurred vision clears when I see his poor, neglected cock weeping pre-cum.

I want to give Connor the best head of his life, so I suck him between my lips and brace both hands on the bed. I bob on his cock with no regard for the mess dripping down his balls to his taint.

He's so big I gag nearly every downstroke, but I don't care even as tears blur my vision.

The harder I work, Connor amps up his efforts on my pussy. An orgasm hits me like a crashing wave. My legs lock and my pussy spasms against Connor's mouth. The intensity of my pleasure has me sucking his cock relentlessly

"Fuck. Baby, you've gotta stop." Connor pants, jerking a hand to where my mouth sucks his cock, stopping me. "I don't want to come yet."

Delirious from my orgasm, Connor has to roll me off him to my back.

I vaguely process his body position on top of me, but I wake the fuck up when his huge cock slams home, deep inside me.

"Connor, oh my god, you're too big," I moan, squirming away from his monster cock.

"No, doll, it's just right. You were made to be filled by me. Relax for me, baby," he coaxes.

It's always this way. The initial shock of being split in half gives way to mind-bending ecstasy.

"I...can't think. Or...move. Please...use me," I whine.

"Fuuuuuck, Delilah." He's feral and I'm living for it.

"You want me to use you? Use this tight little cunt to get off?"

Each thrust gets harder until I have to tangle my hands in the comforter to stay in the pleasure zone.

"Yes. Use me. Take what you need, please. I want you to come," I beg.

"Jesus christ, I love it when you beg for me. Where do you want me to come? I'm close."

"Come inside me."

Connor stops fucking me instantly. "What? Doll, we haven't talked about kids or anything," he says, softly, but not afraid. My heart warms and I know I made the right decision.

"I got an IUD placed four days ago," I admit. We've been so exhausted from wedding preparations and ranch work, we've barely had time to kiss let alone fuck. His eyes search mine, waiting for more explanation, dick still hard inside me.

"It's copper, so it's effective immediately. It's good for ten years, but if we ever decide we want kids, I can get it taken out."

"Did it hurt?" he asks, combing my sweat drenched hair from my forehead.

I don't want to upset him, but I'll never lie to him. "It did—badly."

He tries to pull out, but I grab his ass keeping him inside me.

"It hurt for a couple of minutes, but now I don't feel anything at all. I promise. I got it because I want all of you. I want you to come inside me," I confess.

"You're so brave, doll. I never would've asked you to do that. You're giving me a gift and I want you to know how amazed I am by you." He kisses me deeply, his thrusts resuming in a slow, sensual drag.

We move as one, his hips snapping faster until sweat beads on his brow.

"I'm getting close again," I whine. Connor tilts his hips and the head of his cock hits that magical place that sets me on fire.

"Come for me, fuck, I can't hold it. COME!" he snaps.

A few more pumps and I fall off the cliff into a slow thrumming orgasm, Connor's hot seed filling me until we're spent.

He collapses on top of me, and I rub my hands across his sweat covered back, kissing his neck reverently.

"I love you so much," I say between kisses.

"You have no idea how much I love you, doll," he says into my shoulder.

We lay in bliss for a few moments until his weight becomes too much for me. He rolls off and scoops me into his arms. He walks us to the enormous en suite and I reach to turn on the shower.

We wash off the wedding, sex, and sweat with lazy hands and indulgent kisses. I feel guilty for missing the end of the wedding reception, but only for a moment—because as Connor wraps his naked body around mine beneath the covers, there's nowhere else I'd rather be.

41

Shit. It's barely past lunch and Delilah's already growing suspicious of my odd behavior. I had to silence my phone because CJ's incessantly texting me. Don't get me wrong, I'm eternally grateful for his help. But would it kill him to type a paragraph before hitting send, instead of sending me thirty small texts to get the point across?

I've "had to use the bathroom" several times already. The group either thinks I have a horrific stomach issue, or an online gambling problem.

I'm returning from one such disappearance when I collide with James, coming out of a bedroom that definitely isn't his. Delilah and I clocked them weeks ago and I'm ready to have a little fun.

"Hey man. What're you doing?" I block his escape route, leaning against the wall.

"Uh...nothing...I mean, I came back here to grab a jacket for Harper," he lies.

I know for a fact Harper's building a snowman down by the lake with Mr. and Mrs. Andersen, and she was bundled up within an inch of her life.

"Oh yea? Where's the jacket?" I motion to his empty hands.

"Shit. I'd forget my ass if it wasn't attached to me," he says but makes no move to go back into the room to get the jacket. Liv must still be in there and he's covering for her.

"I can grab it if you want." I move to walk around him, and he practically shoves me to prevent me from going into Liv and Harper's suite.

"Naw, I've got it. Did, uh, Iz find you? She was looking for you a bit ago," he fumbles.

"No, she didn't. Maybe Liv's with her, Delilah's been looking for her all morning," I lie, and James's face pales. I clap him on the shoulder and turn back for the center of the cabin, chuckling to myself at how fun that was.

I'm searching for Delilah when Reid scares the ever-loving shit out of me.

"You and I need to have a little chat," he says, wrapping his arm around my shoulders, leading me to sit by the fireplace.

"Where's—" I try to ask, but Reid answers like a mind reader.

"Greyson drove the Irish twins to town. More like Greyson needed to run to town and the twins stowed-away, leaving him no choice but to bring them. Don't ask me what they're up to. I have no fuckin' clue. But you're lucky because Delilah started asking questions about why you keep running off, and Greyson may have saved your ass," he says, eyebrow raised pointedly.

It should only be James and Liv left in the cabin, and they're otherwise occupied, so I tell Reid the truth. He's already helped me so much and I've come trust him

I'm going to need someone "on the inside" to cover for me anyway.

"I know you'll tell me to piss off for getting all up in your feelings, but before I tell you, I want you to know I had no intention of stealing attention away from you and Izzy's special day." I raise my hands offering peace.

"Yea, piss off. What's going on?" he asks, crossing his leg, ankle over knee.

"Delilah and I are eloping in the morning." Reid's eyes widen comically.

"But she doesn't know yet..." I hedge.

"Explain," he commands simply, face like stone.

"Hear me out. I've dreamed of marrying Delilah since I was a little kid. She's always been it for me. My parents had the fairy-tale marriage, and even with my dad's Alzheimer's, my mom's love hasn't wavered an inch. When Quincy married Sam, I was so happy for them, but I spent the ceremony imagining it was me and Delilah at the altar. I did the same thing yesterday during your ceremony—sorry man, no offense."

"No offense taken." He waves his hand for me to continue.

"I've waited too long for Delilah to be mine, and yesterday, watching you marry Izzy...I can't wait another day to tie myself to her forever."

"That's great, man. How the fuck are you going to pull that off, though? Is that why you've been sketchy as fuck with your phone all morning?" Reid asks.

"Yea. My friend CJ's planning everything behind the scenes—he's psyched to use his 'gay superpowers'—his words, not mine." I chuckle.

"What do you need from me?" he asks, and I'm blown away by how easily and genuinely he offers his help.

"I need you to keep this between us, and Izzy." Reid raises that eyebrow again, pulled taut by the scarring on his face, making him look menacing even though he's a teddy bear.

"I know, I know. It's a huge ask. I just need you to cover for me until tonight. As soon as we leave, you can tell everyone else for all I care."

He considers this, stroking his beard, clearly displeased I'm asking him to keep secrets from his family.

"Fine. But I ain't lying for you. I'll keep my mouth shut, because that's not out of the ordinary. I'll casually suggest to my mom that she occupy the women today—facials or some shit—then you can get your affairs in order without Delilah noticing you acting weird as fuck."

"Thanks, Reid. I owe you one."

"Two."

"What?" I ask.

"You owe me two favors. At any time, no questions asked," he barters.

I take that deal in a heartbeat, shaking his hand firmly.

"Now, tell me how your farrier training's going," he says.

I relax into the couch, glad to have a momentary distraction from orchestrating the most important moment of my life.

"It's going great. I'm over halfway done with the program. I'll get my certificate around the time Delilah graduates from college."

"And you're liking it?" he asks, genuinely curious.

"I am. It's completely different than the department of transportation, but it feels right, you know?" He nods.

"The program director's linking me up with a local farrier who's willing to be my mentor. They'd come to Lucky Spurs, or I'd travel with them, but they'd provide the hands-on experience I need to confidently care for your horses," I assure.

"Whatever you need. I might be the one paying you, but you're the one doing me, and the ranch, a big favor. Farriers get fuckin' expensive, which is why I jumped at your suggestion to work in-house. Just don't get greedy and figure out how much money you could make flying solo and leave us," he says jokingly, but also dead serious.

"Never. I'm grateful you've welcomed me into your family,

and I'd never jeopardize that. You gave me a fresh start, you saved Delilah's internship, hell, you sold me land to build her the house of her dreams. Lucky Spurs is my home, and I'll give it my blood, sweat, and tears 'til the day I die," I promise.

"Amen to that," Reid says.

The front door opens to Greyson stomping inside, cold air whipping in behind him. The twins stumble in giggling to themselves as usual. I love seeing my doll so happy.

If CJ and I can pull this off, she'll be even happier this time tomorrow.

Izzy rounds the couch, sinking onto Reid's lap, wasting no time sticking her tongue down his eager throat. Delilah mirrors her sister's position and wraps herself around me.

"Hey dollface."

"Hey studmuffin."

"I fucking love when you call me that," I growl into her neck.

She's done it since middle school and it's my contact in her phone, but I've always had to hide how much it turns me on. Not anymore.

I pat her ass to get off my lap and lead her by the hand to our suite. As soon as the door snicks shut, I slam her against it and pounce.

I lose myself in her touch.

Her plush lips opening for me

Her hot tongue sweeping across mine

Her hands in my hair. Fuck.

"I love you so fucking much. Don't leave me like that again," I say before sucking her pulse point.

She giggles. "I just went to the store. We weren't even gone an hour."

"Don't care"—*kiss*—"I want you"—*kiss*—"with me"—*kiss*—"always."

Her laughs turn to moans as my kisses trail down to the swell of her tits. The sweater she's wearing is really doing it for me. I push her tits together, dipping my tongue between them.

"Fuck, I love touching you whenever I want. Sometimes it's still like I'm dreaming," I say into her cleavage.

"I know. I love it. It's everything," she pants.

I bend down and hook my arms under her thighs, picking her up and carrying her to our bed. I crawl on top of the bed with her in my arms and lay her back into the plush mattress.

I dry hump her through our jeans like we're making up for all the times in high school we could've been fumbling around in the back of my truck.

She meets me thrust for thrust, but I freeze when she pulls me down by the front of my shirt and licks up the column of my neck, nipping at my beard.

"I want to ride you," she says, and I nearly come on the spot.

Like in a sitcom, I rip our clothes off unceremoniously until we're contorted and laughing. Her laugh lifts my soul every single time.

I lay on my back and help her straddle me. I tried to play it cool when she told me she got an IUD, but I about lost my mind. I love fucking her bare, but coming inside her was life changing. Something about claiming her fed the animal deep inside me, leaving me more satisfied than I've ever been.

Though the intimate part of our relationship is new, our bodies move as one, as if they'd been doing this all along. She positions me at her entrance and drops down onto my aching cock in one shot.

"Connor," she groans, "I'll never get used to how big you are." And if that isn't the best compliment a man could ever receive, I don't know what is.

I grip her hips, helping her fuck me.

"Yea, doll? You like this fat cock stuffed inside you?" She whimpers, spurring me on.

My good girl likes the dirty talk, and I'm here for it.

"Or is it less about how wide I stretch your cunt, and more about how the tip of my dick kisses your cervix with every thrust?"

Her full-body shudder graces me like a king.

"I love when you talk dirty to me. It turns me on so much, Connor."

"Yea? You also like when I praise you like my good girl." She whimpers, her glorious tits bouncing as she rides me.

Her cunt flutters faintly around my dick. "That's my girl."

The rippling around my dick stops—she's not going to get there in this position. I'll happily accommodate her hungry pussy any way necessary.

I thrust into her hard, holding her down, not letting her escape being full of me.

"I want you on your knees, ass up, face in the bed."

She scrambles to obey, knowing I'll only ever take care of her. Her implicit trust makes the beast inside me roar.

I position myself on my knees behind her upturned ass. I take advantage of her vulnerability and lick from her clit to ass. She screams into the mattress, so I do it again.

"You're so fucking wet for me, baby. But I want you dripping by the time I'm done with you." I spit on my hand and stroke my cock, already wet with her juices.

I grab her hips so tight I'm sure it'll leave fingertip shaped bruises, and pound inside her in one thrust. Her screams are muffled by the comforter, her hands frantically gripping at the fabric for stability.

"Next time you can't come, you fucking tell me." I slap her ass, leaving a beautiful red handprint on her fair skin.

"Don't just go through the motions because you think it's what I want, or I'll punish you." I bring my other hand down on her opposite cheek, creating a stunning red mirror image.

"If this is the punishment, I'll take it," she says between labored breaths.

"You'll take anything I give you like the good girl you are."

"Yes. Anything. I want it," she chants incoherently.

"Rub your clit for me, I want you desperate." She shoves a hand between her legs, and her fingers graze my cock with every swirl over her clit.

Her pussy tremors again—sublime pressure building around my cock.

"Fuck! You're so tight, baby. Milk me dry."

My filthy words are all it takes. Delilah comes so hard her cunt chokes my dick. She's so tight I can barely push inside her with each thrust.

"I'm gonna come." I groan as ropes of my cum paint her insides.

I continue to lazily fuck her until my dick softens, and when I pull out, our combined release drips from her used hole. Possessed, I use two fingers to collect the mess and push it back inside her.

"You killed me," she says, falling to her side.

I drop to the opposite side, facing my wrecked doll. I love seeing her destroyed from my dick as much as I love seeing her thrive under my care. Though, I suppose a proper fucking is a form of care.

"Naw, I wouldn't let you die unless you took me with you. I can't live without you."

As we touch softly and kiss sweetly, I remember I have something to tell her.

"Guess what happened while you were at the store?"

"What?" Her face lights with mischief.

"I caught James sneaking out of Liv's bedroom." Delilah slaps my chest, hard.

"No, you did not!" she whisper-exclaims.

"I did. And I fucked with him a bit to see if he'd confess." I chuckle.

"Did he?"

"No. I figure, let them have their fun before Greyson finds out and murders James and puts him six feet under," I say.

We whisper and laugh, enjoying keeping the secret between us.

Somehow, I manage to get to the evening without blowing my cover and ruining my plans. Reid's been making pointed eye contact with me for the past hour, but I'm waiting for the last text from CJ confirming we're good to go.

My phone buzzes, still on silent, but I wait to check it until Delilah turns the other way. Seeing that the plan is in motion, I make a show of checking my phone and "reading a text."

"Shit," I say louder than necessary, and Reid rolls his eyes.

"One of the ranch hands texted. One of the boarded horses is showing signs of colic and he's not comfortable handling it himself."

Izzy folds into Reid, shellshocked. He dotingly rubs her back.

"Reid, if you're comfortable with it, I'll head back right now and get eyes on the horse," I offer—the lie sweet on my tongue.

"That'd be great. Thanks for letting us enjoy our honeymoon." He kisses Izzy's hand.

"You really don't mind?" Izzy asks, concerned.

"Not at all. Delilah and I can be packed within the hour and hit the road. Should have eyes on the horse just after midnight,"

I say, looking to Delilah for confirmation. Her answer will make or break my entire plan.

"We've got this," she assures her sister.

YES! I shout and fist pump internally. I'm going to pull this off.

We make our rounds hugging everyone and saying our goodbyes before rushing to pack our bags. We're out the door and on the road in a wink.

"Why don't you sleep, doll? We've got a four-hour drive ahead of us and you need to rest," I coax.

She yawns. "Are you sure?"

"Positive." I turn up the heater and lower the stereo volume. My doll drifts to sleep in no time at all.

I check the time and am pleased our "four-hour"—seven-hour—drive is on schedule. I set the GPS and turn off the audio notifications.

Settling in for the long haul, I pray my bladder will hold—I intentionally avoided any liquids the last few hours for this very reason.

In less than twelve hours, the woman of my dreams will be my wife.

42

My sleepy eyes open to blackness, hands flying up to meet silky fabric.

"Morning, dollface," Connor drawls. "Don't take off your blindfold. Trust me. Everything will make sense soon."

It'd better because I'm wildly confused. Did he say it's morning? It should be the middle of the night—the drive home from the Dreamhouse is only four hours. My seatbelt's still across my chest, so we're still in the truck.

Connor's door opens before a strange voice says, "Mr. Hayes, welcome. Here's the item you requested, and your keycards, thank you for checking in early. The bellhop will follow with your bags and the valet will handle your vehicle."

We're at a hotel, a fancy one from the sound of it. My door opens, startling me, and Connor unbuckles my seatbelt. He takes my hand and coaxes me out of the truck.

"Trust me, baby," he says.

He carefully navigates me across asphalt, cobblestones, slick hard flooring, and stops abruptly.

Noises overwhelm me without my sight—conversations, laughing, glasses clinking, the ding of the elevator arriving.

Connor leads me onto the elevator and must press the button to our floor—wherever that is. The elevator stops and Connor takes my hand as we walk across plush carpet.

He lets go of me and the beep tells me he tapped the room key to the door, which he pushes open. My blindfold is gently removed, and I blink from the intrusive lights.

"Connor! What in the world?" I chuckle, as he sweeps me off my feet and carries me bridal style across the threshold of the hotel room. He sets me down, holding me to face him, his back to the door.

"What's going on?" I ask, excitement and nerves bubbling in my stomach.

Connor takes me by the hand and leads me through a stunning hotel suite. The entryway opens into a vast living space, leading to the bedroom and en suite bathroom. He stops us in front of floor-to-ceiling windows.

It takes me a moment to register what I'm seeing. The dazzling lights of the Las Vegas Strip glitter brilliantly in the dark. People meander the street, from businesspeople to drunken bachelors and bachelorettes.

"You brought me to Vegas?" I ask, stunned stupid.

When I turn around for Connor's answer, my heart skips a beat.

He's down on one knee. My hands fly to my face, covering my mouth in shock and tears immediately flood my eyes.

"Baby, don't cry, please. I can't take it." He looks terrified I'm crying so I reassure him.

"They're happy tears, I promise."

He clears his throat, visibly nervous, which I find adorable.

"Delilah, I knew from the moment I found you sitting in the dirt you were something special. My heart was drawn to you like a string connected us, pulling me towards you. I didn't know then the little girl in the pretty yellow dress would become the center of my universe and the reason I breathe."

I'm desperately trying to listen, but my heart's pounding in my ears and I'm sniffling back tears. A voice in my head's shouting *IT'S HAPPENING!*

"I've spent my life loving you, taking care of you, and making big plans. It took us a long time to get here, but I wouldn't change our journey because we ended up where we belong.

"Watching your sister get married broke something inside me—my patience. I'm done waiting to make you mine forever. Delilah Anne Tate, will you do me the great honor of becoming my wife?"

Connor pulls a black box from thin air and opens it, revealing a stunning pale-yellow diamond ring in a white gold, vintage style setting. Beside it rests two matching white gold bands—one small and thin, the other large and wide.

I collapse, falling into him, bowling us backwards on the floor.

"Yes. A million times yes! All I've ever wanted was to marry you, Connor. Yes, I'll marry you!" I say through restrained sobs as he holds me tight and kisses the tears from my face.

"Baby, I promise to be the best husband you could ever dream of," he swears, kissing me firmly on the lips.

A knock at the door ends our moment and Connor helps me up to answer the door. To my surprise, a staff member brings in a packed room service cart, while another wheels in a wide clothing rack full of garment bags, loaded with boxes on the bottom rack.

"Is everything to your liking, Mr. Hayes?"

"Yes, thank you. Everything's on schedule, so please proceed with the itinerary," Connor says, so formally it makes me giggle.

I have so many questions I'm dying to ask, but Connor

must've worked tirelessly organizing everything and I promise myself I'll go with the flow and enjoy any and every surprise he has for me.

"I thought you might be hungry, I know I'm starving." Connor lifts the silver domes from the plates revealing decadent pastries, crisp bacon, and cut melon and berries.

My stomach grumbles, and I take a plate from him and pick through the miniature bakery. Connor pops the cork on a bottle of sparkling cider and fills our glasses.

We sit to eat our lovely breakfast—or midnight snack, I still don't know what time it is—and Connor fills me in a bit more on his grand plans.

"I know you would've done some of this with your sister and Liv, but I wanted today to be about the two of us. I'm the only other one here, so, if you're not superstitious about it, I'll have to help you into your wedding dress," he says, a blush coloring his cheeks.

"My wedding dress?" I ask, hope and excitement rising like helium.

He leads me to the garment rack and explains, "I wasn't sure what you'd want, but I wanted you to have choices." He starts unzipping garment bags and I nearly faint.

"I rented a few different wedding dresses. I hope you like one of them but if you don't, I'll find you whatever you want," he says nervously.

Intricate lace, slippery satin, and wispy chiffon delight my senses as I run my fingers over the delicate fabrics.

I pinch my side to prove I'm not dreaming. This is beyond anything I could've ever imagined and this extraordinary man did it all for me. I can't stop the tears escaping my eyes, but I wipe them away the best I can.

"I love you so much. I would've happily married you in our

normal clothes with a twist-tie ring. This is everything. I can never thank you enough." Connor kisses my forehead, gripping the back of my neck.

"Never thank me. This is less than you deserve—you deserve the world, but I'm honored to give you this," he says.

Hanging on the rack are five dresses, all in an elegant off-white. A classic princess ballgown, a tea length satin slip dress, an ethereal chiffon masterpiece, a fitted mermaid gown, and a backless lace mini dress. The styles are vastly different, but somehow, suit me perfectly. I'm blown away by what Connor's put together for me.

A tiny black bag reveals a delicate white lace thong. None of the dresses require a bra, so I strip naked and slip on the thong.

"Baby, you're killing me, how am I supposed to keep my hands off you?" Connor groans, hands balling into fists at his side.

"You're not, I want your hands on me," I say.

His rough hands skate across my body, leaving goosebumps in their wake. He grows hard in his jeans but doesn't act on it. He simply helps me in and out of the dresses, revering my body with gentle touches.

I revel in playing dress-up, trying on each dress and gleefully twirling in front of the mirrored wall. Each dress is met with compliments that make me blush and want to take them off to do other activities instead.

I surprise myself, and Connor, by choosing the backless lace mini dress. It makes me feel delicate and feminine, while sexy and confident. The halter-top drapes elegantly, showcasing my cleavage and is fitted to my waist, baring my shoulders and back. It hangs perfectly to mid-thigh, like it was made specifically for me.

Connor's deft fingers carefully zip the dress, from my butt to the small of my back.

He gathers my hair over my shoulder and marks me with kisses on the exposed skin of my neck. His beard scratches, heating my blood.

A swift slap to the ass sends me on my way, high on his adoration.

As I twirl in the mirror, loving my wedding dress, Connor brings five shoe boxes to the sofa for me to choose from. I pluck a strawberry from the room service tray and delight in the sweet tang on my tongue.

I laugh in glee at the shoes Connor's arranged for me. The open boxes showcase bedazzled white Chuck Taylors, ballet flats, strappy heels, classic pumps, and an impossibly beautiful pair of cowboy boots.

I don't bother trying on the other shoes because I know exactly what I want.

The boots are a delicate snip toe with a slightly higher heel, in light tan leather. Intricate white leather and stitching adorns the boot as if it's draped in lace. My fingers reverently graze the crystals studded into the design.

"They're yours, baby. I didn't think we needed to buy the dress—I mean, I will in a heartbeat if you want to keep it—but I intended on buying whatever shoes you chose along with these boots. They were yours the moment I saw them."

Connor motions for me to sit on the couch and he gets down on his knees, rolling soft white wool socks up my calves, and slips my feet into the boots like I'm Cinderella. He helps me to my feet, and I admire myself in the mirror.

"You look incredible, doll. I can't wait to marry you," Connor says, kissing my beard-burned shoulder, already sensitive to his touch.

"Would you like to choose your jewelry?" he asks.

"My goodness, you thought of everything, didn't you?" I chuckle in disbelief.

He opens a jewelry case revealing pearls, glimmering precious metals, flashy jewels, and a ribbon choker. To his surprise, I choose nothing. When he balks, I explain.

"I want to marry you with only my sun necklace and my engagement ring."

"You can have whatever you want, baby," he assures.

"I know, but all I want is what you gave me." I hold up my left hand, obsessed with my ring, and pinch the worn sun between my fingers with my right.

Another knock at the door unveils a beautician here to do my hair and makeup. Connor steps out to get dressed and she gets to work.

I opt to keep my hair down, pinned behind one ear, so she irons it flat until it shines like silk. She keeps my makeup natural, but glams me up with a smoky eye, something seductive and more than I do myself. The lovely woman packs up and wishes me a long and happy marriage.

Boots thud behind me and I turn to see the man of my dreams looking like he stepped out of a wet dream.

Connor's wearing a three-piece black tuxedo with a white pearl snap adorned with an elegant bolo tie, cowboy boots shined within an inch of their life, and atop his head sits a white cowboy hat.

I've died and gone to heaven. Suddenly I wish the wedding would hurry up and be finished so I can show this man just how *appreciative* of him I am.

"You really know how to stroke my ego." Connor chuckles as my eyes greedily drink him in.

"You're unbelievably sexy, Connor. How did I get so lucky?" I purr, running my fingers along the lapels of his tux.

"I'm the lucky one, dollface. Have you looked in a mirror today?" he jokes.

Connor checks the time. The faintest glow of orange crests over the glamourous buildings on the strip. Getting married at sunrise will be unforgettable.

I'll never stop thanking him for this gift.

43

"Connor!" I exclaim as he leads me by the hand to a white limousine waiting at the valet.

"I've always wanted to ride in a limo." The smooth leather seats are cool beneath my bare thighs and palms.

"I know," Connor says, sliding in beside me, engulfing my knee with his warm hand.

Never having been outside of Colorado, let alone to Las Vegas, I'm spellbound by the neon lights glowing beneath the fading stars, as night melts into morning.

A squeeze to my knee brings my attention back to the incredible man next to me—my fiancé. *Oh my god! Connor Hayes is my fiancé!*

"Do you want to ask where we're going?"

"Not even a little bit," I say honestly. "I don't want to ruin a single moment of what you've put together for me."

I rest my head on his shoulder, careful not to get makeup on his pristine tux. The drive is short and soon we've come to a stop on the notorious Vegas Strip. The limo driver opens Connors door, and he steps out, offering his hand for me to join him.

Dark surrenders to light as the sun teases the sky. Rich navy blue dotted with glitter blankets the heavens, fading to dusty purple as night gives way to morning. Lavender and rose shimmer above the faintest coral kissing the horizon.

"Mr. Hayes, right on time. This must be the lovely Miss Tate," the kind woman says. "We're delighted to perform your ceremony this morning. Please, come with me."

I'm in awe he organized this. I have so much I want to know, but now isn't the time to feed my curiosity. Living in this moment will fuel me for the rest of my days, and I'm determined to memorize it all.

Connor crooks his elbow for me to link my arm through, and we follow the woman into the adorably themed chapel. Iconic scenes flood my memory, like when Mr. Rachel marries Mrs. Ross covered in permanent marker. My smile's so wide my cheeks ache.

This is the best day of my life.

"As discussed, the Sunrise Promise Package includes exclusive use of the outdoor garden ceremony space, music, an officiant, your marriage license, and a photographer. After you say, 'I do,' we'll bring out the cake you requested, and you'll have your first dance. Then you'll ride into the sunrise happily ever after as Mr. and Mrs. Hayes!"

Goosebumps cover every inch of my body hearing *Mr. and Mrs. Hayes.*

It's something I've always dreamed of but never dared wish I'd have.

The woman ushers us through the chapel to the outdoor space, and the pinks and oranges of daybreak are already battling the darkness of the night before.

My bridal cowboy boots clack softly across the flagstone in harmony with Connor's, echoing in the quiet morning.

We stop several paces from an older man dressed in a suit

standing in a charming white gazebo. A carousel-like roof is supported by fluted columns, over a matching flagstone base.

Movement from the shrubbery catches my attention.

"Izzy?" I cry, tears already welling in my eyes.

My Irish twin, best friend and partner in crime for life, is miraculously standing before me in Las Vegas, the morning after her wedding.

"Don't cry twinie! You'll ruin your makeup." Izzy wraps me in her arms, and I try to calm myself while she rubs my back.

I peek over her shoulder at Connor, a serene smile painted on his gorgeous face. *How did he pull this off?*

"Did someone order a Best Man?" Izzy releases me as I do a one-eighty to find CJ waltzing into the space like he owns it.

"You look exquisite, Delilah. Absolute perfection. Wouldn't change a thing." He kisses me on the cheek on his way to stand beside Connor.

They share a bro-hug with lots of back slaps and exchange words I can't hear. Connor hands his cowboy hat to CJ and smooths back his hair.

My sister leaves me to stand beside CJ, who extends his elbow for her to hold.

"Absolutely stunning, Mrs. Matron of Honor," CJ croons to Izzy, who playfully rolls her eyes at him.

Connor's warm hand sweeps the hair off my back, cupping the back of my neck in his safe hold.

"Stay right here, doll."

Soft music plays through the space, making it even more ethereal.

I'm rooted to the spot as my fiancé enters the gazebo. CJ escorts Izzy in as well, him standing beside Connor, and Izzy standing opposite next to the spot that I will fill.

Her eyes sparkle, but not at me—behind me. A calloused hand gently cups my shoulder.

"Reid?" Of course he'd follow his new wife to Vegas, I shouldn't be surprised he's here.

"Are you here to be a groomsman?" I chuckle. Looking all around for Olivia to pop out an announce herself as a bridesmaid.

"No." He stands in front of me, commanding my full attention.

"Every girl deserves the opportunity to be walked down the aisle by someone important to them. If you'll allow me, I'd be honored to give you away, Delilah."

I fan my face, tears dangerously close to spilling past my lashes. I haven't had a dad in a decade, and no one ever filled his shoes. Mr. Andersen's been like a new father to Izzy, and poor Connor, his dad is fading before our eyes.

But Reid, he's taken Connor under his wing at the ranch, mentoring him and becoming close friends. I love him for my sister, and he's always treated me like family.

"I'd love that," I manage to answer through my tight throat.

Reid turns to stand beside me, holds up a bent arm, which I loop my hand through to rest on his forearm.

We take the few steps into the gazebo and instead of standing beside CJ, Reid comes to stand behind Izzy, wrapping her in his arms.

How are they here, doing this for us, instead of celebrating their nuptials from yesterday?

"Mr. Hayes, pleasure," the officiant drawls, shaking Connor's outstretched hand.

"Miss Tate, lovely to meet you," he says, kissing the back of my hand.

Connor's less than pleased and possessively wraps his arm around my waist, tugging me closer to him.

I secretly love it, being cherished and fiercely protected.

The officiant steps back, a knowing gleam in his eye, resuming his post. "Are we ready to get married?"

"You sure about this, doll? Once you're mine, I'm never letting you go."

"I've never been so sure about anything in my life. I've always been yours," I promise.

"Please, stand here for the photographer and join hands." I forgot about the photographer. Glee bubbles inside me at the promise of our day memorialized in photographs. I chuckle at the "X's" taped to the flagstone marking our places.

Connor takes my hands, his thumbs soothing me, any nerves melt away at his touch.

The morning sky is brightening more by the minute, the oranges, pinks, and purples blending into the lightening blue sky. The rising sun creates an ethereal glow over the garden.

I couldn't have planned a more perfect wedding.

"We're gathered here, with this sunrise as our witness, to celebrate the union of Connor and Delilah. Today, we affirm your bond, uniting you as husband and wife."

Connor squeezes my hand, and I beam at him—looking just as excited as me, a glimmer of the boy who I fell for all those years ago.

"Connor, when you're ready..." the officiant leads.

Connor's Adam's apple bobs with a thick gulp, the only hint of his nerves showing.

"I've never doubted the existence of soulmates, because I found mine when I was eight years old. I was riding my bike, and I rode farther than I was supposed to, because something was telling me to keep going. I know now, the heartstring that connects us was pulling me forward to find you. I found a little doll sitting in the dirt in her pretty yellow dress, like an angel fallen from the sky, changing my life for the better.

"From that moment on, I've had a steadfast best friend who

quickly became the love of my life. You're it for me, Delilah, you always have been. Life took us on a winding path to get here, but all that matters is you're standing here with me, and I'm eternally grateful you've chosen me to be your husband. I wanted to marry you at sunrise because you are my sunshine, the light of my life. I promise to love and protect you until my last breath. *As sure as I live, this love that I give, is gonna be yours until the day that I die.*"

Through the happiest of tears pouring down my face, I reply, "*Oh baby, I'm gonna love you forever.*"

"*Forever and ever, amen,*" Connor finishes.

I can't help it—I'm kissing him before my next heartbeat.

The officiant wipes a tear from the corner of his eye before continuing.

"Delilah, if you have anything you'd like to say to Connor..."

A rush of nerves hits—I'm completely unprepared for this moment. But Connor's loving expression tells me whatever I say will be perfect, and I relax.

"This has been the most unexpected, magical day of my life. I always dreamed of becoming Mrs. Connor Hayes, but I never dared hope it would come true. You've been my hero since the day you found me—a broken little girl who needed you more than you'll ever know. Wherever you were is where I wanted to be. The connection between us is something from a fairytale—I was destined to be yours, and you mine.

"I love you for your unwavering loyalty, your integrity, and fierce protectiveness. I love you in the big ways that make you the remarkable man you are, but also in the quiet ways. The way you look at me like I'm the only person in the world. The way you always find me in a crowded room, because our hearts are strung together. The way you stand behind me and give me the confidence to follow my dreams. I've never wanted to be anything more than I want to be your wife. I promise to devote my life to giving you the love you deserve."

Connor sniffs, holding back tears. His quivering lip makes me love him more than ever.

I whisper, "I love you, baby."

The officiant clears his throat, drawing our attention from our little world back to the sun-brightened gazebo.

"Connor, do you take Delilah to be your lawfully wedded wife? To cherish, honor, and love, in sickness and in health, in seasons of plenty and in seasons of need, and to be true to her in all things as long as you both shall live?"

"I do." The heartstring binding us glows golden in the sunlight.

"Delilah, do you take Connor to be your lawfully wedded husband? To cherish, honor, and love, in sickness and in health, in seasons of plenty and in seasons of need, and to be true to him in all things as long as you both shall live?"

"I do." The golden heartstring solidifies into unbreakable, unbendable steel, binding us together, forever.

"You've chosen to exchange rings as a symbol of your unending love. As you place this ring on your love's finger, please repeat after me," the officiant says.

Connor takes the ring box from his pocket and hands me his thick band and holds my thin band between his fingers.

He takes my left hand in his and vows, "With this ring, I choose you through all the changes life may bring us."

The band slides onto my finger, nestling perfectly against my engagement ring.

Our hands dance, shifting for me to hold his left hand between mine. "With this ring, I choose you through all the changes life may bring us."

I place the ring on his finger and my heart skips at how much I love seeing him wearing proof of our commitment.

"By the power vested in me by the state of Nevada, I now pronounce you husband and wife. You may kiss your bride."

Time stops, and in the split-second day overtakes night, Connor slides one hand up my neck and clasps our left hands together between us. I grab onto his shoulder for dear life and our lips meet. His kiss heals every broken piece inside me and promises a lifetime of love and joy, beneath the perfect sunrise.

"I love you, Delilah."

"I love you too, Connor."

We move to a small podium and sign our marriage license, and for the first time, I sign my name *Delilah Anne Hayes*. CJ and the newly minted Isabelle Andersen sign as our witnesses and relief floods my body as the last thread to my parents is cut—never again will I be a Tate.

The photographer ushers us to begin our first dance as a married couple. I laugh with delight as our song plays from hidden speakers. He places his cowboy hat on my head and gives it a little tip-up with his knuckles to see my face. We slow dance, no one to impress, nothing to prove—to none other than the great Randy Travis.

"You're mine, baby, forever and ever."

He presses the sweetest kiss to my lips before I whisper, "amen."

Izzy and Reid slow dance in the shadows, giving us our moment.

CJ gives the photographer a run for his money, snapping pictures on his phone for us.

Our song ends, and we're led back inside the chapel to cut our cake. Airy, sweet lemon crumb is the perfect complement to the tart lemon frosting.

"Mmm! My favorite. Connor, you really did all of this?" I ask, devouring my slice of wedding cake.

"Of course I did, dollface. I've been thinking about this day for a long time. I wouldn't settle for anything less than perfection for my wife." He playfully licks a smear of frosting from the corner of my mouth.

I shiver, both from the wet heat of his tongue, and from being called his wife.

The woman from the chapel boxes the rest of our small cake and kindly escorts us out with our paperwork and instructions on how to get our photos.

Izzy's hand finds mine and gives me a squeeze.

"I'm so glad you came," I say

"Wouldn't miss it for the world."

Reid wraps his arm around her shoulders and tips his head to a car waiting in the valet.

"Livy's going to have a conniption she wasn't here." I cringe.

"We've got it covered. Don't stress about it for a single second," Reid assures.

"Time to get back to our own honeymoon," Izzy says with a wink.

Connor shakes Reid's hand, and hugs CJ goodbye.

Three of the most important people in our lives get into the car to presumably head back to the airport to return to Colorado.

Only half an hour has passed since we stepped out of the limo, and in that short time, everything has changed.

Our limo pulls away from the chapel and we have our first private moment as husband and wife.

I straddle Connor's lap and crash my lips to his. His throaty laugh sends vibrations to my core. I kiss his neck, unknotting his tie, unbuttoning his shirt, and trailing kisses onto his chest.

"Baby, what are you doing?" Connor groans but doesn't stop me.

I wrench his clothes aside to reveal the sun tattooed on his pec. I trace it reverently with my tongue, overflowing with love because he got this tattoo for me years ago, years before he knew I loved him back.

"I love you so much, Connor. I can't find the words. I need you." I'm burning up and need him inside me. He thickens in his pants and shamelessly grinds me down onto him.

"We'll be in our hotel room in a few minutes, and you're going to take your husband's cock into this tight little cunt." I moan at the delicious friction between my legs.

The rest of the drive passes with heated promises and sparks of incomplete orgasms. By the time we get to our room, I'm feral for him.

Connor carries me across the threshold to our marital bed. As soon as he sets me down, I'm on him. I carefully set his cowboy hat on the nightstand before I ravish my new husband.

We kiss and hump like teenagers, and it's hotter and more fun than I could've dreamed. Laughter fills our suite as we fumble out of our boots. I unwrap him from his tuxedo and he takes his time peeling me out of my wedding dress.

Connor lays on his stomach and shoves his shoulders between my thighs, holding me open for him. He licks me through my lace thong, soaked with my arousal.

Nothing will ever be better than this—having the man of my dreams, the love of my life, my husband, bathing me in pleasure.

"Sorry doll, I hope you didn't like these too much," Connor says as he rips the delicate lace from my body and discards it on the floor.

His tongue spears inside me, and I go delirious the same way I always do when his mouth makes love to me. I'm already close from dry humping him in the limo and on the bed, so when his beard scrapes my inner thighs as he sucks my clit into his mouth, penetrating me with two thick fingers, I come.

I'm shaking in the aftermath of my explosive orgasm as

Connor kneels between my legs, trailing wet kisses up my belly and across my breasts. I need him inside me, now.

"Fuck me, husband." Connor's pupils blow, his chocolate eyes going molten with lust.

He fists his cock and smears the pre-cum from his slit down his length. He knows how much I love watching him touch himself.

"You want your husband to fuck you, baby?" He notches at my entrance. "Does my wife need her husband's cock deep inside her?" The tip of his cock breaches my hole, and I tighten around it involuntarily.

"I need my husband's cock. Please, baby. I need you," I beg.

He slides into me achingly slowly, in halfway and back to the tip until I'm delirious.

"My wife," Connor growls as he punches his hips forward, filling me completely.

"Yes!" I cry.

"You're my wife." *Thrust.* "Mine." *Thrust.* "Say it," he demands.

"I'm your wife." *Thrust.* "Yours." *Thrust.* "Always yours." I whimper.

Primal need radiates from him, instinct taking over as he fucks into me with abandon.

"And what am I, baby? Who am I?" he taunts.

"My husband." His thrusts becomes erratic, and I know he's close.

"You're my husband. You're mine." I moan, grabbing his tight ass to pull him deeper, my nails digging into his flesh.

"Fuuuuuck," he groans, spilling into me. My pussy ripples around him as I ride out my second orgasm, leaving me twitching in the letdown.

He rolls off but takes me with him, so I'm sprawled across his chest. We lay together, our labored breaths the perfect soundtrack to this day.

"So, there was no horse emergency at the ranch?" I joke.

His laugh rumbles beneath my palm. "No there wasn't. Reid was a great wingman and doesn't expect us back until after the weekend. I've got you all to myself in this hotel for two more days. I know it's not much of a honeymoon but—"

I cut him off. "This is everything, Connor. This is more than I ever dreamed of. Everything was perfect. I wouldn't change a thing."

"I'm so glad you're happy, doll. It's been a rollercoaster to get us here." He chuckles.

"Fess up, mister. I want to know how you pulled all this off," I say, impressed and still in disbelief this is real.

"I promise I'll answer every single question you've got, but first, let's order some room service and take a shower." He squeezes my ass and slaps it with a loud pop, making me squeal and squirm off him, racing me to the shower.

Soft cotton billows around me as I nestle in to the comforter, reveling in post-consummation bliss. Connor's fine ass waltzes across the suite to get the room service menu and I drool over his half-hard cock hanging heavy between his legs as he returns.

"Breakfast or lunch?" he asks.

It's not even eight a.m., but we ate breakfast in the middle of the night.

"Both." I happily reply.

And together, we cuddle in bed, order enough food to feed an army, and enjoy each other's bodies until we pass out in each other's arms—as husband and wife.

44

"You did not!" my new wife exclaims, her uncontrollable giggling shaking the bed.

"I did. I tripped James when he was carrying the French toast to the table."

Delilah's laughter makes me feel a hundred feet tall.

"CJ wouldn't stop texting me wedding dress pictures and when I told him we were having breakfast, he said if I ignored him, he'd choose for me. He has good taste, but I wanted to pick the choices you'd have. I panicked. I needed to get away from the group for a decent amount of time. So, when James came out carrying a plate loaded with French toast drenched in syrup in one hand, and the powdered sugar duster in the other, I took my chance."

Delilah slaps my chest, and I hold her hand against me, admiring her wedding rings.

"It took us an hour to get that mess cleaned up, Connor! Mr. and Mrs. Andersen played it cool, but I overheard her squealing about their star property being infested with ants because of the sugar," she explains.

It was an impulsive decision, but 100 percent worth it,

because during that hour, I hid in the walk-in closet of our suite, carefully examining dress after dress CJ was sending me. I know more about the differences between tulle, organza, and chiffon than I'll ever admit.

Did you know there's a heated debate over whether a wedding dress should be pure white, off-white, or ivory? They all look the fucking same to me.

I turn to my beautiful wife—I can't believe she's finally my wife—radiating with joy.

"You're not kidding are you?" she asks. "You handpicked every detail?"

"Down to the size of the icing rosettes on the wedding cake." I groan internally, because licking lemon frosting off my new wife's bare tits not even an hour after we said "I do" was fucking unbelievable.

Lemon's always been her favorite, and because I love anything to do with Delilah, it quickly became a favorite of mine as well. I can't see, smell, or taste lemon without thinking of her smiling face.

She snuggles closer into my side, tracing the patterns of my tattoos with her fingertip.

"I assumed CJ had more creative control of everything," she says.

"CJ was a great wingman, but they were my ideas and decisions. He took care of the phone calls, emails, rental agreements, payments, reservations—all the things that would take time and privacy I didn't have."

My stomach dips when she traces over my abs, an enticing tickle drawing to my center.

"We owe him big time," Delilah says.

"I sure do but you don't owe him a thing, doll." I chuckle.

"What does he want?" she asks, knowing CJ can be diabolical when he wants to be.

I groan and cover my eyes with my arm. "He gets to pick my next tattoo. Image and placement..."

"Nooooo..."

"Yes," I say, peeking out from beneath my arm.

"Please tell me he's over what happened in eighth grade, and that your face is off limits..." Delilah whines.

"CJ thinks face tattoos are—and I quote—*so 2018*. Thank god. But no, he's not over the incident. We should start getting used to the idea of a Taylor Swift tattoo on my ass..."

He's never forgiven me for stealing his phone when he was the next caller to win Taylor Swift tickets on the radio.

Delilah groans playfully.

Of course, my sunshine wouldn't make a big deal of me unwillingly getting another woman's face tattooed on my bare ass.

"Can we not talk about this anymore, it's making me nauseous," I joke.

A knock at the door saves me from my humiliation and I pop out of bed to answer it. I don't give a shit if some delivery kid sees me without a shirt on. But I'm sure as hell not letting them see an inch of Delilah's bare skin, laying in our bed in a tank top and panties.

"Thanks, man." I tip the kid and lock the door behind me.

I snag two plates from the kitchen and a stack of paper napkins.

Delilah happy-claps as I enter the bedroom, carrying the pizza box like a butler.

"M'lady," I say, bowing.

We prop the pillows against the headboard and open the box on the comforter. I dish up a steaming slice of meat lovers for my wife, and two for me.

I open a container of ranch for her to dip her pizza in, just the way she likes, and drizzle buffalo sauce all over mine.

"Cheers," Delilah says, gingerly holding her slice out to me.

"Cheers, doll." I clink my slice with hers and we dig in.

We chat between bites of pizza and enjoy our time together.

Delilah sucks the dregs from her lemonade, and I refill it out of habit. Climbing back into bed, she licks her fingers and hands me her plate. I stack it onto mine and set them and the pizza box on the floor.

We snuggle deep into the covers—perfectly content to relax like this. We've been fucking like rabbits, but moments like this are just as intimate and a calming time to connect.

"Marrying you is my dream come true, Connor." She gazes up at me with those crystalline eyes. "What do your dreams look like?"

I huff a laugh, because I'm holding it in my arms.

"You, baby. You're my dream. You, always," I answer. A sweet blush graces the apples of her cheeks.

"I mean, what else? What happens now? Our adventure's just beginning."

I pull her to sit astride me, her creamy thighs bracketing my hips, tiny little panties barely covering her cunt, tank top barely restraining her glorious tits.

"You go first. Tell me what your dreams look like," I prompt, because I want to craft my answer based on what she says.

She gives the cutest wiggle, and I have to will my dick to mind its fucking business.

"Well, in my perfect world, in the perfect life, I'd have you by my side." I pinch her ass to say, *obviously*.

"My mom would be healthy, and we'd have a good relationship—Izzy too—and my dad would come back and apologize for ever leaving us and make it up to us by being a better man."

My heart aches for my fallen angel. Of all the things I'd kill myself to give her, fixing her parents isn't in the realm of possibilities. The wistfulness on her face guts me, because I desperately wish her parents loved her and Iz the way they deserve. The stars fade from her eyes as she comes back to reality.

"We'd live in the white house with the blue door—you know, the one by the library?" she asks. Of course I know, and it's killing me keeping so many secrets from her.

"It'd always have a crisp coat of paint on it and the blue door would never peel. We'd fix the picket fence and sit on the front porch drinking your mom's lemonade, watching the patrons enjoy the library."

She's so pure of heart. I must've done something right in a past life to deserve her.

I can't remember the last time mom made lemonade—not since Dad's condition worsened. *Did Quincy ever make it for Sam?*

"What else?" I ask, hoping she'll continue.

"I'd love my job as an equine therapist and build a renowned program at Lucky Spurs Ranch that would make Reid and his family proud. You'd be a sought-after farrier, and we'd spend our days working at the ranch, nuzzling the horses and eating lunch together under the big shady trees.

"I'd see Izzy and Livy most days, since the ranch is the place that brings us all together. We'd have Sunday dinner with the Andersens and watch Harper grow up. Hope—the paint horse Reid rescued—would be mine."

That's news to me. I knew she loved the damn thing, not that she wanted it for her own. I'll be having a chat with Reid as soon as we get home to make that happen for my wife.

I rub my hands up and down her thighs, covered in goosebumps from the slight chill.

"Harper's a sweetheart," I say. "How do you feel about kids? In all these years, I don't think we've ever talked about it."

"It's not something I ever allowed myself to want. Growing up like me and Izzy did doesn't exactly make me want to bring kids into this world—even if I'd never treat a child the way we were treated. I would've only wanted to have kids with you, and I never thought I'd get to have you," she admits.

"You've got me, doll. Forever and ever."

"What about you?" she deflects.

"I've never specifically wanted kids for the sake of having kids. But I guess I've always imagined my life with the house and the dog and the kids. Like you, I only ever wanted to do this life with you—so I only want to have kids if you want to have kids."

Uncomfortable, she twiddles with the ties on my athletic shorts.

"What if I never want to have kids?" she asks, not meeting my eyes. I lift her chin to force her to look at me.

"Then we don't have kids. It's that simple. *You* are my dream, baby. So long as I have you, I don't need anything else. We're a family, you and me. We don't need anyone or anything else to be complete." Tears shine in her diamond eyes, and she gives me a soft smile.

"What does your dream life look like?" Delilah asks.

Little does she know my dream life is exactly this. Pizza in bed with my soulmate.

"My dream life is yours, baby. I'm only happy if you're happy," I answer honestly.

"Come on, that's a cop out." Delilah smacks my chest playfully.

I chuckle. "Alright, fine. My dream life looks like yours. We live together in the house of our dreams. We both have jobs we're passionate about. We work and enjoy life with the family we've found—us, Quincy, Iz and Reid, Liv, James, Grey and Harper, Mr. and Mrs. Andersen...my folks." I gulp, hit with grief from losing my dad while he's still alive.

"My dad would be better, and my mom could relax. Quincy would be happy again, maybe find love again." Delilah wipes a stray tear from my eye.

"I wish that for her too," she says quietly.

I gently pat her ass, motioning for her to hop off my lap. Sex is suddenly the last thing on my mind. She cuddles in to me like every night and I turn off the lamp. We lay in silence, soaking in comfort from each other.

"I love you, Connor," Delilah says, tipping her head up for a goodnight kiss.

"I love you, doll." I kiss her back tenderly.

It's not long before she falls asleep. I lay awake for a long while, replaying her wishes for her dream life and know I can accomplish most of them.

We've got the marriage and the found family. Our jobs are in the works—it's a matter of time before we've both got fulfilling careers at the ranch. I'm building her the house of her dreams, to replace the one I couldn't buy her. The money I worked to the bone for is going to good use to make her dreams come true. Some of that cash now earmarked for buying her the horse she's fallen in love with.

I find sleep in the blackest hours of the night, at peace knowing I'm making my wife's dreams come true.

45

I'm so close to graduating, I can taste it, but it tastes like ash because I'm so stressed I'm imploding. If it weren't for daily orgasms from my husband, I might've jumped into the Whitetail River and let it carry me away.

Instead of living in newlywedded bliss, I'm a basket case. Of course, Connor's the best husband in the world because he's unfailingly patient and does everything possible to help me—even while finishing his own program and taking on additional responsibilities at the ranch.

I suppose it's timely since my lesson today with Tanya and Biscuit is about emotional regulation. I've studied until my eyes crossed, but I'm anxious to work on it in person.

Crunching gravel alerts me that Tanya's arrived with my best buddy Biscuit in tow. I help back her in and get Biscuit unloaded. She gets him comfortable as we chat about our last lesson, and what to expect today.

"Now remember the belly breathing we've been practicing. You've been practicing, right?" Tanya asks.

"Yes, I have. I'm an expert at this point." I chuckle.

I practice every chance I get. Focusing inward is a challenge, especially when the pressures of the world are so loud.

"Alright, let's move on to desensitization."

Oh, dear god. I wasn't prepared for this. I thought we'd spend the session practicing mirroring. Biscuit snorts, backing up slightly, flicking his ears back and forth—picking up on my anxiety. It's fascinating how in-tuned he is to the slightest emotional shifts.

"No use in fretting, darlin'." Tanya pulls out a crisp windbreaker and pops it open.

I jolt at the sudden sound, and Biscuit retreats a step, tugging on the lead held tightly in my hand. Immediately guilty for upsetting him with my reaction, I take some belly breaths and do my best to center myself.

"Now, I'm gonna walk around like I'm checking the fence. You're gonna do your best not to react. It's natural for you to anticipate his anxiety, which ratches up your anxiety—and that's what'll make him nervous—your energy, not me moving around in the jacket."

The windbreaker swishes and crinkles as Tanya takes exaggerated steps along the fence line. My stomach's flipping because I'm afraid Biscuit will spook, and on schedule, his head rises and nostrils flare. I'm gripping his lead so tight, my knuckles are white.

I relax my hold and loosen my stance, doing my best to act like there's nothing special going on. Biscuit relaxes a fraction, his energy soothing my own, harmoniously flowing between our bodies.

Tanya brushes her hands down the windbreaker loudly and my eyes flick to her, but my body and respiration stays calm. Biscuit flicks his ear but otherwise remains still.

By the end of the session, Tanya's running around like a lunatic, flapping her arms, rustling the windbreaker like crazy.

So long as I stay calm and don't react, Biscuit doesn't give two shits what's going on.

A joyous laugh bubbles up my throat, and I'm thrilled Biscuit remains calm, only a flick of an ear, because he senses my happiness.

"Great job today, darlin'. Looking inward and becoming more attuned to your own emotional shifts will do you wonders in this field. Practice that on top of your other skills until our next session. You're getting real close to graduating. Keep up the good work," Tanya praises.

As her trailer disappears over the hill, warm arms wrap around me, and I melt into Connor's hold.

"Wife." His deep rumble floods my skin with goosebumps.

"Husband," I reply, tilting my head for an upside-down kiss.

I turn and drink him in. He's positively edible today decked out for a day in the stables.

Those goddamn Wranglers hug his thighs and ass so perfectly I'm jealous the denim's touching him so intimately. His cowboy boots are caked with dried mud—I'll have to give them a clean tonight so he can relax. Leather gloves hang from his back pocket, and soft flannel is pushed up to his elbows beneath a new quilted vest.

A worn Broncos cap covers his golden hair from the sunlight and I'm about ready to drag him into a stall and get on my knees for him.

"How was your session? Looked like Tanya was trying to attract a partner to mate with." He chuckles. I love his laugh.

"It was great. We were working on me staying calm in the chaos, because Biscuit senses my anxiety and if I panic, he panics. But since I acted like I didn't care about Tanya's flapping, Biscuit didn't care either. It's like he and I were sharing a brain and a heart. The way he mirrors me is mind blowing."

He pulls me in with an arm hooked around my neck, kissing

my forehead with a loud smack. "I'm so proud of you, doll. You're going to be great at this."

His faith in me means everything, though I have imposter syndrome out the ass and want to crawl in a hole at least twice a day.

"What's on tap the rest of the day, baby? I'm done at the stables. I need to take a shower before class." He holds me tighter. "Wanna join?"

I laugh. "You know how much I like getting clean before we get dirty."

He sweeps me into his arms and jogs the entire way to the truck.

We're about to get very, very clean.

Reid and Tanya arranged for me to go to an equine therapy workshop in Fort Collins, and I was able to register for the breakout sessions I wanted. The workshop was transformative—two days learning how equine-assisted therapy can be life changing for people struggling with their mental health.

Connor had in-person classes for his farrier program, so Reid suggested Izzy go with me. We had such a great time exploring the city and having sister-time. Everything was perfect, until it wasn't.

I attend a session the second day hosted by a renowned equine-assisted psychotherapist. She's brilliant and will no doubt be revolutionary in the field.

Someone asked an innocuous question about what she had to do to get where she was in her career, and her answer pulled the rug out from under my feet.

My head swam in a torrential storm as she detailed everything that must happen after graduating with a bachelor's degree. Two to three years to get a master's degree, thousands of supervised clinical hours, licensure exam, state application for licensing, and ultimately getting certified in equine-assisted therapy.

I'm not naïve, I knew equine therapy was more than leading a horse around a pen—but no one ever spelled out the additional years of schooling, clinical hours, and legalities. Maybe I missed it because I homed in on this specialty so late in my degree program, or maybe I assumed I only needed a master's degree if I wanted to be a psychologist or social worker...

After all this time, I felt like I found my passion, where I belong, my chance to make a difference—and now it feels impossible.

I left the session nearly catatonic and when Izzy picked me up, she nearly took me to the emergency room for how listless I was. I numbly told her what I'd learned in that last session, and how my future's destroyed.

I wanted to drive home immediately. Izzy tried to convince me to get some dinner in my stomach and get a good night's sleep before we made the drive home, but I insisted. She only agreed after I promised to eat dinner in the car.

I managed half a chicken burrito before I couldn't eat any more. We spent the drive in comfortable silence—my sister never prodding or prying—just letting me sit with my feelings in a safe space.

"Baby, what's wrong?" Connor all but shouts.

She brought me to the apartment but couldn't get me up the stairs, so Connor rushed down to carry me. Now I find myself in my husband's arms, being carried up the stairs to our home like I'm made of glass, and I can't bring myself to care about anything.

Izzy helps us inside and Connor sets me on the couch with a

glass of water. She pulls him aside and recounts the disastrous afternoon. She leaves at some point; I don't notice.

"Let's get you to bed. We can talk it all through in the morning. Everything looks better in the light of a new day."

I never for a second doubted marrying Connor—not when I was a daydreaming little girl, and not when he proposed to me for a surprise elopement. His attentive care tonight proves why.

He carries me to the bedroom and gently sets me on our bed. Kneeling, he slides my cowboy boots off and rolls the socks off my feet. When he treats me to the same foot massage he always gives me, I dissolve into tears.

"Let it out, doll. Give me all your pain, I'll gladly carry it for you," he soothes.

And I do. I let my frustrations and sadness drip down my cheeks as Connor sweetly removes my clothes and dresses me in one of his shirts for bed. He brushes my hair and delicately removes my makeup, before tucking me in.

He closes up for the night and is soon wrapped around me, stroking my hair and kissing my tears away.

I've never been more grateful to receive Connor's love.

46

"Hayes!" Reid barks.

Fuck. I must've fallen asleep in the office. I pop to my feet, scrubbing my hands up and down my tired face.

"Sorry, Reid. Won't happen again."

"Sit down," Reid orders, so, I do.

"The fuck's going on with you? Don't bother lyin'." He leans against the doorframe of the office, arms crossed across his broad chest. Not intimidating at all...

"I'm fucking exhausted. Don't get me wrong, I love managing the stables and wouldn't trade it for anything. But I have three full time jobs right now—the ranch, the farrier program, and building the house. I know I did it to myself. It's catching up to me is all," I admit.

Reid scratches his beard thoughtfully. He doesn't have his hat on; he must've come from indoors because I only ever see him in a hat if he's working outside. It's a big damn deal since he spent so many years hiding his facial scarring. Those Tate girls sure have a way of healing a man. Except they aren't Tates anymore—thank god.

Just when I'm sure Reid's about to rip me a new asshole, he stuns me stupid.

"How can we help?" he asks.

"Wh-what?"

"Might take a while for you to get it through your thick head, but you're family. If the Andersens value anything, it's family. So, how can we help?"

I'm a fixer, the one who helps. I thrive when I'm helping others, and I rarely ask for help in return. I've been getting better about it—I asked for Reid and CJ's help pulling off the elopement. I asked for help in one way or another when I took the job at Lucky Spurs Ranch and took a risk on the farrier program.

Reid's been endlessly supportive, and he took a huge chance on me in his business.

He also helped me out when he agreed to sell me the land I'm building Delilah's dream home on. If he gave me a job and land to build a house, he'd probably help me with just about anything. From stories I've heard, the Andersen brothers and Greyson don't let silly things like the law or morality stop them from doing what's right.

"Not used to being the one asking for help," I admit.

Reid chuckles. "Tell me about it."

"I'm so close to getting my farrier certificate—nothing anyone can do to help me there. I've taken to it like a horse with a peppermint and I love it. Have to get to the finish line, you know?" I explain. Reid nods, processing but not interjecting.

"My work at the ranch gives me purpose and I'm honored you trust me with the care of your animals and the boarded horses. They bring me a calm I never expected. When I'm out here working, my hands are busy and my mind's quiet."

Reid responds to my vulnerability with his own. "This land's always been where I go when the world becomes too heavy. Real or not, I've always believed the ranch has a spirit of its own, and lord knows horses heal people."

I think of my wife and how she so desperately wants to work with the horses to help people with their struggles. There's got to be a path forward where she's happy. Because I won't let her give up on her dream because of a master's degree-sized roadblock.

"Exactly, I don't want to give any of that up—shit, not that I'm asking you to do anything about it. The work's the work, it takes as long as it takes."

He continues to nod, his hazel eyes impossible to read.

"Now the house is another story. I bit off more than I could chew trying to get the damn thing built in such a short amount of time with just the two of us." I shake my head in defeat. "I don't know where to ask for help, to be honest."

Admitting it is a weight off my shoulders. Reid takes his time mulling it over so long I grow uncomfortable under his scrutiny.

"Tell you what. Hadn't discussed it with you yet, but I'd like you to focus on your farrier apprenticeship after you finish your certificate program. I'd already been planning on hiring a part-time stable manage or assistant manager to help out. But I know how you love the animals and the work. So, let me give you a choice." He pauses, making sure I'm paying damn close attention.

"Do you want to take the apprenticeship slower, and maintain your workload at the ranch but with a part-time staffer? Or do you want to go full boar into your apprenticeship, and we train a new stable manager, and a part-time staffer to handle the stables?"

I blink at him stupidly. Is he seriously asking me if I want to have my cake and eat it too? Or, to have a buffet of cakes, eat them, and have leftovers?

"Reid...if I slow down, you'll have to hire farriers until I'm done and that's a hefty chunk of money for the ranch—on top of hiring a part-timer."

"Mmhmm."

"If I go full-time into the program, I'd do most of my hours here, reducing your external farrier expenses, but in exchange for hiring a full-timer and a part-timer. Either way will be fucking expensive and a lot of work for you," I say sheepishly.

"What's your point?" Reid drawls.

"I...uh..."

"As much as Lucky Spurs Ranch is my heart, my soul, and my home—it's a business. And sometimes big risks lead to great rewards. It often takes upfront losses to see a return back on new investments—such as bringing a farrier in-house. Decisions at the ranch are solely my responsibility, but if you'd like to discuss it with James and my folks, they'd be open," he offers.

I think it over, fiddling with shit on the desk. I know what I want, but I'm afraid to ask for the help. *Stop being a pussy.*

I clear my throat, sit tall and meet Reid's attention.

"If it's my choice, if my opinion matters in your decision making, I'd like to focus full-time on the farrier program and help train a new stable manager and staffer." I gulp.

"Done." Reid pushes off from the door frame, widening his stance. "What else?"

Is he serious? I can't ask for anything else. Can I?

When I don't say anything, Reid speaks up.

"The two of us have kicked ass on your house build. Haven't had to rely too heavily on contractors, but we're on the final push. If you've got the cash to burn, I'd suggest we hire out a few of the remaining jobs."

I cringe. I wanted to build Delilah's home with my own hands. Maybe asking for help doesn't negate the work I've done...

"I'd also suggest—if you're comfortable—letting the rest of the family in on the plan. You're so close to the finish line. If you'd be willing to tell James, Grey, my folks, Isabelle, Olivia, and your sister, we could knock it out of the park. I know you told CJ. He ain't exactly a builder, but based on your elopement, he's proven he can herd cats like a pro, which we're gonna need." He chuckles.

My hands have tangled themselves in my hair, tugging painfully. Fuck. If I want to pass my farrier program and not let Reid and the ranch down, I need help.

God, how I wish my dad was around. I'd give anything to have his hand on my shoulder and his gruff voice encouraging me. But maybe I could convince Quincy. Being out on Sam's land would be hard on her, but maybe it'd help her grieve and heal as well.

"This close to the end, no one's going to blow the secret. Everyone will want Delilah to be surprised and happy. Ain't no one in the family going to fuck that up for you," he chastises.

"Shit. You're right. I didn't mean to come across as distrustful. I don't want to inconvenience anyone," I say, before promptly receiving a slap upside the back of my head.

"Come on loverboy, we've got troops to wrangle," he says, walking away expecting me to follow him like a puppy. Which I do.

"You can't be serious." Delilah wails as Iz and Liv take off her pajamas and dress her like a Barbie doll.

"Deadly," Liv says—damn that girl's fucking terrifying. James must have balls of steel to deal with that one.

"Chop, chop, twinie," Izzy says.

"I can't go vacationing right now! I graduate in two weeks! I don't have time for this!" Delilah shrieks, expecting to me to save her from her sister and best friend.

"Connorrrrr!" she whines.

"You owe me, Lilah. I didn't get to come to your wedding, you're giving me a girl's trip," Liv says lightly, but completely serious.

I usher the girls out of our bedroom and sit my wife on the bed. Kneeling in front of her, I gently brush her silken hair out of her face and run my thumb over her bottom lip.

"Dollface, you deserve this. You need a break. You've worked your cute little ass off and are so close to finishing. You told me yourself you only have one more session with Tanya, and you'll be observing, not running the workshop."

She objects but I cup my palm over her mouth silencing her.

"Take a deep breath and have some breakfast. Izzy brought Mrs. Andersen's lemon-cream cheese Danish you love. Let the girls pack for you and you're leaving your phone and laptop with me."

Panic floods her eyes. I don't like taking her phone any more than she does, but she needs to disconnect to relax. Plus, I can't risk anyone spoiling the secret.

"We can communicate through Izzy and Liv. You're going to the new library lake house Izzy themed for Swift Property Management to do nothing other than read, relax, eat, laugh, and sleep. Okay? I'm not taking no for an answer, baby," I say with no room for argument.

She gives me the cutest stink eye but melts under my stare. The minx licks my palm, and I remove my hand from her mouth, wiping it on her face.

"Connor!" she squeals, wiping at her cheek.

"Don't lick me if you don't like the consequences." I chuckle.

"You love it when I lick you..." she says suggestively.

Nope. Now is not the time to pop a boner for my wife. There's too much work to be done.

I give her a stern look, trying my damndest not to crack.

"Okay..." Delilah relents.

And just like that, my girl is whisked away into the hills so me and the guys can finish this fucking house. I hate lying to her, but it's a necessary evil at this point. I'll tell her the whole truth as soon as possible.

Standing in our apartment for what's hopefully one of the last times, I focus inward to the heart Delilah owns.

"Almost there, baby. Almost there."

47

"You were right, and I was wrong," I say deadpan.

"Told you so," Izzy gloats, sticking her tongue out at me. I reach out pinchy fingers trying to grab it but she's too quick.

I nearly had a mental breakdown as we drove away from the apartment. There was no way in hell a four-day lakeside vacation was a good idea two weeks before graduation.

But as usual, my husband knows me better than I know myself. I desperately needed the break. I've worked so hard for so many years, the thought of messing up now is terrifying.

Not to mention everything I've worked for may be for nothing—or the first step of many I wasn't prepared for.

I shake the negative thoughts from my head and focus on the girls' conversation.

"You seriously killed it, Izzy. The library theme is on point. Book lovers from all over the world would pay big money to stay at the library lake house," Livy praises.

Izzy blushes under the attention, but she deserves every ounce of pride because she created a true destination.

The lake house couldn't be more than a thousand square

feet. The exterior felt like we were entering a fairy tale like Hansel and Gretel—the cutest woodsy cottage. When the foliage blooms in spring, it'll be ethereal.

Walking inside transports us to a glimmering fae library. Imposing wooden bookshelves line every available inch of the walls, expertly staged with enough books to appear full, but not so many to be cluttered. Twinkling fairy lights weave in and out of the space, casting a peaceful glow over the rainbow of spines on the shelves. Complete with a small rolling ladder in the living space, the library lake house is perfection.

"I accept this as apology for not being in on the elopement master plan," Livy winks at me, "this is way better than back-to-back flights within twelve hours."

Izzy, Reid, and CJ really made generous sacrifices to be there for our wedding and help make everything possible. I'm eternally grateful that the people I love helped Connor pull off the surprise of the century.

Four days are spent luxuriating in the serenity of the cottage, surrounded on three sides by trees that kiss the sky, and a pristine frozen lake. I'm going to beg Connor to bring me back someday in the warmer weather.

"Thank you for kidnapping me, I didn't realize how burnt out I was. Connor was right, I'm so close to finishing, and now I can go into my final session and advisor meeting refreshed," I say on a sigh. He's perfect.

"Do you need help getting upstairs?" Izzy asks as Livy parks in front of my building.

"No, you get back to your husband, and Livy, you get back to whoever you're currently terrorizing," I joke.

Livy's face goes white, but she recovers quickly. How long do she and James think they can keep their tryst a secret?

Back in the apartment, I find my phone charged on the kitchen counter with a text.

> Studmuffin: Welcome home, beautiful wife. One of the mares is foaling and Reid asked me to stay overnight to monitor her. I've got my phone on me, otherwise I'll call in the morning. I love you!

I'm disappointed not to see him; I'd kill for one of his hugs. But I'm proud of him for taking his new job seriously and being Reid's right-hand man.

> Me: Okay baby, let me know if you need me to bring you anything. Thank you for the trip, I really needed it. I love you!

I spend the rest of the evening washing my trip laundry. Connor kept the place spotless while I was gone. It's like he hasn't been home in four days. It's sweet he tidied up for me.

Just in case he's sneaking some sleep between checks, I don't call him before bed. I'm sure he'll call when he can.

"Alright, Ty, you ready to try again?" Tanya asks the hulking military veteran.

We're in the larger pen on her property for the trust-building workshop today. I'm thrilled we have nine veterans from a wide demographic.

Eight of the nine have met Biscuit, Ty outright declined, so Tanya's giving him another opportunity before the session wraps for the day.

Instead of directly addressing Ty, she speaks to the group.

"Biscuit doesn't care what you do or don't say. He doesn't know your history, what you've seen or done. Biscuit cares if you're calm. Now that sounds impossible, right? PTSD is a real bitch, and we ain't tryin' to climb that mountain today.

"All we're doin' today is familiarizing you with the pen and our buddy Biscuit. He feels what you feel and will mirror it back to you. Even if you think you're perfectly fine, Biscuit's body language will tell the truth about what's goin' on in your mind and your body."

She winks at me before kindly tilting her head to the side asking Ty if he'd like to try.

Ty nods once, jaw tight and arms crossed. I have to focus inwards because my anxiety's ramping up anticipating what's going to happen between the horse and the veteran.

Biscuit huffs and shakes his head. Ty stops walking and looks at Tanya like *What the fuck am I supposed to do?* She simply smiles at Ty encouraging him forward.

Ty's agitated and I'm proud he's trying at all. Cold wind passes through the valley, everyone's hair ruffled by the current. It lifts the brim of Ty's baseball cap, nearly blowing it away but Ty holds it on his head. The momentary distraction is enough that Ty's shoulders have lowered, his arms are no longer crossed, his jaw relaxed, and his stance is looser.

Biscuit flicks an ear but is otherwise unperturbed. Ty tenses and takes a few large steps towards Biscuit, causing the horse to shake his head and retreat a step. Wheels are turning in Ty's head as he watches his own emotions play out in real time through the beast.

Tanya resumes conversation with the rest of the group, giving Ty the space to try without an audience. I observe him in passing glances, careful not to make him feel like a spectacle.

Like magic, Ty and Biscuit work things out. Ty smiles at the soft velvet of Biscuit's muzzle beneath his fingertips. Though this isn't an active session for me, Tanya trusts me, and I'm comfortable approaching the duo.

I hand Ty an unwrapped peppermint and with a furrow of his bushy brows, he says he doesn't want a mint.

"It's for Biscuit," I say with a soft smile and motion for him to offer it to the horse.

Skeptical but curious, Ty holds the sweet treat in his open palm and Biscuit greedily gobbles it up. A boisterous laugh escapes the burly man and for a moment he jolts, concerned how Biscuit will react, but his new friend is happy, and peace washes over Ty's features.

Tanya calls it a wrap and thanks everyone for trusting Biscuit today. I love how she makes it about the horse, not the handler. In reality, the therapist or facilitator is merely the bridge between human and equine souls.

"How do you feel, darlin'? Last session under your belt, ready for the next steps?" Tanya asks, getting Biscuit untacked.

"You've been invaluable, Tanya. I'm so grateful for your time, you're a wonderful teacher," I say, her hand bats the compliment away.

"But honestly, I'm lost," I choke out. Tanya waits for me to gather myself.

"I'm not sure getting a master's degree is right for me. But if I don't, I can't be an equine therapist, and everything I've worked for is for nothing." I pluck at a loose thread on my jacket.

"Well, ain't that the dumbest shit I've ever heard." I snap back at Tanya's harsh comment.

"It ain't all or nothin' darlin'. You can help a hell of a lot of people with the education you've got. Correct me if I'm wrong, but it's the horses you love working with, not an unbridled passion for clinical psychology?"

Even the term clinical psychology makes me cringe.

"Right. But that doesn't help me. It just means this isn't the career path for me." Tears sting my eyes, and I brush them away with my sleeve, not bothering to hide my emotions.

"Girl, there you go bein' stupid again," Tanya bites out.

"How many people have you helped these past few months? How many times have you facilitated moments of true healing? We need both, darlin'," she says.

I'm beyond confused and growing embarrassed at her ribbing. "Both what?"

"Therapists and specialists. Folks licensed to provide therapy and seasoned equine facilitators who understand the horses. Ain't one path to healing, it's a team approach."

"I don't need a license? I can still work with the horses to help people?" I ask, afraid to know the answer. It sounds like what she's saying, but I don't want to get my hopes up.

"You could march your little fanny into your boss's office right now and tell him you're ready to build an equine assisted learning program and offer services for team-building, school programs, wellness retreats, communication—hell, anything that doesn't directly treat mental health conditions.

"Can't call it equine therapy, 'cause it ain't. If you want to get some legitimacy behind your program, there's several equine assisted learning certification programs you can finish in no time at all, with your degree under your belt. Hire a licensed equine therapist if your workshop requires it, but otherwise, this is all you, darlin'," she says, simple as pie.

"I've got another session comin' in an hour, so I need to get on it, but you call me if you ever need anything. I'll work with Reid and your advisor on any paperwork or approvals they need, alright? You take care, you hear?"

And with that, I'm left with my future laid in front of me like a yellow brick road.

"Hell yea!" Connor says, lifting me in the air, his huge hands circling my waist. I wrap my legs around his middle and bury my face in his neck.

"All my evaluations are signed and approved...I get to graduate!" I wiggle in his arms.

"I'm so fucking proud of you!" Connor spins us in circles until he's so dizzy, he slides us down one of the stall doors to the hay strewn floor, me still tightly wrapped around him.

"When's the graduation ceremony?" he asks, massaging my hips and thighs.

I chuckle. "I did most of my degree by distance learning. I wouldn't know anyone, and the pomp and circumstance aren't important to me. We can have a celebration at the ranch when my diploma comes in the mail."

"If you're sure, doll, because everyone would make the trip in a heartbeat," Connor assures me. And they would. I'm so blessed to have found such a loving family.

"I have something to tell you too," he says, surprising me. I shimmy my shoulders, excited for his news.

"I finished my farrier program. My mentor oversaw my final shoeing assessment and passed me on the spot. Looks like we'll be checking the mail for two important pieces of paper." His smile could melt the sun, I swear.

I cradle his face, his beard tickling my palms, chocolate eyes gleaming with pride.

"I'm so proud of you, Connor. The past nine months were a whirlwind. Everything in our lives has changed for the better."

A tear escapes and I catch it with my thumb before it trails into his beard.

"We fucking did it, baby. We made all our dreams come true," he says resolutely.

Our lips meet in a tender kiss, joy and relief flowing between us. The kiss heats slowly, a lick leads to a nibble, until his tongue is sweeping into my mouth, making my head spin. He breaks our kiss to trail his swollen lips down my jaw to devour my neck. I tip my head back giving myself over to him, basking in his attention. I couldn't care less we're on the stable floor.

It's moments like this, where no words are required, his soul speaks to mine in a language we've known since he found me sitting in the dirt in my pretty yellow dress.

"Fuck, baby. If you don't stop grinding that sweet little pussy on me, we're going to have a problem."

I didn't realize I'd been humping him, but the warm tingle in my clit tells me he's right.

"We wouldn't want you to have a *problem*, would we?" I taunt, sliding my hand between us to cup his erection through his Wranglers.

"Please, baby," he groans. "If I get to come, please let me blow my load in your cunt. Please," Connor begs incoherently as I jerk him from outside his jeans.

I take his cowboy hat from his head and place it on my own.

"You gonna give me a ride, cowboy?"

His hands bite into the soft flesh at my waist and I relish the sting. I love that I can unravel this man so easily. I've come into my sexuality since we became intimate. I'm on his dick as often as possible. It's become a basic need like food, water, and shelter.

Connor buried inside me is a necessity.

"You want me to ride you, baby?" He rolls his hips into me from his seated position on the stall floor. "I'll ride you hard and put you away wet like the horses. That what you want?"

I'm panting, desperate for exactly that.

I lean in, lips grazing his ear, and whisper, "What I want, is for my husband to fuck me."

No other words are needed because Connor hoists us off the ground using superhero strength and slides me down his front, his cock pressing into me the whole way.

"Turn around," he growls. I immediately obey because holy shit I love it when he unleashes like this.

He smacks my ass so hard I yelp, and grabs me by the back of the neck, marching me towards the back of the stall. He takes my hands and presses them into the cool wood.

"Don't move."

Being blind to what he's doing drives me wild, and he knows it. His rough hands unbutton my Wranglers, unzipping them slowly before slipping his hand into the tight denim to cup my pussy. A whimper of desperation escapes me, needing more of his touch.

His hand's gone too soon, and he focuses on wrenching the tight denim down my ass and hips. The fabric chafes my sweaty body, and as soon as enough flesh is exposed for his liking, he grips my nape again.

"Bend over."

Oh. My. God. I love when he takes charge, letting go of control and giving my body and my pleasure over to him completely. I hinge at the waist, arching my back, my hands sliding down the wall to support my new position.

His boots shuffle back, and I imagine he's admiring the view, or checking to make sure no one's coming. Arousal floods my pussy at the possibility of getting caught. I'm so turned on it hadn't crossed my mind until now.

He draws closer to me, a hand trailing beneath my sweat-soaked shirt under my coat. The fact I'm nearly dressed makes this so much hotter. He won't be able to play with my tits but I'm sure he'll make it up to me with his cock.

"This. Ass," he growls, smacking each side of my ass in rapid succession.

"Fuck, you look so good tattooed with my handprint, dollface." I shiver at the endearing nickname amidst the filth.

He ruts his jean-covered cock between my ass cheeks and I back into the rough sensation.

"So eager. My little wife needs to be fucked, doesn't she?" His question nearly drowned out by my desperate mewls.

"How wet are you, baby?" He doesn't give me the chance to answer.

Instead, he pulls my thong down to see for himself. Cold air hits my bare pussy, and I shiver. It immediately cools the arousal stretching from my pussy to my thong.

"Fuuuuuck, doll, you're soaked. This all for me?" I whimper desperately. "Damn right it is. This cunt knows who it belongs to. Knows I'll always give it what it needs."

Jeans tight around my thighs, body bent forward, the pose is obscene, and I love it. I love being whatever he needs. My thighs are pressed together, and I already know it's going to be a tight fit for him to get inside me.

His belt buckle clangs as he fumbles to get it open one handed, his touch never leaving my body. A flick of a button and zipper being pulled down echo in the silent stables, seeming far louder than they are.

The low, steady rustle of his calloused hand pumping his cock floods my pussy. Arousal drips down my leg and I flush from the intimacy and vulnerability of this moment.

The broad head of his cock pushes between my thighs to my soaked entrance.

"Jesus fuck, your cunt's gonna be so fucking tight. I'm not gonna last," Connor growls, pushing into me inch by inch.

I'm so wet there's no need for him to prep me with his fingers. The friction around my entrance burns, intensifying the pleasure, and the immediate fullness aches deep inside me.

His fist wraps around my braid, jerking my head up from lolling between my shoulders.

He doesn't ease me into it. His thrusts are hard and fast from the jump.

"This. Cunt. Fuck. Always so ready for your husband's fat cock." Connor's jacket scratches the top of my ass, his belt buckle smacking against my leg.

"Always. Please, Connor. Please fuck me," I beg.

"Gonna pump you so full of cum it drips out of you the rest of the day. Gonna nut so deep in your pussy we give your IUD a run for its money."

Oh my god, why is that so hot? That shouldn't be so hot. We don't even want kids—aren't anywhere near ready—but the thought of it slickens his thrusts. He's fucking me so hard I can't breathe let alone speak.

"Your cunt just gripped me so hard, dollface. You like that? You like the idea of me filling this pussy with cum—desperate for me to breed you?" I whimper and push back into his thrusts.

"Because I fucking love it. I'm gonna blow hot cum right into your cervix, baby. Now make yourself come. Flick that clit, baby. I'm close. Fuck," he groans, holding his orgasm back.

I reach between my legs, the fit's impossibly tight but I manage to glide two fingers against the hood of my clit like a "V".

"You're gripping me so tight. Fuck. Fucking come!" he barks, snapping his hips forward one last time and spilling deep inside me.

I don't know if it's his hot cum filling me, the way he's been relentlessly pounding my G-spot with the head of his cock, or his demand, but I fall apart. He strokes his dick in and out of me through my orgasm until I'm trembling.

Connor pulls out slowly, our combined cum leaking down my legs. He gathers it up with his hand and shoves four cupped fingers back into my tender sex.

"Oh my god," I whine. *Why? Why is this so unbelievably hot?*

"You better hold my cum in your cunt, baby, because it needs to stay inside you where it belongs." He slaps my ass again, the sting from the cold intensifying the pain. Surely I have red handprints on my ass cheeks.

He pulls up my thong and jeans for me, leaving me to button and zip them before doing up his own jeans—ever the gentleman, even freshly fucked.

He takes his cowboy hat back from my head and kisses me sweetly on the lips.

"You're a real cowboy now, stud. A farrier to boot," I say.

"I'm not your studmuffin anymore?" he asks playfully.

"Naw, baby, you leveled up."

48

It's the second year in a row I don't get to be with my twin on her birthday. Irish twin, but still, this day is important to me too. Reid whisked her away to god knows where. He's taken to spoiling her rotten and though she protests, she secretly loves it.

Harper was sick, so Greyson insisted we ignore his birthday. He's crazy intimidating, so no one dared argue with him. Connor left a six-pack on his doorstep, knocked and ran like his ass was on fire. I laughed so hard that my big tough husband's afraid of growly Greyson.

Connor's been gone a lot. I'd be concerned if I had a speck of doubt about his loyalty, but I trust him implicitly, I always have. So I busy myself registering for the equine assisted learning program I chose.

Livy's supposed to be coming over for facials and 90s movies, so when there's a knock at the door, I holler for her to come in since I left it unlocked.

I bounce out of the bedroom, giddy to have some girl time—and stop dead.

My mother's standing by the kitchen counter, digging

through my purse. A large man stands menacingly blocking the doorway.

"Mom, what are you doing here? You can't be here. I have a restraining order. You could get arrested," I plead. Even if she's a terrible mom, I can't help noticing she's gaunt and her skin isn't a human color.

She's strung out on something I don't recognize, which scares the shit out of me. I know how she behaves drunk, or high on weed, coke, or heroine. But this is something different.

"Yea, I know, you stupid cunt. What kind of stuck-up bitch gets a restraining order against their own mother? I fed you, clothed you, kept a roof over your head for twenty-three fucking years and all the thanks I get is two useless daughters who opened their legs for men with money instead of taking care of their sick mother."

My stomach clenches with everything wrong that she said. I can't process it before she spouts off again.

"So, you're gonna give me whatever I want. And if you don't, I'm gonna take it," she says, thumbing over her shoulder at the man whose lecherous stare makes my skin crawl.

"Told you she was pretty." The implication makes my stomach roil. The creep eyes me like I'm a steak and he's starving.

"What do you want?" I ask, like a weak little girl.

"You can start by giving me your PIN numbers because I'm taking your cards. Keep money in the accounts for me to spend and we won't have any problems."

Easy enough, I'll cancel the cards as soon as she leaves and call the police.

"As a matter of fact, give me that fucking rock off your finger." She rushes over to me, gripping my left hand between her shaking ones so tightly it hurts.

"The Hayes boy finally make an honest woman out of you? You've been following him around like a bitch in heat for years."

I flinch at her words, hating that she or anyone thinks of me, or Connor, that way.

"Get off me! Get out and I won't call the cops," I plead, wrenching out of her grasp.

She snaps her fingers and the goblin from the front door rushes me, backing me into a corner in the living room. He cages me in while my mom destroys my apartment, searching for anything she can sell.

He's too close. I try to get away, but he grips my jaw, his thick fingers digging into the flesh of my cheeks. Stale booze wafts off him, making me gag.

"Go ahead," Mom says to the man, whose mouth lilts into a predatory grin that has me trembling. "You've got until I'm done searching the place."

Without warning, the front door blasts open, wood splintering as it slams against the wall.

"GET OFF MY WIFE!" Connor booms.

The creep's ripped away from me by the hair, Connor throwing him to the ground like a piece of trash. The clunk of his skull cracking against the hard wood floor vibrates in my bones.

Connor's cowboy boots obliterate the guy's ribs and back despite the fact he's already unconscious.

He whips around to catch me as I fall into his arms, shaking.

"Are you okay?" he asks, checking me for injuries. I think I nod. I'm not sure.

I'm not *here*, because this can't be happening.

The unmistakable click of the hammer of a gun halts all movement.

Connor blocks my body with his own like a human shield.

"Come on, boy. Don't make this harder than it needs to be. I was just explaining to your bitch of a wife how you're gonna support me from here on out as a thank you for letting her live this long," Mom snarls.

When the man groans from the floor, Connor delivers another kick to his side. He steps away from the heap of human garbage on the floor and holds me behind him.

"Sit down, Ivy." His voice is firm but calm. "Put the gun down."

Either she's extremely confident in herself, or too high to make a different choice, but she collapses onto our couch. She slams the gun onto the coffee table, and I flinch, terrified it'll go off. Unconcerned, she fishes a bag of poison and a cloudy glass pipe from her jacket pocket—blackened at the end from use.

I can't look away as she loads the pipe and holds a plastic lighter under the bulb until she's ready to smoke it.

She inhales deeply and twitches like electricity is coursing through her veins. She quickly pales and sweat beads on her pallid skin. Her eyes dart around, rapidly losing control to the high.

Connor instinctively takes a step back, protecting me between his body and the wall.

Her breathing is shallow and rapid, like she can't get enough air. The electricity in her veins is pulsing—her hands going rigid and twitching at unnatural intervals.

Her hand flies to her chest and I know.

She falls forward off the couch, contorting on the floor. Her choked gasp reaches into my chest and tugs on my heart as my mother dies on the floor of my apartment.

"Call 911," Connor says quietly, but he doesn't move to help her. I'm frozen to the spot, too fixated on a chip in the coffee table to locate my phone.

"Delilah, baby, I need you to call 911." He hands me his phone and I dial.

The voice on the other end says something, but I can't make out the words. Connor gently takes the phone from my hand and speaks to the dispatcher in low, clipped sentences. He gives them our address, explains the situation, and tells them there's a gun present.

Long moments pass. Connor walks over to her body and kneels to check her pulse. He meets my dead eyes and shakes his head.

You'd think I'd be crying, or screaming, or begging him to save her. Instead, I can't move. A warm peace flows through me, sickly grateful she's gone.

A scraping noise draws our attention. Mom's accomplice is trying to drag himself to the door. Connor crosses the room in three long strides and holds the guy down beneath his boot.

"Don't move," he spits at the guy. "I'm dying for a reason to bash your face in for touching my wife."

"Police! Show your hands!" Officers flood into the small living space, and still, I don't move. Connor slowly raises his hands in surrender, but walks towards me, nonetheless. He wraps me in his arms, and we stand like a statue as chaos ensues around us.

It happens in slow motion, and super speed at the same time. Their voices come from deep underwater.

One officer gets on the radio. "Dispatch, we need EMS to our location, female, unresponsive, possible overdose. No pulse, not breathing, CPR in progress."

There's no use for them to keep doing CPR, she's dead. The cracking of her ribs beneath the compressions is a sound I'll never forget. Or perhaps, I'll forget it all. I'm not mentally here.

Another officer detains the creep and drags him out of the apartment to the squad car.

An officer tries to talk to me, and I blink back. Connor answers for me. He stays close, one hand never leaving my body.

"Time of death..." I hear the words, but they don't make any sense.

Someone drapes a blanket over her body. A paramedic checks me over for what feels like forever. It could've been five minutes, or fifty. Time passes slowly underwater.

Eventually, the room clears. Mom is gone. The man who grabbed me is gone. The cops and paramedics are gone. I blink to focus my vision and find the apartment in shambles—all of our things strewn around like garbage.

Connor locks the door and walks slowly towards me.

"Come here," he says softly.

I step into his arms and press my cheek to his chest. His heartbeat grounds me. Steady, strong, safe.

Connor leads me to the bathroom. While the water for the shower heats up, he undresses me carefully. We haven't spoken a word.

He guides me beneath the warm spray and tips my head back to wet my hair. His gentle touch breaks me. I heave ugly sobs, and cry into his chest.

Furious at her for dying, for not getting help for her addictions, for choosing any and everything over her kids, for bullying me and shaming me, for never taking care of me.

I rage and Connor holds me together, so I don't fall apart.

He washes and rinses our tired bodies and wraps me in a towel before drying himself. He leads me to our bed and pulls back the covers, helping me crawl in before I curl into myself.

The room goes black, and he wraps around me. He peels the damp towel from my skin and holds me close against his naked body.

"How did you know?" I ask into the dark.

"Livy came over for your movie marathon and the door was wide open. She called 911 and me. She waited downstairs until I got here."

I have no reply, deeply grateful Livy called for help, and that Connor came so quickly.

But there are no words. There's no fixing this, making it better, or taking it away.

Instead, I cling to the arms holding me together, so I don't sink to the bottom of this ocean of despair. The pressure underwater cocoons my senses, and I drift into a dreamless sleep.

"Fuck, we don't need to be talking about this, Quincy. Not today." Connor's sister left her cottage for the first time in what I'm guessing is all week.

"No. It's okay. I need to try to get some normalcy back in my life. I've done nothing but grieve these past two years. I'm tired of people tiptoeing around me like I'm made of glass. It's bad enough they dance around Mom and Dad." She shakes her head, a profound sadness overtaking her posture.

"We don't mean to, I think we're all trying to give you space while we all try to navigate life without..." I trail off.

"Without Sam. It's okay to say his name. In fact, I'd prefer if everyone would. I hate how people act like he never existed at all. HIS NAME WAS SAM ANDERSEN!" She shouts into the starlit sky.

It's New Year's Eve—what would've been Sam's thirty-first birthday, had he not died from an aortic aneurysm, leaving Connor's sister a widow.

Even the thought of losing Connor breaks my heart. She's so brave. I couldn't live without Connor. Surely my soul would follow his. They've been woven together since fate drew his bike to the end of the paved road all those years ago.

Mom's been gone for two weeks. We didn't tell Izzy until she and Reid came back from their getaway. I didn't think she'd much care, and when we told her, she proved me right. Maybe she cried in private or will grieve our mother in her own way.

I'm not mourning in any way I ever imagined. I'm empty and free at the same time.

We refused to go through the trailer post-mortem, and relinquished disposition of her body to the coroner's office. The new sheriff dropped off some original documents, like our birth certificates, that they found in the trailer. We were shocked she held onto them.

Christmas was a somber affair. As a combined family, Andersen-Hayes-Clark-Dalton, we decided to postpone any holiday celebration until spring. I'm continuously blown away by the support from this family we've found.

"Just tell me," Quincy says, growing frustrated. "How did she pass?" she says, softer, apology in her eyes.

"She overdosed on meth and had a heart attack," I say frankly. "Years of addiction caught up to her, and instead of robbing us—or god forbid shooting us—she died."

Both Connor and Quincy gape at me wide eyed, surprised by my cold response.

"I'm sorry, Quincy. I don't mean to be so insensitive. I know Sam..." I trail off, ashamed of my behavior.

"No sweetheart, you're fine. Like I said, we can talk about these things, and nothing you said was untrue. For what it's worth, I'm sorry you won't get to have the relationship with your mom you wanted," Quincy says.

Sadness shimmers in Connor's chocolate eyes, because neither he nor Quincy will ever have the relationship they want with their dad ever again—except instead of death, he's disappearing before their eyes.

The screen door clacks open, startling us all.

"Ball's about to drop," James's floating head says before disappearing back into the main house.

Our blended family has joined to ring in the new year, and to celebrate Sam. We shared memories and stories about Sam throughout the dark hours leading to midnight.

There's no cheering or fanfare when the clock strikes midnight. Mr. Andersen gently kisses his wife, says goodnight to the rest of us, and leads her to their bedroom as she dissolves into tears.

Reid kisses my sister, and they branch off to admire Sam's funny little armadillo collection in the family room.

James gives Harper—asleep on the sofa—a peck on the cheek for his midnight kiss.

Greyson kisses the top of Olivia's head, and they lean on each other for support.

"Happy New Year, Delilah doll," Connor says sweetly.

"Happy New Year, stud."

He kisses me softly, cradling my head in his hands, supporting me as he always does.

"Any resolutions, baby?" Connor asks.

"Just one," I say, gazing at my husband.

"To leave the past in the past. It's a new year. We're married, our past brought us here, but unless it's a happy memory, it has no bearing on our future. We've graduated and despite any hurdles, are embarking on new careers.

"We can't bring anyone back from the dead, but we can cherish the good memories and let the rest fade with time. I want to move forward, not linger on things from the past we can't change."

"I couldn't agree more, doll. We'll go into the new year with our heads held high, side by side. I love you so much," he says, dipping down to kiss my lips gently.

"I love you too. More than you'll ever know."

49

Connor age 18, Delilah age 17

"It's badass, seriously," CJ assures me.

It hurt like a bitch and was weeping with plasma and blood, so the tattoo artist bandaged it so I could put my fucking shirt back on.

"Thanks, man. I always told myself it'd be the first thing I did when I turned eighteen. Thanks for coming with me," I say sincerely. CJ's one of a kind. Love him to death.

"Do you think she'll like it?" CJ asks, driving us back into Swiftwater Valley.

"I mean, probably? She's never had a strong opinion about tattoos, but I've never hidden the fact that I want them. Besides, me, you, and the tattoo artist are the only people on the planet who'll ever know the meaning behind the tattoo."

"You're not going to tell her?" CJ asks, theatrics in full force, flailing his arm in my face.

"Eyes on the road! Fuck no. I'm not telling her. She doesn't need to know."

So what if I'm hopelessly in love with Delilah Tate.

So what if my best friend's the love of my life, but she doesn't know, and will never find out, because she doesn't feel the same way. I refuse to jeopardize our friendship over my feelings.

"Alright, alright, loverboy. Cool your jets," CJ admonishes.

I turn up the stereo and let Randy Travis do the talking the rest of the drive home.

I carefully peel the bandage off my pec, doing my best to follow the tattoo artist's instructions. It stings when I wash it and pat it dry, but the ointment soothes the burn.

The full color sun bursts to life off my winter-paled skin. Rays pour from the sun on all sides towards my shoulder, sternum, and ribcage. The center of the sun is graced with the delicate face of a beautiful woman. The tattoo artist did a phenomenal job bringing Delilah's perfection into ink-form in a subtle, minimalist way that doesn't make it look like I have a photo realistic picture of my unrequited love tattooed over my heart.

The tattoo artist asked me why a sun? And since I don't know the guy and may never see him again, I told him everything. Hours passed as needles punctured ink permanently beneath my skin. I told countless stories about Delilah. From the day I found her crying in the dirt, to the other day when she kissed my cheek and I nearly fainted.

Delilah, my Delilah doll, my fallen angel—is my sunshine. She's the brightest part of every day, fills me with energy and purpose, and always lights my way through the darkest times.

I re-bandage my chest as a precaution. I can't risk anyone bumping me or hugging me too hard and my shirt rubbing against the raw skin at the party tonight.

In a twist of cosmic fate, my dollface and I share a birthday, one year apart. Today as I turn eighteen, she turns seventeen. It breaks my heart I'll be graduating in the spring, and she'll be stuck for one more year. At least Izzy's graduating too. maybe after she's gone, the relentless bullying will stop, since it's not Delilah they're witch-hunting.

My parents agreed to host our annual joint birthday party in our rec room so long as there's "no banging, boozing, or blazing."

I love my dad so much. He's everything a man and a father should be, and I hope to be just like him someday.

If I'm lucky to love someone as much as he loves my mom, I'll have won in life. My heart jerks at the reminder that love will never be with Delilah.

The party's in full swing, and as promised, there's been no shenanigans. We didn't invite a big group, just our best friends and they all respect my folks.

Quincy couldn't come home from college, since she was just here for Christmas, but she called me earlier and wished me and Delilah a happy birthday.

"So what happens now, big guy?" a friend from wrestling asks.

"Got a job with the department of transportation. They'll have me working as a traffic flagger on weekends until graduation. Hopefully I get promoted to highway maintenance," I say, draining a glass of Mom's famous lemonade.

"Dude, you're the only person I know who's excited to work for the DOT. Power to you, man. Should make decent money, though," he says.

And he's right. One of the main reasons I applied for the DOT was the pay structure. I've been saving money from odd jobs over the years, but if I want to get serious about ever buying the white house with the blue door by the library, I need to save some serious cash.

A tender hand touches the center of my back, and I melt, knowing it's her.

"Here's another lemonade, you drank that one so fast I turned right around and got us new ones." Delilah giggles.

She's so fucking pretty. Her white hair's pulled into a half ponytail, with two pieces left out to frame her doll-like face. She's wearing a cute dress she found at the consignment store over Christmas. It's black and covered in tiny white and yellow flowers. It suits her perfectly.

I hope she didn't notice I slipped cash in her wallet when we got home from shopping that day. She works so hard for her money, what little her mom doesn't take, but she wouldn't let me buy the dress for her. So, I "paid her back" on the down low.

"Thanks, dollface." I give her an awkward side-hug and kiss the crown of her head.

"You're welcome." Her crystalline eyes twinkle up at me, and I look away quickly because I don't want to get caught staring like I so often do.

"Are you having a good birthday?" I ask, busying myself with the glass of lemonade.

"It's perfect. Your mom said she'd swat my fanny if I thanked her one more time for hosting." Her giggle tinkles like windchimes, sprinkling goosebumps across my arms.

"Gifts!" someone shouts, and we gather around the pool table at the center of the rec room where a couple of presents are stacked.

My parents already gave me my gift—the title to my car. It was so generous for them to buy me a car when I turned sixteen, but I never considered it mine until I held the pink slip.

I haven't told Delilah because I know for a fact her piece of shit mom didn't do shit for her birthday, and her dad hasn't been home in years.

Izzy, Livy, and a small group of girls scramble for a small pink box on the pool table to hand to Delilah. She slides her fingers beneath the tape and along each edge of the wrapping paper, careful not to tear it, like she always has.

Her eyes shine with pure joy, aimed right at me. What did I do in a past life to deserve her smiles? I'm not the one who got her the gift, but it's me she shares her happiness with.

"A new e-reader! Thank you so, so much!" she gushes, hugging each of the girls.

"We pooled our money and got the newest one, and there's a gift card in the box so you can buy some e-books, but my mom said you can hook it up to the library too!" Livy prattles on.

Tears shine in those diamond eyes, but they're the happy kind, so I stay where I am.

A few more little gifts go to my doll, and her smile widens with each present. She's so thankful it hurts my heart. Someday, I'll shower her with so many gifts and tokens of affection, she'll forget all about how shitty her parents are. Fuck them for making her think she doesn't deserve even the smallest birthday gift.

Only one of the gifts on the table is for me—high school guys don't really buy each other presents—but of course, CJ plays by his own rules.

It's a white envelope with my name scrawled across the front. I tear off the end and tap the contents into my hand.

CJ pipes in immediately. "Sorry, Connor. I thought I was buying a year subscription for online video game play, but I accidentally bought a year subscription to that unlimited e-book subscription. And would you look at that, it's the same company as the e-reader Delilah got!"

He gives me an exaggerated wink. Fucking drama queen. I swear everyone sees right through him.

Delilah must not, because when I hand her the gift card, she cries and wraps both me and CJ in a hug. I'm momentarily jealous before I remember he's blissfully gay.

"You boys are the best!" We each get a kiss on the cheek and whereas CJ is unaffected, I scurry off for a refill of lemonade to hide *my flushed cheeks from everyone and slow my heart rate to non-heart attack levels.*

The party slowly starts to clear out, some people moving to parties that have "banging, boozing, and blazing," while others have curfew. Livy's mom's coming to take her and the twins home, so I only have a few minutes to get Delilah alone to give her my gift.

I find her exiting the bathroom and grab her by the wrist, pulling her out of view.

"Connor." She giggles. "What're you doing?"

"I wanted to give you your birthday present in private." Hopefully it's dim enough over here she won't notice how red my face is.

"Connor...we promised no presents. I can't buy you anything..." she says embarrassed.

"I don't need anything, I've told you a million times. Besides, the people at the store practically threw this at me and begged me to take it, and I couldn't say no." I wink at her, and it's barely light enough to see her blush, meaning she saw mine.

I take a small white cardboard box from my pocket. It's been burning my leg all night and I can finally give it to her.

Despite her protests, she takes the box, adorably excited to open another present.

A gasp is cut off by her hand covering her mouth.

"Connor...it's so pretty." She traces the cool metal on the foam block in the jewelry box.

"Put it on me?" she asks.

I take the box from her and twirl my finger for her to turn around. She sweeps her doll-like hair into a ponytail and my dick jerks at the exposed column of her neck.

My fingers struggle to clasp the delicate chain around her neck. She spins around and bathes me in her sunlight.

"I've never had anything so nice..." she coos.

Perfectly decorating her chest is a small sun pendant. The center is a silver color, and the rays are golden. When I saw it, I knew it was meant for her. I had to dip into my savings, but it was worth it to put joy on her face.

Thankfully, she doesn't ask why a sun, because if she asked, I'd tell her the truth and fuck everything up. If friends is all we'll ever be, I'll be the best friend she could ever ask for.

"I'm never going to take it off," she promises, and I like it more than I should.

"Happy birthday, dollface," I say, squeezing her hand.

"Happy birthday, studmuffin." She squeezes right back.

50

Delilah

"Have you seen Connor?" Izzy jumps out of her skin at my question.

"Oh my god, you scared me! Why are you here?" she scrambles.

"What do you mean why am I here?" I chuckle. "I work here. Why are you being weird?"

Izzy looks over my shoulder and back over her shoulder like we're being stalked.

"I'm not being weird. You're being weird," Izzy says.

With her hair grown out, we look like twins again. She kept it short for so many years, I can't lie and say I didn't miss looking the same.

"You do realize we're basically the same person and I can tell when you're being weird because you're doing what I'd be doing if I was being weird," I point out. "Now, have you seen Connor, or not?"

"Shit! I forgot, Reid asked me to run to Clark's Hardware to pick up something he ordered." She takes me by the shoulders and marches me towards the cars.

"Would you be a dear and go for me? I have...a call I can't get out of. Yea. Forgot about that call I have."

I eye my sister skeptically; there's clearly something going on.

"I just got here, I wish you would've asked me before I left the apartment. I hate to double back."

"Oh, but you will, won't you? Text me when you're on your way back, okay? And text me when you park." Why's she so antsy?

"Okay, sissy. Whatever you say." I kiss her on the cheek and make my way back to town. Maybe I'll stop by Bean & Brew for a hot chocolate and work on my business plan.

"Hey doll, what are you up to?" Connor rubs his sleepy eyes and kisses my cheek as he joins me at the kitchen island.

He looks divine in only low-slung athletic shorts, but bone-deep exhaustion cloaks his features. I'm so proud of him for how hard he's working on his farrier apprenticeship and keeping up with his responsibilities at the ranch. But he's working too hard.

"Just finished framing your farrier certificate and my diploma," I say, bursting with pride, running my finger along the smooth wooden frames.

"I didn't know they'd come yet. That's fucking awesome, baby. Thank you."

"I know, I'm sorry. I didn't mean to hide it from you. Mine came first but I wanted to wait for yours to come in the mail before I framed them together. Sorry for being sneaky."

Connor gets the strangest look on his face. A mix between guilt and panic. "Nothing to apologize for. It's not sneaky if it's for a nice surprise, right? Can't be mad if a person kept secrets to pull off a surprise. Right?" His rambling borders on frantic.

"You're right. It was worth it to see you happy." I smile at him, tipping my chin asking for a kiss. He visibly relaxes.

"What else is on tap today?" Connor asks.

"Well, I know it's technically my day off, but I was thinking about coming to the ranch with you today."

"Today? But it's your day off." He parrots back at me.

I laugh. "I know, but if you're there and my sister's there, I don't want to sit around the apartment all day. Maybe I'll visit Hope if Reid thinks she's ready."

I've fallen more in love with that paint horse every single day. Reid said she's acclimated to the ranch and gave me the green light to integrate her into the equine assisted learning program I'm developing.

Connor scratches his hair feverishly, growing agitated.

"I need to go to the bathroom," he blurts and darts out of the room.

Poor thing's so tired he's glitching like a robot.

I stand back to examine the wall space for where I should hang our achievements. My phone rings and I pause before answering it.

Unknown Number

I don't usually answer unless it's someone I know but I've been reaching out to so many contacts in the equine therapy world, I should answer it.

"This is Delilah."

"Hey, it's Greyson. I'm glad I caught you." That's weird. I swear I had his number programed into my phone.

"My babysitter's sick, and Harper's still on winter break. Is there any way you could come to the store and grab her for me? Y'all can spend the day at our place. She's got crafts and shit she's been dying to do," he says, clearly stressed.

Connor comes into the room, fully dressed, and makes a beeline for the front door. Before I can stop him, he slides into his cowboy boots and coat and is out the door with a "love you" thrown over his shoulder. *What in the world is going on with that man?*

I don't have anything going on anyway. "Sure, I can be there in fifteen, will that work?"

"Yes, you're a life saver. See you soon." And with that, Greyson hangs up.

Why would Greyson call me when Livy and James have been tag-teaming to helping him out? They must be busy today.

Harper's a sweetheart, we'll have a great day and maybe even sneak in some glitter. Greyson hates the stuff and forbids Harper from using it in the house.

I better get dressed so I don't keep him waiting.

"Now that I have my equine assisted learning certification, do you think we can start getting serious about marketing and ordering signage?" I ask James.

"Absolutely, get with Mom, she won't mind you using Swift's resources to get rolling."

"I don't want to take advantage..."

"Nonsense. You're family. What else?" he asks, all business today. He keeps checking his phone, tapping it every ten seconds like he's hoping to get a text.

"So long as you're confident I'm all set on the legal side, you're off the hook," I say.

"You're all set with general liability insurance through the ranch. We've got your participation consent forms and waivers, adults and minors. Your business plan looks phenomenal. I'll get the independent contractor agreement template finalized for you.

"Otherwise, ask Swift's marketing department for our photo

release form and decide if that's something you'd like to pursue," James says, packing away his laptop and notebook, already standing to leave.

"Thank you so much for everything, James. I know you're busy."

"No thanks needed." He checks his phone again.

"Uh, Liv wants to meet you for lunch at The Flying Pig. Do you need a ride, or..."

Why would Livy be communicating through James?

I release a heavy sigh and pack up as well. "No, I have my car. Thanks though."

James is already out the door before I look up from my bag.

Everyone's been acting so weird all month. I've barely seen anyone and we're never together in a group.

I guess this is what being an adult is like. Everyone has their own jobs and responsibilities. Now that I'm getting the program up and running, at least I'll see Reid and Izzy more often.

It'd be nice if I saw my husband for more than blips at a time. He sleeps at home every night, but he's dead tired. He's been too tired to have much sex, and I didn't realize how bad I needed it until I haven't had it.

Connor better be ready to get jumped the second he walks in the door tonight.

51

"Promise you can't see anything?" Connor asks for the umpteenth time.

He stopped me before I could go into the stables and tied a bandana around my eyes. He carried me and set me in his truck, and we drove for a few minutes before abruptly stopping.

He's been guiding me to god knows where on foot and instead of anxiously wondering where he's taking me, I'm thoroughly enjoying whatever has my big strong husband acting like a sweet little puppy.

"Yes, Connor, I promise. My eyes are even closed beneath the bandana, so I doubly can't see anything."

Snow crunches beneath our boots and I'm growing more confused by the minute. We would've reached anywhere within walking distance by now—the barn, the main house, Izzy and Reid's house, the guest houses, even the farthest one.

"Ok. We're almost there," he says, his hands shaking, one holding mine, the other on the small of my back.

Connor guides me to a stop and removes his hands from my body. It's our joint birthday, so I'm not surprised he's arranged a surprise. But I can't for the life of me figure out what it could be.

He removes my blindfold.

"Can I open my eyes, now?" I ask playfully.

"Yes. Open your eyes," he says, taking both my hands in his.

When I do, Connor is framed by the picturesque backdrop of the snow-covered land that makes up Lucky Spurs Ranch. Blurred shapes of other buildings on the property float in the distance, but I can't orient myself to where we are.

"Before I give you your surprise, I have some secrets I need to confess." He gulps.

I know he'd never hurt me, so I'm filled with curiosity instead of dread.

"Remember when you were in third grade and the school office told you you'd won a drawing for a new backpack?" he asks.

"Yesssss..."

"I was sad yours had ripped and your parents wouldn't buy you a new one. So, I took all my allowance and bought you one, and had the office ladies help me give it to you."

My chest tightens, tears immediately pricking my eyes.

"Remember your senior year when the school guidance counselor said you'd qualified for the new free breakfast and lunch program?"

Lower lip trembling, I nod.

"I pre-paid for all your meals that year since I'd graduated, and I needed to know you always had something to eat."

My throat constricts, struggling to swallow the revelation Connor is why I didn't starve that year.

"Remember how you couldn't recall ever applying for the scholarship that paid for all your college expenses these past few years?"

Tears track down my cheeks, frozen from the cold but burning with emotion, but I nod.

"You were working yourself to the bone trying to support

yourself and Ivy without Izzy around *and* paying for school. You were killing yourself. I made your advisor swear they'd never tell you where the money came from, just that it was a scholarship," he admits.

"You...paid for everything all these years? My tuition, books, seminars? My bank account was always full, they told me it was a living stipend..."

Realizations are rushing in faster than the tears escaping my eyes.

Connor tightens his grasp on my hands and swings our arms in and out, nerves showing.

"Remember when you were ten and I promised someday you'd have the white house with the blue door?" he asks.

"The one by the library? It belongs to the town..."

"It's the one promise I made over the years I can't keep, and you'll never know how sorry I am. Baby, I tried everything. I saved every spare dollar I've ever made to buy that house for you, but it wasn't meant to be." Devastation flashes across his handsome face.

"But...we only got together—" *A few months ago...*

"I know. It didn't matter. I promised you'd have that house, and I was hopelessly in love with you, even if you never felt the same way. It was something I had to do, because you deserve everything you've ever dreamed of."

My bottom lip will surely bruise from how hard I'm chewing on it, mind reeling processing the whole truth of how much Connor's sacrificed for me over the years, how he took care of me and kept me going even during the darkest times—knowing he may never have me.

I huff a laugh because it still gets me sometimes how if one of us had been brave enough to confess our feelings, it would've saved us years of unrequited love and heartache.

"I can't give you the white house with the blue door by the

library. But I can give you a white house with a blue door of your own." His chocolate eyes melt in the sunlight.

He releases my hands. "Turn around, dollface."

I'm tremoring head to toe, and not from the cold. I slowly turn around and revel in Connor's warmth at my back.

This can't be real. I'm dreaming, right?

"Happy birthday, and welcome home, baby," Connor says with a kiss to my temple.

An immaculate cabin has been erected on an area of Lucky Spurs Ranch I've never been to. The single-story rancher sprawls so wide I can't fathom how many rooms lie within. Wide, white wooden planks wrap around the façade like icing around a cake.

The front door shines like a sapphire dead center of the structure, flanked with stained glass windows that reflect rainbows from the bright sun.

The roof overhangs the house by at least eight feet, covering an expansive porch that wraps around the front exterior to the sides. *Does it continue around back?*

Knotty wood stained a brilliant chestnut supports the oversized rocking chair by the front door. Large enough for both of us to sit or lay comfortably.

"Connor..." I whisper, leaning into his sturdy chest. His strong arms wrap around me, and I cling to his forearms for dear life.

"Do you want to go inside your new house, doll? How did I not put it together sooner? This is your dollhouse." His chuckle vibrates through my back, and I feel him smile into my hair.

He moves to my side, an arm around my waist, and guides me up the porch stairs onto the patio, and through the brilliant blue front door.

The space is overwhelming, but in the most welcoming,

wrap-you-in-a warm-hug, way. The love built into these walls radiates all around us.

"You did all this?" I ask, incredulous.

"With help from our found family, yes. I couldn't give you the house you dreamed of, but hopefully I've built you the house we'll make a life together in, making new dreams."

I turn into Connor and sob, fingers desperately clutching his coat.

"Please don't cry. If you don't like it I'll change anything you want," he pleads.

"Don't you dare," I say into his chest. "It's perfect."

He lifts me from my hiding place and bends down to my level.

"I can't believe you did this for me, Connor," I say through tears.

"You have no idea the lengths I'd go to make you happy. You've had me wrapped around your finger since I was eight years old. The only difference now, is I'm wrapped around your ring finger, as you are around mine." He smiles that smile that melts my heart and my panties at the same time.

"Before I give you the grand tour, there's something I'd like to show you first." He raises his eyebrows excitedly, and walks us through the living space, combined kitchen-dining room, to a mud room.

"There's someone important waiting to see you." Connor motions for me to go first through the back door.

The back patio opens to a paddock with a small stable big enough to fit two horses comfortably.

I walk slowly down the porch, through the gate into the paddock, quivering the entire way. I look to Connor for permission to keep going and he chuckles.

"Don't keep 'em waiting."

My feet carry me to the expertly constructed stable. I open the man door and sink to the perfectly clean floor.

"Oh my god!" I cry, pouring my heart onto the ground, Connor rubbing my back soothingly, waiting for me to be ready.

He helps me to my feet, and I realize I'm not dreaming. This is real. Connor's made every one of my dreams come true.

"Hey there, girl." Hope's velvet muzzle tickles my palm, searching for a treat.

Not taking my eyes from her, I ask, "How?"

"It was a team effort, really. Tanya witnessed you bond with Biscuit so deeply, she nearly offered to sell him to Reid for the program. But Reid had a better idea. He'd been keeping a close eye on you and Hope and saw something growing there. I told him how much you loved her, and we knew she belonged with you. It's not every day someone meets their heart-horse, but you did the day you laid eyes on Hope," he explains, and I try desperately to absorb every word.

"She's mine?"

"She's yours, baby."

I don't bother drying the tears anymore, rather letting them fall like drops of joy, christening this unforgettable moment.

"Welcome home, Hope. Wanna be my best girl?" I ask, lavishing love on her sleek face and down her neck.

She nickers, leaning into my touch, telling me she's happy to be here too.

A soft snort leads me to the other stall housing a massive bay gelding waiting for a dose of attention.

The horse is a rich chestnut with a striking white blaze down the center of his face. He's stunning. Somehow, he suits Connor perfectly.

"He's a gentle giant. Came in with the last batch of rescues. Maybe he can join your program alongside Hope. Besides, I need a mount if I'm going to keep up with you, because you're going to take over the world, baby." His belief in me never ceases to amaze me.

"What's his name?" I ask in awe.

"Rocket." Connor laughs that deep laugh that warms my heart. "Which is hilarious considering the big guy won't even trot without serious bribery."

I launch into Connor's unprepared arms, and he stumbles back, catching me and keeping us upright. I plant a grateful kiss on his lips, broken by the smile splitting my face.

"Thank you. For everything you've ever done for me. I love you more than the moon and the stars, Connor Hayes."

"It's been my honor. Nothing makes me happier than taking care of you. I love you more than the sun lights the sky, because baby, you're even brighter."

He wraps me in one of his incredible bear hugs around my middle and I yelp.

"Ouch!" *Shit.* I thought I could keep the secret longer than a few hours…

"What? What's wrong?" Connor scrambles, trying to find the source of my pain. I wiggle out of his arms back onto my feet.

"It seems silly now, but I have a birthday surprise for you too."

Connor frowns, waiting for me to explain. I unzip my jacket and shuck it off—his confusion only growing.

I lift my shirt, exposing my stomach. Connor drops to his knees, gripping me by the hips.

Long moments pass where he can't form words, and he doesn't dare touch it.

"It's your sun," I say.

Tears blanket his gaze. "You covered your scar. Baby, this had to have hurt. When? Why?" he stammers.

"Just before you kidnapped me." I chuckle.

"Izzy went with me to the new shop just out of town. My scar was the last part of me I haven't healed from on the inside. And nothing makes me feel more accepted than you. I gave the artist a photo of your sun tattoo and this is what they created. Do you like it?" I ask, afraid of his response.

"Like it? I love it. Baby, it's fucking sexy. You're such a badass." He softly kisses around the tattoo, careful not to touch it.

I pull Connor to his feet and take him by the hand, letting my shirt fall back into place. "I'm ready for the grand tour of our new home, husband."

He makes a show of checking the time before shooting me a devilish grin.

"We best get moving because we've got a lot of rooms to christen before our birthday dinner at the main house."

With that, I scamper away from his wandering hands, laughing from the heart and loving this life of mine.

52

We've all gathered at the main house after a long day of work on the ranch. My mentor came out early this morning so we could be finished before the big event today. He let me take the lead on three of Reid's newly rescued geldings. He only had to step in once, and it was only to point out a tiny imbalance I didn't catch on that first horseshoe.

Reid's praise ricochets in my mind. *You're getting it.* And while the words are practical and not overly complementary, coming from this gruff old cowboy, who uses his words sparingly, it means the world to me.

Izzy and Reid prepped the guest houses for an upcoming family reunion booked at the ranch. This'll be the first multi-cabin booking they've managed. But the single bookings are such a hit there's no doubt they've created a destination people are going to flock to.

Today was monumental. *Hope at Lucky Spurs Ranch* held its first workshop. Delilah put her heart and soul into the program and worked tirelessly to make today a success.

Today, twelve women trusted my wife to introduce them to equine assisted learning.

Delilah blossomed with confidence under the afternoon January sun. She outshone even the brightest star in our galaxy as she connected with the women in that pen.

To celebrate my wife's success, Mrs. Andersen went all out. There's an extravagant spread of food laid out for the occasion. Mom and Quincy got Dad settled in the den and have been trading off sitting with him while we set up for dinner.

I come by to give them a break. I usually sit in silence with my dad but today is different. Today was special.

Delilah used me as a guinea pig for the equine assisted learning program. Me and Hope would be best friends if Delilah didn't solidly own that horse's heart. Through our sessions, I've worked through a lot of feelings about my dad, Quincy, and Sam. I'm so fucking proud of my wife. She's going to help countless people. I should tell Quincy how much it's helped me. Maybe she'd be willing to give it a try.

"Hi, Dad."

He's looking at the TV, not at me, and that's fine. Mom's found it helps to ground him in familiarity when she has to take him out of their house. She always puts on one of his old favorite shows like *Cheers* or *M*A*S*H*. The episodes are humorous and short, and he seems content watching an episode or two while we're at events like the dinner tonight.

"This is a good episode." I chuckle at the screen, but sober when I realize my dad isn't laughing with me.

"They're whipping up a great spread for dinner. Mom said Mrs. Andersen made that potato salad you love so much."

It warms my heart more than I could ever express that the Andersens have accepted my family into theirs with no hesitation. Even after their connection to us, Sam, was gone.

My sister still isn't herself. I worried she wouldn't want to be at the ranch because it reminds her too much of Sam, to spend an evening with her deceased husband's family, but she was excited to come celebrate Delilah today.

"I'm sorry I haven't been talking to you the way I should've been. You're my dad, I love you, but watching this disease take..." My throat clogs with emotion, rendering me unable to finish my confession.

"I'm sure Mom already told you, but I quit the department of transportation, completed all the training, and became a farrier. I work here at Lucky Spurs Ranch. No more long hours alone on the road wishing I was home. Now my home is the ranch, literally and figuratively. I feel like I belong here, Dad."

I think my dad would've been proud of me for the career change. He was always the one trying to get me and Quincy up in the saddle to appreciate Swiftwater Valley as much as he did. It's a shame his wishes came true too late for him to see it.

We sit in silence for a scene of his show before I burst out with a guffaw.

"Holy shit, I still haven't told you the wildest thing of all. No doubt Mom already told you, but I've got to tell you myself." I wait, studying my dad's face, gearing up to tell him the best news of my life, knowing I won't get the reaction I'd wished for.

"Delilah married me. Can you fuckin' believe it? Other than CJ, you're the only person I ever confessed my true feelings to, though everyone seemed to know anyway. All those years spent wallowing, pining over my dream girl—she was in love with me too, both of us too scared to say anything and ruin the friendship.

"She's incredible, Dad. You always loved her to death, but you should see the woman she's become. She overcame her struggles, her parents are no longer poisoning her life, and she worked her ass of and finished her psychology degree. She used it to start an equine assisted learning program here at the ranch to help people work through their own struggles. You'd be so damn proud of her, Dad."

Tears prick the backs of my eyes, because more than missing my dad for myself and Quincy, I miss him for Delilah. My parents always loved and accepted Delilah and Isabelle into our home and did their best to help where they could. Now, not only does Delilah not have parents, but she also doesn't have parents-in-law to lean on and share her life with. Dad literally cannot, and Mom's lost herself in caring for him.

As always, my heart twinges wishing things were different, but I've accepted his Alzheimer's isn't going away, and that it's okay to miss who he used to be and grieve that loss, while still loving and supporting who he is now.

"I love you, Dad," I say, squeezing his shoulder lightly, leaving to get Mom or Quincy to take my place.

I'm a few steps away from the bustling kitchen when my wife nearly bowls me over.

"Oh my god, have you had a lemon bar yet?" Delilah says with a mouth full of lemon curd and shortbread, somehow sounding like she's making love to the damn thing.

"Get a room already," I joke, grabbing her tight ass to hold her against me.

She swats my chest and feeds me the last bite.

"Dinner's ready, your mom made a plate for your dad already," she assures me.

We file into the dining room, starving for Mrs. Andersen's cooking. Plates are loaded buffet style and drinks are passed. Mom gave Delilah her lemonade recipe for her birthday—talk about a sob-fest—and I swear she makes it every chance she gets.

I drag Delilah closer to me by the underside of her chair, so our thighs are pressed together. I wrap my arm around her shoulders and eat one-handed.

"I'm so fucking proud of you, dollface. You looked like you belonged in that pen with Hope. And based on the chatter I overheard, those women were highly impressed. I bet your next workshop sells out with a waitlist."

Delilah smiles, a faint blush covering her cheeks. "You really think so?"

"I know so. You were meant to do this."

How is this my life? How often does a person get everything they've ever wanted without giving up a thing?

I'm married to the woman of my dreams, the one person I've loved since I was a snot-nosed kid. I'm surrounded by the best friends a guy could ask for. I've been welcomed with open arms into a family that found me when I needed them the most. And we've rallied around my dad for his care.

Mrs. Andersen, Liv, Izzy, and Delilah take turns checking on Mom and Quincy. Taking them to lunch or drinking coffee on the porch. Anything to make them feel like individual humans for a little while, not only caretakers. They both seem lighter now that the Andersens have been spreading their unique brand of love and support.

A knife clinks against the lemonade pitcher. Izzy stands and clears her throat.

"Raise your glass for a toast to the world's greatest Equine Assisted Learning Facilitator"—we all chuckle, because it really is a mouthful—"that Swiftwater Valley's ever seen. I think I speak for all of us, when I say we're boundlessly proud of you, Delilah, and know you'll help so many people."

"Cheers," everyone says together.

Reid scoots his chair back, scraping on the hardwood floors and stands to join his wife.

"This ranch has been in the Andersen family for generations, and when I thought all hope was lost, we brought it back to life in a new, unexpected way. The ranch has always been the one place I found peace, and all I wanted was to share that with other people." He wraps his arm around Izzy who looks at him like he hung the moon.

"Isabelle always dreamed of having a place like the ranch she could go and feel like she belonged. So, that's what we created. Lucky Spurs Ranch was born from love and built by this family's belief in me. Little did I know, the ranch would flourish with everyone's dedication and unmatched skills. We've got a herd of rescue horses living their best lives doing trail rides, being pet and groomed by giddy school children, and now working with our girl Delilah to heal people's souls. The horses are in perfect comfort thanks to Connor's hard work and commitment. These horses have never had nicer horseshoes in their life—he's out here giving luxury pedicures to the damn beasts," Reid jokes.

The table chuckles with warm affection, squeezing my heart like a hug.

"Olivia, James, and Greyson, you give so much of your free time to the ranch asking nothing in return, and from all of us that work on the ranch, we are boundlessly grateful. Mom and Dad, I hope we've made you proud. And Quincy, I hope we've done right by Sam honoring his memory."

My sister wipes tears from her eyes, always alone in a room full of people.

Mr. and Mrs. Andersen embrace, heartbroken and bursting with pride simultaneously—watching two of their sons thrive while the other lives only in their memories.

Reid clears his throat from the emotions suffocating him. "Cheers to the Lucky Spurs Ranch family, and especially to Delilah for her successful first workshop."

"Cheers!" Glasses clink and laughter and conversation resumes.

Delilah leans into my hold, nestled where she belongs, right over my heart.

"We did it, Connor. Can you believe this is our life?"

"Yea, baby, I can." I duck down stealing a kiss from my wife.

EPILOGUE

Delilah

We dig into our meals, and deep satisfaction sinks into my marrow. One minute the dining room's alight with a calm joy, the next, Greyson's choking on his food, with James pounding on his back to dislodge the blockage.

Harper, his adorable daughter, is stricken, eyes wide like a baby deer.

"I'm sorry, what did you say sweetheart?" Greyson asks her, hoarse from coughing.

"I...um...I was trying to ask you a question." She flushes a deep red.

"Can you ask daddy again? I think I misheard you," Greyson says.

"I asked how come you don't have a girlfriend," Harper says behind a curtain of her jet-black hair.

Everyone's eyes go wider than hers were a second ago, heads ping pong-ing back and forth with the same *what the fuck do we say* expression.

The story as we know it is Harper was born from a short-lived, casual relationship between Greyson and a woman named Vanessa. She decided motherhood wasn't for her and bolted, leaving Greyson to raise an infant alone. He eventually tracked her down to get the legalities worked out.

As far as I know, she signed away custody and he changed Harper's last name to Clark, effectively erasing Vanessa from history. He hasn't dated since. And by the panicked shock painting Greyson's typically emotionless face, this is the first time Harper's asked this question.

"Well, sweetheart, some families have a mom and a dad, or just a dad, or just a mom. Maybe grandma and grandpa are the main adults, or an aunt or uncle. All families look different," Greyson manages. "Daddy doesn't need a girlfriend. I have you."

It isn't the answer Harper was looking for, and family dinner isn't exactly the best place for such a sensitive conversation.

"But Gramma and Grampa Andersen are in love. And Gramma and Grampa Dalton are in love. Reid and Izzy are in love, Delilah and Connor are in love. Aunt Livy and James are in love," Harper whines.

The temperature in the room drops a solid twenty degrees from the icy glare Greyson shoots at James. I don't dare laugh, because now isn't the time, but the fact the nine-year-old has noticed Olivia and James's behavior proves they haven't been nearly as careful sneaking around as they think they've been.

"Aunt Livy and James are *not* in love," Greyson snaps.

Unperturbed, Harper continues. "But how come you aren't in love? How come I don't have a mommy?"

Time stops, the room so silent the only sound is Greyson's teeth grinding.

"Harper, little love, we'll talk about this later, okay?" he manages.

"May I please be excused?" she asks so quietly I barely hear.

"Of course, sweetheart," Greyson offers, but Harper's already scurrying away.

Uncharacteristically rattled, Greyson looks to Mr. and Mrs.

Andersen. As his pseudo-parents, of course he'd lean on them for support.

"We've got her," Mr. Andersen says as he and his wife follow behind Harper.

"Fuck. FUCK," Greyson barks. "Made it nine fucking years before having to break my daughter's heart. Goddamn it."

"This couldn't come at a worse time..." Greyson groans, head in hands.

"What do you mean?" I ask softly. Connor squeezes my shoulder in solidarity.

"I've got to find a new nanny. James, Liv, you've been life savers helping out whenever you can, but it's not stable enough for Harper and she's been unsettled. It can't be easy watching her friends get picked up every day from school by the same parent, in most cases, a house with a mom and a dad.

"She never knows who's picking her up until we text her teacher. On any given day, she could be walking out to find me, James, Liv, Mr. or Mrs. Andersen, Reid or Iz, and sometimes you or Connor."

"That must be hard, the instability is stressful for you both," I offer, wishing Hope were here to help settle his raging emotions. Is it too much to bring the horse into the house?

Olivia rounds the table to rub her older brother's back. "We'll figure this out, Grey. We knew this day would come. You've got our support," she tries to soothe.

"I've already asked too much of y'all. And don't even bother suggesting Meredith," he snips.

"I hate when you call her that, she's your mom too," Olivia argues. "You know she wants to have a relationship with you and Harper—"

"You stop right there," Greyson interrupts. "No offense, Liv, but I've got my reasons why I don't speak to Meredith, let alone allow her to be anywhere near my daughter."

Olivia Dalton isn't one to back down from an argument but swallows her response and returns to her seat.

"Now I have to rattle my little girl's life even more by introducing some stranger into our home full-time. She won't see her surrogate aunts and uncles as often, and she's asking questions I don't know how to answer." He buries his hands in his hair, his knee bouncing furiously.

"Forgive me if I'm overstepping, but of the group, my schedule is the most flexible," I say cautiously.

"I could pick her up after school every day and bring her to the ranch. She could spend time with me and Hope. Maybe she can find some peace here amidst the chaos. I can easily walk her to the main house when her grandparents get home, and you can pick her up from there."

"Fuck. I mean, that'd be great, Delilah. If it isn't too much of an inconvenience. Just until I can find a nanny," Greyson says, exhausted.

"No inconvenience at all, I'd love to have her," I assure him.

Greyson leans back in his chair, defeated.

"Now I have to find nanny number seven. Maybe seven will be my lucky number."

ACKNOWLEDGMENTS

Holy freaking shit. I wrote a second book. When I came up with the idea for this series, it was incredibly important to me that the stories could be read as standalones but could also be enjoyed as part of an intricately interwoven series. That means I had all five books plotted, titled, and had all main characters chosen before I typed a single word of Bourbon & Backroads.

It still seems insane to me, I started writing Heartstrings & Horseshoes the month after finishing my first draft of Bourbon & Backroads. The epilogue left such a delicious teaser, I couldn't resist diving into book two. It took me longer to write Heartstrings & Horseshoes than Bourbon & Backroads, but that's because I also interwove dual timeline chapters.

I had so much fun calling back to Reid and Isabelle from book one, and teasing books three through five. I love Connor and Delilah in a very special way. In part because I adore childhood crush to lovers as a trope, but also because my husband and I are high school sweethearts. So I had so much fun writing Connor and Delilah's chapters as teens because once upon a time, that was us in a way.

Anyhow, that leads me to the actual acknowledgements. Above all, thank you to you, my reader. Whether you found me through Heartstrings & Horseshoes, Flannel Fiancé, or Bourbon & Backroads, THANK YOU for continuing to be interested in the stories I tell. If this is my first book you've read, I hope you'll stick around because I've got a lot up my sleeves.

With literally no break between projects, my husband

continued supporting me on this crazy writing journey. The things I blurt out at him of an evening on the couch could be anthologized. Surprise, babe! It wasn't just one book, you're in it for the long haul with me!

While not completely understanding, my wonderful kids were the cutest cheerleaders. Asking if I was working on my book (they also called it my "fun work") and being so gentle with my paper drafts and proof copies. Hopefully me sticking to the plan to become a bestselling author will encourage them to chase their dreams someday.

My reader group saved me time and time again. They caught things I missed, didn't think of, or overlooked, and unwaveringly encouraging me. Mom, Debi, Amy, Jordan, and Kayla, thank you from the bottom of my heart.

The list of indie (and some who've gone trad!) authors who inspired, supported, and listened to my endless questions, keeps growing. A few stand out amongst the sea of excellence, and I'm delighted to consider them my friends as well as colleagues. Bonnie Poirier, M.A. Cobb, Michelle Carrero and Kat Brooks, I'm endlessly grateful for you.

Again, my editor Kay levelled this baby up to something I'm extremely proud of. Sandra Maldo created yet another stunning cover I'm thrilled to show off, and frankly, stare at all day.

Thank you for taking a chance on me. Aside from writing stories I love for myself, really all I want is to make you FEEL something. A laugh, a smile, a tear, an irritated scoff, anything to bring human emotion to you from the pages of my book.

xo Amanda

WHAT'S NEXT?

Good news doll, there's more where that came from. There's more stories waiting at Lucky Spurs Ranch.

Book 3 coming June 2026.

Want to know when the next book drops (and maybe get a little bonus content while you wait)? Join my newsletter and be awkward with me online @authoramandajayne on Instagram and TikTok.

ALSO BY AMANDA JAYNE

LUCKY SPURS RANCH

Bourbon & Backroads

Fifty Shades of Flannel

Flannel Fiancé

ABOUT THE AUTHOR

Amanda Jayne writes romance with heart, heat, and humor, delivering rugged heroes, wild-hearted heroines, and deeply satisfying happily-ever-afters.

She's got a soft spot for grumpy men with gooey centers, can't resist when he only smiles for her, and will never say no to a possessive alpha.

When she's not writing your next book boyfriend, she's probably hyperfixating over a new obsession, rearranging her bookshelves, or ignoring her to-do list in favor of *just one more chapter*.

You can find her @authoramandajayne on Instagram and TikTok, and at www.authoramandajayne.com.

Made in the USA
Coppell, TX
19 January 2026